To Maria

ONE WHITE
Camellia

Roy Beck
8-29-07

ONE WHITE Camellia

R. FRANCIS BECKS

Tate Publishing & *Enterprises*

Tate Publishing is committed to excellence in the publishing industry. Our staff of highly trained professionals, including editors, graphic designers, and marketing personnel, work together to produce the very finest books available. The company reflects the philosophy established by the founders, based on Psalms 68:11,

"The Lord Gave The Word And Great Was The Company Of Those Who Published It."

If you would like further information, please contact us:
1.888.361.9473 | www.tatepublishing.com
Tate Publishing & Enterprises, llc | 127 E. Trade Center Terrace
Mustang, Oklahoma 73064 USA

One White Camelia
Copyright © 2007 by R. Francis Beck. All rights reserved.
This product is also available as a Tate Out Loud Product.
Visit www.tatepublishing.com for more information

No part of this publication may be reproduced, stored in a retrieval system or transmitted in any way by any means, electronic, mechanical, photocopy, recording or otherwise without the prior permission of the author except as provided by USA copyright law.

Book design copyright © 2007 by Tate Publishing, LLC. All rights reserved.
Cover design by Jen Reddon
Interior design by Sarah Leis

Published in the United States of America

ISBN: 978–1–6024709–0–3

07.24.04

Raw justice obligates me to dedicate this book to my wife, Helen, who is still as beautiful inside and out as she was when I met her over thirty years ago. Some of our friends refer to her as "The Saint," for having endured living with me for all of these years.

I would also like to include in this dedication the six fantastic children whom Helen bore and whom we had so much fun raising, which, of course, by extension, makes the dedication include the grandchildren whose numbers are still growing.

A fire burns, and sight and sense enflame.
The soul yearns, nor will affections tame.
But great the saints whose love was passion born;
Love's lover changed, not human nature torn.
All good must know of evil's sweet entice.
Our virtue's heights equate potential vice.

Jeanne Anne Trudeau
Sr. Saint Cecelia, opc

PROLOGUE

I began writing this book in the mid 1970s, a few years after graduating from college and taking employment as a newspaper reporter. This book was originally intended to be a biography of one of our nation's more popular and colorful jurists. However, during my research, I uncovered phenomena that refused to submit to reason; at least to reason as applied to any of my previous, personal experiences, nor will these discoveries allow me to return to my former state of blissful, skeptical agnosticism. Early in my adolescence I decided that I preferred peace to wisdom and later added the corollary, "When in doubt, forget it!" This principle served me with such exceptional effectiveness, that when I uncovered the aforementioned anomalies and, subsequently, failed to exorcise myself of those gnawing queries, my mental and emotional stability became shaken. Because of that fact, as well as my rapidly increasing family responsibilities, I decided to delay the writing of this book. I spent the interim concentrating on raising our children with my wife, Helen. But the unsettled mysteries uncovered during the above-mentioned research never left me. After the children were raised and I had more time simply to think, the questioning became more intense... like a voice shouting louder and louder in my head.

Helen recognized my uneasiness and knew of my dilemma concerning that past research. Consequently, she suggested that I try to finish the book. And, obviously, I did.

As stated above, this book was originally to be a biography, which I sincerely intended to draft with an appropriate attempt at objectivity... but that was before I began the research, or at least the personal interview portion of that research. After that, I could no longer be objective. I became too intimately involved in the story and was too personally affected by the persons and circumstances uncovered to qualify as an historian, at least relative to this subject. Thus, the ultimate purpose for writing the book had also changed. Because of my own interactions with and reactions to the story I am about to tell, I am presenting my own experiences leading up to, during and following my research as well as the biographical material, which I uncovered. I hope that when I finish, the reader will understand why.

Since this is no longer a biography, I am also allowing myself the liberty of avoiding the actual names of persons, places and institutions. Also, where unavoidable, I have changed some names even at the expense of an occasional awkwardness. This is done, not only to protect the innocent, but also to protect myself from any legal problems. The actual names are, at least to me and I hope the reader, of little importance. The incidents, however, are very important.

Lastly, I appeal to the reader for insight that might help me to regain my peace of mind. I sincerely hope that somewhere there is a person of sufficient wisdom and diction capable of understanding and expressing how what I am about to relate could have happened. If anyone is so gifted, I ask that he or she contact the publisher of this book who has generously promised to forward all such correspondence to this writer.

R.F.B.

Chapter One

Obviously, more than a few pious souls reading the following chronicle will assert that my introduction into the unusual life of the Honorable Ronald M. VanderLinde was totally out of my control and predestined by a Superior Being for his own benevolent purposes. If true, the pattern of my days was probably established prenatally when I was blessed with that aptitude euphemistically described as the gift of gab.

During my first nine years, my mother of long suffering divided her time between household chores and telling me to keep quiet. Then my tonsils were removed, after which I spent about a week almost mute. The shock from this abrupt lack of sound was such that my mother foreswore all previous admonitions to silence, vowing never again to restrict my verbosity. As a high school student I became a member of the Forensic League and for the remainder of my mother's life, she could be heard at least weekly explaining to relatives and friends, "He joined the debating team in high school and he hasn't stopped since." She would say this jokingly and even somewhat proudly, but there was a melancholy tone in her voice and an expression in her eyes that could only be interpreted as a plea for compassion.

I entered college bearing the reputation of being able to say nothing in twenty thousand words or more, a gift which was extremely useful when required to give an oral report on a subject about which I knew absolutely nothing. I actually did that once and received an "A" for the report.

Being somewhat lazy and more than somewhat practical, I had decided to seek a career promising both financial security and minimal effort. My first studies were in the field of creative writing, intending eventually to become a novelist. However, I quickly abandoned this glamorous goal when I discovered the repulsive reality that, but for a handful of very fortunate authors, the world's literary artists appeared to find great difficulty satisfying their apparently incompatible drives to create and to eat. Consequently, I spent my last three college years wandering through the supposedly non-creative halls of the school of journalism.

Despite an almost religious adherence to the ancient scholastic principle, "Never let your studies interfere with your extra-curricular activities," I graduated with honors. Cum laude's notwithstanding, I was delightfully surprised at the ease with which I acquired a position as a reporter for one of the newspapers published in the large Midwestern city where majestically stands my college Alma Mater and to which is parasitically affixed the suburb where I was born and raised. Though I vainly attributed the brevity of my stay in the ranks of the unemployed to my excellent scholastic record, a charming personality and an obviously attractive appearance, my flattering ego trip became a short and meaningless jaunt when I learned of my new employer's weird hiring practices after only three days on the job.

When I phoned for an interview, I was informed that I would be sent an application, which I was to fill out, "With maximum precision, accuracy, and completeness," and which I was to return promptly with my college transcript and a thorough but succinct resume. These instructions were delivered in an overly instructive tone that was in complete contrast to the soft, gentle voice of the girl who conveyed them. I was quite anxious to meet this contradiction.

I had called on a Monday and spent the balance of the day drafting a very complimentary autobiography. The application form arrived on Tuesday. The original phone conversation made an application in duplicate seem almost natural, but some of the questions thereon were definitely unnatural. That an employer would ask to know an applicant's date of birth is certainly normal operating procedure but that he would request the exact time of day seemed anomalous to the extreme. The form also asked for the precise place of birth: "Note, by place of birth is meant the exact location, that is, the address, not simply the city or state." Though I knew the hospital in which I was delivered, the time of day was a total mystery. When I reached this question I looked up at a decorative wall clock in my room that hadn't kept time for about two years and I inserted the time it displayed. I mailed the application at the post office that afternoon and received a call on Wednesday morning. Miss O'Donnell, as the Personnel Secretary introduced herself, stated that the newspaper had received my application and then added, "If you are still interested, I will schedule you for tomorrow. There are tests that we administer to all prospective employees and they, together with the interviews, will take up most of the day." She apparently assumed that I was still interested, since she failed to wait for a reply and continued, "Can you be here at 8:30 tomorrow morning?"

I told her that I could and that I was impressed with the speed involved in the processing of my application to which she pertly quipped, "We try! Personnel is on the second floor. See you in the morning."

And see me she did... but more importantly I saw her. Sitting behind a gray, office style desk on which sat a small name plate that modestly advertised, "Miss Helen O'Donnell—Personnel Secretary," was exactly what I had seen on the phone: an alert, efficient and most attractive young lady in her early twenties. She was, without a doubt, the quintessence of the dark-haired Irish. Her face boasted of very white, slightly freckled skin framed by nearly black hair and bejeweled with sparkling blue-green eyes. I recalled reading somewhere that the dark-haired Irish were the result of the blending of the original inhabitants of the Emerald Isle with their adopted sons marooned on the Irish shore subsequent to the devastation of the Spanish Armada by the British Navy. As I introduced myself, I reflected that the men of the world owed a huge debt of gratitude to Drake and his fellow buccaneers.

I had fulfilled my proper function as a job applicant by arriving early. It was only 8:20 AM when my lovely escort led me into a glass cubical of a room austerely decorated and furnished with one scratched auditorium type table and just the right number of evenly spaced, wooden seated, wooden backed chairs. Miss O'Donnell placed a large booklet and a sharpened pencil on the table near where I had taken a seat. She counseled, "There's no time limit on the test but try to finish by noon. Some of the brown baggers use this as a lunchroom."

As I adjusted myself on the very hard chair seat and placed my elbow on an equally hard tabletop, I quipped, half under my breath, "They must be masochists."

I was soon agonizing through one of those self-revealing psychological tests that contain such diverse and senseless questions as, "Do you have diarrhea in the morning," and, "What would you rather be: 1) Financially secure or 2) Rich?" I suspect that such tests are aimed not at determining an applicant's mental or emotional state, but rather his or her level of frustration tolerance.

At 11:30 AM I emerged from the transparent cubical, which by 9:15 had become my torture chamber. I numbly indicated to Miss O'Donnell that I had finished the test and that I was hungry. The former was fortunately true, but I had lost any chance I might have had for an appetite somewhere around question 327, "At a large party with whom would you rather carry on a conversation: a celebrity or an average person?" Despite my gastronomic indifference to food, I decided to plead for a lunch break to clear my head before being interviewed by what could be my future superior. Since my appointment with the managing editor was set for 1:00 PM my request was granted. But Miss O'Donnell warned, "Mr. Blakesley is a stickler for punctuality."

My lunch consisted of one hard-boiled egg, a domestic beer and a package of Sen-Sen, the latter prudently added to avoid the risk of creating a first impression as a lush. The egg and beer were dictated by a lack of appetite, a need for emotional stabilization and an extremely strained bank balance. Immediately following graduation, I liberated myself of the $400.00 remaining of the educational endowment left to me by my father by undertaking a month long, post-graduate course in pure fun.

At nine minutes before the hour I was standing at the ready beside Miss O'Donnell's desk. "Follow me," she directed.

As she rose and started towards the elevator, my visual perception, which by now had become sufficiently accustomed to the exceptional attractiveness of her face, broadened to encompass her entire physiognomy. I poetically thought, "Thou art thrice blessed." In addition to a lively, sparkling personality and a captivating countenance, she possessed that special feminine grace that emanates exclusively from the long willowy look. Seeing her at a cocktail party, one could easily mistake her for a high fashion model except that she fortunately avoided that artificial seductiveness that such models often exude. There was nothing artificial or forced or anything other than natural beauty radiating from this daughter of Erin.

When the elevator reached the fifth floor, the opened door revealed a huge room inhabited by a multitude of bustling workers scurrying about in ant like fashion. But for the low ceiling and the pillars that rose strategically throughout the room, it could easily have accommodated two simultaneous basketball games. Particularly noticeable was the stereotypical nature of the office's occupants as well as its ambiance. I was certain that I had viewed this same scene, in miniature, of course, in at least a half dozen late night movies. I felt that Clark Gable must be somewhere about barking out orders in a gruff, surly voice with just that minute degree of softness that revealed his true, tender self. And should I look long enough,

One White Camellia

I would surely find a red-nosed Thomas Mitchell sneaking a quick slug from a ninety proof bottle of cough medicine.

As we strolled down the aisles no one bothered to notice us except for a few overworked heads that rose to take an eye break as Miss O'Donnell strolled by. Our route was simple: straight ahead, then sharp left. As we took the turn I could see a small lonely room far in the distance. It was the only room protruding from the otherwise four flush walls. The wood grained paneling, which adorned the exterior, made it look like a wart growing out of the surrounding green paint. The room was obviously an afterthought added for utilitarian rather than architectural or aesthetic purposes.

One small window glared defiantly from the upper half of the badly nicked, light colored door. The light color and the early American molding on the door looked ridiculous against the dark, plain modern paneling. As a painting the scene could have been entitled, "Frugality."

Moving down the aisle, it grew increasingly apparent that this ugly protrusion was our target. From a distance I could see a sign on the door, which I speculated bore the name and/or title of the occupant. However, as the sign came into focus I realized with appropriate concern that the informative little appendage was a simple sheet of typing paper fastened to the door with transparent tape, stating in a bold legible script, "KEEP THE DAMN DOOR CLOSED." I assumed that the sign was the natural descendent of a line of ineffectual postings probably beginning with, "Please close the door."

When we reached a point about twenty feet from our goal, Miss O'Donnell stopped abruptly with a simple, "It isn't one o'clock yet." Having walked alongside but slightly behind her, I was certain that I had not seen her check her watch. I scanned the walls ahead for the clock from which she discerned the exact time but found none. Though I admired her clairvoyance, I said nothing. I was content with merely observing the irregular, albeit smooth, flow of bodies in and out of the paneled room. Everyone was moving at that quickened pace usually reserved in offices for the last fifteen minutes of the workday. The double time was constant except that each person slowed momentarily on entrance and exit long enough to certify that the door catch was fastened, then sped up again.

Suddenly a small red light lit up directly over the door. With equal and somewhat startling suddenness, all those on their way to the room stopped, pivoted and returned at normal walking speed to their respective desks.

"It's one," Miss O'Donnell informed, moving quickly forward. I took the knob with the gallant intent of opening the door for her but, having caught the prevailing aura surrounding the room, I looked to her for approval before turning. Understanding my caution, she nodded affirmatively, much as a mother would to her offspring as he reached tentatively for a second cookie.

The nameplate on the desk read, "H.H. Blakesley, Managing Editor." Behind the desk sat a middle-aged man of average height, average weight and average everything. He was neatly groomed from his highly polished shoes, through his manicured fingernails, to his perfectly brushed hair. The latter was black with just the right amount of gray at the temples and was divided on the left by a part that was mathematically true enough to qualify as a geometric example of a straight line and that ended precisely at the end of the rear cowlick. About all that could be said of his facial characteristics was that he had two eyes, one on either side of a sharp nose that pointed down towards a pair of thin lips and a narrow chin.

He quickly rose to greet me, very briefly shook my hand and then just as quickly sat down. He wore a pair of plain dark blue trousers that matched the plain blue jacket, which was carefully draped over a wooden bedroom valet standing in a rear corner of the room. There was neither a wrinkle nor fold in either and the creases were still razor sharp in spite of what must have been an extremely active half-day's work. His shirt collar was heavily starched and it tightly clutched a perfectly knotted, contrasting, striped tie that bore a pin, which I cynically suspected had been positioned with a micrometer. Though the men in the outer office wore their sleeves rolled up past their wrists or elbows and had long since unfastened the top button beneath their loosened ties, all of Mr. Blakesley's buttons were firmly in place and his tie, of course, remained as perfectly knotted as when he had put it on.

The editor's office was singular for its uncluttered state in a much-cluttered business. There was a wooden desk devoid of all papers and which displayed only a monogrammed penholder, a phone, a double tier wire basket showing "in" and "out," the fore-mentioned nameplate and an artificial gold tri-fold frame, obviously containing pictures of the family. Behind the desk there resided a cushioned swivel chair containing our Mr. Blakesley and the jacket adorned valet. The only other appointments were a visitor's chair tucked away in a corner near the door and a framed sign that hung behind and above Blakesley's head that read,

> THERE ARE TWO WAYS OF DOING THINGS:
> MY WAY AND THE DOOR WAY.

Miss O'Donnell made the formal introduction and handed Mr. Blakesley a folder, which I assumed contained my resume, college transcript and one of the copies of my application form. Having fulfilled her duties, our Irish beauty left inconspicuously, making certain to close the door tightly. As I heard the door latch click, a very disquieting feeling engulfed me, as though I had suddenly been abandoned by the whole world and left alone to fend for myself in a universe consisting solely of me and some kind of heartless, carnivorous beast. I thought that mine was probably the experience of the applicant for the anti-anarchist police force during his job interview with the police chief in G.K. Chesterton's nightmare, *The Man Who Was Thursday*.

My success in college was due in great part to a system, which I had devised consisting, in essence, of anticipating the material from which each professor drew his test questions. During the first two or three weeks of a course... at least until the first test or quiz, I would take notes almost verbatim from the teacher's lectures and memorize much of the critical material in the text. After the first exam, it was easy to determine from which source each instructor drew his or her test questions (rarely did any draw from both lectures and text). I could then just relax for the remainder of the semester studying only a specific teacher's identified source before each test. This method not only saved me time when studying for exams but also eliminated the need to read the text, had a professor tested only from lectures, and freed me up to study other subjects during classes, whenever the instructor tested only from the text. I had often considered earning a little beer money tutoring my fellow collegians in this time and effort saving ploy, entitling the instruction, "How to acquire a college diploma while learning as little as necessary."

Anticipating interviews with prospective employers, I had decided to stay with a winner and utilize the same effective practice that earned me scholastic honors. The obvious problem with this scheme was that to ascertain what kind of questions each interviewer would ask and accurately determine the answers he wanted me to give, I would be required to condense three weeks of psyching into as little as three minutes. With this in mind, I began analyzing H.H. Blakesley even before we entered the office. That he was neat, punctual and orderly was obvious. The question was whether these characteristics were by nature or by design.

As he began speaking, I noticed that both delivery and content were clear, concise and deliberate. However, his voice, though never changing in sound level or tone, was not without feeling and his facial expressions, though not projecting any particular emotion, were not emotionless. I concluded that he was not a cold automaton. He was indeed a sanguine soul who had apparently realized that his life's goals could best be reached by governing himself on the principles of deliberateness and strict order. The conflict was apparent. However beneficial these principles may have proven towards the acquisition of his goals, they also proved devastating to his stomach. He was frequently popping large white pills into his mouth. As a youngster, having witnessed the agonies of my father's ulcer, I recognized the pills as antacids.

As it turned out, my attempt at a hasty psychological analysis went for naught. The interview was actually a lecture, with my role consisting of listening attentively and trying to show as much interest as possible in an outline of duties required for a fledgling reporter on this particular newspaper.

Skimming quickly through my folder, he began, "Your grades were good but that only means you can write. Our policy is to serve the community by informing, entertaining and stirring our readers in support of issues that benefit the community. The challenge is to avoid overemphasizing any one of these elements. Too much informative copy and your paper puts the reader to sleep. Too much entertainment and you are no longer a newspaper. Too much championing-of-causes and you suffer the ultimate fate of all crusaders: martyrdom. Our cardinal virtue, therefore, is balance. And that's my job: balancing those three ingredients."

Having covered the opening subject of his sermon, he closed the folder and carefully placed it in front of him on the desk. This action was performed slowly as though he were gathering his thoughts before continuing. However, since he had certainly given this same speech on many previous occasions and was reciting what by now must have been a memorized lecture, I knew that this reflective pause was purely for effect. He continued, "I have held my present position for eleven years and I will hold it for many more. The reason for my confidence is that I possess the talent to determine balance instantly, on the run, so to speak. I see each page for which I am responsible in my mind as the news breaks. The moment stories come to my attention I am able to shuffle headlines, copy and pictures so that everything is balanced in tone, content and appearance even before the proofs are typed. If you're impressed, you should be. Mine is a very rare gift."

I dipped my head slightly and raised my eyebrows in an appropriate expression of admiration, but I prudently decided against interrupting verbally even to flatter.

Having received his due adulation he went on, "However, my talents are worthless unless the reporters under me also possess two essential skills, neither of which is necessary to acquire a degree in journalism."

The negative reference to my scholastic excellence was obvious. He elaborated, "First, the reporters for this paper must become adept at dictating by phone, as well as typing on paper, a precise number of words for any story. I permit a variance of ten words over or under. This skill can be learned through practice, but you will be expected to practice on your own time. After one week from your starting date, no copy will be accepted that varies more than ten words from the word limit I establish."

I felt quite certain that the Managing Editor's reference to my practicing and my starting date did not imply that I had indeed been hired. I was practical enough to realize his phraseology probably meant nothing more than a variation on the editorial, "we."

Blakesley paused again to make certain that requirement number one had been thoroughly absorbed and then continued, "The second skill no one can learn. You either have it or you don't. When you get the facts on a story you will phone me direct, unless time permits you to check in with me in person. Summarize the story as succinctly as possible. I will designate the number of words I want and the tone in which you will write the story: informative, light, human interest, humorous, tear jerker, etc. That's the second requirement: to dictate or type an article spontaneously under the pressure of a deadline in any mood I tell you." As though it were an afterthought he added, "By the way, on this paper I do the job that the Managing Editor, News Editor and Copy Editor would be doing on any other paper of this size. So when you're on the phone with me or you're here in my office, don't bother with your name or hello or any other pleasantry. I don't have time."

As he finished this last sentence, he opened the upper right hand drawer of his desk and withdrew a letter-sized envelope. "Ms. Winslow will now test you on these two skills. This envelope contains a news item and four moods, each with a specific number of words. You will dictate four articles, one in each mood and as close as possible to the number of words designated. Give this to Ms. Winslow in the outer office."

The last sentence was delivered with a nod to the door and an obvious reference to the bifocaled woman who had apparently arrived during the interview and who was now waiting outside of Blakesley's office. On the word, "outer," my host reached under his desk and seemingly pressed something. As I rose and turned towards the door, I saw through the window in the door what appeared as a horde of humanity descending on the office, which still included me. I quickly stepped aside to avoid being trampled by eight or ten men and women rushing into the office, either waving papers or gasping short phrases to which they received short replies. The phone rang even before I could return the chair on which I was sitting to its home in the corner of the office. As I finally squeezed through the door, I could see the Managing Editor, phone on shoulder, speaking to several people and reading two papers simultaneously.

I greeted Ms. Winslow and obediently handed her the envelope. She ordered, "Come with me." As we started down the aisle I glanced back at Blakesley's office and, sure enough, the red light was off.

I followed Ms. Winslow down the center aisle about twenty paces, then left ten paces, then right ten until we reached a desk dominated by a typewriter and a large vase of freshly cut daffodils. Ms. Winslow was a large boned, relatively tall woman in her late forties or early fifties. She increased her height to well over six feet with very high heels and a mass of graying hair fashioned in swirling overlapping layers on top of her head. She appeared physically strong, though not necessarily masculine, with level square shoulders and a large bust that seemed exceptionally firm for a woman of her age.

Ms. Winslow ordered me to sit, much as one would give such a command to a dog. She did so verbally and with a hand gesture indicating a metal folding chair beside her desk. Though I politely hesitated, giving her a chance to be seated first, she was not about to allow me this act of chivalry. After waiting as long as I could without disobeying her order to sit, I uncomfortably lowered myself onto the chair only to find as I looked up that she had slid a half step forward and her head was now towering almost directly over mine. She was staring down at me with an expression of superiority effortlessly blended with contempt and remained motionless, seemingly mesmerized by her position of domination. Finally she became aware of the awkwardness of her relative proximity to me and moved to her seat mumbling, "Well let's see what gem Mr. Blakesley has for us today." Ms. Winslow opened the envelope and removed two memo-sized sheets of paper. She began reading, "You are to dictate four articles about the same story. The first, one hundred words, straight news; the second, two hundred words, tear jerker; third, three hundred words, incite populous to action; and the fourth, one hundred words, humorous." As she slid the last paper to the bottom, she glowered at me with an expression that charged, "That should take the cockiness out of you my friend!" Then she read the second note, "The Fire Department removed Mrs. Jones' cat from a tree." She expressed disappointment. Half throwing the two pieces of paper at me she grunted, "That's a snap. The last poor slob had, 'the scientific discovery of a new strain of tsetse fly.' He left halfway through 'Human Interest.'"

The fact that her previous victim had surrendered without completing the test appeared to please our Ms. Winslow. But if her remark was meant as a suggestion, she missed the effect. I felt that a gauntlet had just creased my cheek and I was intent on returning it in exactly the manner in which it had been delivered. I was not about to let this old bat intimidate me into throwing in the towel. Besides, I had always enjoyed a good verbal contest.

She stared at me soberly and piercingly, trying to ascertain whether Mr. Blakesley's challenge had adequately shaken me. I stared back trying to exude an air of nonchalant self-confidence. Realizing that she had failed to disturb my emotional disposition she injected, "I am to inform you that embellishments are permitted." She paused momentarily and then added, "I assume you know what embellishments are?" The words she used and the tone in which she employed them reflected a little of the insult she intended but she let me know with her eyes that the last remark was definitely intended to cut.

I flippantly replied, "Of course. It's something you serve that usually includes artichoke hearts and marinated watermelon rinds."

"Don't be sarcastic," she snapped bitterly. Then, changing to an unjustly injured tone, she whined, "I was only trying to be of help."

I suddenly realized that I had been skillfully finessed into giving her the opportunity to openly express her contempt for me and also into permitting her to make me look like a callous ingrate. She had underestimated her adversary, however. I wore many battle scars from wounds inflicted by the older sister of a neighbor friend during high school and college who had mastered this same art of seducing someone into saying or doing something to which she would retaliate viciously, asserting that her reaction was justified. Through instinctive efforts at self-defense, I had long since developed effective counter maneuvers. In the same injured tone I replied, "I'm sorry, if you took offense. I wasn't being sarcastic. I'm a little tense and I was only trying to relax with some humor." I made a direct hit. She was still staring at me but her eyes went out of focus. She had planned only one assault and had not anticipated a counter attack. Now she realized that I had not only side stepped her big guns but had leveled a volley of my own, accusing her of misunderstanding, of being devoid of a sense of humor and of lacking compassion for a poor frightened job applicant. Nevertheless, she regained her poise in about three seconds. She was shaken but not defeated. As her eyes refocused I saw pure hate. She slowly picked up her steno pad and pencil, placed the lead point with exaggerated deliberateness at the upper left-hand corner of the pad and challenged, "Well?"

I wiggled as far back in the chair as possible, placed my right hand on my knee, reached my left hand forward in a straight-arm position resting my fingertips on the edge of the desk and dictated in a firm, perfectly cadenced, overly articulate voice, "Article number one."

I dictated fluently for about seventy five words, telling the factual story of Mrs. J.J. Jones' valuable Siamese cat who had wandered from its owner's yard and who, when accosted by a large brown and yellow German Shepherd dog, had found refuge in a neighbor's tree. At this point I paused to correct a phrase. "Strike that last sentence." I was about to continue, but Ms. Winslow quickly interrupted, "Real reporters are usually closing in on a deadline. They don't have time to rewrite."

"You're right," I retorted, hoping to leave the impression that I knew the pressures facing real reporters. I finished my straight news item and without hesitation or change in inflection continued, "Article number two."

Unfortunately, I had begun to warm up to this game of mood changing copy and instinctively I succumbed to my innate verbosity. I told the heart rending account of a lonely, widowed Mrs. Jones whose sole consolation resided in her two precious feline companions and how a snarling, vicious, wolf-like dog leaped the Jones' fence and without provocation attacked the beautiful and defenseless female angora that Mrs. Jones anxiously, though proudly, announced was in a family way.

When I finished the second article, my scribe caustically remarked, "I think you were to hold that one to two hundred words. There's enough copy here for a full page feature."

"I'll watch it on the next one," I answered indifferently. The remaining two articles suffered a little in tone but I think I scored much better at the numbers thing.

When I finished the entire assignment, Ms. Winslow let me know that she was relieved that she was finally done with me. "There's a coffee machine against the wall over there. I'll have these articles typed in a few minutes."

I rose with an air of self-assurance and with great concentration made my way through the maze-like aisles to the coffee machine, which stood near the elevators. Half way through my coffee, a lunch-rejuvenated Miss O'Donnell briskly exited one of the elevators. She saw me instantly and chirped, "Oh, hi! How did it go?"

"About as smoothly as a canoe ride down the Colorado rapids," I replied.

She smiled. "Encountered Sadie Winslow, did you?"

"Nothing I couldn't handle," I answered. "What's with her anyway?"

By now I had gulped my coffee and we began winding our way back to Ms. Winslow's desk.

Miss O'Donnell enlightened me about my recent adversary. "As I understand, Sadie's worked at the same job for the better part of twenty years and watched everyone else, men especially, climb the ladder of success. She probably sees every new applicant such as yourself as a young upstart who will eventually by-pass her, both promotion and salary-wise. From the few conversations I've had with her, I've gathered that she's a charter member of women's lib. I don't think she's ever married. She seems to hold men in contempt."

"She certainly did in my case," I laughed. "What a blow to my ego. I thought her animosity was directed at me personally."

We reached Sadie Winslow's desk just in time to watch her adeptly snatch the last paper from her typewriter. She aligned the papers and handed them to my companion grumbling, "More dead wood." She looked at me to make certain that I had heard her. Neither of us said anything. We just turned and started on our way to Mr. Blakesley's office.

"How much longer will I be here?" I asked.

"Just one more stint in the Blake's office," she answered.

"What time is this interview?" I asked.

"Two fifteen." she replied.

"Is H.H. Blakesley always as stiff as he appeared to me?" I inquired.

"He is... here at the office," she responded.

"What about out of the office?" I queried.

"I've never had the opportunity to find out what he's like socially," she exclaimed, "and frankly I have no desire to find out."

Her selectivity in men was both encouraging and disconcerting. I hoped that she was not too selective.

Just about then we reached the twenty-foot way station so we pulled up again. "It isn't two fifteen, yet," I interjected, anticipating her directive.

"You catch on fast," she replied.

As we watched what was now a familiar wave of bodies ebbing to and flowing from Blakesley's office, I inquired, "How was lunch?"

"Are you really interested or are you just making small talk?" she quipped playfully.

"I think both," I answered.

She continued, "I tried a new restaurant today. The lunch was great. I'd like to try their dinner menu sometime."

This sounded like a possible invitation for me to offer her an invitation to dinner but before I could pursue that promising scenario, I was preempted by the infamous red light and the expected stop and return movement of the office personnel.

"Shall we?" Miss O'Donnell said.

This time I opened the door without prior approval. Blakesley made no gesture for us to be seated, so we both simply approached his desk and stood awaiting his pleasure. My escort handed him my articles, which he skimmed through, averaging less than five seconds each.

He began, "The mood and content are fine but the length is terrible... especially this second one." Depositing the papers in the wastebasket beneath his desk he added, "It doesn't make any difference anyway. The job is yours if you want it but do me a favor and decline."

I refrained from answering... I did not know how. I just stared straight ahead, trying to understand Blakesley's last remark. He offered me a job and then told me that he preferred I not take it. In spite of all of the craziness that had transpired since I entered the building that morning, I had steadfastly maintained my poise. However, I was now totally unnerved. I tried to speak but probably for the first time in my life, I could not quite figure out what to say.

"Oh, come on Becks. I'm busy. Do you want the job or not?" he demanded.

I decided to ask for a day or two to think about it and began my request, "Well there are a few other papers that I would like to... "

He interrupted, "Damn it! I know that this late after graduation, most papers have closed applications from this year's journalism students." He again asked the question but this time he paused between each word, "Do - you - want - the - job?"

I still wanted a few minutes to think. So, for lack of anything better to say, I asked, "Well, how much is the salary?"

He did not reply directly but rather turned his head towards Miss O'Donnell. Answering his look, she quoted a substantial monthly figure, which I learned later she was told to offer me by the paper's illustrious publisher. Blakesley shook his head incredulously and muttered, "To think what I started at."

Definitely impressed with the salary offer and realizing that the Managing Editor's patience was obviously wearing thin, I decided to accept his offer. "When do I start?" I asked.

"Monday. But God only knows what I'm going to do with you. You won't even have a desk unless you can find somebody who's sick or on vacation." Then he turned to Miss O'Donnell and for the first time, I caught a tinge of sincere emotion exuding from my soon to be leader. Showing a slight but real exasperation, he rhetorically asked, "How in the hell am I supposed to run a newspaper when the hiring practices are determined by whether or not Venus is flirting with Jupiter in the early morning hours on a particular day twenty-five years ago?"

Returning to me he directed, "If you don't have a typewriter, get one. You'll have to write in your car or anywhere else you can find until somebody around here quits, is fired or drops dead." Then he grumbled, "This is ridiculous." He handed my folder to the Personnel Secretary and ordered, "Get him started."

From recent experience I knew that Blakesley's hand sliding under the lip of his desk was a definite sign of impending danger, so I quickly turned and opened the door. In spite of my alertness, we barely made it through the doorway without being crushed by what seemed to be the unbridled onslaught of the barbarian hoards.

As we retraced our route back to Miss O'Donnell's office, I remembered the promising conversation that was so rudely interrupted by Blakesley's ominous red light. "Would you like to try the dinner menu tonight at that restaurant you mentioned?" I asked.

She did not answer immediately but chuckled softly.

Wondering if I should feel rebuffed I inquired, "What's so funny?"

"Oh, don't be hurt," she counseled compassionately. "I wasn't laughing at you. Since you're asking me out on such short notice, I was just thinking of the fun I could have playing the coquette role, 'Oh, I'm sorry. I'm all booked up for the next three months but I'll let you know if I have a cancellation.'"

"No offense, but I think you'd make a lousy coquette," was my reply.

"So do I," she admitted, still chuckling. "Let's not make it dinner though," she added. "We'll both be tired and you're probably broke. Let's just go somewhere quiet and have a drink."

I really meant it when I said she would make a lousy coquette. Everything about Miss Helen O'Donnell was open, honest and sincere. I could not conceive of her in any sort of artificial role-playing. Admiring her directness I responded, "You're a very understanding young lady."

"You're right," she agreed in a playful banter, displaying the most attractive smile that I was certain I had ever seen. Then she added, "Do you have a car or do you want me to pick you up?"

Her frankness and the ease with which she discarded unnecessary formality were disarming. I assured her that I had a car but then quickly added the caveat, "It's not much of a car but it runs."

Back at her desk she gave me the necessary directions.

For the remainder of the day I was aware of an almost forgotten adolescent excitement. That evening I arrived at her house about ten minutes early and was not surprised that Helen answered the door, sweater over her shoulder and ready to go. She greeted me with a spirited, "Hi!" and then shouted, "See you later... won't be late," to someone inside.

There was something drastically, though not unbecomingly, different about her. As she took my arm and guided me briskly down the front steps, I realized that her hair had changed from very dark brown to a lovely deep auburn. She was apparently wearing a wig that could definitely have been her own hair. Without the wig, her almost black hair made her skin look like soft white cotton. But with it, all of the red highlights in her complexion, as well as the few freckles across the bridge of her nose, came to life. The changed hue also went stunningly well with her simple kelly green dress.

At Helen's suggestion, we stopped at a local restaurant/lounge just a few minutes drive from her house. We took a booth in the bar area, which sported subdued lighting, and a musical combo that played only soft, slow tunes. The relaxing ambiance was exactly what both of us were looking for, especially me, after my weird day at the newspaper. During the evening's conversation, Helen manifested even another attractive facet of her personality. Though I tried to discover as much as I could about her, she tactfully kept reverting the dialogue back onto me. Needless to say, my ego was constantly flattered by her apparent interest in everything about me. By ten o'clock I was a well-read book to her, but all I knew about my companion was that she lived with her parents and three younger sisters, preferred live theater to movies and enjoyed all forms of music. It was only 10:30 when Helen suggested we leave but I offered no objection. Her earlier prediction that we would be tired proved correct. I was really beginning to drag.

On the way back to the house I inquired, "By the way, what's with that Blakesley character? He's a nut. Along with a few dozen other oddball idiosyncrasies, he offers me a job and then asks me to decline the offer. And that salary...! I know from some of my fellow journalism grads that that salary offer was much higher than the going rate for cub reporters. What gives?"

"You'll find out," was her only reply.

I continued to try and pry the mystery from her but she was adamant, so I soon dropped the subject.

At her house, Helen introduced me to her parents who were sitting in the living room watching TV. We exchanged the usual courtesies. Then Helen led me back to the front door. She reached up and kissed me on the cheek, squeezed my hand and whispered, "Thanks. That was just the kind of evening I was in the mood for. See you Monday."

Driving home, I reflected on how quickly values change when you are young. I did not know whether Helen O'Donnell was different than any other girl I had ever known or that somehow I had reached a new level of maturity. I had decided only recently that I still had a lot more wild oats to sow before I would be ready to settle down to one girl. But, though the free and easy life was still appealing, it had changed from a need to a very tentative want in just one day.

While lying in bed my mind wandered philosophically. One new plateau in my life had definitely been reached. I was no longer a societal parasite. I was now a self-supporting, tax paying member of society. And, best of all, I was a reporter for a big city newspaper. Of what I was not aware was that all that had transpired over the last few days was but one more step towards my fateful encounter with the life of Judge Ronald M. VanderLinde.

CHAPTER Two

Monday morning arrived exactly as predicted on my calendar. I reported again to the personnel office, this time to fill out tax forms, hospitalization forms and forms giving my new employer permission to ask me to fill out more forms.

After developing a sufficient degree of paralysis in my writing hand, Helen took me to the third floor city room where she introduced me to the Assistant News Editor, who in turn introduced me to some of my new comrades in arms, one of whom was Hank Chapman, whose duty it was to, "Show me the ropes." Hank was tritely labeled by the Assistant Editor as an, "old pro." Hank later confided that the "old pro" moniker meant merely that he had developed a mastery over Blakesley's two precious requirements. He sarcastically confided, "I think I can dictate a humorously, informative article about my own mother's demise in exactly two hundred thirty-seven words. That doesn't make me a good reporter. It only means that I'm a genius at making the Blake's life easier."

I was delighted to learn that Hank's opinion of our Managing Editor and his ridiculous demands were identical to my own. We developed an instant friendship and camaraderie that has lasted to this day.

On Monday and Tuesday, Hank led me around the city on assignments that were interesting but of little real news value: For the third time in a month a truck capsized on a sharply curved, sharply inclined off ramp on a cloverleaf exit to the downtown freeway tying up rush hour traffic for two hours; a sweet, gentle and petite housewife defended herself from the assault of her alcohol laden, common law husband with a butcher knife (husband not seriously injured but required eight stitches on his left cheek and sixteen on his right hand and fingers); the police were summoned by neighbors to a wealthy suburban home to quiet a boisterous party of teenagers who used the two-week absence of one of the boy's parents as an opportunity to throw a beer party (intoxicated youths taken into custody, parents notified, names withheld from publication); and other similar incidents.

On Tuesday afternoon I dropped into the personnel office to ask Helen to a local amateur production of *The Mad Woman of Chillot*. The performance was being given in one of those semi-round little theaters. In my ongoing cynicism at that time, I pictured the actresses in such presentations as frustrated housewives seeking the opportunity to gain a bit more attention and recognition than they garnered from their domestic careers, and also possibly the opportunity to prove to their husbands that they probably could have made it big in show business, had they not been so stupid as to get bogged down with marriage and kids. I surmised the motives of the men to be no better, but too numerous to catalogue here.

Most of the evening with Helen was made up of small talk, and, in spite of the obvious amateurism, the play was entertaining. Helen insisted we drop backstage after the show to compliment the male lead on his rendition of the Ragpicker. She had obviously seen him in other local appearances, since she told him that she thought this was his best performance yet. I found this, "after show" activity empathetically embarrassing, since most of the performers made fools of themselves eagerly seeking out added kudos beyond the curtain calls. Some of the members of the cast even came out from behind the curtain in full costume and makeup in search of departing friends, relatives and co-workers whom they probably had coerced into buying tickets and who were now being asked to pay the additional price of saying, "I didn't know you were so talented," with as much sincerity as they could muster. Watching the post show performance of some of the members of the audience giving their cajoled applause to their costumed friends, I concluded that there was probably as much acting talent in the seats as there had been on stage.

Fortunately, the Ragpicker was not of this breed. As noted, Helen knew him from performances at other theaters. He was a successful business and family man who simply enjoyed the creative outlet that amateur theater provided... much as some men involve themselves in woodworking or model trains in their basement, adult playrooms. Helen elaborated her compliments with an expression of appreciation for the manner in which the actor had developed the full measure of self-assurance and independence that were essential to the soul of the free spirited Ragpicker without carrying these necessary qualities to the point of arrogance that would have turned his character into a Cyrano de Bergerac. Drama as an art form was never my forte, so I merely added that I enjoyed his performance very much.

From the theater we went back to that restaurant/lounge, which was the location of our first outing, but this time for something to eat. The small talk continued until we pulled up in front of Helen's house where she asked, "Have you met Mr. Holmes yet?"

"Who?" I asked.

"Mr. Samuel Holmes, our illustrious Owner/Publisher."

I confessed that I had never bothered to concern myself with who owned or published the paper and then added, "He probably doesn't know I exist."

"Oh he knows," she rebutted with a playful smile.

"What possible interest would the owner of a large city newspaper have in a relatively unimportant new employee?" I inquired in a rather sarcastic tone.

"You'll find out," she responded in a manner that only increased the mystery.

"Do you know when I'll meet him?"

"Very soon I would guess," she answered, continuing to tease.

"But why would he want to meet me?" I insisted.

At this, Helen reached for the doorknob. "Wouldn't spoil it for you for anything in the world! It's late. Now get out of here."

Before I could object, she threw me a kiss and scooted out of the car and into the house, leaving me sitting in a state of absolute bewilderment.

The following morning I reported to Hank as usual, but instead of a "Hello," he greeted me with the announcement that Mr. Holmes wanted to see me. In spite of Helen's warning of the previous evening, I was, nevertheless, taken aback.

"When?" I asked.

"As soon as you get in.," he grinned.

"Would you tell me what this is all about?" I pleaded.

"Never," he retorted, now chuckling out loud. "You have the experience of your young life coming up. It would ruin it for you, if you knew what to expect. We have a strict code here not to tell new employees about Holmes until they have encountered him. It's a kind of initiation. Seventh floor and don't forget to tell me how it goes."

As Hank turned to go I observed, "You said, 'Encountered him.' Isn't 'Encounter' a little combative for a simple employer/employee meeting?"

"Actually, I thought, encounter was rather euphemistic," he chuckled again.

On the elevator I could not decide whether to be excited, worried or frightened, so I just relaxed and allowed myself to experience all three emotions at once.

When the elevator doors opened I was surprised to find a very ordinary scene. A receptionist was sitting behind a secretarial desk in a plush, carpeted corridor. I approached the desk and announced, "My name is Francis Becks."

"Yes, I know," she replied. "Mr. Holmes is expecting you." She pressed a button on her intercom. "Mr. Becks is here, sir." She rose and led me to a door to the left and rear of her desk.

Samuel Holmes' office was huge. The three walls that were in view as I entered the room were covered with the same wood paneling that decorated the outside of Blakesley's enclosure. It was easy for my imagination to recreate the scene that led to the frugal decision not to waste the scrap materials from the refurbishing of the publisher's office but, rather, to use them to build a segregated space for the Managing Editor. I was certain that someday I would discover a conspicuous opening somewhere in the building from which was extracted the anomaly that became Blakesley's door.

The carpeting was a very deep avocado and even more plush than that in the outer corridor. The rich gold drapes that fell from ceiling to floor and that covered the center half of the wall behind Holmes drew my attention to the extreme height of the room. It appeared that the ceiling and, consequently, the floor above had been removed to make this room two stories high. I could not begin to figure out what purpose this extravagant use of office space could fulfill. The Mediterranean styled desk bragged of rich, natural wood grain, oversized and slightly too elegant. By deliberately concentrating on my peripheral vision I could discern paintings hanging on the sidewalls. They were done in rather exotic hues. In the far right corner of the room stood a gray on gray marble pedestal with white streaks running between the changing shades. The pedestal was the nesting place for an ebony bust of some ancient historical character that I could not identify. The sculptured figure wore a stern expression on his face and a Pharaoh type headpiece aloft. The other corner held a right-angled bookcase of the same style and grain as the desk. It was filled with well-worn volumes of varying sizes and shapes. To the immediate left of the desk was a black twisted, wrought iron planter spewing a profusion of multi-shaded green foliage that spouted upwards, outwards and downwards. Two heavily cushioned black-leathered chairs were residing in front of the desk, properly aligned with the outer edges of the desk but aimed inward so that a seated occupant would be facing directly at the party sitting behind the desk, which, in this case, obviously, was Mr. Samuel Holmes. He was very short and equally thin and his dwarf-like appearance made the huge desk behind which he sat and the immense chair that engulfed him seem larger than they were, which, in turn, made him appear smaller than he actually was.

Holmes failed to rise as I approached his desk and he made no effort to extend to me a hand to shake. He merely motioned to me to be seated, which I did, allowing myself to be absorbed by one of the soft, leather chairs. Holmes raised his eyes to meet mine as I entered the room, but they quickly dropped again, refocusing on the multitude of items that lay sprawled on the top of his desk. There were six or seven books and a black folder in which were bound seventy or eighty typewritten pages. All of these were open and angled towards him. Directly in front of him were several sheets of paper. One was lined and covered with handwritten mathematical calculations. A second showed a large spoked circle with two smaller circles near the center. It was spotted with what appeared to be Egyptian Hieroglyphics and Roman numerals irregularly placed inside and outside of the circles. I recognized the third sheet as the original copy of my application form.

When I had entered, Holmes' hands were under the desk with his forearms resting on his thighs. His head was over the desk and moving quickly in all directions: referring to my application form, then to the scratch sheet, then up to one of the books, over to another book, down to the wheel like paper, etc. After about five trips around the desk, his head finally rose to an upright position though his body remained over the desk. Looking at me intensely and speaking in a soft, sincere voice he asked, "Do you believe in astrology, Mr. Becks?"

I was embarrassed that he had caught me by such surprise that I had allowed my mouth to drop open. If required to compose a million opening statements from an employer to his newly hired employee, I definitely would not have included, "Do you believe in astrology?" I struggled to regain my poise and at the same time to conjure up a reply that could not be taken offensively. I quickly deduced that the publisher was an avid believer. Why else would he begin our conversation with a reference to the subject? However, wanting to leave the door open to the possibility that his remark simply reflected a momentary mental aberration, I decided to play it in a noncommittal fashion. Consequently, I elusively responded, "I've never studied astrology, sir. I couldn't say whether it is a valid science or not."

"Oh, it is a valid science, Mr. Becks. Yes, it is a very valid science. As a matter of fact, it is superior to and supersedes all of the other sciences. You see, Mr. Becks, astrology gives everything, including science itself, its scope, its limitations, its purposes, its very meaning and reason for existence. Do you believe that, Mr. Becks? You should!"

Diplomacy was strongly dictating that I show a willingness to accept some of Holmes' remarks, but, though I am not beyond an occasional exercise in hypocrisy when expediency demands, there are depths to which even I will not descend. I was on a tightrope. How could I admit my real opinion of astrology without biting the hand that I hoped would be feeding me for many years to come? Striving to give the impression that I did agree without actually doing so, I said, "It would be presumptuous of anyone to arbitrarily deny a belief that is held by so many people. After all, there are millions of readers throughout the world who follow their daily horoscopes in their newspapers. Fifty million Frenchmen can't be wrong. Can they, sir?" I answered with a nervous laugh.

"You have made an excellent point, Mr. Becks...yes, a very excellent point."

During these remarks, Holmes' head was nodding up and down as though he were not only agreeing with my statement, but was also listening to what he was saying and agreeing with himself as well.

He continued, "Are you aware, Mr. Becks, that the Zodiac is as old as recorded time and that we find reference to it in almost all civilizations as each became capable of writing a lasting form of communication? Each has its own individual characteristics, but all are the same in that they establish a celestial influence on man. There are many other similarities as well. Does the fact that all of these different cultures, many separated by thousands of miles and impenetrable terrain, nevertheless, developed a Zodiac that may appear drastically different but are essentially the same tell you anything, Mr. Becks?"

Not knowing what this enlightening bit of historical data was intended to tell me, I replied, "I'm not sure, sir."

"It means that primitive men, totally independent of one another and free of the limiting influences of sophistication and materialism, discovered the same truths buried deep within their natures. It is a known fact,

Mr. Becks, that animals have greater sensory capabilities than do men. Isn't that so?" Fortunately he did not wait for an answer. "The reason is that man, depending more and more on his developing intellect, allowed his senses of smell and sight and hearing to fade. So too, primitive man was in great need of all facets of his intellect, not just his ability to reason analytically but also his capacity to reason intuitively. Do you understand what I am saying, Mr. Becks?"

He finally asked a question to which I could answer with unqualified affirmation. I blurted out, "Oh, yes. Completely, sir."

"Good." He went on, "Just as he allowed his physical senses to deteriorate through lack of use, so too, modern man, relying almost exclusively on his powers of analytical reasoning, has allowed his intuitive capabilities to fade and lie dormant. All that is involved in clairvoyance, in the predicting of the future, is a rekindling of man's ability to reason intuitively and to draw upon that vast reservoir of knowledge hidden deep within the nature of each of us. What do you think of that, Mr. Becks?"

I was actually impressed with the logic of his arguments, albeit, they were far from conclusive, as well as the clarity with which he expressed them, so I flatteringly told him so, minus the inconclusiveness, of course. However, I had a strong feeling that neither the reasoning nor the expressions thereof were his, but that he was merely quoting lines from one or more of the worn books resting on his desk or on the shelves of the corner bookcase.

Having completed his course in introductory astrology, Holmes set about instructing me in matters much more specific and far more pertinent to the two of us. He dropped his head over the papers again and exclaimed, "I see from your application that you were born at 12:31 AM, on September 24, 1948. Is that right, Mr. Becks?"

Since the time of day seemed as important to him as the date of my birth, I was not disposed to admit that I had fabricated the hour at which I was born. I nodded affirmatively.

"That was a very exciting time, Mr. Becks, a very exciting time. The heavens were alive with activity."

At this, Holmes began reciting a long list of planetary aspects. He named planet after planet, expounding how each was in conjunction or square or trine or sextile to one or more of the other planets or the moon or the sun. The more he spoke, the more excited he became and the longer became the span between breaths. When he finally completed the list of aspects, he was required to gasp for air. However, he paused only long enough to regain his wind. "I have never seen a nativity like yours, Mr. Becks, never! It's just pregnant with possible interpretations...just pregnant."

Though I had no idea why my "nativity" was so astronomically "pregnant," I quickly extended an appreciative smile to the author of such an obvious pun. But the smile was squandered. Holmes was so intently engrossed in his grandiloquent dissertation that, unbelievably, he was oblivious to his accidental witticism.

He continued, "Would you like to know some things about yourself, Mr. Becks?"

I was obviously expected to say that I was so I replied, "Certainly," with a level of enthusiasm that surprised even me.

For the first time since I had entered the room, Holmes raised his hands above the desk. He reached up to draw one of the books a little closer and to turn a few pages on two others. I noticed that the outer sections of his thumbs and forefingers were encased in transparent, plastic friction tips. I assumed he used them to facilitate the turning of the pages in the books. But I also observed that he clutched a small, white handkerchief in his right hand, which he used to wipe any part of his unprotected hand that might accidentally brush one of the books, a paper, the desk or even his own clothing. He was very careful and such accidents occurred infrequently, but the incidents were common enough to establish a definite pattern.

Bending far forward over two of the books, Holmes began describing me with a long series of personal tendencies and traits, about fifty percent of which were general enough to include everyone I had ever met. When the analysis did become specific, I found about twenty percent of it accurate, sixty percent partly accurate and the other twenty-percent ridiculous, since it directly contradicted the first twenty-percent. Holmes constantly interjected explanations into his evaluations. The reason that I possessed a certain quality, or tendency or characteristic was that a named planet was at the time of my birth residing in a given numbered house and that house was being ruled by a particular Zodiacal sign. I admired the research that must have been involved in such a study, but my appreciation was considerably abated by the occasional inclusion of inconsistencies that were so glaringly apparent that I was astounded that even Holmes failed to see them. One such contradiction appeared early in the analysis. Holmes declared that at my birth Venus and Pluto were sixteen degrees into Leo, the ruler of my first house. Venus, so situated, meant that I was a person who appreciated the good life and that I wanted the comforts it could give without realizing that I would be required to work for them. He then followed Venus with a brief explanation of Pluto's significance at this celestial position. At this point, Holmes erupted into a heightened state of excitement. "Ah, Mr. Becks. This is very interesting... very interesting. Saturn is not in Leo but it is, nevertheless, in your first house. You see, Mr. Becks, your ascendant is two degrees into Leo but Saturn is only one degree into Virgo. This puts Saturn in your first house and that means...," he turned a few pages in one of the books, "that you are hard working, overly conscientious and that you often seek situations in which to satisfy your desire to be punished. Have you noticed that tendency in yourself, Mr. Becks?"

I answered, "Not really, sir," but then quickly added, "Though I could be so inclined without realizing it. Couldn't I, Sir?"

What I really wanted to say was that between Venus and Saturn, my astrological interpreter had just described a hard working sloth that was also a hedonistic masochist.

When Holmes finally appeared to finish my horoscope, I was frustrated to discover that he had not finished at all. "I suppose you are curious why I omitted the positions of the moon and Jupiter," he queried. "I did that on purpose. You'll understand why later."

Holmes had mentioned so many planets in so many houses and Zodiacal signs that I had found it difficult to believe that he had left any unmentioned. I had always enjoyed a bright sun at the beach and I was delightfully aware of the benefits of moonlight illuminating the golden sheen in a girl's hair. However, beyond these simple phenomena, I never bothered to concern myself with the names, numbers or positions of the balance of our neighbors in the solar system.

Holmes now opened the upper left hand drawer of his desk and removed another circled sheet of paper on which was scribbled the same type of hieroglyphics that adorned the sheet already on his desk. "I am about to tell you some things about myself, Mr. Becks, things that may help you understand why I place so much faith in the Zodiac."

He leaned forward even farther than before and his voice took on that soft quality that one uses when he is taking another person into his confidence in matters very intimate. "This is my horoscope, Mr. Becks, a horoscope that has foretold all of the major events in my life; even incidents that occurred long before I knew anything about the science of astrology."

It was difficult for me to determine whether the pause that ensued was a genuine effort to recall past events or whether it was an excuse to give me an opportunity to offer some gesture of encouraging interest in his life history. I decided to remain mute but I rose slightly in my chair and jutted my head forward with as much of an interested expression on my face as I could muster under such circumstances.

If encouragement was what he sought, my actions sufficed. He was soon immersed body and soul in a presentation of the planetary positions at what he identified as his "nativity." The question quickly came to mind whether he would refer to a "pregnancy" of activity among those planets.

"I have a very favorable horoscope, Mr. Becks, a very favorable one. You see, I was born at 2:39 PM Eastern Standard Time on October 10, 1933. And 2:39 PM at 85 degrees North Latitude is 2:11 PM true Greenwich Time, which on October 10, 1933 was 15:26 Sedial Time. You know what Sedial Time is, don't you, Mr. Becks?"

I was getting a strong message that Holmes was trying to impress me with a superior knowledge of time zone differentials and astrological terminology so I decided to gamble. Having spent a summer vacation with East Coast relatives who were sailing buffs, I knew quite well that Sedial Time was a dimension used by navigators to shoot the stars. However, in an effort to flatter my host's ego, I played dumb by responding erroneously, "I'm afraid I don't, sir."

My sensitivity to Holmes' real intent did not fail me. He smiled proudly, obviously pleased with his lexical triumph. He paused just long enough to satisfy his vanity and then, like all truly unlearned, learned men in such a parlance, he made an overly gracious, condescending gesture so as to avoid overly embarrassing his ignorant protégé. Lifting his hands, shoulders, head and eyebrows in an expression indicating that my ignorance of the subject of Sedial Time was of only relative importance he went on, "Well it really doesn't matter anyway. The important thing is that, at my birth, Aquarius was rising on my ascendant and that Jupiter was in my ninth house. A sextile Mars, a trined Saturn, excellently supported Libra and, you may not believe this, Mr. Becks, but Jupiter was conjunct with the Sun. That's right... conjunct with the Sun. The only affliction to my Jupiter was a mild influence by the moon."

Holmes was literally bubbling with pride during the delineation of these aspects as though he himself had been responsible for the hour, day and place of his birth. His enthusiasm was of the contagious sort and I found myself almost blurting out, "Congratulations!" Fortunately, I caught myself in time to avoid such a blunder.

A highly detailed autobiography followed that included the astrological causes for all that had transpired during Holmes' life. Mercury squared to Saturn resulted in a premature birth and the subsequent near fatal lung congestion. However, Holmes' Sun-supported Jupiter brought him through this postnatal infirmity with miraculous ease. Significantly, neither nature nor medical science was given any credit for his recovery. Saturn residing in his first house caused the separation of his parents and gave him an early sense of responsibility. During his last two years of college, he was very interested in religion. This was due to his eighth house Neptune. After graduation his mother discouraged him from entering ministerial studies but rather convinced him to take a prolonged trip around the world to discover what life was all about before determining his future career.

"All of this was predicted, Mr. Becks, all of it! Jupiter in my ninth house, Uranus in my third house and Mars in Sagittarius all indicated worldwide contacts and extensive travel."

The travelogue that followed took us through the Philippines, Japan and the Far East. We stopped briefly in Tibet where an evil aspect of Mercury to Neptune confused Holmes spiritually. He was much intrigued by the Gelugpa Lamas at the Shiigatse Monastery who possessed a worldwide reputation for being guardians of many ancient secrets of life. Holmes even made a decision to remain permanently at the monastery but, fortunately, Mercury moved out of orb a few weeks later, allowing his mind to clear, and he continued his travels.

"The next major incident took place in Marrakech. Disaster befell me there, Mr. Becks, disaster! I went slumming in a dingy little dive on the evening of August 30 of '56. There was a sexy exotic dancer on stage and I fell in love at first sight. Anyone else might be embarrassed to admit this but I'm not. I couldn't help myself. You see, Venus had moved into a very bad aspect to Neptune that night... a very bad aspect. At such a time one can become easily mesmerized by someone else and do things they will gravely regret for many years later. Oh, you're probably wondering why Jupiter failed to come to my rescue. After all, Jupiter was sextile to Venus that night. But in my nativity Mars and the Sun supported Jupiter. On August 30th, Mars not only deserted me but also turned traitor and apparently so afflicted the Sun that it nullified the good aspects of Jupiter. I not only fell in love with the dancer, I proposed to her that very night and we were married two days later. I was helpless, Mr. Becks, helpless!"

Helpless Holmes may have been, but I suspected that he was influenced far more by glands than by planets.

The balance of the trip was now a honeymoon, though... regrettably shortened by some bad news. Holmes had kept in touch with his mother who cabled him in Paris that his father had died of a sudden heart attack. He returned home immediately, bride in hand, and to his mother's delight cured of his interest in the ministry.

Holmes' father had been the president of a large steel fabricating company and had served on the boards of directors of several other local firms. The estate was considerable and Holmes, being an only child, his inheritance was in the millions. However, Holmes was not satisfied in merely sitting back and enjoying his wealth. He spent several months trying to decide on a profession. Then, on November 14, 1956, he and his wife attended a party where he met a professional astrologer who was visiting from New York. She explained the planetary influences on man, and two days later Holmes permitted her to cast his horoscope.

"I knew that I had found the thing for which I had been searching all of my life, Mr. Becks... all of my life. She showed me how everything that had happened to me could have been predicted, even my meeting her. You see, Mr. Becks, on November 14 the moon had moved into trine with Uranus. This aspect indicated that a woman would enter my life for just a short time but that she would have a profound and prolonged effect on my future. Isn't that interesting, Mr. Becks? She told me that Neptune in my eighth house not only creates an interest in religion but also gives the native an aptitude for perceiving the future and a psychic ability to interpret the past. She said that I would make an excellent astrologer. She said that Mars in Sagittarius meant that I was capable of great accomplishments and that Jupiter in my ninth house indicated that I would influence people with my mind. Jupiter well aspected and in Libra meant that publishing would probably be my profession. As you can see, Mr. Becks, that prediction was obviously very accurate... very accurate indeed." He offered this last remark with a sweeping gesture of his right arm, indicating the surrounding environment and, consequently, his position as owner/publisher of a major newspaper.

Holmes then gave the account of how he acquired ownership of the paper. "Though the opportunity presented itself through the death of the previous owner in January of 1957, the best time to start any new venture is when the Sun is in good aspect to Jupiter, which would not take place until early May. I directed my attorney to drag out the proceeding, Mr. Becks. He was successful in finding a legal impediment, so all we had to do was sit back and wait a few months." As he began this last phrase, Holmes sat back in his chair and struck a pose of patient indifference, obviously to give the impression of a four month lapse in time.

As this whole interview had progressed, I had become aware that an extremely soft chair may be comfortable for short stays, but for lengthy visits it can inflict excruciating pain in the lower back and an aching stiffness in the shoulder and neck muscles. The heinous thought of being confined in that chair from January to May shot painfully through my mind. Fortunately, Holmes took only about four seconds of silence to portray the four-month wait wherein he picked up his story on the morning of May 15th when the title transfer was finally consummated.

Next, Holmes began divulging his marital difficulties... astrologically provoked, of course. All of the previous narrative varied from slight interest to abject bore, which was barely tolerable. But now I was expected to listen to a melodrama of an obvious soap-opera genre... and this with intense pain in my back and neck. "It was an ill-fated marriage, Mr. Becks... an ill-fated marriage," he confided. "Oh, it wasn't all my wife's fault. After all, Venus was in Scorpio in my nativity and this usually indicates more than one marriage. But my wife's horoscope was much more to blame. You see, she was born in Morocco on January 4th, 1936. Capricorn was just appearing on her ascendant. Her moon was in Taurus, which accurately described her as being voluptuous, indolent and self-indulgent. Uranus in her fifth house and Venus in her twelfth house said that she would have many love affairs, even affairs with married men. Venus in Sagittarius did mean that she wanted to be faithful in spite of herself. That's probably why she didn't play around at first. But when I cast both of our horoscopes in 1958, I saw the handwriting on the wall. On August 21st the moon would pass in opposition to Mars, which would raise her senses and emotions to a very high pitch. Then, the following day, Venus would move into conjunct with Uranus and would be in square to Neptune. I started warning her as early as January that on August 22nd she would enter a very sensuous state that could lead her to unwise actions and that a person would enter her life that would raise her emotions to the highest degree. She would be inclined towards a deceptive love. She would think that she was in love and she would believe that he was in love with her but all of this would be illusion. With Venus afflicted at her birth and now conjunct with Uranus, she would feel very affectionate and want to be free of all restrictions and inhibitions. I warned her that if she succumbed to these influences, she would have an affair that would lead to an open scandal. Then, from August 24th to September 11th, Venus would be in an evil aspect to Mars.

Her sexual instincts would remain very strong during this period. I warned her that all of these aspects indicated only a short affair, however, nothing lasting but something that she would regret, if she gave into these inclinations. I warned her, Mr. Becks. Honestly I warned her from early January until May 19th when Mars passed into an evil aspect to Saturn. This made her feel abused and ill treated. She screamed at me that night. She told me that my astrological interpretations were driving her out of her mind. Oh, she tried to blame her irritation on me, Mr. Becks, but I knew that Mars and Saturn were the real culprits. She finally said she wanted a divorce and walked out. She could have avoided so much trouble, if she had only listened to me, Mr. Becks, so much trouble."

Holmes made no effort to hide the pathos in his voice. The anguish at not being able to convince his wife was sincere. I almost felt sorry for him but my own excruciating back and shoulder pain prevented me from extending any great level of compassion.

According to the narrative, Mrs. Holmes filed for divorce immediately after leaving her husband and subsequently sought a substantial amount of alimony. "I knew that both my legal and financial chances would be best when Mercury was in good aspect to Jupiter. I was successful in getting the trial date set for October 16th. In the meantime, I hired a private investigator that placed my wife under surveillance. I told him to watch her especially during the period of August 21 to September 11. On the night of August 27th, he photographed her in a very compromising situation with her own lawyer in his backyard swimming pool. I understand her lover's family was out of town for the week. With the pictures as evidence, I was able to file a countersuit for adultery. My attorney tried to dissuade me from using the pictures in court, since such a disclosure could ruin many other lives. He suggested that we present the pictures to the principle only and that we seek an out-of-court settlement, which would avoid adverse publicity. But, as I said before, any affair that occurred while my wife's afflicted Venus was conjunct to Uranus would result in notoriety and scandal anyway. So I saw no reason not to show the pictures in court. Naturally it was messy. My wife's lawyer lost his association with his law firm and his wife left him. But Mercury came through for me. We made a very beneficial settlement. My poor wife received very little money and her lover deserted her right after the trial. The last time I heard of her she was dancing in a go-go bar somewhere on the near West Side. Why didn't she listen to me, Mr. Becks, why?"

This was obviously a rhetorical question so I refrained from replying.

"But then these are not your problems, are they, Mr. Becks? The reason I told this story is to convince you of... how did you put it, Mr. Becks? Oh, yes, 'The validity of the science of astrology.'"

Holmes had spent over a half-hour exposing many personal and even intimate details of his life in an effort to convince me that astrology was credible. All he did accomplish was to prove to me the truth in the sociological axiom that a man's beliefs, even if erroneous, can so influence his actions that his actions can actually bring about the condition that he believed existed in the first place. He tried so hard to win a disciple that, in spite of my aches and pains, I found it impossible to resist all of my sentiments of pity. I decided to give him some small reward. "You are very convincing, sir. I will certainly give the subject a great deal of thought. Who knows, I might become an astrologer myself."

He immediately rebuffed that idea. "Oh, I wouldn't consider becoming an astrologer, Mr. Becks. Your horoscope shows nothing of the insight required for that profession. No, I wouldn't advise that at all. Besides, I have an offer for you that is much more in keeping with your natural attributes. Do you remember that I told you I had deliberately omitted mentioning your moon and your Jupiter? Well, Mr. Becks, we were both born with an excellently aspected Jupiter. Yours was in your fifth house, Sagittarius. It was sextile to Mercury and trined to Venus and Pluto. That is very good, Mr. Becks. It means that you are a person of exceptional good luck but that you are not self-motivated. You need someone to push you to do the things by which you can fulfill your potential. Your moon in Gemini and in your eleventh house tells of a native who would make a superb reporter. On the negative side, you have a tendency towards change. You like to move about, but such moves will cost you financially and emotionally. Also, your security depends on others... not on yourself. Do you see the picture, Mr. Becks? You are a natural reporter and I am a natural publisher. You need motivation and I have the power to influence people. You need the security that others can provide and I am wealthy. You are lucky and I have the ability to turn my associations into gain. If we put all of this together, Mr. Becks, we see that we are mutually compatible. And with your joining my employ at this time while Jupiter is sextile to the Sun, we are destined to be of immense financial benefit to each other. Wouldn't you agree, Mr. Becks?"

Again Holmes failed to await a reply. "Now perhaps you will understand why I directed that you be hired... and at such a generous salary. I want you in my employ, Mr. Becks, and I want you to stay in my employ so that we can both reap the benefits of our association."

There was a deliberate pause to allow me to adequately appreciate his offer. Then, maintaining the same theme but adding a paternalistic overtone, he continued, "If you have any problems with your job, Mr. Becks, feel free to come to me. Oh, yes, and another thing...don't succumb to your tendency to job hop. Trust me, Mr. Becks. Moving about will only bring you misery."

Holmes was leaning forward during his description of our compatibility, but now he sat back in his chair. "I know I should not tell you how much I want you working for me. You could become complacent and slough off on the job, couldn't you?" He snickered as though he had put a naughty thought in my head. Then changing his expression to one of indifference he went on, "But that wouldn't matter, would it? Even if you did nothing but draw your paycheck, someday, somehow you will bring me great financial gain. Jupiter has never failed me."

All of the mysterious things that had happened within the past week now made sense: the speedy handling of my application, the application form itself, Blakesley's offer of a job while requesting that I decline the offer, the inflated salary. They all fit.

Holmes was peering at me intently. He was looking for some sign that I would accept his advice to resist my, "Tendency to job hop." I acquiesced. "I'm certain that I will be very happy here, sir."

He smiled confidently, seemingly satisfied that he had succeeded in all that he had intended with the interview. Since he said nothing further, I surmised that our meeting had ended. I rose very slowly out of consideration for the condition of my back. I extended my hand but Holmes declined my offer. Instead he gestured with his head towards the circled paper on his desk that bore my horoscope. "You may have that, if you wish, Mr. Becks. I have another copy for my files."

Since the paper was directly under my outstretched hand, I simply dropped my arm and picked up the paper. "Thank you, sir," I said, trying to sound as grateful as possible.

As I turned to leave, I was congratulating myself for the manner in which I had handled this bizarre episode. But as weird as the interview may have been, nothing in it prepared me for what I was about to confront. As I pivoted, I was frozen in a state of absolute paralysis. Now facing me was the wall through which I had entered the room and which stood behind me during the interview. The entire surface consisted of a huge, brightly colored, highly detailed mural of the traditional astrological wheel placed on a sky blue background. The wheel was covered with a myriad of symbolic figures displaying persons, animals and things. It reached from ceiling to floor and dramatically demonstrated that the reason the ceiling slash floor above had been removed was to make the height of the room as high as the width of the rear wall to allow for the unbelievable size of the wheel.

The cause of my immobility was obvious to Holmes, who said enthusiastically, even lovingly, "Magnificent isn't it? I spent $20,000 to have it designed and all of the details researched and another $25,000 to have it painted by one of the nation's leading muralists."

Though my back was to him, I could sense Holmes' face broadened in that special smile reserved to express the pride of ownership. I strongly felt that I was expected to say something in admiration. "It's . . . " I paused for several seconds, grasping for a phrase that would express my feeling and at the same time offer some degree of adulation. Finally I blurted out, "It's. . . it's very expressive, sir."

At that point I wanted out of that room more than I wanted anything else in the world, but when I looked for the door I could not see one. I knew that I entered through that wall so there had to be a door but it was obviously camouflaged as part of the mural. A momentary sense of desperation, even terror, swept over me. It was as though I were trapped forever in a nightmare. My eyes ran frantically back and forth across the wall until a small shadow indicated the possibility of a doorknob. I quickly walked (almost ran) to where I thought the knob was and reached for it. But my hand froze in midair. There was a picture of a scantily dressed woman on the wall where the door probably was located, and the knob, if that is what the shadow was, was located, not on, but uncomfortably near a part of the female anatomy towards which a gentleman does not reach unless he knows the lady very well. At that, a desperate voice in my head yelled, "It's only a picture, you jerk!" and I flung my hand onto the knob. But, in spite of my excusatory rationale, I muttered an instinctive, "Excuse me," under my breath as I turned the knob, opened the door, rushed through and closed it quickly behind me.

Finally outside of Holmes' office I simply paused and gave a deep sigh. The receptionist heard me and turned her head in my direction. I was aware that when I had arrived earlier at the seventh floor, I had been preoccupied with the anticipation of my interview with Holmes. Consequently, I could not be certain that what I now saw was nothing but an optical illusion resulting from the emotional shock of my recent adventure into the world of the occult. The receptionist appeared as though she properly belonged among the seventeenth century practitioners of the black arts. She wore long black hair that reached to her waist. Every strand was stiff and straight. Her narrow lips were covered with a purplish lipstick and her near black eyes, deep-set and slightly slanted by high cheekbones, were heavily outlined by dark eyeliner that gave her eyes an even greater impression of being sunken into her head. All of this was placed on a nut-brown complexion that gave off a slightly gray hue. Though she was sitting, I could see that she possessed that same tall thin figure with which Helen O'Donnell was blessed. However, on the receptionist it in no way radiated the cheerful, bright, willowy grace that was so becoming to Helen. Rather, her narrow shape made the receptionist look sinisterly reptilian. As our eyes met, I felt an awkwardness that was akin to embarrassment... as though I was standing before her spiritually naked. She seemed not to be looking at me but into me, reading not just my mind but also my very soul. Needless to say, I nearly ran to the elevator. The period during which I waited for the elevator doors to open was probably no longer than usual but it seemed interminable. I could feel the receptionist's eyes burning through the back of my head. When I entered the elevator, I pressed the button for the fifth floor but, as I descended, I realized that I was in no condition to return to the city room. I was not only trembling within, but my whole body was shaking. My vanity would not allow me to display such emotional instability before my peers, so when I reached the fifth floor, I simply let the doors open and close and pressed the button for the second floor. I decided that I was in need of a compassionate ear to help me settle my strained nerves. By the time I reached the personnel office, my hands had stopped shaking and my legs had regained most of their strength. I felt reasonably certain that I could conceal my inner turmoil. My confidence was ill founded, however. Helen saw me coming and while I was still twenty feet from her desk, she chided, "I see you've met Samuel Holmes."

"Does it show that much?" I queried timidly.

"Don't be ashamed," Helen offered understandingly. "Everyone wears that expression of bewildered disbelief after encountering our eccentric publisher."

"Hank Chapman used that same word, 'Encounter.' He said it was a euphemism for what really happens. I'm inclined to agree with him. I think assaulted is more like it."

Helen laughed in agreement and I requested her company for a cup of coffee and a little light conversation before I returned to work. I was surprised that it was only ten o'clock. Helen condescended and notified the switchboard accordingly. We went to the basement snack bar that doubled for a coffee shop and the main in-house lunchroom for most of the newspaper employees. It had been economically converted for that purpose with painted concrete block walls, a painted concrete floor and an inexpensive acoustical tiled ceiling. Ten or so rectangular tables and about seventy-five wooden folding chairs, both identical to those that furnished the testing room in the personnel office, stood uninvitingly around the room. The lack of comfort assured the company that no one would extend his or her coffee break or lunch period beyond the allotted time. One wall of the basement was lined with vending machines. One offered dark colored hot water, which the sign on the machine deceitfully described as coffee. Another vending machine tendered tuna fish, egg salad and chicken salad sandwiches from which all taste had been extracted with meticulous efficiency. Still another displayed a variety of leather-crusted pastries filled with flavored gelatin and an occasional small piece of fruit, which one could conclude had been inserted by accident.

I bought each of us a cup of so-called coffee and we sat at one of the tables. In spite of my tenacious efforts to rend from my mind the unpleasant ordeal with Holmes, my efforts were without success. Consequently, I decided that the best course was to talk the subject out of my consciousness. "Are all of the employees working here astrologically compatible with Holmes?" I asked.

"Not all of them," she answered. "When we interview for an open position or when people walk in off the street such as in your case, I have orders to send the original copy of the application to Holmes. If he determines that an applicant has astrological potential, I receive an order that he or she is to be hired. If the horoscope is adverse, I get a verbal, never a written, instruction that under no circumstances is that applicant to be offered a job. In most cases, however, the people who apply fall into neither category and the department heads are free to use their own judgment."

"Do you mean," I reacted in disbelief, "that should a Pulitzer Prize winning journalist apply for a job, he would be turned down because of a faulty horoscope?"

"Well," she admitted, "I doubt that anyone of that stature would want to work for this paper but, if he did, I honestly doubt that he would be hired."

Considering my brief experience with Holmes, I vocally contemplated, "I would say that you're probably right."

"By the way," Helen inquired, "How does it feel to have the kind of job security that Holmes has laid on you?"

"Frankly, I don't feel all that secure," I replied. "With a character like Blakesley as the Managing Editor and Holmes for a publisher, I have to wonder how long the paper will stay in existence." Then I added, "Who does the policy making anyway?"

"As best I can determine, we have no policy," was her answer. "Holmes told me in my interview that his horoscope made him the champion of the underdog, the poor and trade unions. I've seen a few editorials aimed in that direction, but besides those, we seem to be in favor of whatever is popular at the moment. I understand that Blakesley has the job of picking the political candidates that the paper endorses. But all he really does is wait until the final week before the election and then endorses the candidates that the polls say will win. That way, after each election, the paper can claim that it represents the views of the people in this area and at the same time brag that it exerts great influence on the community."

"But that's a contradiction," I interrupted.

"I suppose that's true," Helen agreed. "But both images sell papers so I doubt that anyone around here would bother to concern himself with anything as inconsequential as a contradiction."

By now our coffee was cold and I had relaxed enough to reenter the workingman's world. When I reached the city room, the Assistant Editor told me that Hank Chapman had been sent to cover another accident on the freeway and that I was now on my own. A short while later I was given my first solo assignment. I was off and running as a reporter for a big city newspaper.

CHAPTER Three

My next year and a half as a reporter was not uneventful but it was consistent. Though I enjoyed the challenge of writing copy about a variety of topics in the different moods that Blakesley ordered, I found myself completely inept at staying within his allotted number of words. Consequently, I was summoned to the Managing Editor's office two or three times a week to be the recipient of what were, to my mind, irrationally, abusive dissertations about my mathematical deficiencies: some were pointed, some caustic, some darn right profane, but all were cuttingly nasty. Blakesley's numerous tirades included such classic utterances as, "For your edification and enlightenment, Mr. Becks, allow me to inform you that the number one hundred fifty falls quite regularly between the numbers one hundred and two hundred. Very rarely, and I mean very rarely has anyone discovered this number lounging between three hundred and four hundred." Another gem involved a poignant essay on the sociological importance of words. "Communication, Mr. Becks, is an indispensable function for any form of social interaction and words are one of the most useful tools available for this purpose. Therefore, when I say the words, 'Two hundred,' I am attempting to convey a thought from my mind to your mind. However, when you respond to those words by submitting five hundred words of copy I, being a reasonably rational person, must conclude that there is some sort of communicative problem here. And so, since I know that my gray cells are intact and in good working order, I have deduced that there must be some malfunction among yours. In short, you must be a bloomin' moron." The last phrase of course was delivered with increasing decibels and emotional intensity. On one occasion Blakesley even offered to pay the tuition, if I took a first grade course in arithmetic.

At first I was not at all certain that I was as secure in my job as Holmes had tried to make me feel so I made a sincere effort to comply with Blakesley's numbers. But about three months after I had started working for the paper, Blakesley concluded one of our more abrasive sessions by admitting that he had become so completely disgusted with my performance that he had pleaded futilely with Holmes to allow him to fire me. Hearing this, I realized that there was little that I could do or not do that would jeopardize my job. After that, I missed Blakesley's word count even farther than I had previously. To this day I am not certain whether I simply became complacent or if I was deliberately trying to make my editor's life even more miserable than I had prior. I must admit that the latter concept was a delicious consideration.

During these distasteful meetings the red light over the editor's door was brightly gleaming, broadcasting my plight to all in the city room. By late summer, I had spent so much time in Blakesley's office that the fifth floor personnel were referring to the light as, "Becks' Beacon."

Socially my life was definitely on the rise. Helen O'Donnell and I went out regularly and I was beginning to know more about drama and the theater than I thought I would ever want to know.

Under Helen's inducement I even became involved in a production of *The Man Who Came To Dinner* that was being presented by the young adult group at her church. Rehearsals started in August and the performances were held during the last two weekends in September. I was assigned the job of lighting director and for several nights a week for the weeks preceding the performances I was engrossed in an effort to project the right colored lights at the correct spot on stage at the precise moment that the play director wanted.

There was a matinee and evening performance on each Sunday and we sent out for supper so that the cast would not be required to remove their makeup and costumes between shows. On the second Sunday I brought along a flask with which to celebrate after the final presentation but imprudently decided to start early, between shows, and more imprudently, I ignored the fried chicken. In short, I drank my supper. The bourbon hit my stomach much more quickly and with a greater impact than I had anticipated. By six o'clock I was on stage, blissfully high, and reciting some poetry that I had read as required reading in college and had enjoyed enough to submit to memory. Some of the poems were humorous but a few were serious and quite meaningful, especially for a cynic. The cast and stagehands were sitting in the audience eating their suppers and some of them were squirming with embarrassment at my uninhibited flamboyance.

Fortunately, I sobered up before the evening performance, which, unfortunately, turned into a shambles. The doorbell failed to ring at one point during the first act and the main character, Whiteside, and his secretary were required to ad lib for several minutes. Then, early in the second act one of the performers skipped two pages of the play. A second actor attempted to return to the spot in the script at which the omission took place. This so confused another member of the cast that he stood mute and petrified staring at one of the side drapes behind which sat the equally confused prompter. The panic on stage was only exceeded by the panic of the actors behind the backdrop. One of the female leads that was by nature a dominating, take charge type, decided that she could salvage the scene and made an unscheduled entrance down center. Her action startled those already on stage and the result was that a full seven pages of the manuscript were skipped. At this, the director who was sitting in the audience admiring his creative handiwork darted back stage and ordered the curtain drawn. That night I discovered that Sunday night church audiences would enjoy anything offered to them. At the end of this comedy within a comedy, they gave the cast a standing ovation.

Driving home, I apologized to Helen for having made a fool of myself between performances. She mused thoughtfully, "Some of those poems were lovely. I didn't know you were that sensitive or that deep. Were you required to memorize them in school?"

"Not really," I admitted. "Those poems had some ideas and expressions that just seemed to hit a responsive chord. I've never thought of myself as sensitive or deep actually... just a person who enjoys living things when I run across them. I like to try to feel the feelings of the poets and novelists or any other kind of writer while I'm reading their creations."

My eyes were mainly on the road but occasionally I looked over at my companion. She was sitting at the far edge of the seat leaning mainly against the back seat but partly against the door in an angle that turned her slightly towards me. Her expression was reflective. "That's the same thing." she philosophized. "Only a person who is sensitive can appreciate the joys and sufferings of others. And only a person who can feel compassionately and empathetically with others is capable of really loving. And as far as I'm concerned, real loving and real living are the same." She paused momentarily and then added, "I was pretty sure there was something beneath that glib, nonchalant exterior you usually project." Again she paused, and then uttered pensively, as though she were almost reluctant to admit it, "Now I know."

This was an exceptional mood for Helen. I had never seen her so consistently somber before. She was never frivolous but she had always impressed me with her genuinely wholesome, lighthearted approach to things.

Ignoring her comment about my glibness I pondered out loud, "And only a person who is capable of a profound love can know that living and loving are synonymous."

Neither of us spoke for the remainder of the ride to Helen's house nor while we walked to the door. Standing in the inner hallway we simply looked into each other's eyes trying to see if what we heard each other say was in truth what and who we were. Helen was the first to break the silence. "Well, it's finally happened to me."

"To us," I countered.

We were exhausted from the afternoon and evening performances and were both in a very simple, tender and caring mood. Consequently, what I considered our first truly loving kiss reflected those gentle sentiments.

My Christmas present to Helen three months later was a ring, which she insisted that she help me pick out. The style was simple and the solitary stone was delicately, almost precariously, set. In spite of my objections it was also relatively inexpensive.

During the months before and after our engagement, I became thoroughly acquainted with Helen's family. Her mother was relatively short and of average weight with hair that was in the last stages of turning silver gray. Her simple meat and potatoes table was attractive and tasty and her house was neat with a heavy emphasis on comfort, especially for her husband whom she frequently treated as lord of the manor. She possessed a very quick wit but her humor was never cutting or at the expense of anyone else's feelings. She was religiously orientated and totally dedicated to her family.

Mr. O'Donnell was the Irish Catholic version of the WASP: hard working, bigoted and overly protective of his job, home and family.

He was an ironworker and a foreman for a large, local construction company. His face was red and leathery and showed the affects of exposure to year round weather.

Helen's three younger sisters were delightful. Each had a strikingly different personality and each was what I like to call, "a liver." When they were happy, they were ecstatic. And when they were unhappy, they acted as though the entire world was falling apart around them.

Bridget was seventeen and in her final year in high school. Her hair was sandy red and on occasion she would succumb to tempers of absolute despair over the multitude of freckles that dotted her otherwise very light complexion. "How can a boy even see me through all these ugly spots," she would complain. On a few occasions I tried to convince her that her affliction only enhanced her beauty but she would not be consoled. I finally decided that periods of melancholy were normal for an adolescent girl and I contented myself with telling her in various indirect and subtle ways that she was pretty.

Colleen was fourteen and just beginning to show her entrance into womanhood. She was a bit awkward, having recently added some six inches to her height and her medium shaded skin, which blended quietly with her dishwater blond hair, bore none of the freckles which were so devastating to her older sister. Colleen was the scholar in the family and, though she spent most of her free time reading, she was sweet and charming and demonstrated a capacity for conversation that was considerably beyond her years.

Then there was Kathleen. I think that every Irish family has a Kathleen. She is usually the "baby" of the family, seemingly delicate and helpless (though not really) and a creature whom everyone she will ever meet will enjoy spoiling. I knew early in my relationship with Helen that a priceless bonus to that relationship would be my opportunity to watch her younger sisters grow through nature's process of turning awkward, moody, even hysterical little girls into lovely, graceful, mature young women.

The next significant incident on the job occurred in early February. My occupational security allowed me to ease into a complacency that apparently was not limited to the numbers game. On this occasion of interest I was assigned to cover a double, three-alarm fire in an empty warehouse on the Near East side. By the time I had reached the scene, flames were leaping from every window in sight as well as through the roof. The fire department had given up on the warehouse and the firemen were concentrating their hoses on the surrounding buildings in an effort to prevent the fire from spreading. The temperature was only slightly above zero and a fierce, rapidly changing wind was whipping the freezing spray from the hoses in all directions covering everything within a two-block radius with a thick icy glaze.

Never having been attracted to the particular stimulants enjoyed by the

Polar Bear Club members, I parked my car three blocks from the fire and remained comfortably inside. From experience I knew that the important facts for such a story were the number of fire companies called to battle the blaze, the estimated loss to the owner or owners and the speculated cause of the fire, all of which I could attain from the Fire Chief after the excitement and, in this case, after the danger of pneumonia had passed.

However, I was not permitted this prudent exercise in preventive medicine. One of the fire companies that was ordered to move its equipment from in front of the warehouse to a position two buildings down the street was hindered from doing so by a thick layer of ice that had frozen a hose to the pavement. While three firemen were struggling to loosen it, the brick, front wall of the three-story warehouse toppled forward on top of them.

It was a horrifying sight and, though I knew that my presence would interfere rather than aid the rescue, I instinctively bolted from the car and ran to the accident. By the time I had reached the scene the other firemen were successfully clearing the rubble covering the fallen men. All of the newspapers, as well as the radio and television stations, were represented and the reporters had gathered in an empty storefront across from the warehouse. I joined my colleagues and we watched as the men were placed on stretchers and carried to nearby ambulances. All three of the firemen appeared conscious, though in a great deal of pain. As the sirens blared and then faded, one of the reporters collared an Assistant Fire Chief who gave us the identity of the injured men with the stipulation their names be withheld until the next of kin were notified. He also added that, except for some very deep bruises and bad lacerations and what appeared to be a crushed leg, the men seemed to have miraculously escaped any life threatening injuries. Since the fire was finally under control and the unheated store was offering little protection from the cold, I decided to leave the scene.

Though it was not yet noon, I decided to call it a day work-wise. It was Friday and Helen and I had planned to leave immediately after work for a three-day weekend of skiing in the Pocono Mountains. When I reached the downtown area, I stopped at a sporting goods store to pick up a few pieces of skiing apparel and to phone my story to the paper. I also needed to cash my check and convert some of it into traveler's checks. The shopping plus the banking, the latter of which was greatly delayed by the Friday payday crowd took much longer than I had expected.

I was surprised that it was almost 4:30 when I arrived at the newspaper to pick up Helen. As I entered the building the switchboard operator signaled to me. She informed me that Blakesley had left a message to have me report to his office should I return to the paper. I asked the operator to tell Helen the reason for my delay and I jaunted blissfully up to the Managing Editor's office expecting another lecture on mathematics. However, as I entered his office I sensed something different about Blakesley's ire... somewhat ominous, as a matter of fact.

He was holding a copy of one of our competitors' papers in front of him and without dropping it he grunted caustically, "You composed an interesting story about that warehouse fire, Becks. And believe it or not you came reasonably close to the correct number of words."

Sliding the paper into his lap he continued, "I assume that reporters from the other papers were on hand to cover the story too?" Not knowing where this conversation was leading I simply nodded affirmatively. "Would you like to see your story, Becks?" he goaded playfully. A copy of our afternoon edition was lying flat on his desk. He picked it up and turned to one of the inner pages. "I regret that the story was not of sufficient importance for us to give you a byline. That way the whole world could know who it is that makes my life so miserable."

He passed the paper to me opened to the page that bore the warehouse fire story. It was a short article with a small headline that read factually, "East Side Warehouse Destroyed By Fire." I scanned the copy briefly; confirming that it read mostly as I had dictated and then looked back at Blakesley, still bewildered by the cause of his obvious irritation.

The Managing Editor raised the other newspaper from his lap. "Would you like to see how our competitors handled the story?" he sneered wryly.

He continued to hold the paper in his hands but turned the front page in my direction. A fifth of the way down the page glared a large, bold headline, "TWO FIREMEN DIE IN WAREHOUSE BLAZE." Immediately above the story was an editorial entitled, "WHEN WILL CITY ORDER ABANDONED BUILDINGS DEMOLISHED?"

I quickly read the first few paragraphs of the editorial, which stated that if the city building inspectors were doing their jobs, empty, deserted firetraps such as the warehouse would be condemned and torn down before they could become tombs for our valiant fire fighters. The editorial went on to offer a thousand dollars as the initial donation for a fund it was starting to help the family of one of the deceased firemen. The family was shown in a four by six portrait lower on the page. The picture showed the fireman and his middle-aged wife surrounded by upwards to ten children ranging in age from the baby in its mother's arms to a boy of about sixteen.

One White Camellia

A photograph of the fireman in uniform was also shown. The second victim was a nineteen-year-old rookie, whom the lead story described, quoting one of his superiors, as, "One of the brightest and nicest kids that ever joined the department."

Blakesley held the paper in front of me far longer than I would have normally expected. I assumed that he knew that the more I read the more uncomfortable I would feel. If so, he was right. When he finally decided that I had enough time to realize the journalistic importance of the story he lowered the paper and in a soft, stabbing tone he snarled, "I think you missed a few facts, Becks."

Naturally, I tried to defend myself. Partially stammering I protested, "The men were still alive when I left the fire. I had to get what I had back to the paper before the deadline."

Blakesley snapped back angrily, "Don't try to snow me, Becks. I happen to know that the paper before me has exactly the same deadline we have. Now, unless one of its reporters can foretell the future, I would say that you had as much time to get as many facts as your counterpart on this paper." During this tirade Blakesley's voice rose consistently and considerably in volume and as he concluded with the phrase, "this paper," this paper came flying across the desk at me leaving me standing with egg on my face and a large, unfolded, partially crumpled, papery bundle in my arms.

"It seems, Becks," Blakesley continued, now with an expression of exasperated despair, "That I not only cannot trust you with submitting the correct number of words but that I also cannot trust you to cover a story with any level of competence. That creates a problem for me, wouldn't you say?"

At this point in the conversation I was not about to say anything.

"Since I can't fire you, and, since it would be devastating to the morale in the office, if you were just to sit at your desk all day long doing absolutely nothing, I have decided on an alternate course of action. I understand that your cousin's husband with whom you are currently residing was recently appointed City Purchasing Agent for the new administration. Such a contact within the inner circles of the mayor's office can be invaluable for a newspaperman. How would you like to cover City Hall?"

For a split second I was delightfully surprised. Such assignments are considered plums, and usually awarded to reporters who have proven their journalistic excellence over many years of story chasing. But I quickly realized that there was something amiss here. My friend, Hank Chapman, had been given the City Hall beat only a month earlier and I understood that he was doing a good job on it.

Blakesley caught my initial delight and moved quickly to dispel any inference that he was offering me a promotion. "You know, of course, that we already have a good man covering the administration. I am assigning you as his assistant. The way I see it, if you should be lucky enough to accidentally stumble on a story, I can count on Chapman to follow up and...." Blakesley leered at me adding a deeper contempt in his voice, "Get all of the facts."

He paused to enjoy the pleasure of twisting the knife he had plunged into my ego. "By the way, let Chapman write the copy. You just pump your cousin-in-law for material. That way I'll have you out of my hair and, for the most part, out of my life."

Blakesley did not extend the courtesy of telling me that the meeting was over. He simply reached his hand under his desk and started reading a few memos from his "in" box. Though he no longer paid any attention to me, I was certain he was mentally watching my person swinging in the breeze.

The statement that the Managing Editor had made about my cousin-in-law's appointment was a reference to a topic that had a much more personal bearing on my life than simply the occupation of an in-law. A few months earlier I had attended a wedding of a cousin whose family my family visited a couple times a year as I was growing up. As it turned out, one of the bride's sisters grew up to be a serious status seeker. When her husband was recently rewarded for political patronage with his new position as Purchasing Agent for the city, she felt that they deserved to live in a domicile in keeping with her spouse's newly attained station. Consequently, she enticed her hubby to move into a luxury, two-bedroom suite on one of the upper floors of a high rise that was part of a downtown urban renewal project. Unfortunately, her husband's new title was much more prestigious than his new salary. Since the apartment building was only a five-minute walk to my paper, my cousin convinced me of the benefits of sharing the apartment and the rent. I never really liked the girl while we were growing up and was less enamored with her when she became an adult, so the offer of shared accommodations was not at all appealing. However, the convenience was, and, since the apartment would have been out of my price range too, the shared rent idea was very attractive. So I accepted the offer. After all, I would be getting married in a while, at which time any discomfort in those living arrangements would instantly evaporate.

As it turned out, I was often required to exercise a great deal of patience with the unnatural accommodations. However, now that I was assigned to cover City Hall there was a definite advantage in living with my, as Blakesley put it, "cousin-in-law," especially since there were so many scandals being uncovered by the new administration about the corrupt practices of their predecessors.

After twenty years of domination by one political party, the people of the city had decided that a change was in order. Everyone knew that there was graft, payoffs, kickbacks and miscellaneous conflicts of interest for the two decades during which the former political dynasty manipulated the city government and its coffers. But the electorate never bothered to unseat the thieves as long as the administration continued to provide adequate public services and as long as the political profiteers had the decency to keep their unethical dealings discreetly out of the limelight.

During the recent campaign, however, the mayor, in a vulgar gesture of over confidence agreed to a late campaign television debate with his eager, young opponent. During the debate the challenger accused the mayor of a flagrant exercise in conflict of interest in awarding a contract for garbage removal to a company, which was owned by the mayor's two brothers and with which it was suspected his honor, himself, was a silent partner. However, these charges had been leveled before and answered by the mayor's press secretary as being perfectly legal in the first case and totally false in the second. The egregiousness of the first accusation was further exacerbated by the fact that the company in question submitted a bid significantly higher than the lowest bid offered. The defense argued that the law did not require acceptance of the lowest bid but rather, "the best bid," which opened the door for awarding the current contract to the mayor's brothers' firm, which had provided extremely good garbage removal for longer than the mayor had been in office.

The mayor began by nonchalantly repeating the patent argument for awarding the contract to his brothers but then, in an expression of absolute arrogance, he admitted on public television that he was a silent partner in the company adding that the extra financial gain was his rightful due. "After all," he boasted, "look at all of the good I've done for this city over the past twenty years."

Prior to the debate the polls had predicted that the incumbent would be returned to office by a considerable margin. But the television indiscretion violated the second rule of corrupt government, i.e., keep your thievery out of sight. By admitting his partnership in the garbage removal company the mayor had so insulted the electorate that a week later they elected his young upstart opponent. Even my analytically cautious Managing Editor had been caught off guard by the sudden change in political popularity. The paper (read Blakesley) had naturally endorsed the incumbent just before the debate. The Editor now was forced to compose an editorial explaining why the newspaper was correct ten days earlier in endorsing the previous mayor but why it is now in total support of the people's new choice of city leadership. It was a masterpiece of rationalistic hindsight deserving of an award for fiction.

My cousin's husband had been a friend of the challenging mayoralty candidate's family and, at my cousin's urging, had accepted the responsibility of coordinating the letter-stuffing portion of the campaign. Initially there was little hope of unseating the incumbent, of course, and the opposition party simply sought a candidate who would enjoy a few months in the limelight but had no real future in politics that might be jeopardized by the embarrassment of an overwhelming defeat.

My cousin's desire that her husband become involved in the campaign rose mainly from the opportunities that such activities provided for her to rub shoulders with the political and financial powers within the city. The ultimate success of the election and the grateful appointment of her spouse as City Purchasing Manager were an unexpected bonus for her.

The new regime was elected in November and took office in early January. Since the incoming mayor had run on the usual platform of reform politics, promises of clean, honest government and a quick prosecution of any members of the previous administration who had been involved in illegal activities, these themes dominated his inauguration address. From November to January the incinerator in the City Hall basement was in constant use, rendering to ashes any documents that could be in any way incriminating. So thorough was the carnage that when the staff of the new administration took over, they were seriously hampered from executing their duties by the lack of any records of current government business.

Though thousands of documents could be destroyed, hundreds of memories could not. After twenty years in control of the city government, the previous mayor and his cronies grew so overconfident that they became overtly obvious about their improper shenanigans. They had openly revealed their illegal practices to many of the civil service employees who probably thought their bosses would stay in charge forever and for fear of recrimination remained mum to the outside world as long as the old regime remained in control. But now that the crooks were thrown out of office the indictments landed fast and furiously on the basis of eyewitness accounts and first hand knowledge by these employees who were anxious to vindicate themselves as well as to gain favor with their new supervisors. Some even hid documents from the incinerators' devouring flames in order to prove their accusations. My proximity to the newly formed cabinet proved, as Blakesley had predicted, "Invaluable." My cousin's husband, obviously motivated by vanity at being a member of the mayor's inner circle, willingly provided me with information regarding anticipated indictments long before the stories were given to the general public, which, in this case, meant the other news media. Consequently, I frequently scooped all of the other papers on city government matters.

Hank Chapman knew that I enjoyed writing and that I would be dissatisfied with just gathering information for his copy, so we worked out an arrangement wherein I wrote the stories and Hank edited them adding or deleting from my articles in order to meet the correct number of words.

By late summer the team of Chapman and Becks was recognized by our colleagues as a power with which to be reckoned. Many of the reporters from the other papers and the radio and television stations began following us around City Hall, entertaining us at lunch and devising various natural and some very unnatural schemes by which they could engage us in conversations during which we might accidentally reveal some of our not yet published news items. Eventually the mayor received complaints from the editors of the other papers about my unfair advantage. Consequently, at the request of my related informant, I occasionally leaked a minor tidbit of not yet publicly known information to one of my fellow reporters. I felt no scruples about taking advantage of my position and I mentally established a scale of values representing benefits versus rewards: the better the meal to which I was treated, the better the news item that I accidentally revealed.

The whole process proved so satisfactory that after a while even Blakesley began to warm up to me, and Holmes was bragging that it was his knowledge of astrology that had predicted my benefit to the paper and had provided him with the foresight to hire me. On the occasion that our paper published the exclusive account of the facts leading to the upcoming indictment of the former mayor, Holmes publicly patted himself on the back by openly advertising that he was rewarding me with a nice raise.

Socially and occupationally, everything was going my way and it could not have happened to anyone who would have enjoyed it more. I was the envy of my profession and the recent increase in salary enabled Helen and

I to move our marriage date forward to mid January. Lady luck or fate, or whatever it is, was certainly smiling in my direction. But I was soon to find out the truth in the adage that fortune is a fickle mistress.

It was a brisk but beautiful autumn afternoon when disaster struck. Bernie Saunders, who was a classmate and fraternity brother of mine in college, had secured a job on the sports staff of one of the other papers in town. Because his natural beat was the various athletic arenas in and around the city, I considered it rather odd when he began making frequent visits to City Hall. Then, when he displayed an interest in rekindling our old acquaintanceship, I realized that his efforts at friendship were probably by order of his Managing Editor. Early in our renewed relationship I tested my suspicions by a feigned accidental slip about a new scandal that was due to break in a few days, but had not yet been written up. The item appeared in Saunders' paper that afternoon.

Though I knew our friendship was a sham, I never called him on it, since he frequently provided me with complimentary tickets to athletic events.

On the ill-fated Saturday our mutual alma mater was scheduled to hold its annual Homecoming football game. Bernie, having been assigned to cover the event for his paper, invited me to join him in the press box. The admission was free and the seats were the best in the house, so I accepted.

Not wishing to appear a total freeloader I offered to drive. My means of transportation at the time was the same ancient vehicle that had carried me on my multitudinous excursions during college and, which I was now nursing along with infinite gentleness while I attempted to save enough money to purchase a new model. Unfortunately, just two days before the game my aging companion of many travels expired on the freeway in an ignominious departure to that big parking lot in the sky.

My first and only warning of trouble came from the oil indicator light on the dashboard. Since I was on a limited access throughway, and, since I was approaching my intended exit, I decided to gamble for the mile and one half remaining on the freeway. My decision proved automotively fatal. A sudden cloud of black smoke bellowed up in front of me totally blocking my view. I tried to remain in my lane as I quickly slammed on the brakes. However, because of my lack of view and the skidding due to my sudden braking, I barely avoided an accident with a passing car into whose lane I had partially swerved. By the time I exited the car and precariously made my way through the traffic to the safety of the median strip, my car was an uncontrollable blaze. Except for the lane, which was presently being blocked by the fire, the traffic continued past the passengers gazing at the conflagration and extending sympathetic looks in my direction. I felt self-conscious as the solitary ornament on the dividing strip and embarrassed to be the object of so much pity. In, what I can see now as a silly gesture, I put my hands on my hips and stuck my chin in the air in a pose of pride. After all, that fantastically exciting Chevrolet bonfire whose flames were streaking gloriously skyward in unabashed splendor was mine and mine alone.

The freeway incident was premature and I realized I would have to settle for a late model used car. Helen drove me to several car dealerships on Thursday and Friday evenings, but I could not find a car with which I was satisfied.

My cousin's husband had intended to sleep in on Saturday morning and to spend the afternoon at home reviewing bids for a new communications system that was expected to speed up police response time to emergency calls. He graciously permitted me to borrow his car for the day. It was a beautiful, fire engine red, domestic sports car with every extra imaginable, which he had acquired only two months earlier.

Hank Chapman had succumbed to a severe case of strep throat, which meant that I was the only reporter covering City Hall for our paper. But, since there was practically no one at the city administrative offices, I had no qualms about leaving my post for the balance of the day.

The game was scheduled for noon and it was about ten thirty when I picked up Bernie at his paper from which we drove to the stadium. Homecoming games are usually scheduled with weak opponents in order to give the alumni a feeling of pride in their alma maters. However, on this occasion the Athletic Director either miscalculated the strength of the visiting team or he was at a loss to find an opponent that was weaker than the home team. At half time our glorious warriors were still looking for their initial first down; a commodity, which the team seated on the opposite side of the field seemed to accumulate with unhindered ease. As the bands took the field at the intermission, the scoreboard trumpeted the embarrassment: 42 to 0. Bets were being taken in the press box as to whether our unworthy opponents might reach the century mark before the game was over and whether our heroes would find the strength within their souls to gain even one first down.

Shortly after the halftime, Bernie received a telephone call from his paper. He said a few words and then hung up, explaining that the connection on the press box phone was so bad that he was unable to hear the party on the other end of the line. He left our perch high above the stadium to call back from a lower level. When he returned he said that one of the reporters on his paper was writing a feature about Detroit's current issue of sports cars and that pictures of all of the models had been secured except the one in which we had driven to the game. He then asked if I would permit a photographer from his paper to photograph my cousin-in-law's car. At worst I could be charged with only a minor breech of loyalty and with a sudden mischievous impulse I agreed. Bernie relayed my approval to his paper. Although I momentarily caught the inconsistencies: first, that there was now no difficulty with the phone connection and also that the photographer needed my permission to take pictures of a car sitting in the middle of the stadium parking lot, these thoughts were driven from my mind by an outstanding trap by the left guard followed by a beautiful piece of open field running that covered eighty yards and that left at least seven of our gallant defenders in his wake lying spread eagle on their faces.

The stands began clearing early in the fourth quarter and the parking lot was nearly empty when we approached the car. The photographer was waiting for us and, though I initially objected to his request that I pose with the automobile he convinced me to oblige with the argument that he wanted candid shots that would not look like extractions from the manufacturer's advertisement brochures. I suggested that Bernie join me in the pictures but he insisted that he had never been photogenic. The photographer took several pictures using the stadium as a background, some with me standing beside the car and some with me sitting in the front seat with the door open. When he finished this series of shots he said that a picture of this muscle car motor would be great, so I opened the hood. At this point Bernie engaged me in conversation and I paid no attention to the activities of the picture taker. My host was offering me a couple of tickets for the pro football game that was scheduled for the following day. He said the tickets were at his apartment and he suggested that we drop in there for a drink and maybe order out for pizza.

When the photographer was finished and we started home, I turned on the radio to catch the day's college scores, but Bernie requested we play the cassette recorder instead, since he had found a tape in the glove compartment of a combo that he said he liked. After we arrived at Bernie's apartment and while my host was getting the drinks and ordering the pizza, I tried again to hear the scores on television, but again Bernie objected, saying that he was having trouble with the set and that the repair man that he had called recommended that he not play the set, lest he possibly do more damage. We spent the rest of the afternoon eating, drinking and comparing editors. Needless to say, my accounts were much more entertaining than his. About 5:30, I called home to find out if my cousin's husband needed the car before supper. My cousin answered the phone and said that her husband had been called to City Hall earlier in the afternoon for an emergency meeting and that Blakesley had just called insisting that I report to his office as soon as possible. She added that he sounded very upset.

 I left Bernie's apartment immediately and drove downtown mulling over the various possible reasons for Blakesley's summons. As I approached the newspaper building weird things began to happen. The windows on the fifth floor were open and heads began to pop out along the full length of the building. Since the final edition had certainly gone to press and was probably already on the streets, I could not imagine why so many of the personnel were still in the office, let alone sticking their heads out of the windows. As I passed below I could not see the fifth floor but I could see masses of shredded newspaper, torn sheets of paper, rolls of toilet tissue and other miscellaneous debris descending on the car. When I turned from the main thoroughfare into the driveway leading to the rear parking lot a similar quantity of litter of like substance fell from the skies. As I stepped from the car a huge cheer soared through the autumn air. With memories of the triumphant Lindbergh running through my mind I ascended in the elevator fully expecting to be overwhelmed by a worshiping mob congratulating me for an heroic accomplishment the nature of which no one had bothered to inform me. Instead, a frighteningly motionless city room engulfed in a ghost-like silence greeted me. Everyone was sitting perfectly still at his or her desk and every head was bent downward, as though engrossed in the paper beneath it. I stopped at the Assistant Editor's desk to ask what was going on but he simply replied that Blakesley was waiting for me. As I continued towards the Managing Editor's office, I realized that something of catastrophic proportions had occurred. For the first time since I had joined the paper over two years earlier I saw no one in Blakesley's office or showing any sign of wanting to enter while the red light was off. To say that the infamous light was off and that there was no human activity surrounding the office was like saying the sun had risen in the West and set in the East on a given day.

Blakesley began with a voice that was obviously strained by restraint, "Would you have a seat, Mr. Becks?"

I drew the chair from the corner of the room and seated myself in front of his desk.

"I understand that you attended a football game this afternoon," he commented softly, still trying to control his emotions.

I tried to alibi. "There was nothing going on at City Hall, so I...," but Blakesley cut me off.

"Is it true that you used your cousin-in-law's car?" By now the anger within was starting to come to the surface.

"My own car caught fire Thursday and...," again he interrupted. "A brand new sports car isn't it?" he sneered almost through clenched teeth. I gave up trying to answer him verbally and simply nodded my head.

"Well, it seems that a little incident did occur at City Hall this afternoon. The mayor called a press conference. He disclosed another scandal. Does that interest you, Becks?"

To this point I was quite tense, but now I relaxed. Blakesley's remarks seemed to be leading towards a rebuke for my having deserted my post, thus allowing the other papers to scoop us on another disclosure of corruption in the previous administration. Every major figure in the former government had already been indicted on multiple counts of fraud and another indictment would only be anti-climactic and of minor news value.

Blakesley sensed my sudden apathy, which made him even more irritated than before. "It was a very interesting news conference. It was covered in great detail by every other paper in the city. Doesn't that bother you just a little, Becks?'

Helen and I had planned a quick dinner before attending a road company performance of *The Fantastics* so I decided to play the humble sinner in the hope that Blakesley would cooperate with a short sermon; thus enabling me to make a quick departure. "I know I shouldn't have gone to the game, sir, but nothing was happening at City Hall and I was offered press box seats for our Homecoming game."

"Ah, yes," Blakesley broke in. "Our game, you say. You went to the game with Bernie Saunders, I hear."

I was impressed and somewhat annoyed at the thoroughness of Blakesley's intelligence gathering and I showed my irritation at his apparent invasion of privacy. "Yes. What was wrong with that? Bernie and I were classmates."

"Do you consider Saunders a friend?" he snapped with a sarcastic grin.

"Not really," I countered trying to mimic his sneer. "Bernie provides me with comps to games occasionally, but I wouldn't say we're close."

"I wouldn't say that either," Blakesley responded, obviously ignoring my rather argumentative reaction. Interjecting a satirical tone he added, "I think your Mr. Saunders used you today, Becks."

I was now very confused and I must have let it show. Blakesley paused for a moment to relish my bewilderment before continuing his assault. "And you allowed a photographer to photograph you with your cousin-in-law's nice new car."

"This must be it," I thought to myself. Blakesley was upset because I allowed a competitor to photograph the automobile. "Look," I countered snidely, "Permitting a fellow journalist to take a few pictures so that he can complete an assignment on something as insignificant a subject as sports cars can hardly be called a serious breech of loyalty."

As I was uttering this last sentence, I was growing more and more aware that there was something wrong here. My rationale that this whole episode was about a rival's newspaper article did not jibe with the wild ticker tape welcome from the city room staff or the emotional intensity of Blakesley's interrogation. As I completed my defense, my voice grew slower and lower in volume knowing that there was probably a more ominous shoe to fall.

"So that's what they told you," Blakesley replied sardonically, "...a story about sports cars. Well I suppose you could say that. At least it was a story about 'a' sports car."

I had never enjoyed cat and mouse games especially when I was the mouse so I decided to challenge my adversary into a direct statement of the problem. "Look, if you have a gripe, tell me what it is so we can both get out of here. What do you want, anyway?"

Blakesley finally let all of his anger come to the surface. He rose from his chair, picked up a newspaper that had been lying face down on his desk and throwing it as hard as he could in my direction he screamed, "Your head for starters!"

I raised my arms in self-defense just in time to shield my face from the papery projectile. It hit my forearms and fell to the floor. The front page was in full view. I could see that it was the final edition of the newspaper for which Bernie Saunders wrote. The front page resembled one of those sensationalistic tabloids that cover most of the page with one large photograph. However, in this case the front page showed at least a half dozen pictures of various sizes and subjects, including one of me wearing a pompous smile while sitting in the front seat of my cousin's husband's car. Another photo was an enlargement of the serial number superimposed on a photograph of the car motor with the position of the engraved number circled for easy identification. Directly under the headline was a large photograph of the mayor standing at a microphone and flanked by two men whom the citation described as irate automobile sales representatives. Immediately below that picture was a flattering likeness of my cousin-in-law taken nine months earlier as he was being presented to the news media as the Purchasing Manager for the new administration. The bold black print across the top of the page read, "REFORM MAYOR FINDS CORRUPTION IN OWN RANKS."

I was so taken back by the items staring up at me that I forgot that Blakesley was even there. I reached down, picked up the paper and buried myself in the copy.

The story told of two sales representatives from different automobile manufacturers who had complained directly to the mayor that the City Purchasing Department had misplaced their bids for fifty new police cruisers for which the city had recently signed a contract. The contract had been awarded to a third company whose bid had been considerably higher than the other two but who had won out by default. The two disgruntled challengers claimed that when they complained to the Purchasing Manager's office they were both told that their bids were not considered because they had been miss-filed and not discovered until after the bid deadline. They said that they suspected some hanky panky, since, unbelievably, an identical incident had occurred under the previous administration for which the former Purchasing Manager had been placed under indictment only three weeks earlier. The incriminating evidence in that case was a very expensive luxury car. On this occasion the two injured firms, recognizing the similarities in bidding processes, notified the mayor who had the police undertake an investigation, which uncovered that my cousin's husband had taken ownership of his new sports car one month subsequent to the signing of the contract for the police cruisers and that he had done so without any significant withdrawal of funds from either his checking or savings accounts. A further, more thorough examination showed that he did not take out a loan for the car either. All of which naturally led the mayor to suspect an illegal kick back.

Obviously, enjoying revenge for having been scooped on so many previous occasions through what they considered my unjust advantage, the newspaper emphasized with agonizing repetition my identity as that City Hall reporter who had first revealed to the public the details of so many of the scandals that were the humiliation of the former administration. The said newspaper also dwelled at great length on my relationship to the accused and the embarrassing fact that I had spent the day driving around in the fire engine red evidence.

When I finally finished the story I dropped the paper to my lap and looked blankly ahead, reflecting on the nightmarish nature of the situation. Blakesley had been standing the full while that I was reading but now he gradually eased himself down into his chair. The motion brought me back to reality. I knew that my Managing Editor had carefully planned his next remarks so I tried desperately to think of something to say that might throw him off balance or put him on the defensive but the shock of what I had just learned left my wits dulled. I could only look at him helplessly hoping that he would make a swift and mercifully clean cut when he brought down the ax.

However, our past relationship left no room for such kindness. He began angrily, raising his voice at almost every other syllable for vindictive thrust, "Do you know, Becks; that it took six months to regain the circulation we lost as a result of your warehouse fire blunder? God only knows if we will ever recoup the readers we lose from this fiasco... unless, of course, they consider our front page a supplement to the comic section and buy our paper for entertainment only. How can anyone trust a paper who boasts of a reporter who can't see a story when he's living with it twenty-four hours a day and even riding around in it on the day the story breaks in all of the other papers? If Joseph Pulitzer had created a prize for journalistic incompetence you would win it without contest for the next ten years. And would you like to know the most devastating thing of all? My albatross will stay around my neck. In spite of today, Holmes still won't let me fire you."

Blakesley's arms reached skyward resembling the hell-imprisoned creatures in medieval paintings pleading for reprieve from their torments.

"No man deserves this!" he yelled pathetically. Then returning to me he leaned forward and with clenched teeth he vowed with as much venom as a voice can convey, "But, damn it, Becks, I'm going to get rid of you. Someday, somehow, someway I'm going to get you completely out of my life. And don't think murder hasn't crossed my mind. Before you got here today, I had some of the most delightful fantasies. I think the one I liked best was when I took that picture of you sitting in that car with that stupid grin on your face and tattooed it on your forehead. Tell me, Becks, how would you like to wander around City Hall wearing a permanent portrait of your horrendous incompetence for all your peers to see?"

Blakesley's fantasies were morbidly entertaining but they failed to frighten me. I knew that he was far too deliberate to allow himself to succumb to any act that might expose him to a charge of felonious assault.

Retreating to an only slightly more civilized tone, he begrudgingly grumbled, "I honestly do not know what I'm going to do with you in the future. But for now I'm adamant about one thing: to get you as far away from me as possible for as long as possible. So I want you to listen very carefully. I'm going to give you a few simple instructions that you are to follow to the letter...unconditionally...without exception. And believe me, if you foul up on this, you will carry the imprint of my foot on your fanny as long as you live.

"The Assistant News Editor will give you an out-of-town assignment, which should take you two or three days to complete. Being you, it will probably take more. Regardless, you will find some reason to extend the assignment for a full week. Do you understand what I'm saying?"

I nodded that his message was clear.

"You will then take the two weeks of vacation you have coming, though I don't know what you've done to earn it. Then you will call in sick for at least one more week. That will keep you out of my sight and out of my hair for four weeks during which time I will decide on your future. And, if you were inspired to use the time to look for another job, please be my guest. You might be extending my life about fifteen years."

His instructions completed, he returned to his previous abusive self. Rising slowly from his chair he hurled his right arm, hand and forefinger straight out and bellowed at the top of his voice, "Now get the hell out of here!"

Considering the high emotion of the scene I decided to wave the courtesy of replacing the chair and to exit as quickly as possible. The city room was still fully occupied and all eyes followed me down the center aisle. Most of the faces bore expressions of inquisitive concern but no one was insensitive enough to ask me what happened, though I was certain that they could see some of Blakesley's gestures through the door window and a lot of his yelling certainly could have been heard outside of the Managing Editor's cubicle. A few of the more anxious types appeared relieved, probably because there were no obvious signs of blood and two or three alarmists seemed excessively surprised, again, probably because I was still ambulatory. Sadie Winslow sat rigidly at her desk projecting a scowl that visually articulated her disappointment that I was still breathing.

Since the show was now over, the audience quickly dissipated. When I reached the Assistant Editor's desk, he looked up at me with compassionate understanding and asked simply, "Rough?"

"Rough," I admitted.

He graciously avoided dwelling on my embarrassment and went directly to my assignment. "Did you hear that former State Supreme Court Justice VanderLinde died early this morning?"

I shook my head, no.

"He was a native of our city and very popular in the liberal urban areas of the state. Holmes said something about both he and VanderLinde being champions of the underdog, the poor and the trade unions. I've been directed to have you write a weeklong series on the former Justice that would paint him as a hero to our readers. VanderLinde retired from the bench about six months ago... reportedly for health reasons. Rumors were that, since he knew he was dying, he wanted to spend his remaining time speaking out on social issues. He gave several speeches, the last of which was delivered three week ago at a labor union convention and included some drastic changes in our Federal, State and Local tax structures. According to Holmes, the unions have taken up some of the reform ideas and there are rumors they might push them at all levels of government. Because of Holmes' affinity for the unions, he wants Justice VanderLinde's speeches before union groups played up big with a positive approach to the tax reform ideas. He intends to follow the series with an editorial endorsement of the plans."

"Does Holmes know what the reforms are?" I asked.

"Who knows," the Assistant Editor returned. "Apparently, the ex-Justice's horoscope was in synch with Holmes,' so anything VanderLinde promoted, Holmes has to agree with."

I shook my head mockingly, and then inquired, "When does the series start?"

"Tomorrow," he responded. "But the lead off article is written. It contains the vital stats: dates, place of birth, elected and appointed positions, etc. Give us a couple of days of flattering in-depth stuff, and then hit the speeches, especially that tax reform thing." He paused for a short second then added, "VanderLinde was a colorful as well as a popular figure, so our morgue is loaded with pictures of him... we'll take care of that end."

After I commented that I was glad that I would not be required to concern myself about pictures he continued, "Since the justice spent a great deal of his adult life at the state capital, you'll probably find most of the more current personal material there. His older brother is a Jesuit priest and is currently a retired professor at his order's university in the eastern suburbs. Try to get hold of him for an interview. He's probably at the capital for the funeral. You'll need most of tomorrow for research. Can you leave tonight?"

Since I knew how my cousin would take the sports car disaster, I appreciated the excuse for a quick departure and a lengthy absence from the apartment. I told the Assistant Editor that I could leave shortly after dinner.

I expressed my gratitude for his considerateness and, after making a couple of phone calls, I left the office physically drained and mentally overactive. Though it only took a minute or two to get home, I felt uneasy riding in the now infamous "kick back."

When I arrived at the apartment, my cousin's husband was sitting alone in the living room. His elbows were resting on his knees and his head was in his hands. He was staring straight ahead. Earlier, when I was taking the beating that Blakesley was inflicting, I divided my feelings towards my cousin-in-law between anger at placing me in such a vulnerable and devastatingly precarious position and bewilderment at how he could have been so stupid as to try the same scam for which his predecessor was currently under indictment. After all, he was the person who leaked the crime story to me before the rest of the papers became aware of it. I could only surmise that the automobile representative who instigated the previous kick back scheme had suggested it before the previous Purchasing Manager's crime had been uncovered. But when I saw my cousin's husband sitting there, totally destroyed, and because of her self-centeredness, absolutely alone, I could feel nothing for him but pity. I walked up to him and extended my hand. He looked up at me with a pathetic look and clasped my hand, but neither of us spoke. He was so completely disorientated that I was not certain that he even recognized me.

From the time I entered I could hear my cousin in the bedroom wailing uncontrollably. I tried to avoid her and went directly to my room to pack. However, halfway through my packing she joined me. I did not stop what I was doing nor did I bother to extend my condolences. She was bestowing enough pity on herself. "I knew I shouldn't have married that bum," she blubbered. "What's going to happen to me now? We have practically nothing in the bank and, if he goes to jail, I'll have to go to work. Even if he's acquitted, we'll still be outcasts. I'm certain we're the laughingstock of the city." With this she broke into tears again and went back to her bedroom.

I wanted to tell her to shut up and try to think of what her husband was enduring but I knew that magnanimity was a virtue, which she had never and probably would never experience. I also wished that I could make her realize that her obsession with status was probably the reason that her spouse had succumbed to the temptation but, again, I knew that such an admonition would be futile. My cousin had never permitted herself to feel guilt. Whenever anything went wrong, she would usually find some reason to blame someone else for the problem. And, when she was obviously at fault, she would avoid culpability by becoming angry at the person she offended, often reasoning illogically in an effort to prove that the injured party or parties deserved what she did to them.

When I finished packing I simply told her that I had an assignment at the State Capital and that I would be gone for several days. Crossing the living room on my way to the door I observed my cousin's husband still sitting in the same position and still emanating the same shocked condition. I said goodbye but in his stupor he failed to reply.

The quiet elevator ride was a comforting relief after enduring the shrill pitch of my cousin's wailing. My mind had finally slowed to a normal pace and I could reflect a bit more objectively on the day's events. Leaving Blakesley's office, I had felt that the world on top of which I had been sitting had rolled over and I had been flattened beneath it. But in comparison to my cousin-in-law I was the blessed among the blessed. I still had a job and there was someone who I hoped still loved me. With Blakesley spending four full weeks devising a suitable punishment for my malfeasance, my future was bleak. But dismal as it appeared, I did still have one.

Chapter Four

I had called Helen before I left the newspaper to brief her on my sudden change in fortune, or, more accurately, misfortune. I had also made a reservation for the thirty-minute plane flight to the State Capital for which Helen offered to drive me to the airport.

Helen and I had been saving our vacation time for a January honeymoon but Blakesley had preempted our plans by his sentence of a month in exile. When he ordered that I take my vacation immediately, I wanted to object, but the circumstances being what they were, I did not feel that I was in a position to bargain. During our ride to the airport I tried to apologize to Helen for having ruined our honeymoon plans, but her delightful, positive approach to things rendered my apology unnecessary.

"So we get married on Saturday and go back to work on Monday," she philosophized. "I'm sure there are a lot of beautiful marriages out there that somehow survived that dire fate. Besides, Fran, with a little work we should be able to extend our honeymoon for at least twenty years."

We exchanged knowing smiles and I felt my negative mood start to turn slightly more positive. However, because of the warehouse fire flub and now this recent blunder with my cousin-in-law's car, my self-confidence as a journalist as well as my self-esteem were very much weakened. I had even begun to wonder what Helen really saw in me or if she might be having second thoughts about marrying such a goof-off. My pride would not let me admit how shaken I was, so I asked her simply, "Why are you attracted to me, Hon?" As soon as I said that, I knew that I had so abruptly changed the subject that I might as well have just openly acknowledged my insecurity.

Helen seemed taken back a little, but then she laughed and responded, "Well, as I was growing up I used to bring sick and injured stray cats and dogs home and nursed them back to health. Maybe that's what appeals to me."

"Ouch!" I groaned. "The thought of you marrying me out of pity really hurts."

"Oh, no!" she appealed. "Oh God, I'm sorry. I didn't realize you were that down on yourself. I was just kidding. I thought you were too, asking me what I saw in you. I thought you knew how much I love you and why. I definitely don't see you as a stray cat. I want to marry you because I not only love you, I like you too... you are my best friend. One of the things I like most is that you still have enough boyishness in you that I know you'll be a great father for my children."

"No greater than you'll be a mother for mine," I responded.

We were just pulling up to the departure entrance at the airport. Helen put her hand on my face and turned it towards hers and with the warmest most assuring expression she said, "Feeling better? I wish I were going with you. We all need support at times and right now you sure do, don't you?" With this she gave me a very loving kiss. "You just remember how much I love you, okay?"

"You sure know how to make a guy feel better," I whispered gratefully.

When I reached the ticket counter I discovered that there was a forty-five minute delay in my flight. My soon-to-be-bride's outgoing compassion had both picked me up and relaxed me. I suddenly realized that I was hungry. I used the time awaiting departure to have a snack and to decide my course of action once I arrived at the Capital. I remembered that John Keating, who was a couple of years ahead of me in college and a fraternity brother, was originally from the State Capital and that his father ran a newspaper there. Recalling that John was by no means the independent or self-reliant type I assumed that he probably eased into a position on his father's paper. I decided to use this contact to obtain as much information as I could for the series on Justice VanderLinde.

My previous air travels had been by jet, and I was a bit concerned when I climbed aboard my plane. It was one of those semi-retired propeller crafts that the airlines used as puddle jumpers. As we began taxiing for take-off I started reading the copy of the proofs for the following day's article on the former Justice that the Assistant Editor had given me. I did this both to get a running start on my research, but also to take my thoughts off my precarious means of flight.

The biographical summary was appropriately cursory but it did contain a sufficient amount of details to make interesting reading. This, plus a few bits of copy from the archives at our paper that Holmes definitely wanted included in my series, provided me with a good overview of the former Justice. By putting all of the material together the biography was quite thorough.

Ronald M. VanderLinde was the youngest son of Mark VanderLinde, a Dutch immigrant who had settled on a farm in the northern part of the state. Ronald was the only child born to Mr. VanderLinde's second wife, Kathryn. The future Justice had two half brothers and three half sisters by his father's first marriage.

The elder VanderLinde presumably was a successful farmer but it appeared that he was an even more successful inventor. Through his agricultural efforts he had acquired three large parcels of productive farmland during his first fifteen years in this country. However, his major financial achievements came later when he developed a simple, farm-oriented adaptation to the newly introduced horseless carriage. Presumably the royalties from his first invention spurred his creative genius. During the years that followed he applied for patents for a variety of agriculturally advantageous gadgets. When Mark VanderLinde died, in the late thirties, his estate must have been considerable. From some of the info, I could surmise that he avoided the economic disaster of the great depression by having all of his assets in productive farmland with no debt. Consequently, though my research papers did not reveal it, he must have left each of his surviving children a substantial bequest.

The younger of Ronald's two half-brothers died during the influenza epidemic that followed the First World War and the married half-sisters died during the fifty's and sixty's. Only his brother, Steven, and his oldest sister, Agnes, both of whom were members of Catholic religious orders, survived Justice VanderLinde. The houses at which they were assigned were located on opposite sides of the main metropolis at which I lived.

Steven had attended a Jesuit high school on the near west side of town and entered the Jesuit Order immediately following graduation. The Reverend VanderLinde was published as a Theoretical Physicist but apparently was little known in his field. He retired from teaching in 1968 after celebrating his fiftieth anniversary in the Order. He was presently residing at the east side university at which he had spent most of his teaching career.

Agnes had entered religious life when she was seventeen. She had joined a contemplative order of nuns where she had taken the name Sr.

Mary Agnes, OPC, and where she had recently been appointed Mother Superior.

Ronald VanderLinde was born in 1913. He attended his parish elementary school and the same high school from which his brother, Steven, had graduated ten years earlier. Ronald obviously shared the intellectual gifts of the family, receiving his Bachelor of Arts degree magna cum laude from the Jesuit University to which his brother had been assigned. He acquired his law degree from my own alma mater and then enrolled for studies in international law in Europe. A year later he was accepted to the bar back here in town and joined a small but well-known law firm from which he practiced from 1938 to 1941. Shortly after the start of World War II he enlisted in the Navy and was attached as a medic to a Marine combat unit.

At this point in the article I discovered why Samuel Holmes wanted the subject to be treated as a heroic figure. The story dwelled at length on Justice VanderLinde's military adventures. Ronald VanderLinde received four separate citations for valor including the Navy Cross and was twice awarded the Purple Heart. Here my Assistant Editor had attached a note with a cross-reference to an item from the archives. The reference note indicated that Holmes desired that this citation be played up big and in detail including the printing of the entire citation attendant to the Silver Cross with a picture of the medal incorporated with the article. I considered this a bit exploitative but being aware of Holmes' flare for the dramatic, it was at least consistent. The citation and the paragraphs related to the incident for which the medal was awarded told of a medical assistant attached to a combat Marine battalion who entered an open area following an unsuccessful charge by his unit, which had suffered severe losses and had fallen back momentarily to regroup before attempting another assault. Though the Marines had brought their wounded back to the security of their previous position, one of their men who had fallen into a crater had been overlooked. When the young medical assistant saw the wounded Marine trying to crawl out of the shell hole he ran to him in spite of a fierce cross fire and continued to treat his wounds even in the face of an enemy counter attack. Mortar and artillery fire repulsed the Japanese but a piece of shrapnel from an exploding shell seriously injured the medic's left leg. Ignoring his own condition, he continued his medical attention to the fallen Marine. Though the citation ended here, another note in Holmes own hand writing stating, "Must include," was attached to an English translation stapled to a Japanese newspaper article. The Japanese article appeared to refer to the same incident for which the Silver Cross was issued but took up where the citation ended. It seems that when the medic had done everything he could for the Marine, he stayed in the crossfire to administer to the Japanese soldiers that had been wounded during the counter attack. One of the wounded enemy soldiers was an officer who, after the war, became a member of the Japanese government. The translation said that with the cooperation of American military authorities the Japanese official discovered the identity of the medic who he was convinced had saved his life at great risk to his own. In 1948, this Japanese official persuaded his government to issue a Japanese citation for bravery to Ronald VanderLinde. He was given a medical discharge in January, 1944 having lost a leg to amputation and returned to his law practice after a period of rehabilitation. Two years later he ran successfully for a seat on the Common Please Court where he served for two more years until his appointment to the State Supreme Court. His tenure with that body continued until the spring of 1972 when he retired. He spent his last six months lecturing before a variety of audiences on a wide range of topics.

It was about 9:00 PM when my plane landed and, though I was quite tired from the emotionally exhausting experiences of the day, and in spite of the fact that it was Saturday night, I decided to call John Keating from the airport in the hope of establishing my itinerary for the following day.

I had never become close to John in college. Though we were fraternity brothers, we were not in the same class and John was not the type of personality to which I gravitated naturally. Even in his early twenties he reminded me of those kids that I knew in grammar school whose parents were overly strict. Such youngsters were usually abnormally sedate and well behaved in the presence of their superiors, but who were equally mischievous elsewhere. I think what bothered me most about these hellions was their sneakiness; one could almost say cowardice. They would only become devilish when there was little or no chance of their being caught. Quite often, they would devise fiendish acts and then talk someone else into doing them, making absolutely certain that, should anything go wrong, they could protect themselves from accusation or punishment. It was John who instigated most of our fraternity pranks. Not surprisingly, he routinely appointed himself as lookout. Of course, once or twice he deserted his post when danger of being caught arose. It was just such an occasion when we were discovered in the school printing office changing the type to insert a few four letter words into the Dean's introductory remarks in the university's literary quarterly. John's explanation for not warning us of the approaching guard was that he became nauseous and was in a nearby lavatory. No one bothered to challenge his excuse but we soon wised-up, insisting on a second lookout during our furtive antics.

When I phoned John, I explained my assignment and asked if he could offer any help in my research. He confirmed my assumption that he had taken a job with his father's paper and he added boastfully that he had recently been promoted to Assistant Editor. He further assured me that his paper's morgue probably held all of the information that I would need. "VanderLinde was a colorful and newsworthy character," John asserted. "I think we have everything on him including what he had for breakfast. We knew he was dying so we had a full-page feature ready to go as soon as he decided to make the big scene. It'll be in tomorrow's issue."

John explained that he often had work to do on Sundays and that Sunday was no exception so we agreed to meet at his paper relatively early the next day. The airport information service was very helpful in securing a car rental and a hotel reservation and I began adjusting to my new environment. State capitals are notorious as overgrown rural towns but because of their large transient tourist and business trade their travel accommodations are quite often the best in the state. This was exceptionally true of our capital, to my delight. I was able to find a very comfortable room at a moderate price with a dining room that offered an exquisite and eclectic cuisine.

The drain of the day took over when I reached my room and I was out before my head hit the pillow.

After a delicious breakfast I went to the newspaper building where John showed me around. The complex was only about a third of the size of my newspaper building back home. The tour naturally included John's new Assistant Editor's office, name and title on the door, etc. Considering our past relationship, I suspected that showing me his new status position was possibly the main reason he came into work on that Sunday. He bragged that he had a dinner engagement with a few of the state's legislative bigwigs that evening, but, if I finished my research early enough, we could go back to his house for a drink and to catch up on old and current events.

I buried myself in the newspaper's morgue where, with the help of the paper's current feature and a voluminous quantity of subject clippings from various publications, including a few national magazines, I was able to outline most of the series and draft the next two articles. John had offered me the use of the new copying machine and I took full advantage of it.

Justice VanderLinde's life was a journalistic treasure. It was punctuated with unusual, interest grabbing incidents that were strewn throughout an epic tale of what one could only call the unexpected. Earlier, I referred to a scene from a novel by G.K. Chesterton called *The Man Who Was Thursday*, which was recommended to me by a friend in college. She told me the entire story before I read the book. But, when I did read it, I could not believe what she said would happen next, really would. Yet, when it did, it was as natural and of-course-ish as the sun rising and setting each day. Justice VanderLinde's life history read exactly like that. In the theater they refer to "a play within a play." VanderLinde's biography was a series of extraordinary events within extraordinary events and each fell nicely, or perhaps neatly is a better word, upon each other, when looking backwards at them. But before they happened they could not possibly have been anticipated.

As I scanned the various clippings, I compared the facts therein with the copy of the proofs from my own paper that I had read on the plane and with the feature to appear in John's paper. I found no significant inconsistencies but slight anomalies did appear, mostly involving omissions. The three that were most obvious occurred during the period of Ronald VanderLinde's life between his graduation from law school and his appointment to the State Supreme Court. Two clippings, which I reviewed, mentioned that two months before he received his law degree Ronald M. VanderLinde and a girl identified as Jeanne Anne Trudeau announced their engagement to be married. But nowhere in any of the articles did I find any reference to that marriage or any other marriage. Neither was there any further mention of the girl named in the announcement. I concluded that the marriage did not occur and that Justice VanderLinde had remained a bachelor for his entire life.

The second oddity dealt with the post-graduate course in international law for which the future Justice traveled to Europe. None of the biographical summaries or isolated clippings stated that he received any degree or comparable certification from abroad for having completed his studies there. Since young VanderLinde had returned home in time to be accepted to the bar only one year after traveling abroad, and, since he began a domestic practice of law removed from international legalities, I surmised that he had never completed the course in France, though no explanation was given for his premature return home.

The third and last peculiarity that I considered significant came to light from a disclosure statement of finances, which the newly appointed Justice offered apparently in response to a recently passed requirement of all state appointments. Justice VanderLinde reported total net assets of only twenty-five thousand dollars though another article stated that he had received over two hundred thousand dollars from his father's estate. That estate money plus his income for having practiced law for several years and having served on the Common Pleas bench for two years, made his net worth seem quite paltry and left questions concerning the disparity.

The remainder of Justice VanderLinde's life was free of such aberrations and, since no one else seemed to be bothered by those that I noted, I decided to join my colleagues in the blissful see-no-evil approach. Drawing from the many articles and clippings, I was able to fill in the details for the biographical portion of my series. What follows here concerning Ronald VanderLinde's history is a composite summary from a multitude of news articles, clippings and sundry notes and memos garnered from the morgue of John's paper. I was surprised by the volume and the diversity of sources but did somewhat understand, since, as John had said, "The Justice was a very colorful and newsworthy character," and because this was the chief newspaper for the State Capital. (I will relate this biography as though telling a story rather than as it appeared in my series to avoid the cumbersomeness of constantly referring to references, though I will mention sources in general terms as appropriate.)

My own paper had dwelled at great length on the young VanderLinde's military exploits but it made no connection between his battlefield heroics and his future successes with the electorate. John's paper, on the other hand, residing in the State Capital, emphasized the political ramifications relevant to all that occurred in Ronald VanderLinde's life.

According to John's paper, the young attorney had entered the race for Common Pleas Judgeship after less than five years of actual law practice. He apparently had no expectation of winning, since he made no effort to campaign or to secure support for his candidacy from the news media or from the local bar association. He was obviously engaged in the age old, political process of placing his name before the voters to see what drawing power the name itself would have and by this means determine his future in the political arena. Being on the ballot also enabled him to begin familiarizing the electorate with his name should he at some future date seriously consider running for an office that he desired and for which he was properly qualified. However, fate stepped in. A week before the election the unusual story concerning the Japanese governments awarding of a medal for valor to a member of its enemy's forces broke over the national wire services. Of course, the bizarre account was covered in detail by the local papers with a full explanation of the young lawyer's military career including his many citations for heroism from his own country. The stories also mentioned that Ronald VanderLinde was presently a candidate for the bench. The publicity provided the attorney with instant recognition and an easy victory at the polls.

After relating this account, the writer of the feature in John's paper, obviously reflecting the high political environment of the State Capital, inappropriately but consistently, editorialized about the deficiencies of our democratic process with an electorate that votes neither on the issues nor on personal qualifications, but rather for a familiar or popular name.

The inexperience of the young jurist apparently proved no serious handicap or, if it did, the subject was not covered in any of the articles or clippings. Further, though there was no indication from any source that Ronald VanderLinde sought publicity or notoriety, there was ample evidence that these two phenomena sought him. After only two years with the Common Pleas Court a case was brought before him that propelled him again into the public eye and, according to the article, which I was reading, he gained the prestige that won him his appointment to the State Supreme Court.

Definitely, no incident in the jurist's life was covered by more copy than this case. The voluminous articles and especially the background material enabled me to acquire a great deal of detail. But in order to grasp the whole story, particularly the chronology involved, I had to use a large table in the paper's morgue room plus several smaller ones and even a few chairs on which to lay out all of the items pertaining to the case. The tale was convoluted, but made fascinating reading.

The trial involved a child custody suit that resulted from the after affects of a disaster that had befallen a young couple. A blind twenty-three year old woman named Alice Harwood had sought a permanent stay to a temporary restraining order that her mother, Mrs. Mildred Schaffer, had won several months earlier that in effect placed Alice Harwood's three year old daughter, Elizabeth, in her grandmother's care and barred the child's father from having any contact with his daughter.

The story, apparently, took on a life of its own both because of the extraordinary circumstances involved in the case and because of that strange journalistic phenomenon that occurs occasionally when a page fourteen article catches the public interest and, subsequently, drives the various media to make it a larger than life front page spectacle.

Young Alice had lost her sight in an automobile accident at the age of five. Her mother had failed to notice a stop sign and had hit another car that was passing through the intersection. The impact of the collision sent Alice flying forward where she struck the dashboard with sufficient force to sever the optic nerve in both eyes rendering the five year old instantly and permanently blind. Mrs. Schaffer was divorced but according to one of the in depth accounts, had received a substantial alimony settlement, which enabled her to devote nearly all of her time to the care of her handicapped daughter. As was pointed out at the trial before Judge VanderLinde, the mother attempted to make the girl a virtual recluse as she was growing up, refusing to allow her a normal social life. But when Alice was about nineteen, a family moved next door that included a young man who was just beginning, what was to prove, a successful career in commercial art. Jim Harwood, who worked out of a studio in his mother's house, frequently had the opportunity to converse with Alice over the back yard fence. Mrs. Schaffer, in what Alice's lawyer described as a tyrannical demonstration of over-protectiveness, forbade her daughter to date. Nevertheless, the young couple eventually declared their intention to marry. In spite of her mother's vehement objections, Alice and Jim Harwood married shortly after Alice's twenty-first birthday. The newlyweds placed a small down payment on a modest three-bedroom frame house on the opposite side of town from Mrs. Schaffer. Jim Harwood's mother was widowed and when Alice became pregnant, the elder Mrs. Harwood sold her home and moved in with her son and family. With Alice's youthful energy and her mother-in-law's eyes, the accommodation apparently made for a well-ordered household.

However, when the baby was a year and a half old, Jim's mother came down with a case of pneumonia, which required a week of bed rest. The illness created no serious inconvenience, since Jim was able to take some time from work during his mother's convalescence. But one afternoon, while the baby was taking a nap and Jim was in the back yard mowing the lawn, Alice decided to please her husband by making him a cup of coffee. She accidentally turned the wrong knob on the range placing a full flame under a skillet of bacon grease left from brunch. After a short time the grease ignited and the flames leapt to some nearby curtains. When Alice smelled the smoke she ran onto the back porch shouting the alarm to her husband. Jim led her off the porch and away from the house where he ordered her to stay while he rescued the baby and his mother. By now the kitchen was ablaze, so he was forced to circle the house and enter through the front door. He darted up the stairs and went first to the nursery where he picked up the sleeping infant and then ran to his mother's bedroom, which was at the rear of the house, and directly over the kitchen. By the time he opened the door to his mother's bedroom the room was a raging inferno and he realized that there was nothing that he could do for his mother. When he turned towards the stairs he saw that they too were on fire. He ran into the bathroom where he soaked several towels with water and wrapped them around the baby. Reentering to the hallway he could see through the smoke that the stairs were now a wall of flames. He clutched the towel-enshrouded child to him and dashed into the flames. As he descended, the stairs collapsed beneath him and he and the baby plummeted downward crashing on top of the steps leading to the basement. Jim was rendered momentarily unconscious by the blow from the fall. When he came to he found himself lying on the concrete floor at the foot of the basement stairs with little Elizabeth standing beside him screaming. Jim had broken his left hip in the fall and his trousers were on fire. In spite of his condition he was able somehow to rewrap the baby in the dampened towels and drag himself and the baby up the basement steps. About halfway up, a bottle of alkali, which his mother had used for cleaning and which was on a shelf near the stairs, exploded from the heat, hurling its contents into Jim's face. He was blinded by the contents but he continued his ascent. When he reached the landing he groped for the doorknob, opened the side door and stumbled into the driveway where he collapsed. A neighbor dragged Jim and the child away from the burning house and used the still damp towels to extinguish the flames that had consumed much of Jim's clothing and hair and had burned major portions of his flesh.

In spite of third degree burns over much of his body, Jim recovered but was rendered a permanent invalid. The multiple skin grafts that were performed during his six-month stay in the hospital were aimed at saving his life rather than his appearance. When he was discharged, a large part of his body including his face were hideously scarred. He had also lost both of his hands to necessary amputation and the exploding alkali had so badly burned the corneas of both eyes that he had joined his wife in the limiting world of perpetual blindness. The medical expenses had exceeded the couple's savings and the insurance money from the house barely covered the mortgage. During Jim's stay in the hospital, Alice and Elizabeth lived with Alice's mother but when Jim attempted to rejoin his family, Mrs.

Schaffer refused to allow him to do so, apparently still angry at him for violating her wishes and marrying her daughter. She had further anticipated that her daughter would probably want to be with her husband so she secured a temporary restraining order prohibiting Alice from taking the child from the grandmother's care hoping that Alice would decide to be with her baby rather than go with her husband. But, since Jim was a total invalid, Alice chose to care for her husband hoping eventually to regain custody of her child.

Jim and Alice lived in a public housing tenement on the near West Side with an inadequate monthly welfare check as their only financial support. Through help from the Legal Aid Society, Alice immediately started the process of returning Elizabeth to her parents. But it was six months before the case was brought to trial. How Alice managed to care for herself and her husband during this time was not related in any of the accounts but it could be assumed that their existence was abnormally difficult.

Judge VanderLinde was presiding over the court to which the case was assigned. And with the zealous reporting of the weekly suburban paper that served the community in which the Harwood's lived before the fire, the trial was projected into the limelight. A week before the trial, the paper printed a lengthy article outlining the history and circumstances leading to the litigation. One of the larger daily papers apparently recognized the human-interest value of the case and followed the next day with their own page thirteen article. In subsequent articles the daily noted that the reader response was immense and, consequently, moved the coverage to the front page. Not wanting to be outdone, the balance of the newspapers in and around the city picked up the story. By the time the trial started the copy was so prolific that it was the hottest item in town. I even found subject clippings from John Keating's paper in his morgue as well as from several other down state papers and three national magazines, though the latter were after-the-fact summaries.

Though the public sympathies lay unanimously on the side of the young couple, the testimony at the trial led in the opposite direction. Mrs. Schaffer's attorney called the couples social caseworker to the stand and with the proper questions forced her reluctantly to admit that with the meager and obviously inadequate, in-home governmental aid available, Alice Harwood could not care for her husband and child without the real possibility of another accident similar to the one that had cost Mr. Harwood his mother, his hands, his eyes and which had nearly cost little Elizabeth her life. A psychiatrist also offered expert testimony that constant exposure of the child to the horrific appearance of her father would probably cause her irreparable emotional and psychological harm that would, by the time the child had reached adulthood, result in a morbid and distorted coloration of reality.

Mrs. Schaffer then testified that, though she was neither young nor rich, she felt capable of supplying the material and parental needs of both her daughter and granddaughter, but that she was certain that she could not possibly provide for the additional care required for her son-in-law.

On cross-examination, Mrs. Schaffer admitted that she had opposed the marriage in the first place and, further, that she still harbored ill feelings toward Jim Harwood for having taken her daughter away from her. When it was brought to her attention that her income from real estate rentals and stock holdings was sufficient to provide domestic help and even nursing care for her son-in-law, she insisted that she would not spend one penny for the care of someone who had taken her daughter from her and that she would refuse under any circumstances to allow her daughter's husband to live in her home. Later, outside of the courtroom, when asked why she would not use her substantial wealth to aid the couple and their child in a manner that would allow them to live independently yet safely apart from her, she was quoted in one of the newspapers as angrily declaring, "It's my fault that my daughter lost her sight, so it's my responsibility to take care of her. I'm not going to pay someone else to do what I should do." According to the referenced article, that blatant outburst of uncontrolled guilt was shouted over the futile efforts of Mrs. Schaffer's attorney to stop her from talking.

Alice Harwood's legal-aid attorney argued that this was not a case of child neglect or of unfit parenting. He pointed out that Jim Harwood had certainly proved his love, devotion, and dedication to the well being of his daughter by having sacrificed his limbs and sight to save the child's life. And, though Alice Harwood was handicapped there was no evidence that she was anything but a devoted mother. The attorney also brought forth another qualified psychiatrist who stated that it was his professional opinion that the child would experience no long-range harm by seeing her father's distorted appearance. The attorney then pleaded for the integrity of the family, but he offered no rebuttal to the charge that, if the court were to give the child to its parents the child would be placed in future danger from another accident.

As the trial drew to a close, Mrs. Schaffer's lawyer apparently realized that neither Alice nor Jim Harwood would be called to testify and, further, must have noted that it was Alice alone that had sought custody of the child. Before summarizing his case he subpoenaed the father who objected to testifying but who finally took the stand after being gently prodded by the judge. The attorney asked Mr. Harwood why he had not joined his wife in the suit. Jim Harwood simply responded by pointing out the obvious: that he was no longer able to provide for his family. He then added, "Since I can't take care of them, I don't think I'm qualified to decide what's best for them. And that's what I've been told is what the court is suppose to do. I just decided to trust the court and hope that it will make a good decision and take care of Elisabeth and hopefully Alice too. The attorney then rather cruelly asked Jim Harwood if he did not consider the arrangement offered by Mrs. Schaffer whereby she would provide for his wife and daughter to be in the best interest of his family. Mr. Harwood simply repeated that he no longer had the right or authority to make such judgments but, if that were the decision of the court, he would accept that resolution.

The trial only lasted two and a half days and, though the outcome appeared obvious, Judge VanderLinde stated that he would not render a decision until ten days from that date. However, in postponing the decision he made some enlightening comments, "Pure justice is not always just. Sometimes, under extraordinary circumstances, it requires extraordinary efforts by those whose responsibility it is to administer that justice. This court could not look upon Mr. Harwood nor listen to his selfless remarks without concluding that this was indeed just such a case. For that reason I am asking the indulgence of all of the parties concerned to grant a postponement of ten days before we present the decision."

The publicity concerning the trial continued during the interim and, in spite of Judge VanderLinde's departing remarks, several reporters and editorialists, reflecting the mood of their readers, de-cried the expected miscarriage of justice. However, no one could offer a sensible solution other than the obvious: place the child in the permanent custody of the grandmother with hope that Alice Harwood would join the child, and to place Jim Harwood in an institution as a ward of the state.

Photographs taken of the exterior of the courthouse as the parties entered on the day of the decision showed a surly mob estimated in the hundreds who were held in check by an elite police cordon whose job it was to provide protection for the principles on entering and exiting the courthouse. There were accounts of vulgar shouts and at least one tomato hurled at the grandmother as she ascended the courthouse steps and sympathetic calls of support for the young couple as they arrived.

Many of the papers accurately summarized Judge VanderLinde's decision but the aforementioned suburban weekly printed the entire text of the ruling. I am also including the text in total here, since it was an obvious manifestation of the wisdom, compassion, and judicial instincts of the man who soon would become a dominant figure in the state judiciary and about whom this book is centered.

> Let it be stated at the offset that this court recognizes its obligations to provide justice to all parties that come before it.
>
> Let it further be noted that we intend to use the full authority granted to this court to achieve that justice while at the same time abiding by the limitations placed upon us by law as interpreted by the precedents and traditions of our legal system.
>
> In the case before us we are obliged by law to afford primary considerations to the health and safety of the child whose custody we are here asked to decide.
>
> We have heard testimony from a qualified social caseworker that the child's parents, regardless of their devotion and love, because of their unfortunate physical disabilities can not provide minimal assurance that the child will not be placed in jeopardy without additional in-home care, which is unavailable from present social service programs.
>
> We have further heard the maternal grandparent testify that she is unwilling to provide such care either personally in her own home or through financial contribution for care elsewhere that would include all three members of the Harwood family. Though it may be argued that this grandmother has a moral obligation to so provide, she is not required by law to do so, nor is this court empowered to so order. However, this grandparent has testified that she is willing and able to provide and care for the child and its mother without the presence of Mr. Harwood.
>
> As for the contradictory psychiatric testimony concerning the possible affects on the child from exposure to her father's physical condition we can only conclude that the science of psychiatry is not yet sufficiently advanced to be able to determine with any degree of accuracy what affects, if any, would be

incurred by this particular child through such exposure. Therefore, on the grounds of inadequate evidence we must dismiss any consideration of this testimony.

With these realities before us we are limited in our possible courses of action. But as we have stated, though the jurisdiction granted this court places limitations upon our considerations, the principle of justice to all fixes heavy obligations upon those appointed to interpret and to administer the law.

We have before us a young couple that, through no serious fault of their own, is unable to provide the minimal safeguards to health and safety for their offspring. No evidence has been offered that either the father or the mother is other than loving and devoted parents. Certainly the father has proven by his act of self-sacrifice and by his testimony here that his first concern is to the well being of his wife and child. Any decision by this court that would deny this father the aid, comfort, and support of his family without exhausting all possible resources no matter how unusual would be to render a verdict against this court and the society, which created it and empowered it to make such decisions.

Further, any action that would require a wife and mother to make a choice between her husband and her child is certainly uncivilized, if not, inhuman, since it would be a sentence of a cruel punishment for which she has committed no crime.

Though the law in such cases is clear, the obligation to justice is equally clear. This court has no power to order either the grandparent or the County Welfare Department to provide services that would enable these parents to adequately care for the child while the family remains intact. However, it does have the right, and in this instance, we believe the obligation to suggest and persuade the appropriate administrative bodies to employ extraordinary services that are within their jurisdiction to so provide. Through the excellent cooperation of the administrators of the County Welfare Department, an experimental project has been formulated, which, if successful, we believe will fulfill all of the requirements of law and justice.

This court has inquired of authoritative parties within the County Welfare Department as well as other Federal, State and Local, governmental agencies and has formulated a tentative arrangement. We have ascertained that there are unfortunate single women with pre-school children who are unable to adequately support themselves and their offspring through meaningful employment due to their obligations to their children and who, like the Harwoods are trying to cope with meager welfare subsidies.

We have further learned through personal interviews with several of these young women, who have been psychologically screened and found to be mature and socially adjusted individuals, that some would be eager to share a dwelling with the Harwood family; to act in the capacity of homemaker and to provide any additional care required by the handicaps of the members of the family.

On further inquiry we have learned that the estimated cost of combining the needs of two welfare recipient families, even while providing a modest salary to the single mother for her domestic and personal care, would be less than the total current outlay from all agencies combined for the needs of both families as separately.

Therefore, it is the decision of this court that Elizabeth Harwood be returned to her parents with the condition that Alice and James Harwood accept the domestic accommodations herein outlined and with the further condition that the County Welfare Department hire and appoint a suitable single mother to act in the domestic capacity we have described.

Since it is recognized that this is an experimental program for which there is neither adequate precedent nor predictable outcome, this court recognizes its obligation to review periodically the progress of this accommodation.

Therefore, we order that the County Welfare Department provide this court, on a regular basis and at suitable intervals, a report concerning the health and safety of the child under this program.

Let the Bailiff note that it is so ordered, adjudged, and decreed.

The newspaper accounts told of a joyful and tumultuous reaction in the courtroom followed by prolonged cheers as the news of the decision spread to the people standing in the corridors and outside of the building.

Judge VanderLinde refused to be interviewed by reporters after the trial, but the head of the County Welfare Department was apparently more than willing to share the limelight with the judge. It was not clear whether the decision to hold a news conference was at the request of the media or the Welfare Chief, but in it he reluctantly admitted that the suggestion of combining the needs of two welfare recipients into one at a savings to the taxpayers was initiated by Judge VanderLinde. However, he quickly added that he has always welcomed such innovative concepts and accentuated his intention to carefully study this accommodation and, if successful, to develop a broader program based upon this principle. When asked where the Harwoods would be living, the Welfare Chief said that a friend of the court had donated a single dwelling for their use, but that the location was being withheld from the public in order to minimize unnecessary pressure to the family and thus permit the experimental program to be evaluated under as normal circumstances as possible.

All of the papers heaped extensive praise on the young jurist. One of the more imaginative editorialists even drew a parallel between Judge VanderLinde's decision and the decision attributed to Solomon when he ascertained the true mother of a child, which had been claimed by two women, actually characterizing Judge VanderLinde as a modern day Solomon.

John Keating's paper naturally emphasized the political ramifications of this trial by ascribing it as the primary cause for Judge VanderLinde's appointment to the State Supreme Court. The trial took place during a bitter gubernatorial campaign in which the incumbent's opponent, because of a substantial, but apparently necessary, raise in the state income taxes was seriously threatening the incumbent governor. At the same time, one of the members of the State Supreme Court died less than two years into a four-year term on the bench. The governor's political advisors convinced him that by appointing young VanderLinde to fill the vacancy he could capitalize on the positive publicity of the trial and possibly be enveloped by and included in the aura of wisdom that presently surrounded the Common Pleas Judge.

According to John's paper the appointment was made only one week after the close of the trial and the newspaper, further, adroitly theorized that the legislature, many of whose members were also up for reelection, must have realized that a quick ratification would be politically beneficial to them and that a negative vote would be grossly imprudent. Consequently, many members of the legislature disregarded the youth and judicial inexperience of the appointee, and ratified the appointment of Ronald VanderLinde almost unanimously.

Ronald VanderLinde's career as a State Supreme Court Justice proved almost as colorful and newsworthy as the antecedents to his appointment to that bench. Justice VanderLinde became an attractive anomaly on the court. He was sometimes, though not too often, the sole dissenter in otherwise unanimous decisions. The articles and editorials that frequently popped up in the files of the morgue concerning the Justice's opinions reflected more confusion than analysis. John's paper frequently admitted that it could not label Justice VanderLinde as either a liberal or a conservative. On interpretation of the State Constitution the Justice always argued that our form of government from top to bottom was created to protect the weak or minorities from the tyranny of the strong and the majority. But when applying legislative law to a given case he argued for a strict interpretation of the law as written. This was, of course, directly contrary to some of his more liberal colleagues who attempted to, as later critics of progressive courts would say, "Create new law from the bench." Instead, Justice VanderLinde, after writing a decision, would point out the deficiencies in the law under consideration. Sometimes he would even offer possible corrections, but would always recommend that the legislature amend it, and here he appeared to enjoy injecting a playful barb at the legislature for having written a less than perfect law. He suggested they correct it, "By employing a little common sense."

The one consistency about which the critics of Justice VanderLinde, both positive and negative, readily agreed was that in all of his decisions he was brutally logical. Before one of the Justice's later reelections, John's paper offered a lengthy editorial recommending Justice VanderLinde for reelection, but with qualifications. In the editorial the writer commented on what the editorialist referred to as the Justice's obsession with logic. He gave Justice VanderLinde credit for being exceptionally skilled in the subject, stating that his mastery of logic was probably a reflection of his Jesuit education and then added sardonically, "Aristotle, himself, could probably have written most of Justice VanderLinde's opinions." There was a colorful account in several of the papers about an anecdote during a trial before the State Supreme Court that seemed to touch a few people's funny bones. After Justice VanderLinde had wrapped a question to an attorney arguing a case before the court around a list of logical syllogisms the conclusion of which was that the attorney's position was ridiculously illogical, the attorney responded with, "Well certainly, Justice VanderLinde, if you insist on being logical. But..." and then simply restated the attorney's previously stated view as though the Justice's logic was irrelevant. The above mentioned editorial that stated Aristotle could have written the Justice's opinions also concluded with a caustic remark that the Justice's frequent application of logic to matters before the Court as, "...judicial irrelevance."

Perhaps the main reason that the media had difficulty labeling Justice VanderLinde as either a conservative or a liberal jurist is that, though he was what is called today a "strict constructionist" when sitting on the bench, he was extremely progressive giving speeches away from the Court. Even in the late forties he was arguing the causes of civil rights before the concept had become popular. He was also about twenty-five years ahead of most of the nation in their opposition to the death penalty for capital crimes. An article reported him as saying in a commencement address before his alma mater, "Using electrocution as an example, the act of putting a person to death for a capital crime is not the act of one man, an executioner, in a state prison, pulling a lever. This is a societal act and each one of us as members of that society are equally responsible for the death just as though we individually pulled that lever. So, unless I am willing to pull the lever to kill another human being, I cannot justifiably support the death penalty. And, if you find the concept of pulling the lever as repulsive as I do, then perhaps you also feel as I do that deliberately and with premeditation to take another human life except in self defense or to protect the helpless is actually to reduce oneself, as a human being, to the same level as the criminal being executed."

Back in the fifties and sixties, many of Justice VanderLinde's opinions in and out of Court were not popular with the electorate as evidenced by the frequent articles and editorials that I found in the newspaper morgue. But his willingness to face his critics without rancor apparently won him great personal respect. His solitary dissents even earned him fanciful nicknames such as the Lone Ranger of the State Supreme Court with appropriate editorial cartoons. All of the above frequently placed his name in the papers, which made him a familiar figure to the voters who continued to return him to the bench for almost twenty years.

John Keating joined me in the paper's morgue room at about 4:30 PM and asked if I had found what I needed. I told him that I had enough material to complete the first half of my assignment, but that the paper wanted the last articles to concentrate on the Justice's recent speeches. I said that there was considerable copy on the speeches, but most of it consisted of summaries with only brief excerpts. I asked John if he knew where I could find the complete texts. He replied that the Justice himself was the only probable source and suggested that I contact Justice VanderLinde's brother, Steven, who was probably in the capital to make the funeral arrangements. John was unable to tell me where Steven was staying so I decided to attend the deceased Justice's wake in the hope of making contact.

At this, we left the newspaper building for the drive to John's house. John lived in a relatively new home that was part of an upscale development in an exclusive suburb of the Capital. The houses were at least one hundred fifty feet from the street on lots that obviously had been carved from a wooded area. Several fully-grown trees dotted each parcel of land, which, for esthetic reasons, had obviously been selectively spared the bulldozers' onslaught. No two homes on the street dared to be alike and John's house was chosen to represent the English Tudor era. The grounds were maintained in such exquisite condition that I had to assume they were under the care of a professional landscaper. The type of grass in the lawn was uniform throughout: bright green and totally free of weeds. A variety of round and pointed evergreens bordered by brilliant red ferns ran along the front of the house and covered the bottom quarter of the large framed windows whose small rectangular panes spoke well of the architect's research into eighteenth century English design. Freshly trimmed short hedges also lined either side of the last fifteen feet or so of the winding sidewalk that led to the front door.

I had followed John to his house in my rented car and, though he had driven to the rear, I parked in the driveway near the walk. John joined me at the front of the house and escorted me through the front door, which lead into a center hall, marble-floored foyer. As John took my coat and hung it in the guest closet under the stairway, I glanced around observing the elegance of his home. A study led off the foyer to the left and the living room to the right. I was somewhat surprised at the small amount of floor space afforded the study as compared to the size of the rest of the house and the spaciousness of the living room. The study was paneled and the drapes and furnishings were definitely masculine but the living room was as feminine as a ladies boudoir. The davenport, chairs, tables and lamps were all French provincial. The curtains were sheer and their tiered, folded design could only be defined as frilly. The wallpaper was a slightly off-white linen texture with frequent gold threads running downward weaving in and out in two or three inch lengths. The far wall held a raised fireplace that was inserted into glazed, pale green bricks that covered the entire wall from ceiling to floor. The bricks were set directly on top of one another rather than in the more usual and more structurally firm staggered pattern. The upholstery was all crushed velvet with a davenport in soft gold and the chairs in equally soft green. The carpet was an unbelievable white-white on which no one would ever dare walk.

After John hung up our coats he must have seen me mesmerized by the inaccessible character of the living room. He quickly ushered me into the study without comment where he offered me one of the three chairs that barely fit into the room. Before I sat down I instinctively looked for an ashtray, but there was none in sight. As I eased into my chair, I drew a pack of cigarettes from my shirt pocket and asked John if there was an ashtray handy.

John tried to smile, but failed. He replied meekly in a half whisper, "My wife doesn't allow smoking in the house. She says that the odor gets absorbed into everything and she hates the smell."

I uttered a mildly surprised, "Oh," as I slipped the cigarettes back into my pocket.

John was the beer-drinking champ of our fraternity and he was noted for the exotic liquor supply that he kept in his room. With recollections of John's reputation still vivid, I fully expected him to offer me a drink of the alcoholic variety but instead he sheepishly inquired, "Would you like a soft drink?" Noticing my surprise he quickly added in his previous semi-whisper, "I'd offer you something stronger but my wife's father drank a little too much, so she refuses to allow alcohol in the house."

Since I had entered the house, John's conversation had been limited to his wife's list of forbidden acts. I sarcastically considered suggesting a conspicuous sign on the inside of the front door similar to those posted on the inside of hotel or motel room doors that list at length the rules of the establishment but charity inhibited me.

John flushed at each admission that he had abdicated his authority in his own home. On reflection, I truly considered his plight a delightful display of poetic justice for having grown up without bothering to develop any personal character. Nevertheless, moved by feelings of compassion, I casually interjected a remark about the good old days at college in an effort to change the subject away from his embarrassment.

John was obviously relieved. I had no sooner opened the door to our mutual past than he took off on the, "Do you remember..." theme. After a few inconsequential recollections, John predictably brought up our infamous fraternity card files. One contained all of the jokes that any fraternity member had ever heard dating back at least fifty years. Frats used this file simply as dumb cards with which to refer on a social engagement in case the conversation came to an embarrassing halt. The jokes were filed alphabetically by subject and sometimes included both a clean and a dirty version, depending upon the libertarian or conservative attitudes of one's partner for the evening. I often wondered why supposedly witty college students would need such a crutch, but I figured that some of the frats were not as at ease alone with the opposite gender as they were with the guys. I considered using the joke file a couple of times, but never did. I envisioned myself during a break in the conversation reaching into my shirt pocket, pulling out a card, glimpsing at it and then saying, "Oh, by the way, did you hear the one about, etcetera, and so forth." The image of such a farcical scene was far more embarrassing than any momentary lapse in conversation.

The other card file was far more useful. Each card contained the vital statistics of a large percentage of the girls on campus. The file was used quite frequently by many of the frats in anticipation of social activities. The cards listed each girl's name, address, phone number, grade, major, estimated height, weight, female dimensions, comparative attractiveness (though this item was always considered a subjective evaluation), conversational skills and expected culinary drain on the wallet. This last item came in very handy if you were low on cash at the moment. Needless to say, I definitely used this file.

Our trip down memory lane was enjoyable, but was cut short by John's wife, who entered the front door obviously miffed. She was carrying several boxes and bags... more than she could handle easily, with names on them telling that she had been shopping at some rather expensive women's apparel stores.

"Oh, there you are," she snapped bitingly. Then, still looking at John but obviously speaking to me, she continued snidely, "Whose car is that in the driveway? I had to park behind it." Flipping her keys at John, while still trying to balance the packages, she barked, "You can put it in the garage."

John squirmed in his chair for a second and then tried to divert her attention from her annoyance, "Dear, I'd like you to meet, Fran Becks, an old fraternity brother."

I smiled trying to ignore her rude entrance, "I'm very happy to meet you, Mrs. Keating. You have a very beautiful home."

My effort at cordiality went for naught. John's wife looked at me coldly and turning away, she muttered, "If you'll excuse me, Mr. Becks, I have to get ready for this evening."

As she started up the stairs, John called after her, "Dear, Why don't you bring Mary Beth down. I'm sure Fran would like to see her."

Connie Keating was still in view. She stopped at about the fifth step and looked back at her husband with an icy stare. "I'm not your slave girl," she scowled, barely moving her lips. "If you want to show off your kid, you get her." With this, she continued her ascent and disappeared from view.

John tried another smile, but it broke into a nervous laugh. He caught himself quickly and then, probably realizing that there was no longer any use to pretend an amicable marital relationship, he relaxed and with a sigh muttered sarcastically, "Must have been a rough day at the Country Club." Then adding a touch of helplessness he groused, "Probably had a run in with her boyfriend."

I simply failed to know how to respond, so John broke the silence, "Did you see all of those packages? Sometimes I think she just married me so she could buy a new outfit for every social engagement... and with my job and family connections we go to a lot. The real problem is that her idea of value shopping is that it isn't quality unless it's very expensive. She was just a secretary when I joined the paper after college. We got married about six months later." He hesitated and then, mostly musing to himself he added, "What a mistake that was."

Realizing that any further conversation would be clouded by John's embarrassment at my knowing as much as I did about his personal life, I made my apologies and left.

It was about 6:00 PM when I arrived back at the hotel and, though I was hungry, I decided to shower and change before eating dinner.

I phoned Helen from my room to let her know that with a little luck and the cooperation of Steven VanderLinde, there was a chance that I could be home by Monday evening. She told me that Blakesley had called Sunday afternoon after failing to reach anyone at my cousin's apartment. He wanted to make certain that I was on my assignment and he asked Helen to pass along the message that, in spite of everything that had happened, Samuel Holmes wanted me to be assured that he still wanted me on the staff. Apparently, Blakesley had informed Holmes of the read-out that I had received and of my month long exile. The publisher was probably afraid that I might have been overly offended by Blakesley's invective, and that I might have considered quitting the paper, which, of course, would have denied him the financial rewards that his precious horoscope had predicted from our association. Even conveying the message through a third party must have been agonizingly difficult for my beloved Managing Editor and the humiliation could not have happened to anyone more deserving.

I arrived at the hotel lobby about 7:00 PM where I purchased a newspaper and scanned the death notices for the location of Justice VanderLinde's wake. The paragraph concerning the former Justice read:

> Ronald M. VanderLinde (former Justice of State Supreme Court) beloved son of the late Mark and Kathryn, brother of the Reverend Steven, SJ and Sister Mary Agnes, OPC (Agnes) and the late Paul, Henry, Joanne Baldorf and Theresa Yurik. Friends received at Joseph Wensink Funeral Home, 4823 West Fairfield Blvd. Sunday 2:00 to 5:00 PM and 7:00 to 9:00 PM Funeral Mass, Sacred Heart Church, Monday, October 26, at 10:00 AM Interment, Holy Cross Cemetery. Please omit flowers. Donations to the Cancer Foundation will be greatly appreciated.

Naturally, disturbing Steven VanderLinde for my intended purpose while he was receiving the condolences of the Justice's friends would have been grossly inappropriate, so I planned to arrive at the funeral home at about 8:45 PM and wait until he was able to leave before approaching him. The clerk at the newsstand gave me directions to the mortuary and I discerned that I had about an hour to relax and enjoy my dinner in the hotel restaurant.

Halfway through the entree I was surprised to see John and Connie Keating entering the dining room. After a brief encounter with the maitre d,' they were led to a table directly beside the one along the wall at which I was seated. During the trip through the dining room Connie Keating drew the attention of almost everyone present. She wore a black cocktail dress that would have been appropriate in a nightclub in any large city. However, in the sort of towns that make up most Midwestern state capitals and in a hotel restaurant, it was provocative to the extreme. John's wife was a typically attractive young woman with natural blond hair, blue eyes and, though attractive, she was thin and only modestly endowed. However, she obviously knew the power of feminine suggestiveness.

As the Keatings approached, I recalled the embarrassing episode of that afternoon. Not wishing to rekindle John's discomfort, I hid one side of my face with my hand and turned my head towards the wall pretending to read the newspaper that I had laid on the table. They joined two other couples that were already seated.

The Keatings' table allowed two people to sit on each side and one person at each end. John sat closest to me but facing away and his wife, Connie, sat beside him to the left. Across from John was a tall, black-haired gentleman with an athletic build. He sat very erect, and the lack of any gray in his hair and the appearance of the woman to his right, who was probably his wife, placed his age at about forty. His wife was a mousy little woman: very small in all dimensions with dull brown hair. Her voice was shrill and whiny, and I thought I noted a nervous quiver on the very few occasions that she spoke. Both her hairstyle and dress were about ten years behind current fashions. The other couple were older and probably in their sixties. Both were portly, but were stylishly dressed. Their demeanor projected an air of mature self-confidence. Each sat at one of the end chairs; the woman on the women's end and the man on the men's end of the table. Since the seating arrangement appeared to have been previously determined, and, since it placed the three men at one end and the three women at the other, I concluded that this was a business rather than a social gathering.

With auditory concentration and periodic side-glances, I entertained myself during the balance of my dinner by observing the activities at the adjacent table. I was close enough to hear the normal toned conversations, which consisted mainly in casual small talk. However, by the arrival of the second cocktail the discussion between John Keating and the elderly gentleman revealed the purpose for the dinner engagement. John was being asked to persuade his father to tone down the paper's editorial attacks on some issues in exchange for future services such as inside scoops on controversial legislation and, when possible, about rumored indiscretions of individual legislators. All of the latter was, of course, expressed in the usual deniability code so popular among politicians.

Meanwhile, the elderly woman excused herself and was joined by her mousy companion. The black-haired gentleman appeared to be listening to the progress of the agreement being reached by the other two men. However, his attention was regularly interrupted by remarks directed at him by Connie Keating. The quick and frequent pivot of his head away from Connie and to the other two men disclosed his preference for the male conversation. But Connie was not to be denied. After several verbal efforts to gain his attention, she turned slightly sideways and leaning forward, in order to place an elbow on the table, she probably exposed more than even that dress was intended to reveal. On his next look at Connie his attention was all hers.

The return of the other two ladies brought them towards the corner of the table between Connie and her bewitched friend, both of whom were totally absorbed with each other. The approaching women were obviously aware of the flirtatious intrigue. When they reached the table the smallish one stood beside her husband and stared glaringly down at Connie who, though recognizing that she had been caught in the act, demonstrated no embarrassment or guilt. She simply rose upright with an exaggerated and deliberate slowness while projecting a haughty expression that shouted, "Get away from me kid, you bother me. He's mine, if I want him."

I was so deeply engrossed in the soap opera-like scene that I forgot my original intent to avoid recognition and Connie's arrogant physical maneuverings swung her around in her chair just far enough that she could see me, whom she recognized immediately. The result was momentary confusion. John, who had risen to welcome the ladies back to the table, saw the surprised expression on his wife's face and turning around to see the cause also suddenly recognized my presence. He tried to follow his welcoming of the women with an introduction of me to his dinner companions, but his efforts were wasted because of the other more exciting activities. The elderly woman returned to her seat, but was deeply engrossed in the counter-play between Connie and her adversary. The mousy woman continued glaring down at Connie while complaining to her husband about a nasty headache, and asked that he take her home. When the dust had settled, and the younger couple had exited, I had accepted John's invitation to fill one of the empty seats for my post-meal coffee.

I had the choice of sitting across from John, which would have probably made me look like I wanted to eavesdrop on his negotiations with the senior gentleman or across from Connie Keating who I felt, under the circumstance, would probably prefer silence. So I decided on the latter. Unfortunately I miscalculated Mrs. Keating's audacity. Even though the elderly woman was within earshot of her remarks, she began telling me about her recent table encounter with the gentleman who had just left. Her remarks were not as an attempt at a defensive rationale or even as an explanation, but rather as simple, casual small talk...as though her behavior was as natural as breathing. I just sat and listened because

I really did not know how to react nor did I really care about the matter. She told me that Harry Wilson was a popular, former state football hero from a rural district who was a rising young star in the state legislature. She further added the rumor that he was being groomed for the governor's mansion. She then stated, with what was to me unbelievable, if not audacious candor, that, she had only married John so that she could meet people like Harry and that, if Harry did become governor, she intended to be the first lady of the state, adding, "Who knows, with a little luck and a lot of push, someday I may even become first lady of the nation." Then she added sneeringly, "Not that lifeless little twerp he's married to now."

I looked into her eyes and saw a fierce determination, the likes of which I had never seen before. I responded almost as a reflex, "I'm sure you will be."

I was dumbfounded as to why Connie Keating would tell me these things, since I had only met her that afternoon unless she was not telling me at all but was declaring her intentions to the woman at the end of the table who was probably the wife of one of the people who would be grooming Harry Wilson for the governorship. However, regardless of her reasons, I could not help but feel sorry for poor John. He was not the type of person for whom one would vote the fullness of life's joys and riches. But even he did not deserve to be used in the manner in which his wife described her marital attitudes and intentions. I knew that John could not defend himself, so I decided to return her candor in like fashion. Rising from my seat, I drew my coffee cup to my lips and looking down at Mrs. Keating, I commented simply, "I'm sorry, but I don't find unbridled ambition attractive. It leaves too much blood in its wake."

I denied Connie Keating the opportunity to respond by turning immediately to John and the elderly gentleman and, thanking them for allowing me to join them, I explained that I would need to leave right away if I were to arrive at the funeral home in time to see Steven VanderLinde.

As I moved to leave, I passed my eyes one last time over Connie Keating's nasty stare. I sensed a strange bitterness but I felt no apprehension. Mrs. Keating was not a person of natural charisma. She could only attain her goals by constant effort, which self-preoccupation left her staid and, consequently, vulnerable, or, at least, easy to defense for anyone of flexibility and wit. Though I was now no longer looking at her, I smiled blithely as an added needle before my face passed from her view.

I left the dining room with a feeling of conquest similar to that I assumed the knights of old must have felt after successfully defending the honor of the weak and helpless at the joust. It was a pleasant feeling and a substantial boost to my confidence...just the ego lift that I needed as I left the hotel to interview the Reverend Steven VanderLinde, SJ

CHAPTER *Five*

I arrived at the funeral home about ten minutes to nine expecting most of the mourners to have come and gone, but the parking lot was still overflowing and the surrounding streets were lined with cars displaying license plates from a multitude of states; even the District of Columbia. I was required to park almost a mile from the mortuary. It had started to rain intermittently and, unfortunately, the period of time at which I arrived included one of the "on" rather than an "off" rain period. It was a cold rain. The temperature had dropped into the thirty's as a cold front moved across the Capital. Long-range forecasters had accurately predicted an early winter that year. Fortunately, I had worn an insulated trench coat that evening so when I entered the funeral parlor, though my head was wet and cold, the rest of me, under my coat, was quite dry.

Though the funeral home was quite large for such an establishment, it was in no way close to the size needed to host the crowd that was still present. I slowly maneuvered myself through the human throng into the room where the casket resided. It was closed and in simple good taste but, obviously, one of the more economical models. Though the death notice in the newspaper requested that flowers be omitted, there was a significant floral display surrounding the casket. A few feet in front of and to the side of the casket stood a tall, moderately built, gray haired man in the usual priest attire who was greeting the incoming visitors. I assumed that this was the deceased Justice's brother, Steven. Though he was probably in his seventy's, he stood exceptionally erect, an impressive posture considering that he had obviously been standing and greeting people for hours. Reflecting on this fact, I was struck by the sincere, gracious ease with which he greeted the mourners. Steven VanderLinde exuded that simple, non-ostentatious self-confidence that one seldom sees, but which demands respect when so encountered.

I realized that it would be rude and, consequently, grossly inappropriate for me to approach Fr. VanderLinde during the wake concerning my request to view his brother's papers and the alternative of asking him in the parking lot afterwards, considering how tired he would be, also seemed intrusive. But my desire to complete my work in the Capital and return to home and Helen overwhelmed my sensitivity towards the priest's physical condition, so I decided on the parking lot stratagem.

I was definitely concerned that my stopping him on his way to his car might irritate him resulting in his refusal of my request. I, nevertheless, counted on the, "Charity to others," that people of his profession are supposed to possess.

What I did not count on was the wake continuing for at least two more hours. It was after 11:00 PM before Fr. VanderLinde was able to leave the funeral home. Though he walked erect and seemingly unaffected by the day and evening ordeal, I had to assume that he was exhausted. Though my conscience was yelling at me to leave the poor man alone, my selfish desire to get home won the day. "Fr. VanderLinde," I uttered hesitatingly as I approached him. He turned and acknowledged me. I apologized for bothering him after such a long day and quickly introduced myself, mentioning the paper for which I worked and the task to which I was assigned. I anxiously searched for some expression of annoyance at my intrusion, but was delightfully surprised to see none on his face or in his eyes. Recognizing no negative reaction, I continued, asking him if he knew where his brother's papers were located, especially the drafts of his speeches. In a soft but clear voice, amazingly strong considering his hundreds of greeting remarks throughout the day, he responded simply, "Most of the Judge's papers are in the library at his house." Then he added, "I'll be spending a few days there organizing his belongings including his papers." He hesitated thoughtfully for what seemed an unusual length of time, which hesitancy I attributed to his simply trying to get his wits about himself under the fatigue he must have been experiencing. Then he offered, "I'll be tied up most of tomorrow with the Funeral Mass and the internment... and there's a reception scheduled afterwards that I'm certain will take up most of the afternoon. But, I'm staying at Ron's house while I'm here. If you would like to come over early tomorrow evening, we could both go through the papers. I'm curious myself as to what's there." Though I was a little disappointed that I could not get at the speech drafts until the evening, I certainly understood the reason for the delay and offered no objection. After I agreed to meet him the following evening, Fr. VanderLinde gave me the address of his late brother's house and drove off.

The rain had stopped, but it was not a pleasant night, as a cold dampness hung in the air. By now my hair was dry, but I felt chilled and uncomfortable. However, I was only half conscious of the discomfort. I imprudently stood in the parking lot for some time musing over the priest's gracious tone concerning my research and mentally organized my prospective series from the information I had already acquired. Anticipatory organization of my articles was a frequent wont of mine, which did not always serve me well. The warehouse fire episode was a good example. I assumed things that were not always there.

It was quite late by the time I arrived back at the hotel, so I decided to wait until morning to call Helen and let her know that I would be remaining at the Capital for an extra day or two. I also felt a chill while I was making arrangements with the desk clerk for my increased stay.

The following morning I felt a bit tired, but wrote the feeling off as not having slept well in a strange bed. I saw no reason to attend either the Funeral Mass or the cemetery internment so I speculated during breakfast as to how I could beneficially spend the day while waiting for my later trip to former Justice VanderLinde's home. I was quite intrigued with the character and general demeanor of Fr. Steven VanderLinde whom I had met the night before and with whom I would be spending at least one evening. One of the articles, which I had read earlier concerning Ronald VanderLinde mentioned that his brother, Steven, was a Theoretical Physicist and added further that he was published in his field. I decided to visit the library of the state university located in the capital to see if I could locate any of Steven VanderLinde's works.

My visit to the university library was both informative and rather disappointing. I liked Fr. VanderLinde during our first encounter, perhaps only because he refrained from biting my head off for bothering him after such a grueling day. I speculated from his easy self-confidence that he was probably, at least a medium sized giant in his field. But I could only find one book written by him and that volume, published at least forty years prior, except for some serious dust, appeared brand new, as though no one had ever read or even opened it. Professor VanderLinde's contribution to the study of Theoretical Physics was apparently not sufficiently impressive for this university's teachers to recommend to their students for added reading.

At this revelation I reviewed the large tome that listed all of the Who's Who of the scientific world and which also offered a brief biography of each individual's accomplishments and contributions to their respective disciplines. Though Steven VanderLinde's name did appear, there was no mention of any such accomplishments or contributions, not even a reference to the book, which I held in my hand and which was colorfully entitled, Does Existence Really Exist? And subtitled, How Our Physical World Reveals Spiritual Realities And Vice Versa. I assumed that the editors of the scientific listings as well as most of the scientists listed considered Fr. VanderLinde's book a religious work rather than an addition to the study of physics, especially since it was coming from a, "Reverend," with an, "SJ," after his name.

Except for a brief lunch, I spent the balance of the morning and most of the afternoon trying to find out if, "Existence Really Existed," as explained by Fr. VanderLinde. I had taken two semesters of high school Physics and, though I found the subject interesting and did actually enjoy the course, I often was required to read the material two or three times to comprehend most of the more intriguing concepts. Interest and enjoyment not withstanding, my innate laziness prohibited me from even considering physics as a life's work. It was with these memories of the subject, that I scanned Steven VanderLinde's literary offering.

As best I could understand the book, and I admit without embarrassment that my understanding was minimal, Fr. VanderLinde was attempting to marry the Natural Sciences and Theology, a feat that had certainly been attempted by many great minds in the past. Fr. VanderLinde proffered that he himself was taking a different ploy: starting with Thomas Aquinas's major thesis that all of creation must reflect its Creator and using logic, or at least general philosophy, as a tool, pointed out how the laws of physics, as they are unfolding in our twentieth century can explain many of the previously unexplained mysteries of religion. The author apparently was saying that God intended us to look at nature in order to know Him; that, just as a beautiful sunset is a finite reflection of the beauty of God Himself, so too, as we grow in a fuller understanding of the laws of nature, through that understanding, we can grow in a fuller and deeper understanding of who God is. Fr. VanderLinde was quick to point out that God is not the sunset. To say that would be pantheistic. "But, just as a superior painting of a beautiful sunset by an accomplished artist is not the artist, it does manifest both the interior comprehension and appreciation of esthetics and the painting skills of the artist that enables him or her to reproduce on canvas the abstract beauty within the sunset. Then too, God, though not being the sunset or even the beauty in the sunset, possesses the aesthetic, or abstract beauty that is reflected in that scene."

The author quoted many philosophers and theologians over the centuries that expounded this thesis and parallel theses, such as that the order within the universe must reflect the fact that God possess order and that He likes order. Fr. VanderLinde asserted that this concept was often referred to in moral theology as the Natural Law. But then he took this supposition a step further. This idea was probably his and the reason that he wrote the book: That, not only general attributes within nature; such as order within the universe, reflect the nature of God, but that specific laws; such as the particular laws of physics, as we are discovering them in our time, can be used to explain specific theological mysteries, which God has revealed to us through Scripture and the prophets, if only we are willing to look beyond the empirical evidences uncovered through theory and experimentation and search more deeply into that evidence: not being content with what is unveiled, but perhaps try to uncover why reality is what it is and, in addition, reach for the answers as to what God is trying to tell us with the evidence.

It was here that the Theoretical Physicist lost me. He began explaining a long list of laws of physics and their mystagogical counterparts using elaborate philosophical justifications and jargon both of which I was not familiar. It was about four o'clock when I realized that I had gotten in over my head; that I was reading the material two and three times in a vain effort to understand it, much like my experiences with the subject of Physics in high school, so I decided to finish my stay at the university library and find a place to eat before driving to my evening meeting with Steven VanderLinde.

I was not certain what Fr. VanderLinde's meaning of, "early evening," was, so I picked seven o'clock as my arrival time, hoping that he would have completed his dinner and be ready to go right to work. When the priest greeted me at the door he appeared as gracious as he seemed the night before. After welcoming me, he offered me a cup of coffee or other beverage and led me into the former Justice's library/den. The room was very large compared to the rest of the house indicating that originally the library was probably two rooms. I had a sudden flashback to my entrance into Samuel Holmes' two-story office and the reason therefore. Fortunately, none of what followed included any experience similar to my initial encounter with the newspaper owner/publisher. Most of the walls were lined with bookshelves, which were naturally filled with a plethora of volumes; most of which I assumed were legal reference sources. There was a large desk in front of a draped window and three wooden file cabinets at strategic locations around the room, two uprights and one lateral on which resided a coffee maker (coffee still warming) and variously designed mugs.

There were two large boxes setting on the desk, that Fr. VanderLinde explained contained a lot of his brother's personal papers and which he had retrieved from the attic. He steered me to the file cabinets with the admonition that, if Ronald had kept the notes or actual copies of the speeches, they would probably be there. As I began scouring through the files in one of the cabinets, Fr. VanderLinde commenced his own forage through the material in one of the boxes on the desk. As he did so, he started up a casual conversation mainly inquiring about my past history and me. After asking the usual questions such as where I grew up and where I went to school, he then inquired, in a matter of fact tone, "How long have you been working for the paper?"

"A little over a year." I responded.

"Do you like to write or is writing just an occupational tool?"

I was unable to see where the priest was going with this question and answered, "I think it's both. I do like to write but writing is also a necessary skill for any reporter."

"Yes, of course, that's true," he admitted and then continued. "I suppose what I'm asking is whether you like to delve beneath the surface of a story... learn what's going on within the characters involved... what motivates them... what their strengths and weaknesses are... who they really are."

A brief reflection passed through my mind that Fr. VanderLinde's question would be more appropriate coming from a psychology professor than from a physics professor, but I was curious about his reasons for asking the question. I responded truthfully, "Reporters are seldom allowed the privileges of such in-depth analysis. We're confined to the facts, the facts and only the facts, at least, if we're being true to our profession." But then I confessed, "But it isn't always easy. Actually it's the in-depth stuff that interests me the most... not just what happened, but why it happened."

For a reason I could not quite understand, I found myself opening up to this man that I hardly knew almost as though we were long lost friends. I continued, "I hated history in high school and during my first semester in college because it seemed to be only about names and dates and places. But then I explained my aversion to my history professor who admitted that he had the same repulsion to the subject until one of his professors turned him on to some books that took an entirely different approach. I was studying European History at the time and my professor gave me a book on the period that told the story from the decisions made by various leaders and how those decisions reflected the philosophical ideas being advanced by the intelligencia of the time. The author pointed out that by reading the ideas of the thinkers, an observer could predict what decisions and actions, subsequently, would and did take place. In other words, European History was not just a series of things that happened, but rather a development of thought from which you could see why what happened, happened." I added, "I really liked history when presented that way."

When I finished this dissertation, I thought that I was probably rambling about things for which Fr. VanderLinde had no interest. Surprisingly, though, he appeared very interested. I passed off his positive reaction as simply an expression of his priestly generosity, but then he interjected an interesting comment, "The Holy Spirit works in subtle ways."

There was a lapse in the conversation and we both went back to our rummaging: I in the files, and he in the boxes. After a few minutes Fr, VanderLinde broke the silence with some further personal queries. "Are you religiously oriented, Mr. Becks?"

That question should not have surprised me coming from a priest, but it did not follow naturally from our previous discussion, nor did it flow easily from where we were or what we were doing. I hesitated, trying to figure out how to answer honestly without offending my host. My quandary must have been apparent as Fr. VanderLinde interjected, "I'm sorry. I think I caught you off guard. I didn't mean to challenge your religious convictions or non-convictions, but I do have a reason for asking what I did."

The disarming manner with which he salved my concerns about answering made me want to respond with absolute openness. "I am not religiously oriented, Father. I'm engaged to a wonderful girl who is. She's Catholic and goes to Mass every Sunday. Sometimes she even drags me along. In Lent she often goes during the week... and she's very active in her parish. But I'm afraid religion has never been one of my big interests." I felt compelled to add, "I'm sorry."

Fr. VanderLinde smiled. "Don't apologize, Mr. Becks. I hesitate to ask this but I think I must. Are you an atheist, an agnostic, or a believer who is just not affiliated with a formal religion?"

"I think I'm an agnostic actually," I revealed with continued openness. "I just never thought much about God or even if there is one. I've always been a skeptic about everything, even religion. I'm not bragging about it. It could be a natural outflow from my revulsion to the discomforts of guilt. If there is a God, then I have to be extra responsible for my actions, and that just seems like too much work." Then I quipped, "And besides, I like to sleep in on Sunday mornings."

"So do I," the priest admitted. "That's why I take advantage of my seniority and insist on saying the twelve noon Mass in the university chapel... except during professional football season. Then I take the ten-thirty." We both laughed.

The balance of the evening moved along without much significance. About nine o'clock I found the files that included the notes and, in some cases, copies of the actual speeches, but I could see that Fr. VanderLinde was obviously tired. He was sitting behind the desk, reading material from the boxes. Periodically his eyes would close and he would doze off for a bit. I was also extremely tired... more so than I thought I should have been. Since I now knew where the speeches were, I suggested that we try again the next day to finish our research. Fr. VanderLinde made no objection, commenting that the following day was open for him too. He told me to leave everything where it was. I quickly acquiesced. I was surprised that the drive back to the hotel took so long. I was very anxious to get to bed for the night.

The following morning I woke about 6:30 AM feeling quite sick. I felt like I had a fever, since even the covers hurt against my skin and I had periods of chills. I tried to get a couple more hours of sleep, hoping that the additional rest might make me feel better, but my efforts were in vain. I just lay there feeling miserable. Fr. VanderLinde had invited me for breakfast at 10:00 AM, commenting that he planned to say an early Mass at a nearby parish. I wanted to call off the trip to the former Justice's house and just spend the day in bed, but my desire to get back home motivated me to get dressed, and go... albeit, with much difficulty. I experienced even greater difficulty driving to the house. When I walked the approximately twenty paces from the car in the street, to the front steps, up the steps and to the front door, I had to stop three times to catch my breath. Opening the door, Fr. VanderLinde took one look at me and alarmingly declared, "Good Lord, you look terrible."

"I feel terrible." I admitted. "I think I almost passed out a couple of times in the car on the way over," I added.

"You're sweating and you're very pale," the priest observed sympathetically as he ushered me to a chair in the dining room. "Coffee?" he inquired. "There's probably some aspirin upstairs in the medicine cabinet."

"I had a real problem walking from the car to the front door," I complained. "I've never experienced anything like that."

"I'm not an MD," he explained. "But that sounds like it could be pneumonia. We better get you some help." Fr. VanderLinde checked the phone book for the nearest hospital, then took my arm and helped me out of the house. We decided to take my car so the Father could watch over it if I had to stay in the hospital, which I did. Steven VanderLinde's diagnosis of pneumonia was right and the emergency ward personnel arranged for a room for me until I recovered.

Father left as I was being wheeled to my room with the remark that there was probably nothing that he could do for me at that time. As he was leaving, I asked if he could bring me the speech materials so that my stay in the hospital would not be a total waste of time. He acknowledged that he would bring them to me later that afternoon.

It was already three o'clock by the time I settled into my hospital room. I felt frustrated and irritated from the inconvenience. I also felt stupid for not having at least attempted to dry my hair when I arrived at the mortuary. It was one thing to walk for about ten or fifteen minutes in a cold rain. It was quite another to stand around in the funeral home with a wet head for an hour or so while my hair was air-drying. That neglectful omission was probably the cause of my medical problems.

With an IV sticking in the back of my hand and while lying in a hospital bed wearing one of those silly gowns with the open back, I managed to dial the phone to let Helen know the latest episode of my not very pleasant downstate soap opera. Her sympathy did not totally cover up her disappointment in my delayed trip home, but, of course, there was nothing either of us could do about it, so we just engaged in small talk. Helen did offer to take some time off work and come down to the Capital to keep me company, but I told her about Steven VanderLinde's offer to bring the speech papers to me at the hospital. Though Helen was sensitive enough not to mention that she had no plans for her leave time at work because she no longer needed it for our honeymoon, thanks to my debacle at the paper, the thought went through my head and added to my already negative feelings about myself. Apparently using that feminine attribute that allows mothers to know what their children are doing without actually seeing them doing it, Helen sensed that I was really down in the dumps. She began saying simple but meaningful things that she often does and that quite often bolsters my ego. Consequently, we ended our conversation on an up note. I simply tried to get some sleep while I waited for Fr. VandeLinde's return.

I did catch a short nap before my newly found guardian arrived with the speech files. In the past I had seen Fr. VanderLinde pause thoughtfully before saying something, but he seemed exceptionally reflective during the beginning of this visit to the hospital. He arrived while I was eating my dinner and was relatively quiet while I was completing what I could of my meal. I really, as yet, had very little appetite. Finally he began speaking, seemingly choosing his words with extreme caution. For the first time since we met, he appeared tense or, at least, somewhat lacking in that easy self-confidence that I had admired earlier. Before he finished his first sentence, which was unusually lengthy for him, I interrupted, "Is there something wrong, Father?"

He looked at me with a penetrating stare as though he was trying to read what was going on inside of me. Suddenly, he must have noticed that his demeanor was making me ill at ease. As though snapping out of a trance, he blurted out, "I'm sorry," then continued, "You were observant to notice that I was preoccupied."

"I hope I'm not offending," I interjected, "But it was rather obvious."

"I'm sorry," he repeated and then added, "It seems I'm apologizing to you a lot. It's just that I have some very weighty issues on my mind and some difficult judgments to make."

"More profound than whether existence exists," I chuckled.

"Oh, I see you know about my failed contribution to the world of theoretical physics," he responded, also laughing. "That book laid a large egg. I thought I had some good ideas there but I guess no one else did. That was my doctoral thesis. I was a young warrior at the time it was published, quite full of myself, and my professional ego was bruised from the lack of acceptance by my peers. But I got over it. Fortunately, I had a very practical, wise old Jesuit as a spiritual advisor. I used to tell my colleagues, though, that I was just ahead of my time."

"You might be yet," I sympathized. "Look at Galileo."

"Did you have to bring that up?" he retorted. "We religious scientists are still embarrassed about the Institutional Church's treatment of that poor fellow."

I looked at my new friend and happily observed, "You look a little more relaxed now than you did when you arrived...a little more lighthearted."

"I am...thanks to you," he affirmed.

We both smiled sincerely at each other. "But that doesn't solve my dilemma," he divulged, continuing the suspense that he had carried with him into the hospital room. "I'm hoping you might be the one that can do that."

I was dumbfounded by this revelation. "Hey, I couldn't even understand all the stuff in your book after reading it several times. How can I solve a problem for you? Right now I'm flat on my back in a hospital bed with this blasted IV sticking in me and I'm still having trouble inhaling and exhaling."

He chuckled and rejoined, "Unless you totally stop inhaling and exhaling I don't think your current and, hopefully, temporary breathing problems will inhibit you from accomplishing what I have in mind." Again we laughed. "But seriously, I have a major request of you. My brother, Ronald, was not just a popular judge; he was also a very unique individual. Who he really was and, perhaps more importantly, why he was who he was is a story that both he and I believe should be told, not for his sake, but for the good, or perhaps more accurately, the goodness of humankind. He made me promise on his deathbed that I would find someone who could and would write the story as it really happened. It's a very earthy tale and at the same time a lofty, spiritual, even mystic tale; ecstatically beautiful and also heinously ugly. Ronald was a total person, Mr. Becks," Then he interrupted, "By the way, can I call you by your first name? I don't think we need to be formal anymore."

"Sure, you probably saved my life by bringing me here," I quipped. "That has to make us personally close in some way."

"The kids at school call me Father Steve but most of my fellow Jesuits and my lay colleagues just refer to me as Steve. You can use whatever you're comfortable with. What do you go by?" he inquired.

"Fran...short for Francis," I replied.

"As I was saying," the priest continued, "Ron was a total person. Even as a little boy he lived every moment to the fullest. As an adult he loved and hated, not just unconditionally but absolutely, without limits of any kind. Most of us, if we hope to get to heaven, grow in goodness little by little, day by day, over a lifetime and hopefully reach some acceptable level of holiness before we die. Others, like Ron...St. Paul was probably of the same sort...are, as I said, total people. Conversion from sinfulness to sainthood happens to them in a flash, like getting knocked off a horse by a lightning bolt. Ron wanted his story told, not because of vanity or pride... just the opposite. There were parts of his life that show him in a very bad, I might even say evil, light."

"I find that hard to believe," I countered. "All of the stories that I read about him pictured an extremely generous and selfless person: those heroic episodes during World War II and his various judicial decisions that came down as protecting the weak and helpless for which he took a lot of heat. By the way, did he have a death wish during that battle with the Japanese?"

"No...not at all," Father Steve responded. "As a matter of fact, he wanted to stay on this earth as long as he could to do as much good as he could to make up for some things that he did earlier in his life. That's why I asked you last night if you liked writing in depth about people and events...find out the real motives for why people do things, not just what they did. After Ron died I prayed almost continually to the Holy Spirit to direct me to someone who could write his real story in the depth, which would be required to fulfill my brother's wish. When you introduced yourself to me in the funeral home parking lot as a reporter, the first thing that ran through my mind was whether you might be the one...whether you may have been sent to me for the purpose of writing Ron's story."

By now, physically, I was feeling considerably better than earlier. I was still very weak and achy, but whatever they put in the IV must have been potent because I was alert and interested in the conversation. However, with my non-religious attitude, I could hardly see myself as the answer to anybody's prayers. Many of those little things that had transpired between Fr. VanderLinde and myself that were somewhat bewildering were now explained, but not in what I would consider a rational manner.

"You sound like your suggesting that I write your brother's story," I queried incredulously, "which sounds basically like a deeply religious narrative. Father...Steve...I told you that I'm probably an agnostic...certainly a skeptic. I look at almost everything through a cynic's eyes. When I can't find answers to questions, I drive the questions out of my mind. I'm very good at that. I'm probably one of the last people in the world you should want to write the former Justice's story."

I looked for disappointment in the priest's eyes but saw none. I was about to continue my objections as to why he should look elsewhere for a writer when he interrupted, "I considered your cynicism and skepticism and even your non-belief at great length last night and concluded that such a person as yourself is exactly what is required. Some pious, religiously oriented individual would naturally be inclined to interpret everything in a religiously positive way. As a scientist I've been required to approach physical reality as well as theory with absolute cynicism. That's why many people find a conflict between religion and science. Scientists are skeptics and believe nothing unless its proven and sometimes not even then, whereas religion depends a great deal on faith in spiritual realities that cannot be proven or, at least, appear non-provable."

"That's what you tried to do with your book, wasn't it: marry religion and science?"

"After a fashion," Fr. Steve cautiously admitted. "I simply tried to convince both disciplines, theology and science, that they need each other. Neither one can develop effectively and fully unless it applies to itself the discoveries and understandings developed within the other discipline. Science and theology are siblings, born of the same Parent... Siamese twins, if you will, that can not be separated without seriously limiting the development of our understanding of both."

I was impressed. Even with my limited knowledge of both religion and science, Steven VanderLinde's elucidations were clear and described a rational, symbiotic need between science and theology. His explanation did not, however, convince me that I should be the writer of his brother's life story.

Fr. VanderLinde was apparently aware of my continued reticence and started to continue his persuasions but stopped in mid-sentence. "You must be tired. I hope I haven't worn you out," the priest apologized compassionately.

"I am a bit drowsy," I admitted.

"Why don't you sleep on it," he suggested, "I'll check with you tomorrow." Then he playfully jibed, "I'd suggest you pray on it but that might conflict with your agnosticism, so I'll do the praying for you."

"Uh, oh," I joked in return, "Now I'm in real trouble."

We both laughed and Father handed me some files, which I assumed contained the speech materials. Before he departed he informed me that it would probably be the following evening before he could return, since he had arranged for an appraiser to evaluate and tag the belongings and furnishings in his brother's house. Through a short factual exchange, the priest explained that he felt he should be present with the appraiser, since it would give him an opportunity to see what was in the house and isolate what he or his sister might want to keep: mostly Ronald's personal objects and papers and some books that Fr. VanderLinde had asked his brother to donate to his university's library. I assumed that the balance of the furnishings and the house itself would be sold and the proceeds donated to charity, since both he and his sister had taken vows of poverty... a topic that I had learned about in one of my discussions with Helen and about which my innate cynicism rebelled. I felt that leaving one's financial security to someone else was both dangerous, if they failed their responsibilities, or an opportunity for abject laziness, if the vowee was inclined to shirk his. Helen retorted that my view on the subject was shallow and that, besides, the system had worked successfully for thousands of years.

I would like to have started reading the speeches and accompanying notes immediately after the priest left, but, though it was only about six thirty in the evening, I felt very tired. I hardly rolled over on my side before I was out and stayed asleep till morning, except, of course, for those brief and dreaded blood pressure and temperature checks throughout the night.

When I woke about 7:00 AM, I could tell that my fever had broken. I was also very hungry, which made me feel well enough to want to leave the hospital. However, the nurse insisted that my check out date and time were the doctor's call and that he would be in later. While I was waiting for the resident's visit, I began reviewing the speeches and notes in the files. Fr. VanderLinde was thoughtful enough to include a couple of writing pads in one of the folders and with a pen, which I borrowed from the nurse, I started outlining the articles.

The speeches covered a wide variety of social subjects. I looked for and quickly found the commencement address that expressed the former Justice's views on the death penalty, which was delivered well before he retired from the bench. I read it carefully, since I did not completely agree with the overall concepts proffered in the speech. I was willing to admit to myself that I was impressed by the unique approach he employed, insisting that supporters of the death penalty assume the responsibility of personally acting as the hangman, and that I was also hard pressed to fault the reasoning he employed. However, I had grown up in a modified eye-for-an-eye environment and capital punishment for very serious crimes always made sense to me. Most of the other speeches also flew in the face of much of my early nurturing, which was basically a combination of a strict Teutonic work ethic and a God-helps-those-who-help-themselves approach to social issues superimposed by or perhaps included in traditional Puritanism. I personally resisted much of these influences of child rearing, but I generally accepted them as reasonable social values, mainly, I suppose, because I wallowed blissfully in a protected environment and never had any of the values involve me personally.

The doctor rolled in around 10 AM and informed me of what I already knew: that I was much better and my fever was gone. He also added that he wanted to see a picture of my lungs before he would consider releasing me and that he usually keeps patients with pneumonia in the hospital for at least three days. I appealed for a quicker release but he insisted on viewing the x-rays before he made a decision.

I was assigned a double room the day before, but there was no one in the opposite bed at that time. Shortly after the doctor left an elderly gentleman was wheeled in on a gurney and slid onto the second bed. He appeared very ill and either asleep or unconscious. Though I was not insensitive to his ailing condition, I was happy that he would probably not interrupt my reading and outlining...activities in which I was engrossed during the balance of the morning and all of the afternoon. As I began reading, I was not aware that I was feeling uncomfortable. And when I did become aware I thought my feelings were simply a negative reaction to the ideas being advanced by the former Justice. I discovered myself concentrating full bore on an attempted analysis of those concepts in a semi-conscious effort to justify my life-long conservative upbringing. However, by reading each speech and its accompanying notes in chronological order, I not only acquired a penetrating understanding of the socio-politico-economic philosophy of the former Justice, but something more personally relevant was taking place. I was also being impressed...almost overwhelmed...by a portrait of a unique person. I was getting a hint of what Steven VanderLinde meant when he described his brother, Ronald, as a total person. What disturbed me was that I was beginning to know and admire the former Justice, possibly even like him; as though he were someone with whom I had been a friend for a long time. The whole ordeal was, at best, weird and like nothing I had ever experienced before. I was the friend of a dead man whom I had never met when he was alive. Incredulously, I was definitely intrigued by the former Justice's life and depth of character and, much against my will, I wanted to know more about him. Further, I could not expunge that desire. That is what scared me. For one of the few times in my life I had somewhat lost my mental self-control. I could not simply say, "The hell with it," which I had done a thousand times while slipping into that safe, blissful world of non-concern, that had served me so well on so many occasions.

Fr. VanderLinde arrived shortly after supper—a meal that I inhaled as eagerly as I had gobbled down breakfast and lunch. By this time, the gentleman in the adjacent bed was awake. He obviously recognized Fr. Steve as a priest and indicated a desire to speak to him. Father looked at me as though to say, "Excuse me," and walked to the man's bedside, where he bent over placing his ear by the patient's mouth. There was a short exchange of whispers. Then Father made a crossing sign over the man before turning back towards me. Both men were smiling. It was obvious that the encounter pleased them, and I assumed it was probably personal, so I paid no attention and started a conversation with my visitor as he reached my bed.

"Thanks for the writing pads," I began. I told him that I had spent much of the day outlining, but that the actual drafting would have to wait until I could get to a typewriter at home. I asked him when he was planning to return up north and he revealed that the real-estate agent that he had contacted to sell the house had cancelled his appointment that day and could not reschedule till late the following afternoon. He added that, since he had no pressing business at the university, he planned to stay the extra day, which would also give him more time to package up the items and books that he planned to keep.

After I gave him the doctor's prognosis Fr. VanderLinde suggested that, since I would probably be kept in the hospital till the day after next, I could ride back with him. I told him that I had flown down and had planned to fly back but after the uneasy feeling from the puddle jumper, prop plane trip to the Capital, I really would appreciate a safer ride home. However, I cautioned, "I hope you're not planning a two hour appeal for me to take on you brother's biography. I read some of the speeches and had a very bad reaction."

"Oh, didn't you like them," he inquired with concern.

"No, I thought they were good speeches. Naturally, I didn't agree with everything he said but that wasn't the problem." I hesitated and Father did not interrupt, waiting for me to explain. "I don't know whether I should admit this..." again I hesitated, "But I was intrigued by your brother... not by his ideas only, but by Ronald VanderLinde the person as reflected in the ideas expressed in the speeches." I continued, "Maybe you set me up by describing him as a total and unique individual... maybe I was looking for something extraordinary or unusual and, therefore, read more into the speeches than was really there. However, while I was reading the material, I experienced something, and I use this word with the utmost reluctance, spiritual, or, at least, internal."

The priest smiled at me. Then he interjected, "Have you finished your evaluation of the speeches?" he asked.

"No," I disclosed. "I read a lot of the files you had given me but I would like to study some of the speeches considerably more. I'd like to finish reading all of them before making any firm judgments. You know, I found myself mentally arguing with your brother and I would like to complete my debates with him." After a short pause, I added with self-disgust, "I don't believe I said that. I especially don't believe I meant it. I don't think I've debated anybody about anything more serious than a traffic ticket, since my freshman year in high school."

"Your cynicism?" he conjectured.

The priest looked at me reflectively for a moment then began the inquiry I knew he would eventually advance and for which I anticipated with dread since his entry into the room. "Have you considered my suggestion about writing Ron's story," he inquired with only a slight tone of appeal in his voice.

I waited for more: an overwhelmingly persuasive argument; an attempt at playful cajoling, even an overbearing insistence that I write the former Justice's biography. But he offered nothing further. He simply, calmly observed me while waiting for my reply. "This is a really nice guy," I thought. I did not want to burst his bubble, but I was not prepared to acquiesce to the writing of the story, which I told him in those exact words. But then, for a reason I cannot comprehend to this day, I also added, "But I'm not prepared to say I absolutely won't."

The instant I completed that sentence, I felt a lump in my throat, a knot in the pit of my stomach and every muscle in my body tightened to the texture of a rock. "What's going on? I've always had control, but now I'm losing it. It's got to be you, Father. You seem to be destroying every defense mechanism I've ever had. You know, I feel scared, like I'm lying naked under a burning sun."

Fr. VanderLinde looked down at me and smiled gently. Then he playfully goaded, "Welcome to the human race."

I'm not ready for this, Father," I confessed.

"Who among us is?" was his only retort.

"Can you wait till I get back home before I decide?" I pleaded.

"I'll have to," he responded. "I have to find somebody to write the story and I don't know anyone here at the Capital. If you won't do it, I'll have to wait until I get up north to look for another writer."

It was about eight thirty when Fr. VanderLinde left. I picked up the speech material and read for a while. When I stopped to take a drink of water, I saw the elderly man in the opposite bed laying on his side looking at me. As I observed him he made a slight motion with his hand. I did not know what his gesture meant, but I thought perhaps he wanted something, so I got out of my bed and walked over to his. I bent over much as Fr. VanderLinde had earlier. The gentleman whispered very softly but audibly, "He's a nice priest, isn't he?"

I nodded my head affirmatively.

Then he said bluntly, "I'm dying and I want to pray, but I can't. Will you pray with me?"

My mind began running at the speed of light with such thoughts as, "I can't remember ever having prayed in my entire life... I have never even thought of praying before and don't think I know how... but the poor man looks so pathetic and helpless and, if I tell him that I don't believe in God, it could disturb him deeply in his final hours or even minutes. He wants to pray, so isn't that enough? Certainly a Loving God, as most of the modern day evangelists are touting... wouldn't He know this poor man wanted to pray and wouldn't that be a prayer. But this old man seems such a simple person. He wouldn't understand such mental gymnastics. However, I don't want to lie to him... not on what is probably his deathbed." I took a deep breath and asked, "What kind of a prayer do you want to say?"

He looked into my eyes and whispered with a simple sincerity, "I just want to tell God that I'm sorry if I hurt Him and I want to say thanks for what He gave me."

"I think you just told Him, don't you?" I asked.

"Maybe," the man replied. "But it just doesn't feel right. Won't you say it with me?"

He had backed me into a corner. I either had to tell him that I didn't think there was a God or I had to actually pray. My better instincts took over and I found myself saying with the old man, "God, forgive me my offenses against You and thanks for everything you ever gave me."

With that the gentleman smiled and put his hand on mine. I felt a gentle, but sincere squeeze of gratitude. As I raised upright to return to my bed, I thought I heard the man mutter something. Though I cannot be certain, I think he said, "I'll remember you." About what and to whom I could not imagine and, since he was so weak, I could not bring myself to ask him to repeat or explain himself.

On my way back to my own bed I thought, "This has been one hell of a day." But I did feel rather good about myself. Since I began reading the speeches that morning, I had felt emotionally and psychologically off balance. Now, I felt... comfortable was the only word I could think of.

During the night I was awakened by a flurry of activity at the opposite bed. As the commotion drew to a halt, I heard someone say, "He's gone. What's the time of death?" Someone else answered, "Three fourteen."

Oddly, I did not feel regret, but rather a warm peace. Almost instantly, I fell back to sleep.

Chapter Six

When I woke in the morning, the adjacent bed was empty and neatly made with the sheets tightly tucked in, awaiting another patient. The bed looked cold and sterile as though no one had ever slept in it. The scene made me wonder whether anyone cared that the old man had died. He knew he was dying and the medical staff probably knew it... so where was his family? I reflected on what it must be like to die alone... not just physically alone but really alone: when no one else knows or cares that you are dying or have died.

I suddenly realized that I was entertaining rather morose thoughts, so I reached for the speeches and started a reread of some of them to continue my posthumous "debate" with Ronald VanderLinde over his varied opinions.

On the previous day I began by organizing the speeches both chronologically and topically. When I found the recent speech to a labor union group outlining a tax reform plan, I decided to wait until I got back home before reading it. The Assistant Editor had told me to play this speech up big in my series about the former Justice so that Holmes could follow the series with an editorial supporting the tax plan. Consequently, I figured that I would make that speech the center of the last article of the series and I could read the speech before that writing.

Reading through the material I also had other reactions. I was initially disappointed in the former Justice. Everything that I had read thus far in my research into his life, even those things that reflected the views of his critics, pictured him as a brave heart: willing to... almost hoping... to face a hostile response to his many maverick ideas and beliefs. But my original, admittedly cursory, review of the speeches seemed to indicate that he was usually preaching to the choir, that is, he delivered his propositions to audiences that would certainly not react negatively to his comments.

Almost all of the addresses were offered either at Labor Union conventions or similar gatherings that considered him a judicial defender of their causes, or at college and university commencement ceremonies, mostly of the Catholic school variety, which, of course, reflected his own academic upbringing and religious beliefs. However, as I started reading the texts, the thought came to me that, in order for anyone to speak at such affairs, they must be invited. And such groups would only invite someone to speak who was on their side, that is, someone whom they expected would say things the audiences would like to hear or, at least, would accept. Further, I was not long into the texts before I realized the former Justice was not actually trying to avoid controversy, even with his friendly audiences. He either picked combative issues for a given speech or interjected totally original ideas into well worn issues... ideas that would require considerable reflection before they could possibly be considered palatable, since they would require discarding long accepted, one might say, comfortable positions or conceptual certitudes.

As noted, many of his addresses were delivered at college commencements and academic society gatherings so they were heavy in source references and quotes from famous and brilliant minds whose group presence on this planet spanned millennia. However, I soon discovered that one of the pundits from whom he occasionally quoted was that early twentieth century British armchair, philosopher and social commentator, G.K. Chesterton whom I mentioned before. This reference source surprised and flatteringly pleased me because, as I stated much earlier, I had actually read something by Chesterton. Though most of the former Justice's references were of the heady or profoundly philosophical sort and not reflective of the breed of author with which I kept company during my school, that is, serious reading years, I was, at least, slightly acquainted with this author.

As also stated earlier, the book of Chesterton's that I had read was *The Man Who Was Thursday*, a short, rather wild novel, which Chesterton himself described in his introduction as a "nightmare" rather than as a novel. At my reading of this book I was intrigued by the author for several reasons, though I actually only read it to impress a girl I was dating occasionally at the time. And though the novel raised some annoying questions in my mind, as was my wont in those days, I quickly exorcised myself of any disquiet through mental disregard.

Some of the speeches were quite interesting and perhaps can enable us to see the intellectual processes as well as the depth of thought of the former Justice, much as the judicial decision concerning the young handicapped couple gave us insight into his compassion, wisdom, and intense sense of justice. For this reason I am including verbatim excerpts from a couple of the speeches as well as the full text of one of the others.

Again, many of the non-union speeches were delivered at Catholic college and university commencement ceremonies and often dealt with religious or, at least, ethereal matters. Further, all of the speeches were presented in a friendly, chatty oratorical style. At one small Catholic girl's college, for instance, the Justice concluded his introductory remarks with the following playfully disarming prognosis:

> I'm going to talk to you today about a very popular topic about which most everyone thinks they know everything, but about which, I contend, most everyone knows very little. And that topic is "love." Further, I am going to predict that you are probably not going to like a lot of the things I tell you about love. And, lastly, I am going to make another prediction. In my undergraduate days, I knew several young ladies who attended this school and I knew them as very highly spirited indeed, albeit refined and cultured, of course. I also suspect that nothing has changed, since the order of sisters who run this and similar establishments has a fine reputation of sending their graduates into that staid, and rather boring, male dominated world not just well educated but as forthright warriors, ready to do some dominating of their own... in a refined and cultured manner of course. For this reason, I consider it a distinct possibility that before I have finished my explanation of what I think love is, I might be thrown bodily from this stage. But, hey, I've always liked a good confrontation and, Heaven knows, I have many scars to prove it.

What the former Justice had to say about the topic of "love" was indeed unique, at least to me, and I assumed, to the audience at the school commencement as well.

The definition of love proffered in this speech was spiritual, dealing exclusively with the intellect and will. But he described love's functioning in very practical terms and its resultant effect as being both practical and spiritual, which seemed, at least on the surface, to be inconsistent (originally I typed, "illogical," but, considering the Justice's reputation as a "brutal logician," I decided to use, "inconsistent"). I was not so much confused, as unconvinced by the speech, since it promoted concepts totally foreign to anything I had previously considered. But I was interested enough to resolve to discuss the matter more thoroughly with Helen when I got back home. Naturally, this intention surprised me, since it meant both that I was sincerely interested in something quite profound and, secondly, that I was insightful enough to see some elements within the speech that, if accurate, could indeed enhance a true marital relationship. As a consequence, I tucked this speech into a folder with an identifying tag so that I could go over it with Helen later.

Another speech was of a similar vein, that is, on a topic treated in an unconventional manner with possibly unpopular ideas and even admonishments. It was religious in nature and given before a group, which was identified on the title page: THE FIRST FRIDAY CLUB Friday, February 1st, 1952.

From the location of the gathering...a large banquet hall in a downtown hotel not far from my newspaper office building...and from the introductory remarks of the address, I could discern that it was probably presented to a group of Catholic businessmen following a Mass at the nearby Cathedral. The introduction included a reference to a "Devotion to the Sacred Heart," about which I was ignorant. Helen had mentioned her own "devotion" to Mary, Jesus' mother, and she also spoke of other devotions to some lesser-known saints but I had never heard of the Sacred Heart. I mention it here only because Justice VanderLinde makes reference to it in one of the most poignant parts of this speech. To further demonstrate the Justice's propensity for charging headlong into controversy, I am including the pertinent portion of his remarks to The First Friday Club here. For the full understanding of how this speech must have been received by this audience one must remember that it was delivered in 1952...several years before the civil rights movement became a popular cause, even for liberal whites:

> There has been something bothering me lately about which I wish to engage you today.
>
> About two weeks ago, on a return flight from New York City where I attended a gathering of State's Justices, I met an old classmate of mine from my undergraduate days. As I seated myself next to this gentleman, we recognized each other immediately. I remembered him, because he stood out as the only Negro student in two of my classes. He also was dominant in

our Public Speaking Class for his obvious gift in that area. He had one of those deep baritone voices that reverberate with heavy over and under tones. Without question he was the best public speaker in our class. Everyone assumed that he would use this gift in whatever he chose as his future career.

During the hour and a half flight back home we caught up on our activities since college. He admitted that he had followed my judicial escapades in the papers. Then he started relating his recent history. He confided with quiet pride that he was married and had five children and added that he was a teacher in an inner city Junior High. I sympathized that it must be hard to support a family of his size on a teacher's salary at which he disclosed that he had hoped to get promoted to Principal or, at least, Assistant Principal by continuing his education at night. He revealed that he had acquired no less than three masters degrees in that effort but, then, reluctantly added that, since the promotions did not come, he was now teaching night school at a county community college for extra income.

That wonderful resonant voice was still apparent and I made a comment on how his students must sit up and listen in his classes with that strong dominating voice bouncing off their eardrums. Then I remarked that I was glad that he did not let his vocal gift go to waste. At this he went silent. With a lot of diplomatic prodding from me he finally disclosed that he was returning from a job interview in New York City as a prospective announcer for a network show on that new television media. He hesitated for quite a while before he added that the producer was obviously stunned when they first met and quickly told him that the job had already been filled, though he learned from other applicants that, in fact, it had not yet been filled. All I could think of was, "What a God-awful-waste."

When I arrived home, this incident was still fresh in my mind and, as I was checking my mail, the first piece I opened was an invitation to speak at this gathering this morning. The topic of my talk to you was obvious.

I know the last thing you wanted to hear from me this morning is a sermon and I am probably the last person in the world qualified to deliver one, but your going to hear one anyway, that is, if you are willing to remain in your seats till I'm finished... and let's hope the Holy Spirit is somewhere nearby to guide my words.

Most of you attended Mass over at the Cathedral this morning and I assume that most, if not all of you received Communion, since that is an essential part of the Sacred Heart devotion. And though I am certain that most of you believe that the good nuns taught you everything you would ever need to know about the Mass, I am going to tell you some things that you probably do not know... things, which I discovered from recent readings and which I believe are applicable to this presentation.

If one combines a couple of long accepted Catholic theological teachings, and applies a little simple logic to the Eucharistic concepts held by theologians of the early church, a description of what happens at every Mass is as follows: each time a wafer of bread or drop of wine is consecrated anywhere in the world, every member of the Mystical Body of Christ; the church militant here on earth (which, of course, includes all of us), the church suffering in purgatory and the church triumphant in heaven (and, if St. Thomas Aquinas is correct, all of the angels in creation), are united with Christ our Head... buried in ecstatic union within His Sacred Heart, if you will. And when we receive Holy Communion, as part of our participation in a specific Liturgy, according to this triumphalist view of the Mass as held by those early Church writers, we are all carried by Christ to the throne of our Heavenly Father and there offered in sublime sacrifice with and by Christ to our Father in reparation for our individual sins. Calvary redeemed mankind for all sin. And the Holy Sacrifice of the Mass, which is a continuation in time of Christ's redemptive act on Calvary, enables each of us individually to sacrifice ourselves with Christ in reparation for our own personal sins.

Those of you who have not heard of this triumphal concept of the Mass may be asking as I did when I first read about it: how can all of the members of the Mystical Body of Christ be present, simultaneously, in every Consecrated Host and every Drop of Precious Blood everywhere in the world? Well, in my research into this matter I was pleased to discover that St. Thomas Aquinas and Blessed John Duns Scotus, as well as, most of those brilliant, 13th century scholars had a similar problem with how Christ could be present in Heaven and, at the same time, present on every altar throughout the world. Fortunately, a colleague of these great thinkers came up with an answer to both their query and the one I just mentioned: A gentleman by the name of Richard of St. Albert's proffered that, since God is omnipotent and can do anything, if He wants to have Christ present in Heaven and, at the same time, on all of our altars, he can do it. And, according to Scripture and Conciliatory dogma, He obviously does it. And, though I am not arguing from Scripture or Conciliatory dogma to prove my point concerning our presence in each Host, etcetera, the brilliant theologian, Gregory Dix, points out that virtually every pre-Nicene author, both Eastern and Western did indeed advance this concept: a process, which, of course, is perfectly possible for an Omnipotent Being.

Now, to put these two concepts into a coherent single thesis: most of us live in totally, or near totally, all white neighborhoods and the Negroes of this metropolis live mainly in the inner city, isolated from the whites. Under some circumstances Negroes do live in the suburbs such as a family who lived in the basement suite of a medical building where the father was the janitor. As I understand it, the children even traveled every day across town to the inner city Negro community to go to school. Yet, someone recently threw a brick through their basement suite window, obviously telling the family that they were not welcome there.

Now I would like to ask each of you, "If a Negro family moved next door to you, would you and your family welcome them as you would a white family: chat with them over the back fence, borrow or lend tools, invite their kids into your yard or house to play with your kids? Or would you shun them. Treat them in a manner that said to them that you were not happy with them living in your neighborhood and hope that your personal rejection would make them want to move back quote... with their own people... unquote.

Now let's take a look at scripture. Christ says that the way we treat other people is the way we are treating Him, since He resides in each of us. Further, St. Paul writes that, if any member of that Negro family next door were the only human being that ever lived, God the Father loves him or her enough that he would send His only Begotten Son down to suffer and die just for that Negro person.

Now, it is Christ, residing within each soul, including the souls of the members of that family to which I would like to draw your attention and the fact that Christ is united with those members through the infinite binding power of His love for them. Also, I would like to add that we are all children of God and heirs of heaven and God's love, which is the Holy Spirit, lives in each one of us, including the members of that family.

Now, let's put all of this together: If I treat a Negro abrasively or hurtfully, for no other reason than his race, can I rationally walk up to the Communion rail to receive our Divine Lord in, "His Sacrament of Love," becoming totally one with Christ... after figuratively sticking a finger in His eye with my treatment of my Negro neighbor? I am not saying that you should not receive Communion because of such negative attitudes. I would certainly not be presumptuous enough to act as anyone else's conscience. God knows I have trouble enough with my own. But I am here today to ask you to think about that question: If you treat Christ badly, as He resides in someone of another race, simply because of the persons race, do you have the right to receive that same Christ in Holy Communion?

I simply ask you to think about that.

The entire speech ended there and, though I initially considered that an awkwardly abrupt conclusion, on second thought, I realized that, under the circumstances of historical time, audience, etcetera, this must have been a traumatically effective finish.

Lastly, I had originally decided to include here the entirety of an address to a labor union convention, since I considered this speech an enlightening manifestation of the how and why the Justice was considered a union worker's judge. This speech is also as telling of the intellectual propensities of the man as I could find among the speeches. However, it was quite lengthy and made up mainly of quotes from a particular Papal Encyclical, which I feel, would be tedious reading for the non-legal or theological mind. Therefore, my ultimate decision was a brief summary here with the entire speech presented in an Appendix of this work. However, its reading is recommended for the fullest understanding of Justice VanderLinde, both as Judge and man.

It was apparently given as the welcoming or keynote address before the union convention and was apparently delivered somewhere in the middle of Justice VanderLinde's tenure on the State Supreme Court.

The speech begins with an expression of gratitude for the invitation to speak at the convention because, among other reasons, it would require the Justice to reread a Papal Encyclical by a Pope Leo XIII who, the Justice contended, was, at least in his opinion, the, "...most brilliant Pontiff in the two thousand year history of the Church," and whose writings, Justice VanderLinde enjoyed reading even for entertainment, because the words, "...even in translation...flow like lyric prose."

When the speech reached the meat of the subject matter, it began that entrée with a carefully drawn delineation of Pope Leo's logical arguments laying bare the fatal flaws in socialism, Communism, and Fascism. It then gave proof for the valid existence of labor unions and the do's and don'ts for unions, owners, and government.

For me, three concepts stood out. The first concerned what Leo referred to as, "The great mistake...the notion that class is naturally hostile to class, and that the wealthy and the working men are intended by nature to live in mutual conflict." The pontiff argued, "So irrational and so false is this view that the direct contrary is the truth. Just as the symmetry of the human frame is the result of the suitable arrangement of the different parts of the body, so in a state is it ordained by nature that these two classes should dwell in harmony and agreement, so as to maintain the balance of the body politic. Each needs the other: capital cannot do without labor, nor labor without capital. Mutual agreement results in the beauty of good order, while perpetual conflict necessarily produces confusion and savage barbarity."

The second idea offered concerned the encouragement of worker ownership, or purchase of stock, in the company for which a laborer works. The arguments given are the same as those offered today but, we must remember, this encyclical was written at the end of the nineteenth century, which makes the suggestion considerably before its time.

Lastly, the Justice advanced a very practical rationale for union members avoiding violence in their own best interest as those interests are presented before the courts.

After reading the entire text of this speech I lay back for some not so deep reflection. My first thought was a question whether a mid-twentieth century group of blue collar workers would possibly be interested in the ideas of a nineteenth century pope, even if he was as smart as the Justice claimed. At one point I tried to imagine myself as a high school drop-out (because no matter how hard I tried I could not get decent grades) getting a hard hat job, a wife and kids, a house mortgage and then taking off a few days to attend a union convention only to hear some obviously highly educated judge relating what some religious leader of a religion other than mine said about labor unions over sixty years earlier. But somehow it must have worked. The Justice apparently had some success at delivering this type of speech to this type of audience, since the papers Fr. VanderLinde left with me indicated that Justice VanderLinde had been asked to speak at, and so spoke at, such union conventions on several occasions during his tenure as a State Supreme Court Justice. I wondered if the Justice possessed a special kind of charismatic attraction or if he were being invited to speak at these affairs simply because of his reputation as a union friendly jurist... flattery, if you will, to entice him into keeping his union friendly sentiments.

The second question that came to mind was, "What kind of a person apparently enjoys reading Papal Encyclicals for entertainment?" After spending the day in gray cell overdrive, reading, writing and engaging in demanding legal discussions with colleagues, if I wanted to experience something lyric, I would have put on some records rather than reading Encyclicals no matter how lyric the prose is in translation.

I do admit I was impressed by the Justice's final recommendation that the union members avoid violence. I had never thought of it directly, but it does seem that judges do react negatively to anyone perpetrating physical violence and often give the benefit of the doubt to the non-violent party.

These thoughts returned in the morning and were floating through my head while I waited to be checked out of the hospital and for Fr. Steve to arrive. But, overall, I was somewhat down.

The speeches were supposed to be the main research material for the series of articles that Holmes wanted me to write, but I was not feeling at all confident. I questioned whether I was still depressed from the pneumonia or that the speeches, though apparently very insightful and reflective of the Justice's socio-political leanings, to me at least, failed to present anything like an overwhelmingly captivating picture of the former Justice VanderLinde. I certainly gained some knowledge of attractive traits and attributes from the newspaper articles and from the Justice's military exploits, but those stories had already been printed years ago. My hope was in the speeches, and, though they were interesting, somewhat intriguing, and certainly displayed unique attitudes and opinions, I did not consider them adequate biographical series material... at least not of the blockbuster character that Holmes was expecting.

The hospital exit routine went as one would have expected and Father Steve arrived about 10:00 AM My strength and breathing were not yet normal, but the internist promised they would probably improve over the next week or two. I waited at the entrance of the hospital while Fr. VanderLinde brought the car around. I was a little surprised the car he borrowed from the University for his trip to the capital was a large four door. The priest explained that he knew he was going to be bringing a lot of things from Justice VanderLinde's house back with him, especially a lot of books, so he borrowed the only full sized automobile the University owned. When I stepped into the passenger's seat from the wheelchair in which the hospital personnel pushed me to the entrance, Father Steve cautioned, "I hope there's enough room for your legs. I had to push the seat as far forward as possible to fit everything in the back seat."

As I was settling in, I looked back at the books and paraphernalia piled to the ceiling in the back. He resumed hopefully, "I left enough room in the trunk for a decent sized suitcase. I hope you traveled reasonably light."

I assured him I had, since I only planned to stay a day, or day and a half, tops. "Pneumonia was not part of my itinerary," I complained.

My legs were a bit cramped, but by turning slightly sideways I was reasonably comfortable and, since I still had that harrowing plane flight to the capital in my memory, I was able to convince myself that I could stand almost any level of physical discomfort for only a couple of hours.

Fr. Steve had driven me to the hospital earlier in the week in my rental car in order to get it off the street. I figured he must have switched cars when he got home and pulled my rental deep into the driveway where it had apparently sat since. When we arrived back at Justice VanderLinde's house he let me out and told me he would follow me to my hotel and wait for me while I got my things and checked out. He said he had called the hotel the night he took me to the hospital to explain the reason for my extended stay.

I responded gratefully, "That was nice of you. How did you know where I was staying?"

He admitted, "There were some registration papers on the front seat, so I took a chance the name of the hotel on the papers was where you were staying."

"The old scientific, analytical reasoning ploy." I chuckled.

"I wish all of science were that easy," he responded. "And while your checking out, you might ask the clerk if he or she knows where the nearest drop off spot for your rental car is. After the hotel, I'll follow you, and we can take off for home from there."

"Sounds like you thought it all through," I acknowledged.

And, to my surprise, everything went as planned. "Just about the only thing on this trip that had," I mused as the car turned onto the ramp to the relatively new interstate highway north. I gave an apparently loud sigh of relief, because Father Steve inquired if I were ok.

"I am now!" I articulated in an intentionally emphatic tone. The priest laughed.

(I have chosen to include most of the conversations between Fr. Vander-Linde and myself during our trip north and as completely as I remember them because I firmly believe that the knowledge of this interchange is an imperative ingredient for a real understanding of this story. There are some further insights into the character of the former Justice VanderLinde, but, in this case, and, more importantly, there is relevant information about why I took the decades long sabbatical from the final writing of this book after the interviews to which Father VanderLinde directed me. I apologize to any readers who might find the conversations tedious but, as I said, I believe these exchanges are important. Also, I have included an oration, of sorts, by Father VanderLinde, the professor, that occurred during the trip, that, though the subject of the discourse is not really relevant to this book, again, I believe that what the priest said and the demeanor with which he delivered it can give insights into the fullness of the persons with whom I garnered the information for the book.)

The automobile was relatively new and with the weight of the books et al, the ride was very smooth. We each retired to our own thoughts for a few minutes before I broke the ice, "Well, we might as well get into it," I opened.

"I thought you wanted to wait until you got home to make a decision," Father Steve countered; then added, "You also asked that I not make our trip up state a two hour argument in favor of your writing Ron's biography."

"I changed my mind... about our discussion that is. I realized that the topic would probably be clouding both our minds during the trip and, so, we'd both be biting our tongues for a couple of hours. So we might as well get it over with."

There was a brief silence. I surmised Father Steve was loading his argumentative guns, but when he began his remarks, they were not at all in the form of an argument for my accepting the project he was requesting of me...just the opposite. "You may not believe what I'm about to say, considering my remarks to you thus far, but I really don't want to place the burden of Ron's biography on you. I don't want to put it on anyone."

"Now I'm confused," I retorted. "You seemed so anxious to get somebody to write your brother's story and now your saying you're reluctant to ask anyone to do it?"

"I'm certain that what I've said sounds strange," he admitted. "I don't want to discourage you from taking on the task, but I feel I have to warn you. Sometimes the things you'll discover will be pleasant, even enjoyable, but other things may be, depending on how sensitive and empathetic you are, down right repulsive, and consequently, painful to reflect on."

"I find that hard to believe," I countered simply. "From what I've run into thus far concerning Justice VanderLinde, I haven't found anything distasteful or leading me to believe he was anything but a decent human being. As a matter of fact, I've grown to admire him as a jurist and I certainly respect his intellect...though I didn't always agree with his opinions...and I found myself actually, personally liking the guy, at least to the extent one can get personal with someone you've never met." I hesitated for a few seconds and then protested abruptly, "Wait a minute, are you trying to maneuver me into accepting the job of writing this bio by making me so curious about your brother that I'll do it just to find out what the mystery is?"

Fr. VanderLinde looked over at me and shook his head. "I'm sorry you think that I could be that devious, Fran," he uttered in a mildly hurt tone. "Your cynical nature must run very deep. I assure you, I had no such intention." He glanced over at me again with an expression indicating he was trying to observe from my facial expression whether I believed his disclaimer. "We all have a bit of cynicism in us, Fran, but if carried to extremes, like all extremes, it can be destructive and self-limiting." Then he muttered softly, mostly to himself, "In medio stat vertus."

"What?" I inquired.

"In the middle stands virtue," he explained.

There was another short reflective pause. Then I started up again, "Now, I feel silly. I think I just made a fool of myself, Father."

"Don't dwell on it," he responded. "We all make fools out of ourselves from time to time. Think of how I felt from the reaction, or lack of reaction to 'Does Existence Really Exist?'"

We both chuckled and then went silent again. I finally reopened the previous conversation, "Was he really that intriguing?" I inquired.

Father VanderLinde hesitated longer than I expected. "Yes...yes, he was," the priest responded thoughtfully. "I'm in a bit of a bind, here," he proclaimed. "His life before the war and before his judgeships was, indeed, very intriguing, but most of it is also very personal. I really don't think I should reveal any of those matters to you or anyone else except the one who has agreed to write Ron's story."

The priest's voice tapered off there, and he quickly added, "You know what I just did? I gave you more ammunition for you to accuse me of enticing you into writing the story by creating mystery. I'm sorry. Again, I have to say that was not my intent...and, you'll probably just have to trust me on that. I guess we'll see if you have any anti-cynicism genes."

Again, there was a short lapse. This time Father Steve broke the silence. "As I said, I'm in a bind. The balance of the subject matter is personal and I don't think I should share it with you unless you agree to write the story and, yet, it is in fact the personal and intriguing incidents that would probably convince you to do it."

"That is a problem," I sympathized, "But I think my greatest reluctance comes from the fact that I'm just not sure I want to embrace that much extra work and pressure at this time in my life. I'm hoping to get married soon and from what my fiancée says, we'll probably start a goodly sized family right away. She says she wants six kids and all of them by the time she's thirty so she'll still have the strength to chase them around the house. And she wants them boy-girl, boy-girl, boy-girl."

"Sounds like quite a young lady. She obviously likes children. That makes her a winner right there. Congratulations...I'd like to meet her someday. Also, sounds like you are going to have your hands full with both your new wife and that bevy of children."

"That's what I'm talking about," I began my response. "With that kind of responsibility I don't think I could spend the time necessary to research and write the Justice's biography...at least not for the next many years. Remember, I'll still have to make a living and, with the brood my future wife wants, and I must admit I sort of do, too, I'll probably have to work two or three jobs to support them in the style to which I've always wanted to become accustomed. I'd really like to spend a lot of time growing up with my kids."

"Oh, you admit you're still a child," the priest chortled.

"You better believe it," I admitted. "I don't mind accepting adult responsibilities, but I don't want to become like all those adults I see. I've resisted that from my junior year in high school. Really, adults appear dull and boring to me. They all seem to have lost the magic in life. I was watching a three or four year old in a park one day... reading his face and eyes as he played with things and on playground equipment and it was one of the most beautiful things I've ever seen. Everything he did... it was like it was for the first time... like the entire world was magic. I don't remember experiencing that in my own youth. And I decided I wanted to experience that newness and magic with my own children... through my own kids when they get that age." After a pause I added, "That's one of the reasons I decided to give up the freedom of single-hood... though not the only one, certainly. Finding someone like my Helen and not wanting to let her get away was the biggest reason."

I pulled up short with that... apologizing, "I'm sorry, Father, I was really rambling there, wasn't I... and about things you either care little about or have deliberately deprived yourself of in your calling."

"You needn't apologize," the priest salved. "Yes, I deliberately deprived myself of some of what you say, but I've seen things similar to what you experienced with the boy in the park with many of my students, only on a more mature level when they really, and I mean really, discover the universe and all of its magic. And I was pleased with how you reacted to the little boy's wonderment. You displayed a good deal of empathy. That is a noble attribute. Not everyone has it. It's my opinion, empathetic love is the next step up in human evolution, possibly even leading to mental telepathy."

"Whoa," I reacted. "Now you're getting over my head."

"Too far over to comprehend," he muttered to himself, "But not too far to experience."

This time there was a prolonged stillness except for the usual monotonous traveling automobile sounds. My mind traveled as well. Since I heard nothing further from Father VanderLinde, I wondered if that meant he had given up on the idea of my writing his brother's biography. I felt a bit sorry for him. He had promised his brother on his death bed that he would find someone to write the story and, though Father Steve seemed in very good health for a man of his years, he had to feel an abnormal pressure to find that person before he himself left this planet... but I was not sorry enough to relieve him of that pressure.

My thoughts also, naturally ran to Helen and from there to those children she wanted. I started imagining what it was going to be like being a parent, flying model airplanes with my boys and driving my daughters to sleepovers. I pictured the girls and I engaged in fun type, laughing conversations on the way to their friends houses... conversations they would probably forget by the next day but which I hoped I would never forget... like my memory of the eager, excited eyes of that boy in the park.

After my mind returned to the present I looked over at Father Steve. He appeared a little more somber than earlier. I wondered if he too was worried about whether he could keep his promise to his brother. Out of sensitivity to his possible negative thoughts I decided to switch gears. "Do you still do any teaching, Father," I inquired.

"No... not really," was his simple reply.

"What do you do on campus?" I continued.

"Oh, I give retreats and days-of-recollection to members of various student body organizations. And, of course, I say Mass and hear confessions. Believe it or not, I even give pre-Cana, or to you, pre-marriage counseling. And I read a lot. I like to stay abreast of the latest developments in physics and cosmology."

"Do you write anymore?" I queried hoping not to hit a nerve.

"Not for publication," was his rather terse reply. But then he added, "I do keep notes of reactions and musings about what I read. Without hesitation the priest suddenly took off verbally, not speaking rapidly but uninhibitedly... somewhat like he was lecturing to a class of students or, at least, to himself. It was the first time I saw him exhibit something other than that peaceful self-confidence. "I don't know how our knowledge of science has come this far this fast," he blurted out. "Most scientists today seem more interested in furthering their own reputations and careers, getting themselves published and, of course, winning a Nobel Prize, rather than applying their efforts at furthering mankind's knowledge of the universe God created for us to play in. I read article after article and paper after paper proffering a plethora of theories, many with only a miniscule attempt at validating the theories. It's obvious, at least to me, they are simply trying to throw as many ideas as they can at the wall, in the outside chance that one of them will stick; or rather, in the hopes that at least one will prove to be true and the author of that idea will win a Nobel Prize.

I honestly believe that one of the biggest obstacles to the development of our knowledge of the universe is the Nobel Prize. Everyone seems to have a major portion of his attention on The Prize, which effort is distracting them from their real work of real discovery."

I was surprised at this display of intensity... even passion. Further, I wondered whether Father VanderLinde was still somewhat sensitive about his own failed publication and the thought even ran through my mind that his outburst might have been a release of a pent-up reaction to that rejection. But, he said he had gotten over that years ago. His outburst made me question whether that was really true, so I cautiously returned, "Father, you seem to feel very strongly on this subject. Is it possible you still have some buried, bruised feelings from way back when?"

"I don't think so," he replied in a reflective tone. "Though its hard to be objective about one's own emotions. After my book was published I wasn't hurt because people criticized my ideas. I was hurt because I had put so much effort into the hypothesis and apparently no one in the field of theoretical physics even bothered to read it, let alone criticize the ideas either pro or con. But as I said earlier, I got over that relatively soon with the help of a wise counselor. Actually, the whole episode helped me get my values straight. I'm still very interested in science, but on a value scale of one to ten it dropped from eight or nine to about three or four. Consequently, I quickly found my niche: carrying out my priestly functions and teaching young men about, as you put it, the magic in the universe they live in, and, above all, motivating them, not just to discover, but to really want to discover." After a reflective pause, he added, "I've truly been a fortunate and happy man these past decades."

Father Steve looked over at me and offered a smile that demonstrated that he sincerely was happy. I could not help but think that I had just heard the explanation for why he manifested that quiet self-confidence for which I had admired him since we met.

Actually, though I did not want to admit it, my mind was wandering during his derision of his scientific colleagues. I was contemplating different scenarios by which I might be able to fulfill Fr. Steve's request. "Did your brother give you a time limit on how soon he wanted his story told?"

"Not really," Father Steve answered. "Why, what are you driving at?"

"I just thought that, if we could put off the writing of the biography for twenty years or so, until my future kids are pretty well raised and my future mortgage is pretty well paid off, I might finally have some leisure time. Could I tackle the biography then?"

"Well, yes and no," he countered reflectively. "The most important part of your research will involve interviewing people. Some of them possess very essential knowledge of Ron's life during a crucial period. And most of these people are up in years... including myself." Few of us will still be around in twenty years. Am I right in assuming from what you just said that you are interested in writing the story, after all, if we can work out the logistics? If so, I'll divulge why your proposition creates problems that we'll have to work out."

"Good heavens," I blurted. "You did it. You got me to accept the job, if we can work out the 'how.' Did you know you were getting to me? I mean, I know you're smart and clever, but I haven't really considered you cunning or manipulative even though I accused you of it a while back."

"I don't think I bear those negative traits... at least I hope not," he responded. There was a pause. Then he returned to the question, "Will you write the biography, if we can work out the timing?"

"Talk about a hundred and eighty degree turn around," I grumbled, then acquiesced, "Yes, I'll do it, if I can, but it's going to take something to figure out the timing."

Having received my assurance that I would write his brother's story, if possible, Father Steve started opening up a little. He explained that he could actually tell me just about everything I would need to know and would learn from others, but he knew he could not possibly be objective and some of the material would be very personal. Father Steve told me Ronald had given him permission to divulge anything his brother had ever confessed to him in the Sacrament of Confession, but the priest declared adamantly that he could not bring himself to violate the secrecy of the confessional even if a penitent gave him permission. "After all these years of protecting that secrecy, I can't just violate it like that. I'll be relating things to you and I'll steer you to the people that can tell you what happened, but if any of the matter involves anything Ron told me in confession I can't bring myself to reveal it."

I think he was letting that sink in before he added, "And, though I'm not a biographer or even a writer of your type, I think you should learn this story chronologically... as it happened, if you will, and from the people who lived it so you can experience the maximum impact... because, believe me, Fran, there will be impact. There is to me, even now, each time I think about it."

I considered the intensity of those last remarks to simply reflect the priest's deep involvement in his brother's life, so I continued, "But now we have to figure out the 'when' and 'how' of the interviews and other research." I inquired further, "I assume there is going to be other research?"

"Yes, of course," the priest responded. "You'll want to look over some of Ron's more controversial judicial opinions. I don't know how much you paid attention to such things as you were growing up, but Justice VanderLinde created a lot of waves in and out of judicial circles during his years on the bench." But then he added, "But those things can wait. Ron received his bachelor's degree from the school to which I'm assigned and his law degree from one of our neighboring universities." Father Steve named the university and I admitted that that school was my Alma Mater. "That's great." the priest asserted. That should make your research there easier. I'm certain all of Ron's judicial decisions can be found in that university's law library any time in the future. And you've already done some of the research on his life for your newspaper series. The only immediate requirement is the interviews of the elderly people you will need to see, and I will contact them to tell them you're coming and to let them know about your quest."

I laughed. "Did you use that word 'quest' deliberately, Father? You make it sound like I'm Sir Lancelot or one of those knights of old, and I'm being sent out to search for the Holy Grail or something."

"If I did, it was a Freudian slip," he returned. "Actually, that's not too far from the truth."

"Now you're scaring me," I admitted. That sounds like a lot more than the job I accepted," was my reaction.

Father VanderLinde spoke softly. "Don't worry, Fran. If what you're intending to do is of significant importance, the Spirit'll see you have the wherewithal to do it. He always does," the priest added reassuringly.

Even with Father Steve's guarantee, I was still uneasy. "I've never experienced celestial help before, Father, and I don't expect any now."

"How do you think you got here today? Think of all the things that happened to you that brought you down to the Capital to research your series about my brother. Do you think that all of that just happened by accident... that everything we run into in life is just meaningless fate, if you will?"

"Yes," I snapped.

"Skeptical agnosticism raises its head again, huh?"

"Call it what you want," I grumbled sullenly.

"I hope I didn't dissuade you from writing the story," the priest commented apologetically.

At this I yanked myself out of my mental morose by telling myself, "A story is a story is a story. How tough will it be and how much help will I need from anyone…the Man upstairs or anyone else. I'm a good writer and I know how to research so what's the big deal." Those thoughts and Father Steve's momentary silence allowed me to relax and regain my composure. Finally I said, "No, Father. I'm still on board." But then, to lighten things up a bit I joked, "But let's keep things down here on earth where I know what's going on…after all, I can only write sensibly about things I understand and religious or, so called, spiritual matters ain't one of them."

Father responded in like manner, "Well, I'll try. In my line of work, it may be hard for me to keep my mind on the ground at all times when I'm talking to you. But, as I said, I'll try."

We both smiled at each other and then there was a long silence. I was engrossed in the mental gymnastics involved in figuring out how I could fulfill my obligations to my job and my soon to be wife and still work on the necessary interviews before real family responsibilities demanded all of my time.

I was so engrossed in these thoughts that as I was thinking of them, they started coming out of my mouth without my realizing it. I was snapped out of my revelry when I heard Father Steve say, "You're very right. Your responsibilities to you family and especially to your new wife are paramount. The project I gave you has to take a back seat to them. Work on the story only when you're filling in the gaps between your primary responsibilities."

"I think I just got a sermon about what I've been saying all along," I playfully admonished my companion.

"Touché!" the priest acknowledged with a smile.

I rejoined my previous musings, "I can probably knock off the newspaper series in two or three days tops. My Editor wants me to take the next three weeks off. I could do some of the interviewing during that time period unless Helen has some chores for me in preparation for the wedding. I do have a wedding coming up, you know. But weddings are usually a bride's party, so I may not be too involved there…but I want to be available if Helen needs me for anything. And I will have assignments at work." At that, I looked over at Father Steve. "I guess I'll probably have to organize my time. I don't think I've ever had to do that before, Father... I mean really organize my time." I playfully complained

"It might be good for you. Who knows, you might acquire a profitable new skill," he chuckled.

By this time I estimated that we were about halfway home. We both went silent for a while until I commented. "I'm still pretty weak and I feel kind of tired. Do you mind if I take a nap for a while?"

"Not at all," the priest responded. "I think I know where you live so I'll wake you when we get there."

And that was all I remembered until Father Steve did in fact wake me and I recognized that we had arrived at my complex.

We exchanged phone numbers and my companion reached in the back and handed me a shoebox. "Did your series research tell you Ron studied international law in Europe after his law school graduation?" The priest asked.

"Yes," I answered, "But he came back short of a year. Did he graduate over there?"

"No," was the simple answer. "That's what's in the box," indicating the shoebox I was holding. "He was going with a young lady and was actually engaged to her when he left for Europe. They were planning to get married when he returned and got a job somewhere. When he left, the girl was a senior at a nearby all girl's college. The box has the letters she sent Ron while he was in Europe. Ron kept them and they were among his things at the house."

"Are they important to the story?" I asked.

"Very," was Father's only reply.

"Did he marry the girl, Father?" I inquired.

"No," was another one word reply.

"Then why are the letters pertinent to the Justice's story?" I continued.

Then Father Steve smiled gently, "The letters will be self explanatory, and through them you'll find out why he returned so soon, and when you finish your research you'll know why they're important. Don't rush yourself," he advised compassionately.

With that, Father helped me get my suitcase from the trunk. He offered to help me with the luggage but I was certain at his age he would probably have as much trouble as I would. When I got to the apartment I was delightfully surprised to find that my cousin and her husband were not home. A note on the dining room table said they had decided to take a short trip away from the reporters and television cameras. The note failed to say where they went or when they would return and at that point I really did not care.

I called Helen to tell her I was home but also told her that I was very tired and wanted to get some rest. She offered to come over to make me some supper but I said I just wanted to sleep as long as I could. I lay down without unpacking, and sleep I did. It was only mid-afternoon but I had always missed my own bed when I was away from it. Consequently, I slept like a log until the following morning.

At discharge at the hospital the nurse gave me a bottle of anti-biotic and an exaggeratedly clear set of instructions as to how and when to take them, which I followed scrupulously except during that night of sleep. And when I traveled from the hospital to my hotel in the Capital I carried the pile of speech files in my lap, which of course, made that short ride even more crammed than it otherwise would have been. Consequently, when I put my suitcase in the trunk of the car for the trip home, I jammed the files into it so that I could be a little more comfortable during the much longer balance of the trip. However, the file jamming was considerably difficult in my weakened condition. I used all of the strength I had at the time but I did not consider the jamming that vehement. Nevertheless, that morning, when I opened the suitcase to unpack, the papers and file folders went flying rapidly upward before they spread themselves out around the room. I just stood looking at the mess, contemplating whether the bad luck with which I was afflicted during the trip had followed me home. I had another cup of coffee before I started inserting all of the papers in their appropriate folders and then rearranging the folders again in chronological order.

I called the Assistant Editor to let him know that I was back in town and that I would phone in my first article for the series before deadline that day and that I would be doing the same for the following two articles. He told me that Blakesley had informed him about my stay in the hospital and also told him to remind me about playing up the tax speech to the union group in the last article. I told him I had it under control. He concluded the conversation by telling me that Blakesley was naturally upset about the delay in my article. Our illustrious Editor had begun the series on the previous Sunday and Monday and expected me to finish with the last three articles in the Tuesday, Wednesday and Thursdays issues. With my delay due to pneumonia, a gap would occur from Tuesday until I could continue the series, which infuriated Blakesley immeasurably. He had to either try to give the readers some kind of excuse for why there was a lapse in the series or act like the lapse was intended. Naturally the editor decided on the latter in spite of the inconsistency. Who ever heard of a series that was not serial? The Assistant Editor must have heard me chuckle because he added that Holmes was glad about the delay and hoped that the last article on the taxes would appear in the Sunday paper, which had our largest weekly circulation. I learned that our Owner/Publisher told Blakesley he could put his editorial supporting the tax plan in that issue. Holmes claimed that my pneumonia was caused by our mutually beneficial horoscope though I failed to see how a possible life threatening decease could be of benefit to me.

The next three days went quite well. The articles came easily, especially the last one concerning the novel tax plan. Fortunately, it was more factual than philosophical or theological and, therefore, easier to summarize with no analysis necessary. Helen dropped over after work on Friday to make me supper. We spent that evening continuing to formulate our wedding plans. I told my soon-to-be-bride that, since I would be off work for the next three weeks I could do any pre-wedding running around that she might need. She indicated that she appreciated the offer, but that she had most everything under control that could be done two months in advance. She recommended that I just try to recuperate so that I would be back to normal by wedding time. She joked that she wanted me in a total state of physical, mental, emotional and psychological well-being when I said my, "I do," so that I could never say I didn't know what I was doing when I married her. Of course, I returned the joke by telling her that she was the crazy one for marrying me. She did remind me that picking out and ordering the tuxedos as well as the liquor for the reception was the groom's job. She also asked me to go with her when she picked out the ornament for the top of the wedding cake. I told her that I did not know why she wanted me along for that decision, since the top was usually just a bride and groom figurine, but she said she had something different and original in mind, so I agreed.

Helen spent much of the weekend with me too, helping with some housework and my laundry. I had been thinking about the Ronald VanderLinde biography since I had arrived home and on that Saturday night, after an exceptional meal, I decided to inform Helen of the unusual and auxiliary obligation I had accepted. We spent several hours discussing, not just what it was that I agreed to undertake, but also the how and when; much as Fr. VanderLinde and I had hashed over the topic on the trip home. Fortunately, with Helen, I felt more supported and I experienced more of a feeling that she was not just telling me that I had a problem, but was really trying to help me figure out a solution. She suggested and I concurred that my three week suspension from the newspaper would probably be a good time for me to get as much of the interviewing done as possible that Father Steve said he would set up for me. Sunday night I went to bed secure in the fact that my near future, at least, would sail through reasonably smooth waters. I could not have been more wrong.

Chapter Seven

I waited until about 10:00 AM on Monday morning before I phoned Father VanderLinde to tell him my plans to spend much of the next three weeks interviewing for his brother's biography. He had insisted that, "I perform the interviews in the order in which he would direct me," as he put it, so that I would get the maximum impact...whatever that meant.

When he answered the phone and after we exchanged the usual pleasantries, I filled him in on my plans. He expressed his delight and appreciation and then asked whether I had read any of the letters from the box he had given me. I admitted that I had not looked at the letters yet, since I had spent the weekend writing the series of articles for my newspaper and had been continuing my recuperation. He naturally acknowledged that he understood and that there would be plenty of time in the next three weeks for me to go over the letters and to complete the interviews.

After informing Fr. Steve that I was feeling much better and that I was anxious to get going with the interviews, he suggested that I spend Monday and Tuesday reading the letters carefully, during which time he would contact the persons that I would be interviewing to let them know who I was and why I would be visiting them. He also reminded me about the multitude of Ronald's judicial opinions that were buried in school law libraries, but I told Fr. Steve that I felt I had enough of that type of material. However, I added that I would look into it later, if I felt I needed it for the biography.

After I hung up the phone I took the box of letters into the living room, and, with a fresh cup of hot coffee, I began what was to be a traumatic turning point in my life.

(Naturally, I do not intend to present the full content of all of the letters here. But there are passages of some of the letters that are extremely pertinent to the story at hand, and, consequently, copies of those sections will be displayed. Further, some of the excerpts that are exhibited may not seem important at this point in the narrative but their relevance will become apparent later. Lastly, though I read the letters in chronological order, on some occasions, I will display the context rather in order of topic for ease of reader understanding. Nevertheless, the dates of each letter will be shown.)

All of the envelopes were simple in design and of the ordinary stationary variety. The return addresses all read, "Jeanne Trudeau," and showed her address at an all-girl's college not too far from the university at which Fr. Steve resided and from which his brother, Ronald, graduated. The letters were addressed to Ronald VanderLinde at the Sorbonne in Paris, France. Fr. Steve had also cautioned me to read them in chronological order, so I checked the postage dates on the envelopes to make certain the letters were in order before I removed and viewed the first letter. There were about forty envelopes in all and the postage dates indicated that they had been mailed at near weekly intervals.

At the start, the content of the letters were obviously written by a young woman to her beloved who was away and going to be away for some time. They were personal, but not necessarily intimate…at least, as I said, at the beginning. (Note that, for brevity's sake, the non-pertinent material in the letters that contained relevant matter has been expunged.) After three or four letters I could tell from remarks that Jeanne Trudeau had written, that Ronald was probably writing to her on a regular basis as well, since she appeared frequently to be responding to something he had relayed to her. I also began feeling somewhat like a snoop…like I was eavesdropping on a couple of lovers as they sat on a park bench, holding hands, and vowing how much they loved each other. In addition, there were, naturally, remarks concerning activities in which Jeanne was involved, mainly at her school, and obvious responses to things Ronald was telling her about his activities at the Sorbonne.

But somewhere around letter seven or eight the letters became what I would describe as, "substantive." One of the topics she brought up, which seemed interesting, but relatively irrelevant as I read the material, would indeed prove of immense importance later during my interviews.

Apparently Jeanne and Ron had discussed a home that they planned to have after they were married. Jeanne described how she thought it should look and how she hoped to furnish different rooms in the house: even how she envisioned the flowers and shrubbery around their future home. The pertinent portion of that letter read as follows:

R. Francis Becks

Oct. 8

I've been daydreaming a lot lately about our home-to-be. It was embarrassing the other day. One of my teachers asked a question in class and called on me when my mind was at the house we're planning. I was mentally planting flowers. I think I've planted that same flowerbed at least a dozen times, and each time with different flowers or arranged them in different ways.

I think most people think of their first house as having a white picket fence, with white siding and green decorative shutters and a green roof. But I think that white and green are too stark and the combination is cold. And I've never liked fences. Fences are made to keep people away. I like inclusive rather than exclusive. And I like soft and warm rather than stark and cold. How about beige siding with medium brown shutters and a light to medium brown roof? We'll have all the green we need in the bushes and grass and leaves. And speaking of flowers, Father Castione planted some roses near the entrance to your university driveway that is the most beautiful color I've ever seen. They're a very warm peach. When I saw him the other day I asked him what they were called. He said they're "Sonia Roses." I told him I wanted that kind of roses for my wedding bouquet. He smiled and said they're one of his favorites too. Charlie said that he has been to Fr. Castione's room in the priest quarters to pick up some seedlings for the horticulture lab. Charlie said Father's room can hardly be called living quarters. He said there's a bed, a chair, a desk, and a bookcase; all of which are hard to find under the plant life and other planting debris. Charlie said there is hardly room to walk. He said there are plants and pots and bags of topsoil and fertilizer everywhere. The room was simply horticulture or the means of producing horticulture.

I've thought a lot about the inside of our house too. We'll need to have enough bedrooms for us... and our future kids, of course. So we'll need at least a three, and probably a four-bedroom home. By the way, I've been thinking about them lately too. Our future kids, I mean. I'm glad we decided to have a bunch. It's funny. I've never told you this, but, since I was about sixteen, I've felt like I already loved the children I would someday have. I never told you about those feelings because I'm sure it sounds crazy. It's easier sounding silly in a letter. And, of course, we'll need plenty of bathrooms. When I grew up we only had one bathroom and it was awful in the mornings when we were all trying to get ready for school, especially when we became teenagers. Families should not start the day with everybody irritated and yelling at each other because they can't get into the bathroom.

I've been thinking about the furnishings too. I don't want things to look either heavily masculine or frilly feminine. But, at the same time, I don't want them to look boringly neutral either. I have to work on this. Let me know what your thoughts are, that is, if you have time to think about such mundane things. Your last letter sounded like you were having trouble with your professors giving their lectures in French. I won't say I told you so, but I told you to spend more time with that French course last year.

I think I've worked out our bedroom, though. I'd like to find drapes as close as possible to the hues of those Sonia Roses I mentioned before. Actually, I'd like to do the whole bedroom in earth colors... you know, browns and oranges and peaches and medium to dark greens. As I envision it, the walls should be light beige... and the furniture would be a double bed with a simple headboard and footboard. And, of course, we would have a chest of drawers for you and a dresser with a large mirror for me with a matching nightstand and appropriate lamps. I think I'd like all of the furniture in the house to be in a traditional style... not any of the periodic or peculiar fad styles. I think the bedroom set should be made of warm, deep shaded oak or a medium, cherry but brown rather than red stain. And the bedspread should have some greens and tans and oranges... as I said, in earth colors, but all in soft hues.

On the walls we would probably have a crucifix over the bed but not one of those sick-call crucifixes. Hopefully, we won't need one of those for a few decades. And I know I would like a copy of van Gogh's "Irises" on one of the walls. Our Esthetics Class took a trip to the Museum recently and they had a print of "Irises." I didn't want to leave. I just wanted to stay looking at the painting for hours. I think it's the most beautiful painting I've ever seen.

I hope we have wall-to-wall carpeting in the bedroom and not just throw rugs. I grew up in Canada and floors without carpets are so cold when you get out of bed in the morning and no matter how hard you try you always end up missing the throw rugs and stepping on the cold floor.

You'll probably be able to use one of those valet stands that men like to hang their suit coats on when they come home from work... at least I think they do. I've only seen them in movies. And we could have a plant stand, if there's enough room.

Speaking about enough room, there's something I've wanted to discuss with you. I know one of the other bedrooms should be set up as a nursery, but I would like to have a crib and a rocker in our bedroom too so I can have our newborn babies close and so I can nurse them in our bedroom, for at least the first six months or so. I'll try not to wake you or, at least, not keep you awake, if the baby wakes up hungry during the night.

I know we don't have to decide on these things until you come home, but I'd like you to have some time to think about them.

I think that's enough for now.

I miss you very much and love you even more,
Jeanne

As I said, I felt like I was snooping on the couple by reading the letters, but the readings did give a bit of an insight into the characters of both subjects, especially Jeanne Anne Trudeau. She seemed like a sincere and caring young lady. Sometimes she seemed a bit frivolous, but that might have simply been an effort to find something to say every week. On other occasions she was surprisingly deep for an unmarried girl in her early twenties. She definitely had a leaning towards the arts or esthetic things in life such as when she talked about van Gogh's *Irises* painting and her admiration of the Sonia Roses. I would learn later that her major was English Literature and that she also liked to actually compose her own poetry and music. She must have been a moderately accomplished pianist as well, since she made reference on a few occasions to playing the piano at school functions both at her college and at Fr. Steve's University.

Apparently the two schools conducted some joint activities, since Jeanne referred to such ventures on several occasions in her letters, especially concerning an organization she referred to as the Sodality. From what she said in the letters she was apparently a member of that organization at her college and that Ronald may have been a member of his university's Sodality during his undergraduate days.

The dates on the letters and the postmarks indicated that the letters began in the middle of July, which meant that Ronald had probably left for France in the late spring or early summer, shortly after graduation. Portions of several letters dealing with a specific topic, stemming from Jeanne Trudeau's Sodality activities illustrate some degree of the depth of her character. For that reason the pertinent portions are included here. They are drawn from five of the letters and begin a little farther into her letter writing. A sixth letter that also deals with the Sodality subject was written at the end of the forty letter writing period but will be presented later, since its major impact had to do with much more serious matters.

Sept. 17

I was organizing a joint Day of Recollection with one of your old friends in the Sodality who told me that a Franciscan priest from the inner city put out a call for help. The priest is the chaplain at the County Juvenile Detention Home and at the County Work House for men and the Women's Correction Center. He asked if any of the guys from the Sodality would like to give one–on–one religious counseling to the boys at the Juvenile Home and counseling and lectures on religious topics at the Work House. Apparently the priest also asked the guys to ask us if we would be interested in doing the same for the girls at the Detention Home and for the women at the Women's Center. I asked the girls in my Sodality and a few showed some interest. Fr. Castione has become sort of my spiritual advisor lately, so I asked him what he thought of my participating in this counseling/lecturing thing and he said he thought I would be good at it. Besides, he thought it could help me develop a deeper empathy for people to see first hand what less fortunate souls are enduring. So I've decided to give it a try.

Oct. 24

I've been spending an afternoon each week with the Franciscan chaplain I told you about. His name is Father Bernard Schwengler. He's the nicest person. He's very warm and very sincere and there is a beautiful expression of peace in his voice and on his face and especially in his eyes. I sometimes think that's what Jesus must have looked like. He's a perfect Franciscan. I read a biography of St. Francis of Assisi that Father Castione recommended, which said that St Francis made each person that he talked to feel that the Saint thought that person was the most important person in the world. That's just the way Fr. Bernard treats people. I alternate weeks between the Juvenile Home and the Women's Correction Center. The other girls from school, here, have dropped out of the program and I certainly understand. We get locked in with the inmates and it can get scary. But there's something about this that I like, especially with the girls at the Juvenile Home. The women seem hard, or maybe tough is the right word. But the young girls are just mixed up kids who grew up in bad environments...you know...poverty or abuse or such. They are obviously craving for attention and love. Every time I leave, I feel like I'm deserting them. Some of the younger girls will ask when I'm coming back, and when I say two weeks, their eyes go sad, and I try to find a reason to leave quickly. I don't want them to see my eyes start to water. I think they need me to be caring, but still be strong.

I asked one of the Social Workers what the main causes for juvenile delinquency are, and she rattled off several things like poverty and poor schools and abusive parents. But when I asked, "How about divorce? Every girl I've talked to comes from a broken home or one where there's only one parent."

She just countered matter-of-factly, "Oh, yes! That's the main reason but we can't do anything about that so we just try to put Band-Aids on after the damage is done."

Ron, please promise me we won't ever get a divorce. Think of what it would be like to hurt your own children like that.

It's funny. I just realized last week that when I'm with the girls, I don't talk religion even though that's what I'm there for. But according to Fr. Bernard that's ok. He quoted what he said was a famous saying, "Always preach the gospels and, if necessary, use words." I liked that. So I guess I won't worry about my failure to give formal religious instruction.

With the women at the Correction Center it's a different story though. I don't go one-on-one with them... at least, not yet. They stay their distance so I just lecture on different religious subjects that I think they might care about. There are usually about ten or fifteen at my talks. They don't have to come to the talks, so I don't know whether they're interested in what I'm saying or they just come to have something different to do. I do try to converse with them before and after the talks, but, as I said, they're not very communicative. Maybe they'll open up when they get to know me better. I'd like to get to know them. I have class soon, so I'll write you next week.

Boy, I miss you!!!!
Jeanne

Dec. 30

I attended the joint Sodality Day of Recollection at your alma mater last Saturday. We originally planned it for the Thanksgiving weekend, but all kinds of problems came up, so we postponed it till the Christmas break. Your brother, Fr. Steve, conducted it. It was great. I was really surprised. Even at his relatively young age he already has a reputation for being the brainy sort with a good mind in physics. I didn't realize he was so religious and spiritual too. He stressed commitment: commitment to God, to our families, to our friends, but also to abstract things like truth and justice and love and even commitment to ourselves: always being who we really are and who we were meant to be by God and not try to present ourselves as somebody different. He said when we get up in the morning, we should have a short conversation with God, like, "Ok, God. Since I'm still alive, You obviously don't want me in heaven yet; which means You still have work for me to do down here. So show me what my job is today." I was really moved. I'm trying to get into the habit of saying that prayer or something like it in the mornings. I told him afterwards how much I appreciated the Day of Recollection and how surprised I was, since I always thought of him as mainly a physicist. He said that he was first a priest, then a teacher, and only lastly a scientist. I couldn't help but think that he really had his head screwed on right.

It's one of those miserable early winter days today when it can't make up its mind whether it wants to rain or snow. Yesterday it rained too, but it was warmer and the rain was sort of nice, at least, for this time of year. I spent some time just looking out the window at the rain and thinking about some of the things Father Steve said at his Day of Recollection… what God wants me to do and I put my thoughts into a short, simple poem:

A Raindrop And I

A raindrop falls upon the ground;
A little splash its only sound.
And there it lies
And there it dies…
Its life was but a minute's fall.
And here I stand upon the ground;
A lot of noise my ev'ry sound.
God gives me years,
So many years
Before my soul He'll fin'lly call.
And as my body lies in ground,
My soul will hear the choirs resound
And God will say
With no array
While stand I there before His throne.
'This raindrop in its minutes fall
Gave all it had and all it could.
So in your years before my call
Did you give all you knew you should?'

I know it's no great work of poetic art, but I thought it might help you understand what affect your brother's talks had on me.

The fourth letter concerning the Sodality is the first that can be considered of an intimate nature and because it is, I hesitated to include it. However, I feel that it is necessary in order for the reader to fully understand the two people about whom this book truly evolves and to lay the groundwork for an important incident later on.

Jan. 22

Two of the women at the Correction Center actually started talking to me yesterday. They're probably in their late twenties and both are pretty. But their facial expressions are a bit stiff and the tone in their voices was kind of hard. Fr. Bernard said most of the women in the Correction Center are there for soliciting. I'm sure you know what that means. I've never been able to understand how a woman could do that... sell her body, I mean... unless maybe if she was starving. I think it would be so demeaning. I always felt that such activity would destroy a person's self-esteem. That's why I wanted to talk to them... to see if what I was thinking and feeling about them and their lives was true. When I give my talks I think I see a combination of sadness and emptiness in most of the women's eyes. So when the two opened up to me yesterday, I tried to read inside of them. I wanted to make sure I wasn't seeing simply what I was expecting to see.

I didn't ask why they were in the Center, but it was obvious from what they said and how they said it that they were there for soliciting. They seemed to be trying too hard to be nonchalant about their situation. It was easy to see their flippant attitude was a veneer. As the conversation went on, I began to realize that these women were basically the same as the girls in the juvenile home... just older and incarcerated for perhaps more serious offenses. Thinking about it afterwards, I concluded their work probably didn't destroy their self-esteem. Things probably happened earlier in their lives, while they were growing up, that destroyed their self-esteem and, as a result, they found it easy to earn a living by soliciting. I think my job here isn't to preach religion, but to pay attention to them and listen to them and make them feel that I see them as important and valuable to me, so I can help them see themselves as important and valuable and that way try to rebuild their self-esteem.

I don't know if I should tell you this, but when I got home yesterday I couldn't help but think about us. You know... that time you tried to get me to do it with you. I meant it when I said I didn't judge you. Believe me, my feelings were just as strong. I wanted so much to be like that with you. I really hoped you understood. When I was about thirteen I was at a May Crowning at school and I felt so close to Mother Mary and I made a deal with her. If she found me a good husband who would be a good father for our children, I promised her I would stay a virgin until my wedding night and that I would stay faithful to my husband forever. I know it's hard to be chaste now, but our lives together will be wonderful after we're married.

I've also been thinking about how hard it must be for you in Paris. Staying pure, I mean. Your last letter hinted that you were having some problems in that area. I know they're freer about those things in France, but all virtues are hard precisely because we have to say no to ourselves about something we want. That's what makes them temptations. But the greater the temptation the greater the virtue when we overcome it. I jotted this down yesterday:

A fire burns, and sight and sense enflame.
The soul yearns, nor will affections tame.
But great the saints whose love was passion born;
Love's lover changed, not human nature torn.
All good must know of evil's sweet entice.
Our virtue's heights equate potential vice.

I hope you won't fall and I'm praying for you. But I want you to know that I'll understand and won't stand in judgment, if you do. Though, if you do, I think I hope you won't tell me.

I just thought of something. Remember, I told you about a biography of St. Francis of Assisi I read. Well in it there is a passage in which St. Francis and St. Clare were in a barn at night and the neighbors said the barn glowed with a beautiful light. I have a theory about that. I think all goodness radiates beauty and when the goodness is great enough the radiation glows with a beautiful light that some people call a halo. And I think St. Francis and St. Clare had possibly fallen in love with each other and, on that night, they had a perfect opportunity to violate their chastity, but out of love for God they overcame their temptation to sin and prayed together instead. The goodness was not just turning the temptation into virtue, but by being chaste, not for fear of hell or fear of the shame of getting her pregnant out of wedlock, but purely out of love for God and the desire to please Him, and not offend Him. I think such an act of goodness would certainly produce a beautiful glow in the night surrounding the place where they were at... a beautiful halo of chastity. Please know that I love you and miss you and am praying for you hard and often.

> Jeanne

This last letter is very revealing, not just of Jeanne Trudeau and Ronald VanderLinde's premarital sexual relationship, or non-relationship, but also of Jeanne's innocence that hovers on naiveté or even prudishness. She seemed squeamish about even mentioning words like "prostitute" and "sex" even in the indirect, non-interaction of a letter and even to her fiancé. This was, however, the nineteen-thirties and I understand that the prudishness of the Victorian Era was still a societal influence even in the United States at that time. But more importantly, as noted above, this revelation of that particular part of their relationship is a necessary ingredient in a more serious event to be encountered later.

But before we leave the Women's Correction Center subject, there was one letter written later, through which we can see very deeply into the soul of Jeanne Anne Trudeau. After expressing a sincere empathy for the painful helplessness she apparently sensed that the women were experiencing, she described those thoughts and feelings to Ronald VanderLinde in, at least to me, a remarkable poem for a girl of her age and living in her protected circumstance.

Jan. 28
   I've really been able to get an insight into why the women at the Correction Center are who they are and what they are. As I said before, bad things happened to them in their youth that robbed them of their self-esteem. And now they feel they're doomed... that nobody can really love them, not even God.

They've lost their virtue of hope so I'm trying to give it back to them. I've written a sonnet on the subject.

A Sonnet On Hope

When time has taken charge of newly babes
And borne these hapless reeds to lands unknown
Where beautied demons tell enchanting fab'es
And ev'ry perfumed breeze is wayward prone.

Oh, pity then the soul who sees her will
Both weak and warped; her heart corrupt and cold;
Who nears despair, when trying fails. . . yea, still
Enslaved; ensnared in habits hardened hold.

Poor wretch, fear not a fated doom.
Your prayers, though seem unanswered never die.
Through years of failing strife, strife's grace will loom
Till grace meets habit at an equal vie.

    Then only gentle winds of peace shall blow,
    And God's own happiness your heart will know.

There were several other matters of interest also manifest in the letters. We mentioned Jeanne Anne Trudeau's artistic and esthetic propensities earlier and have sampled some of her poetry. This positive engrossment in things beautiful was evident in many of her letters and some had bearing on our story. A few of those excerpts follow:

Jan. 3
Hi Ron,
    It's hard to realize that I have only one more semester of college. I have to pick a couple of electives; one in my major. I think I'm going to take the "19th Century British Poets" course. I've always liked that romantic period, especially Keats and Shelley and that group. I think I've read Keats' "Ode On A Grecian Urn" at least two dozen times. "Forever piping tunes forever new."
    And talking about tunes, the Music Department is holding

a concert this spring and the Music Director asked me to play a piano solo. She wants me to play Pachelbel's Canon in D. I've always liked that piece. I think it's one of the most beautiful pieces of music ever written, but I think it's most beautifully rendered with strings not by a solo piano. We have some excellent violinists and one of my friends plays the cello like she was born with it against her knee. So I suggested that the Director use a string quartet instead of me on the piano, but she insisted that I do it. So I'm committed to the Spring Concert. Fortunately, I have a light load this last semester so I'll have time to practice. It pays, taking heavy academic loads early on.

Speaking of Pachelbel's Canon, I think I'd like it played somewhere during our Wedding Mass... maybe when I take my bouquet to the Blessed Mother's altar... or as we leave the church... or maybe both. I don't think you can get too much of Pachelbel.

Feb. 11

Boy, did I get an eye opener when I started into the 19th Century British Poets course. When I took that first year English Lit. Survey course we just skimmed through the most prominent poets of that era, like Keats and Wordsworth and Shelley, but there were some others, I don't want to call them "lesser" poets, that were really great too. I feel like a miner who just struck gold. We spent several days on Gerard Manley Hopkins, the 19th century, Jesuit poet who coined the words, "inscape" and "instress." I wish now I had taken the course in Scholastic Philosophy that was offered as an elective in my Junior year. Apparently, Hopkins centered his approach to poetry and esthetics on the individualism of Blessed John Duns Scotus's philosophical system as opposed to St. Thomas Aquinas's universals. We discussed the concepts of the systems in class and I agree with Scotus, at least when it comes to art and poetry and esthetics. I'm not a philosophy major but I think the big argument between the Scotists and the Thomists is silly. I think they're both right. It's like looking at one of those optical illusion pictures. If you look at it one way it shows one image. And, if you look at it another way, it shows a different picture. I think, to understand some realities, like objective truth and objective morality, St. Thomas's system is right and to understand other realities, like art and beauty, Scotus's system is right. I tried to explain my opinion in class but I failed miserably. No one seemed to understand what I was saying. But then the brilliant Scholastic philosophers apparently didn't think of that view either, so I'm probably wrong.

We got snowed in today so all of the classes are canceled and I have several hours of extra time, so I'm going to copy something from the Introduction to my textbook on Hopkins (*Poems and Prose of Gerard Manley Hopkins* by Penguin Books). It's very important to me, and I hope you'll find it, at least, interesting:

"...He eagerly observes the growth and disintegration of anything from a cloud to a bluebell. But he is mainly interested in all those aspects of a thing that make it distinctive and individual. He is always intent on examining that unified complex of characteristics, which constitute, 'the outward reflection of the inner nature of a thing'—its individual essence. He was always looking for the law or principle, which gave to any object or grouping of objects its delicate and surprising uniqueness. Very often this is for, Hopkins, the fundamental beauty, which is the active principle of all true being, the source of all true knowledge and delight—even of religious ecstasy; for speaking of a bluebell he says: 'I know the beauty of our lord by it.'"

"Now this feeling for intrinsic quality, for the unified pattern of essential characteristics, is the special work of the artist, whose business is to select these characteristics and organize them into what Clive Bell has called 'significant form.' So too Hopkins must have felt that he had discovered a new esthetic or metaphysical principle. As a name for the 'individual-distinctive' form (made up of various sense data), which constitutes the rich and revealing 'oneness' of the natural object, he coined the word; inscape and for that energy of being by which all things are upheld, for that natural (but ultimately supernatural) stress, which determines an inscape and keeps it in being—for that he coined the name instress."

That's exactly how I feel about esthetics. Father Castione said he grows flowers because he sees a finite reflection of the face of God in each flower. I've always been so frustrated. I've been trying to say those things since I was about five or six years old. But I couldn't explain in words what I was experiencing in my heart and mind until I heard Father Castione say it and when I read that passage from the Intro to Hopkins. When I was looking at a brilliant, multicolored autumn scene or a beautiful flower or even a little baby I often thought, "This must be what God looks like, at least in miniature." Father Castione said there's a Latin proverb that says, "Nemo dot quod non hot:" one cannot give what he does not have. In other words, God couldn't have created the wonderful things He put in the universe if He didn't have them in Himself. He also said that St. Ignatius Loyola told the Jesuits to look at the goodness and beauties in nature to discover the goodness and beauty of God. Anyway, the whole thing has been quite an experience for me. I hope these ideas didn't bore you with your staid, logical, legal mind.

But the 19th century poet I especially wanted to tell you about is Dante Gabriel Rossetti. He was a painter as well as a poet, but it is his poem, *The Blessed Damozel* that I really want you to read. I still have an hour and a half before I have to go to supper, so I'm going to copy part of the poem here. You can read it at your leisure. I wouldn't think of "forcing" the whole poem on you. Let me know what you think of it. Lyrically it's not the greatest piece of English literature...I mean it doesn't flow smoothly. But there aren't too many John Miltons around. Anyway, to me, it's one of the most beautiful love poems I've ever read, except for the last stanza, of course, which I fully intend to change. How's that for audacity. I can hear you now. "That's just like a female. Declaring she really, really likes something, then immediately tries to change it." Well you knew what I was like when you proposed to me. So keep quiet and read. *The Blessed Damozel* starts with the opening stanza that tells the reader where she is:

> *The blessed damozel leaned out*
> *From the gold bar of Heaven;*
> *Her eyes were deeper than the depth*
> *Of waters stilled at even;*

> She had three lilies in her hand,
> And the stars in her hair were seven.

A little later the poet says how long she has been gone:

> Her seemed she scarce had been a day
> One of God's choristers;
> The wonder was not yet quite gone
> From that still look of hers;
> Albeit, to them she left, her day
> Had counted as ten years.
> (To one, it is ten years of years.)

Then the poet heard his beloved in Heaven speaking:

> She spoke through the still weather.
> Her voice was like the voice the stars
> Had when they sang together.
> 'I wish that he would come to me,
> For he will come' she said.
> "Have I not prayed in Heaven?—on earth,
> Lord, Lord, has he not pray'd?
> Are not two prayers a perfect strength?
> And shall I feel afraid?
> 'When round his head the aureole clings
> And he is clothed in white,
> I'll take his hand and go with him
> To the deep wells of light;
> As unto a stream we will step down,
> And bathe there in God's light."
> We two will stand behind that shrine,
> Occult, withheld, untrod,
> Whose lamps are stirred continually
> With prayer sent up to God;
> And see our old prayers, granted melt
> Each like a little cloud.
> 'We two will lie I' the shadow of
> That living mystic tree
> Within whose secret growth the Dove

> *Is sometimes felt to be,*
> *While every leaf which His plumes touch*
> *Saith His name audibly.*
> *'And I myself will teach him,*
> *I myself, lying so,*
> *The songs I sing here; which his voice*
> *Shall pause in, hushed and slow,*
> *And find some knowledge at each pause,*
> *Or some new thing to know.'*

But the poet interrupts to object:

> *(Alas! We two, we two, thou sayst!*
> *Yea, one wast thou with me*
> *That once of old. But shall God lift*
> *To endless unity*
> *The soul whose likeness to thy soul*
> *Was but its love for thee?)*
> *Then his beloved in Heaven continues:*
> *'There will I ask of Christ the Lord*
> *Thus much for him and me: -*
> *Only to live as once on earth*
> *With love, only to be,*
> *As then awhile, for ever now*
> *Together, I and he.'*
> *She gazed and listened and then said,*
> *Less sad of speech than mild, -*
> *'All this is when he comes.' She ceased.*
> *The light thrilled towards her, fill'd*
> *With angels in strong level flight.*
> *Her eyes prayed and she smiled.*
> *(I saw her smile.) But soon their path*
> *Was vague in distant spheres:*
> *And then she cast her arms along*
> *The golden barriers,*
> *And laid her face between her hands,*
> *And wept. (I heard her tears.)*

As I said, the theme is beautiful until you reach the last four lines of the last stanza. I have much more confidence in love and prayer than that. I once heard that St. Augustine said that the Holy Spirit was the Love between the Father and the Son, which Love binds the Trinity together and makes one God out of Three Persons. I think real love is the most powerful force in this world and the next, and can achieve anything. I honestly believe that, since the woman in the poem made it to Heaven, it means that God and her were bound together through their mutual love for each other. And, if she and the poet, who's still here on earth, truly love each other, through the uniting power of that love, together with her simultaneous love of God will make love for God grow in his heart too, and he'll end up in heaven united with her forever. When the poet asks, "Shall God lift to endless unity a soul whose likeness to thy soul is but its love for thee?" my answer is, "Absolutely! And precisely because of that love." So I rewrote the last stanza:

(I saw her smile.) But soon their path
Was vague in distant spheres:
No mind; she knows through faith in love
That if not now then soon.
For Love that binds is ever true;
No need for foolish tears.

How does it feel to be engaged to someone who feels bold enough to rewrite the classics. Scary isn't it. I guess that's enough for now. Give these things some thought. I'm interested in knowing what you think of them.

With more love than you can imagine,
Jeanne

If these preceding letters paint a basic portrait of Jeanne Anne Trudeau, the last letters will surely display a gradual changing in character or personality or whatever it is that makes a person the person he or she is. That so great a change could take place within only the next few months is remarkable in the least and nearly unbelievable. But this is only one of the "unbelievable" incidents involved in this story and one of the most important reasons I took a thirty-year sabbatical between my research for this book and the writing of it. The next letter of import was written only one week after the one that included the poem by Dante Gabriel Rossetti and many of the remaining letters follow a similar vein, but each with increasing intensity.

Mar. 5

Father Castione has been a big help to me lately... I mean spiritually. I think I'm growing even closer to Mother Mary every day. I didn't think I could admire and love her any more than I did but my insight into who she was and is is growing in leaps and bounds and through my insights into the depth of her goodness my understanding and love of Christ is also growing.

Before you left I told you I was going to try to go to Mass in the mornings before class this year, if my schedule permitted. And as I said in one of my earlier letters, my class load is light so I've been going. Some mornings, after Mass, I just want to stay in the chapel and remain spiritually in union with Our Divine Lord. I know I always am one with Him but I want to be constantly aware of it and not be distracted by everyday things. I've grown to love Him so much. I keep seeing Him hanging on the cross with the blood flowing from His head and hands and feet and from His side and He's looking down at me, obviously in tremendous pain, and He's saying, "See how much I love you." And I want to run to Him and bury myself in His Sacred Heart and, at the same time, I know I've committed sins. I hope I haven't committed many and that they were not very serious and they didn't offend God very much, but I know I have committed some. So, at the same time that I want to run to Him, I want to run away in shame. The pain of the conflicting feelings is terrible.

I told Father Castione about this and he said that John Henry Cardinal Newman described that same thing in his poem, *The Dream Of Geruntius*. He said that Newman believed that when a person dies and his soul sees the infinite Goodness and Beauty that is God for the first time, he would desire with his whole being to run as fast as he could and bury himself in this Goodness and Beauty. But, at the same time, for the first time he also sees the Infinite Good Being that he has offended by his sins and, therefore, sees for the first time how terrible his sins really were, and out of shame, he would want to run away as fast as he could to hide. Father said Newman believed that this is the greatest suffering in purgatory: the fiery pain of a soul being torn apart by these two, total and opposite desires. And because of my recent experiences I believe Newman was absolutely right. I also think that as a soul is experiencing these total and conflicting desires the soul would be living and experiencing a perfect act of contrition: regretting totally, having ever offended God by committing sins; wishing with his entire being that he had not committed them and, of course, intending never, ever, ever to offend God again by committing any sin in the future.

On another note, I've also started to question who I really am. I know that sounds silly. But, Ron, I don't want ever to be phony. I always want to be who I really am... who God really intended me to be. I think that's the best way for me to be able to do the most amount of good in my life.

Mar. 15

I was surprised and a bit disappointed by what you said in your last letter. I know you're much more pragmatic than I am, but I want to share my spiritual experiences with you too. I do admire your logical skills but sometimes I wish you would just relax and let yourself feel things or perhaps let your thoughts become spiritual experiences. I think marriage makes two people one in more than physical and emotional and even psychological ways. I think a couple should share everything, including their most private thoughts and spiritual happening, if they're going to become completely one. Isn't becoming totally one, what love and marriage are all about?

You know I've always had a deep affection for Our Blessed Mother and Our Divine Lord. It's just that it's growing. It doesn't mean I love you any less. In fact as my love for them grows, I feel my love for you growing too. I miss you more and more every day. I can't wait for you to come home.

Since I read your last letter I've been doing a great deal of thinking. I hope you're going to Communion at the Sorbonne because that's the best way for us to be and stay close, even though we're thousands of miles apart... both receiving Communion... both receiving Christ in the Blessed Sacrament...

both becoming totally one with each other through our union in and through our union with Christ. I've been working on a sonnet about this idea:

A Sonnet On The Blessed Sacrament
(How the uniting power of Love within the Mystical Body of Christ enables all of its members to become totally one with each other through reception of Christ's Sacrament of Love.)

What love is there that seeks not to possess
All the beauty and the good beloved,
And does not seek in intimate caress
A oneness more than but a hand engloved.

Vain lovers seek a union but in flesh;
To find but only fleshly beauty gained.
When personness eludes, desire fresh
Is still the state, though satisfaction feigned.

But yea, the greatest lover of them all
Devised a scheme: His bride entire to wed;
Love's unity in full, desire's fall
To all partaking of His angel's bread.

Our gain: we two completely one
While jointly in communion with God's son.

Mar. 23

Thus far I've been able to leave the chapel in the mornings to get to class on time, but my classes are becoming less and less important to me. I just want to spend all day just meditating on Christ and everything about Him and being in total union with Him.

Father Castione said that I've been talking so much about "love" that I should spend some of my Sodality, mental prayer time asking the Holy Spirit to tell me what "love" really is. And, you know, he's right. Everybody talks about love, but everybody seems to have a different idea about what it is. Some people say there are different kinds of love. You know, one love for

God, and another for our parents and children, and a different one for friends, and, of course, a totally different one for our spouses or romantic interests. But I've been meditating on the subject lately, with the Holy Spirit's help, of course, and I think there's only one kind of real love and we can see it in Christ's actions. I've been giving this a lot of thought. (Maybe too much. I received a C- in a Shakespeare test two days ago. I think the teacher took it easy on me. I probably should have failed it. I was up until 2:00 AM the night before just thinking about, "What is love?")

The way I see it, love is made up of two acts of the intellect and two acts of the will. The first three acts are easy. In an apologetics course we learned that the object of all love is goodness. I think St. Thomas Aquinas said that. So first, the intellect sees or recognizes or acknowledges goodness. And I think beauty is something that radiates from all goodness. I think I told you about this a few letters back: if the goodness is great enough, the radiance increases to the point that it becomes a beautiful light that we call a halo. So after the intellect perceives goodness it then appreciates the beauty radiating from it, though I think appreciates is a weak expression for what we experience. It's much more intense and dynamic than simply appreciating. Then comes the first act of the will. We desire to become totally one with the goodness and beauty our intellects have absorbed. I think this much is all automatic. Once we see or acknowledge goodness the rest of the first three acts follow instinctively. And I think the first act of the will is what Christ experienced at the last supper and is the reason he created the Eucharist: so that he could become totally one, physically, emotionally, psychologically, spiritually and mystically one with His beloved people of God. And the second act of the will, which is the tough one, Christ showed us in His Passion and Death. The second act of the will is a willingness to sacrifice of self for the happiness and well being of the beloved. And it is through that willingness to sacrifice of self for the beloved that creates the binding force between the lover and the beloved, and they become one.

When I told Father Castione about my definition of love he was impressed. He said I might have figured out something important. Please tell me what you think of it, Ron.

With sincerest love,
Jeanne

While reading this letter I realized I had read that description of love somewhere else and after only a short reflection it came to me that those were almost the same words Ronald VanderLinde used to define love in that speech at the girl's college. He must have gotten the ideas from this last letter. Again, I promised myself to discuss that definition with my Helen.

Mar. 30

I called your brother, Father Steve, this past week for a favor. I've been wondering lately what it must be like to be a member of a contemplative order like the one your sister, Agnes, belongs to. It must be wonderful to be able to spend most of the day in prayer and spiritual reading. I know we're supposed to make everything we do throughout the day a prayer by offering it up to God in our morning prayers but I really enjoy spending time just talking to Christ and Our Heavenly Father and telling Them how much I love Them and trying to know more and more about their Goodness so that I can love Them more and more. So I asked Father Steve if he could get hold of your sister at her Convent and ask her if I could come over this weekend to find out what it's like behind those cloistered walls. He asked if I was contemplating entering the religious life, but I told him I wasn't. I was just curious to know what contemplative life was like.

He called me back the next day and said he made an appointment for me with Sister Mary Agnes this coming Saturday. He said he was glad that I had asked him to arrange a meeting because it gave him an opportunity to drive over to the convent and visit with her. He said he hadn't seen her in quite a while.

April 5

I met your sister, Agnes, or should I say, Sister Mary Agnes, last Saturday. She's really sweet: so gentle and soft-spoken. I guess that's part of the contemplative life style. After I told her I was curious about the goings on in a contemplative convent she asked the same question Father Steve asked if I were thinking of becoming a nun. I laughed and said, "No. Unless your order is accepting married women." I reminded her that I was engaged to be married to her brother.

She didn't laugh and uttered, half reflectively, "I've never known of anyone inquiring about a specific religious order unless they had some inclination towards entering."

I assured her I was just curious and apologized if she got the wrong impression from Father Steve's call.

She was very informative, both about the general logistics and the activities of the nuns. When I asked her what made her decide to enter a contemplative order, she questioned me again about my possible intentions and I assured her again that I was just curious.

She said it was easy for her to accept her vocation. (I liked that expression, "Accept her vocation." It emphasizes that a vocation to the religious life isn't a willingness to give up other attractive things in life, but is rather a gift from God; a wonderful blessing bestowed on nuns and priests.) She said her attraction to the Convent and to Contemplative life started very early. She said your father stopped at the convent to drop off some of the food he grew on the farm on his way to the farmer's market. She said she started tagging along when she was only three or four years old and she played with the External nuns that met the public and went with your father to the chapel to pray. Then she said something very strange. She said that every time she was in the convent she had the same wonderful feeling that she had when her mother held her on her lap at night. She said that she would fall asleep there and wake up the next morning in bed. She added that she felt absolutely at home at the convent, even before she was old enough to enter school.

When I asked her how old she was when she entered the Convent she said, "Seventeen."

At that I had to ask if she finished high school. She openly admitted that she didn't go to high school because her mother died during child birth when she was thirteen and, since she was the oldest girl she had to be the mother of the house: doing the house work, cooking and washing and the like until her father married again. She said that she only finished the eighth grade, but that was all she needed, since she only needed basic reading and math skills, which she already had.

I'm sure you know all this, Ron, but I thought you might like to know what I learned about your family.

Sister Mary Agnes admitted that she was very disappointed when her father wouldn't take her on his trips to the market when it was a school day or later when she needed to be at home to make meals for the boys. But she said she understood. However, according to her, that didn't make it any easier. She added, "Sometimes, afterwards, when I had time to be alone I would cry. Especially after my mother died. I longed for that feeling that I had falling asleep on my mother's lap or with her arm around me and the convent was the only place I could find that feeling."

I asked her if she still gets that feeling, since she's been living at the convent. Her answer was, "At the beginning," which she asserted with a beautiful smile. But the feeling soon changed to a different, but just as wonderful feeling: one of being in total and constant union with Christ. She said she thinks her initial attraction that made her feel at home in the convent, like she was in her mother's arms, was just a path that God took her through to get to the contemplative life and thus to her current and blessed union with Christ.

I was very interested in everything she was saying, and it must have been obvious to her, since she opened up to me so fully. I felt that I had made a close friend even though I'm out in the world and she's in a cloister.

Still miss you and love you,
Jeanne

April 12

It's Easter Sunday night. Actually, it's Monday morning. I just got in from the Easter Mixer Dance between our two schools. Charlie and Diane were going and didn't want me sitting at home just because my fiancé was thousands of miles away in a boring place like Paris, France. So they invited me along. I was a bit hesitant but I decided at the last minute to go with them.

I went to Easter Mass at the University this morning because they were having a Bach Mass in the auditorium with the school orchestra and choir. It was awe-inspiring... talk about pageantry.

After the Mass I saw Father Castione and asked him if the flowers on the temporary altar were his creations. He said that some of them were. He showed me one bouquet of white blooms that he said he was very proud of. He had been trying for years to develop a species of white camellia that would bloom in the spring to join the lilies as Easter flowers and he said that he finally succeeded. He said, in nature, white camellias only bloom in the fall of the year. The blossom was intriguing. I don't think I've ever seen a camellia before. I told him that the petals looked like they were made of wax... like they were artificial, but he said, that though they may look like wax, they are really very delicate and bruise easily. Since Mass was over, he told me to take that bouquet home. And I did. As a matter of fact, since I knew most of the guys would be giving their dates corsages for the dance, and, since my guy wasn't here to give me one, I pinned one of the camellias in my hair for the mixer.

Which brings me to the most important part of this letter... and the most difficult thing I have ever done. The part that I've been torturing over all week. The beginning of this letter was just nervous prattle... an effort to put off what I'm going to tell you now.

I made a Holy Week retreat this past week. It went from Palm Sunday through Holy Thursday.

After talking to your sister, Agnes, the Saturday before, I began to feel very uneasy. That's why I was glad I had arranged to make the retreat... to give myself some time to really think about everything that's been happening to me in the past year. Ron, I've been asking myself all year, "Who am I. What does God want of me?" I can't describe how much I love you and how much I want a family and children of my own to hold and care for. But there is another part of me that just wants to bury myself in Our Divine Lord's Sacred Heart and never ever leave there. Even as I was talking to your sister, I didn't have an inkling that I wanted to become a cloistered nun. But when I got home everything in me or about me started falling apart.

I have to be who I am and that's so hard because I want to be a wife and especially a mother with little children. But I also know I'm a child of God. Ron, I know now that I'm meant to be a Bride of Christ, now and forever.

Please, Ron, forgive me, but I'm going over to your sister's Convent tomorrow to enter as a postulate. I'll tell Father Steve before I go and we can probably communicate through him or through your sister, if there's anything to communicate about.

I hope so much that you understand why I'm doing what I'm doing. I love you so much and I don't wish to hurt you in any way. But I feel this is what God wants and, therefore, it's what I want and I hope you will want it too. Ever since I can remember I have loved goodness, and beauty and I've tried to bring as much of it into the world as I could. And I always thought the best way for me to do that was by joining with God to create new little beings that I could teach to know truth, and appreciate beauty, and love goodness, and have their own goodness loved, and help them eventually become totally one with God in heaven. And after I fell in love with you I figured I could unite with both you and God to create those wonderful beings. But now I believe, that in the fullness of contemplative life I can help God create more goodness and beauty here on earth than I could in any other way... I wish to be a mother to all of the souls that God has made. And through my prayers and acts of penance help everyone in the world find their way home to the bosom of their loving God.

But, Ron, it's very important to me that you realize I'm going to enter a religious order, not because I lack those human feelings that bring married couples together. I still have all the feelings and emotions and even passions that a wife and mother would have. It's just that the primary object of those feelings has changed. Remember the poem I sent you a few months ago:

A fire burns, and sight and sense enflame.
The soul yearns, nor will affections tame.
But great the saints whose love was passion born;
Love's lover changed, not human nature torn.
All good must know of evil's sweet entice.
Our virtue's heights equate potential vice.

Ron, believe me, I haven't turned cold towards you. I know it must seem that way, but I haven't. My physical passion has changed to a passion of the spirit...a passion of the soul... just as strong and just as real. My previous desire for the physical and emotional ecstasy that I've heard married couples feel has changed to a desire for the spiritual and mystical ecstasy of union with Our Divine Lord. I know that I haven't experienced what the Saints have in such ecstasies, but I've known a touch of it and I believe those experiences are but a hint of what heaven will be like.

But it's so important to me that you understand that what I'm doing does not mean I don't love you or that I am not experiencing the very deep feelings that are in me.

As I was just writing here at my desk, I looked across the room at the mirror on my dresser and saw my reflection with the white camellia still in my hair and I realized that the camellia is a perfect example of what I'm trying to say. I spent a little time drafting a poem:

One white Camellia now adorns my hair.
Look upon this bloom; behold my soul there.
This flower's wax like petals cold appear,
And feign an artificial form.
Shallow eyes would see them as austere,
Though they be delicate and sensitive and warm.
One white camellia now adorns my hair.
Look upon it, love. Behold my soul there.

Ron, someday we will be united in the bosom of Our Heavenly Father. God will indeed lift our souls to endless unity because of the binding power of His love for us and the binding power of our love for Him and precisely because of the binding power of our love for each other.

Goodbye, for now, Ron. Looking forward to being with you forever in heaven.

Jeanne

As the content indicates, that was the last letter in the box. I finished it Tuesday afternoon. As I read the letters, I highlighted the parts which I considered pertinent, so I spent the balance of the day sorting those letters with highlights into an orderly form.

When I finished that chore, I gave Father Steve a call to inform him of my reading completion and to set up my plan of attack for the interviews. And, of course, to discuss the somewhat agonizing goings on between Ronald VanderLinde and Jeanne Anne Trudeau as reflected in the letters.

Father Steve was very happy with my progress and after a short conversation relative to the drama related in the letters, he told me that my first interview would be with his and Ronald's sister, Sister Mary Agnes. He acknowledged that he had spoken to her and told her about my project and what I would need to know. He added that he had instructed her to only tell me the things that happened concerning Ronald up to a given point, after which he would direct me to another interviewee. After giving me directions to the Convent, he surprised me with an odd farewell, even for a priest. He said, "May the Holy Spirit be with you and guard you from harm." I may have been mentally tired from all of the reading, but his departing phrase, indicating that I would need the protection of the Holy Spirit, made me feel as though I was about to enter the gates of hell, or, at least, a lion's den. And, as it turned out, my feelings did not prove too far from fact.

Chapter *Eight*

Thirty minutes after I had finished the phone conversation with Fr. Steven VanderLinde in which he directed me to my first interview for the Ronald VanderLinde biography, I abruptly realized how befuddled my mind had become from my absorption in the story. I had agreed to a 9:30 AM appointment at a convent on the extreme outskirts of the city, which would have been at least a forty-five minute drive from my downtown apartment if I had a car, which, of course, I did not. After a distasteful consideration of using public transportation and shoe leather to reach the convent, I called Father Steve back to tell him of my transportation dilemma. His reaction was a surprising, "Good."

When I inquired why my situation was, "good," he responded positively, "I can drive you over, which will give me the opportunity to set up another interview for you with one of the other nuns at the convent." He continued, "I didn't want to simply talk to this other nun over the phone. Her's will be a sensitive interview and may be difficult for her. I want to talk to her in person and explain the why and what-for of the interview. I can do that while you're talking to Sister Mary Agnes."

At this I interjected, "And the drive over will give me an opportunity to ask you about things which Jeanne Trudeau wrote in the letters that confused me, or at least, were not clear from the letters."

He agreed to enlighten me concerning matters that I had already encountered, but added, "But, as I've told you before, I want you to learn the story as it unfolded... as the participants lived it. I'll resist telling you anything that you will or may uncover through your future interviews."

The next morning, I was waiting for Father Steve as he pulled up in front of my apartment building. I was experiencing a little nervousness in anticipation of the I-knew-not-what. As I climbed into the passenger seat, we exchanged greetings and I added, "Boy, you look chipper for this early in the morning."

Fr. Steve countered, "Early? I've been up for hours. I said the 6:30 Mass at a neighboring parish this morning. And I'm looking forward to seeing my sister. I feel ashamed to admit it, but I was thinking about that this morning. It's been almost a year since I actually saw my sister in person. I've talked to her on the phone, of course, especially since Ron became seriously ill. But, none of that was in person. And, naturally, such visits require my going to see her. I'll certainly be required to begin our greetings with a big mea culpa."

I laughed, "You may not believe this, but I actually know what that means."

We drove a short while before I broke the silence. "You really sandbagged me," I started.

"I think I sort of understand what you mean, but I'd like you to elaborate," was his retort.

I thought for a second and then began, "Before I agreed to write your brother's biography I told you that I was a cynic of the first order. I not only never consider anything below a very superficial level; I don't want to consider anything subsurface. It's called living in peaceful oblivion. And then you give me these letters to read that start out simply enough but gradually descend to a depth of... I don't know what to call it... humanness, personness... some abstract condition... I doubt there's even a name for it."

"Oh there's a name for it," the priest responded half reflectively. "It's called, 'holiness.'"

"Well, from what I read over the last few days, it's a world that, literally, scares the hell out of me."

"That's natural," he replied. "It holds a picture up in front of our eyes of what we know we're supposed to be like as opposed to what we know we really are like."

I felt a cold shudder go through me. I responded accusatorily, and yet my feelings were more defensive than aggressive. "You know you Catholics have the reputation for having created guilt, don't you? Don't you guys feel guilty about giving people guilt feelings? Guilt has caused a lot of mental and emotional problems for a lot of people. That's one of the reasons I'm so cynical... to avoid guilt and all of the problems it creates."

"Only one of the reasons?" he countered in playful inquiry. "Guilt itself has developed a bad and, I think, undeserved reputation. Actually, guilt is good. When we do something bad, our ids tell us we're not the person our egos want us to be, and that conflict between the id and the ego, which causes that uncomfortable feeling, we call guilt. And the pain of that feeling instinctively forces us to try to get rid of it, which we can only do successfully by returning to that good person our egos want us to be. And the only way we can do that is by becoming sincerely sorry for the bad thing we did and promising ourselves we'll try not to do it again."

"But, a lot of people suffer and are even crippled for much of their lives by guilt feelings," I countered.

He answered, "That's because they don't handle guilt correctly. They try to excuse themselves…to convince themselves there was nothing wrong with what they did. 'That guy deserved a punch in the nose.' Or, 'I'm sorry for what I did, but, if that guy says or does the same thing I'll punch him in the nose again.' Sincere sorrow for our wrong actions and a firm purpose of amendment…that's how we get rid of guilt and free ourselves from its debilitating affects."

I really did not like the sermon Father Steve was preaching but I had no rebuttal, so after a short pause I changed the subject. "I didn't see Jeanne Trudeau's last letter coming. Even after she visited your sister in the convent the week before. Her decision to enter the convent at such short notice floored me."

"Imagine how it felt to Ron," the priest responded.

"How did he take it?" I inquired.

"That's what you're about to find out," Father Steve replied. Then he added pensively, "There is something of serious importance that I should tell you before you begin the interviews…to sort of brace you for what you're going to encounter. You're going to meet, what I call, 'total people.' I mean that both my brother, Ron, and Jeanne Anne Trudeau lived every moment to the full. People like them love and hate totally, with their entire beings…without reservation. I don't know if you saw that in the letters, but it will become blaringly obvious to you in the interviews. As I said, try to brace yourself for it. It can get a bit overwhelming at times."

At that, the conversation ended until we turned into the convent parking lot.

"Well, here we are," Father Steve commented. Then, before he reached for the door handle he turned to me and uttered softly, "May God be with you."

Again I felt a cold shudder.

The convent building was larger than I had expected. From the parking lot I could see that behind the convent proper was a large, apparently, uncovered area surrounded by a rather high brick wall. I assumed that this was a courtyard of sorts for private, outdoor prayer, as well as a place where the nuns could possibly do some flower or vegetable gardening.

As Father Steve and I ascended the front steps, I could almost feel the austere atmosphere of the convent. Since I had not as yet seen anything of a foreboding nature, I passed off the feeling as an anticipatory predisposition from the little I knew of contemplative, convent life. Father Steve pressed the doorbell button. After a short wait the church like door opened, displaying a petite nun in the usual attire that greeted us with a gentle smile and equally gentle acknowledgement. Father Steve told the nun that we had an appointment to see the Mother Superior.

We waited a short while in the vestibule, which exhibited the ambiance as I imagined the interior to be: tall ceilings; simple grained, wood wall paneling, and a hardwood floor with a large dark green carpet of plain design. There were a few moderately sized pictures of saints on the walls and a large crucifix over a doorway to an adjoining room that appeared to be one of several parlors for conversing with visitors. The few items of furniture that could be seen in the parlors included high, wood-backed and somber looking cushioned chairs. The walls, high ceilings, floors, and hanging pictures in the parlors were identical to the vestibule décor and, though not repulsive, did portend an uncomfortable stay, at least to me.

Soon we were joined by an elderly nun in the same attire as the one who greeted us at the door. With the lengthy habit, the black head veil, and white bib apparel, it was hard to ascertain her age. But on reflection of the newspaper biography, which I read on the plane to the State Capital, I placed the nun in her early-eighties. She was slightly hunched over and held a cane, but her voice was soft as cotton and her smile was warm and gracious. I was obviously, though not offensively, non-existent during the affectionate verbal exchange between Father Steve and his sister. It was obvious that they were both very happy to see each other again. When Sister Mary Agnes got around to me, she greeted me cordially and confirmed that she knew why I was there and the information Father Steve wanted her to relay to me.

At this point another nun seemed to appear out of nowhere and was standing next to Mother Superior. She looked as though she was near Sister Mary Agnes' age, though with the habit, again, I could not be certain. The Abbess introduced her to Father Steve, who immediately went with her into one of the open parlors. Sister Mary Agnes led me into another parlor, where we sat across from each other.

I had brought both a tape recorder and a notepad and pen to take notes. I began by asking Sister Mary Agnes if she minded if I recorded our conversation, since I am sometimes unable to translate parts of my rapidly scribbled notes. She graciously approved my request.

Sister Mary Agnes hesitated for quite awhile before she started speaking. At first she was looking at me intently, but she was not staring. Rather, she bore a thoughtful expression on her face as though she was sizing me up... or, at least, trying to see something in me that would make her feel comfortable recounting to me what she was instructed by Father Steve to tell me. Then her expression changed, though she continued to look right at me. I tried to read the focus in her eyes to determine whether she was actually seeing me or not really aware of where she was looking... that she was simply gathering her thoughts as to how to begin our conversation. When she did begin, her first remark was a rhetorical question, "You're not Catholic, are you Mr. Becks?"

"No," I answered, "but I'm engaged to a Catholic girl and I've learned a great deal about your faith from my contacts with her over the past year or so."

"Are you aware of how seriously Catholics treat the Blessed Sacrament?"

"You mean Communion?" I asked.

"Exactly," she confirmed.

"Well, I know you regard the wafer with a great deal of reverence. I've gone to Mass with my fiancée and I saw people kneel to receive Communion from the priest and kneel for quite awhile after they get back to the pew. My fiancée told me that Catholics believe the host, I think she called it, is really Jesus as both God and man only in the form of a piece of bread." I looked at the nun to try to figure out whether she would be disturbed by my next statement, but I said it anyway, "I'll be very honest with you, Sister, I find such concepts very hard to believe, but I do know that I don't know everything, so I'm not going to argue against such ideas."

"At least you're honest," she replied, "Especially in matters like we are dealing with here, that could be a most important attribute." Then she continued, "But, when I tell you what I'm going to tell you, I would like to ask you to try to imagine how a believing Catholic would react to the events. You'll need to do that to enable yourself to understand the what and the why of the things that happened."

I instinctively responded, "I'll try." But I was not certain of what it was that I was going to be trying to do.

We both looked at each other inquisitively for a few seconds before Sister Mary Agnes began her tale.

"I had been a nun in this convent a little over ten years when Sister St. Cecelia entered. By the way, at the beginning of the story, at least, I'm going to use Sister St. Cecelia's lay name, Jeanne. It'll be easier and maybe clearer. Jeanne had just broken off her engagement to my brother, Ron. We had a nice talk about a week before she came to the convent to enter our order. And, though she seemed like a serious enough girl, serious enough to be able to make up her mind about entering religious life, the Abbess, our Mother Superior at the time, was not sure, at least when Jeanne first walked through the door. Usually young women spend considerable time thinking and praying about such a serious step before they enter. And, during the conversation we had the week before, Jeanne insisted that she did not have a vocation to religious life. That's why I was so surprised when she showed up on that Monday morning. I remember it was a Monday because it was the day after Easter. I was the External at the time: the nun who answers the doorbell and has contact with visitors to the convent. I was stunned when I opened the door and saw her standing there. I thought she had left something behind from her visit the week before. But she looked directly at me and in a soft but firm voice said, 'I've come to join. I'm becoming a contemplative. I've come to become totally, constantly and forever one with Our Divine Lord.'

"When Mother Superior was called to meet Jeanne, the Mother was concerned at first, since, as I said, Jeanne had shown no earlier interest or inclination towards entering. Mother asked her the usual questions to try to determine how much commitment she had to this drastic lifestyle change. When Mother asked her simply, 'Why do you think you have a vocation to the contemplative life?' Jeanne looked at her and with a very matter of fact expression on her face and in her voice said, 'Because My Divine Lord wants me to be totally one with Him now and forever and that's what I want also.' I've never heard anyone ever say anything in that tone of voice... with that much absolute certainty and yet with so much simple sincerity. I think that must have been the tone in God's voice when he said, 'Let there be light.' And I think Mother Superior must have recognized that unique certainty also because she allowed Jeanne to enter the convent on that very Monday morning.

"Since I was somewhat familiar with the new novice, Mother gave me the job of showing her the ropes, so to speak. Jeanne was a happy and energetic young woman and eager to help in the convent chores in any way she could. She and I struck it off well right from the beginning. But she had a stubborn streak. She would never let anyone interrupt her when she was in private prayer. We have certain periods in the day devoted to private prayer, and Jeanne was very jealous of that time. She was totally generous with everybody about everything else, but not her time in prayer. I expected Mother to tell the new postulant to be more charitable and a little more flexible on this issue when unexpected things come up, but she didn't. I was surprised. Our Mother Superior at the time was a firm, but caring, director. She bore her responsibilities very seriously. She was extremely conscious of her obligation to watch over the physical, emotional, and spiritual well being of the sisters in her charge as well as the convent and our religious order. That's why several incidents that occurred during this period surprised me.

"Since I had grown close to Jeanne, I think I paid a little more attention to her than I had to the other sisters. And I noticed that after Jeanne made that statement with such certainty about her vocation on Easter Monday, Mother gave a little more space to her than she gave to the rest of us. She seemed to allow Jeanne a trifle more leeway than she would have allowed the other sisters. I don't know if the other sisters recognized this but, if they did, none ever complained. At first, I thought that Mother may have been afraid of Jeanne. But when I watched Mother looking at Jeanne and when I listened to the tone in Mother's voice when she talked to Jeanne, I could see there was no concern over a personality threat... just the opposite. There was an almost pious respect... like Mother knew God had sent us something very special in Jeanne Anne Trudeau, soon-to-be, Sister St. Cecelia and God wanted us to let her do her thing because it was God's thing too. And that attitude towards Jeanne came to full necessity in what happened only a week after she entered our convent.

"It was the following Saturday when my brother, Ron, arrived, banging viciously at the front door of the convent. As I said, I was the External at the time. When I opened the door he apparently didn't recognize me and I didn't recognize him. I mean, I only saw him maybe a half dozen times in our lives. I entered the convent before he was born and he seldom visited me here. He was closer to our other brothers and sisters and when our two brothers died during the post World War I flu epidemic, I understand he grew much closer to his brother, Steven, who was sort of his hero... probably because the two of them received most of their father's brains."

At this point Sr. Mary Agnas paused and asked if I wanted to interject any thoughts or ask any questions. Actually, I was quite absorbed in her story and was anxious that she continue. She had obviously just gotten to the good part, that is, "How did Ronald VanderLinde react to his fiancée's entering a convent?" So I commented simply, "No, please, go on."

And she did. "As I said, I didn't recognize him at first. But not only because I hadn't seen him for a long time but also because his face was extremely red and distorted in an awful expression of anger and even hatred. Ron pushed past me. He was yelling, 'Where is she? Where is Jeanne Trudeau?' He went quickly to the door leading to the cloister and burst through. 'That's the cloister!' I yelled. 'Men can't go in there! You'll be excommunicated!' But he didn't pay any attention to me. He was yelling at the top of his voice. 'Jeanne, where are you! Come here! I've got to talk to you. Jeanne, you can't do this! We love each other too much!' He went charging back and forth in the hall. The sisters were scrambling to hide. Some went into their rooms. Others hid where they could. This went on for several minutes. Mother Superior came out of her room and yelled at him to get out and threatened to call the police. He was working his way down the hallway and finally entered the chapel.

"As I said, he was yelling constantly and at the top of his voice... calling for Jeanne. I didn't know where Jeanne had gone. I found out a few days later, after the dust settled, that when Ron first entered the vestibule yelling, Mother ushered Jeanne into the Abbess' office and Mother hid her in a closet.

"When Ron entered the chapel there were several nuns there either fulfilling their Perpetual Adoration Hours before the Blessed Sacrament or engaged in private prayer. And when he burst in yelling, they just started yelling back at him to leave. But that just made him angrier. Finally, he went up to the altar and took the Monstrance that holds the Blessed Sacrament and threw it as hard as he could. When it hit the wall it broke and the Blessed Sacrament flew out onto the floor. The tabernacle door still had the key in it from morning Mass and Ron opened the door and pulled out the chalice. He hurled that against the wall too. The Consecrated Hosts flew all over the chapel... on the seats and kneelers and, of course, onto the floor. I could hear the nuns in the chapel yelling, 'That's a sacrilege! Don't you know that? That's Our Divine Lord.' But he yelled back, 'I don't give a damn, you hear!' All your pious goodness can go to hell as far as I'm concerned. And you can all go to hell with it.' Then, with a horrible deliberateness, he growled very loudly, 'Goodness! I can't tell you how much I hate goodness!' With that Ron charged into the public portion of the chapel and exited outside from there.

"When the noise stopped, the nuns in the chapel ran to Mother's room yelling that Ron had strewn the Consecrated Hosts all over. When Jeanne heard that she ran to the chapel yelling, 'Oh, no... no... Lord, please no!' When she entered the chapel she burst uncontrollably into tears. She saw the chalice lying on the floor and ran to it and started picking up the hosts and putting them in the chalice. And as she picked up each host, while she was crying bitterly, she kissed it and placed it gently into the chalice. While she was doing that she kept saying over and over, 'Please, Lord, I'm sorry. You know he didn't mean it. Please forgive him... please forgive both of us. It's my fault, too, for wanting to be one with you more than with him.' She just kept picking up the hosts and kissing them and pleading for forgiveness. The priest must have consecrated a lot of extra hosts that morning because there were dozens strewn around the chapel. About the time she had picked up nearly half the hosts, Mother Superior entered the chapel with a few other nuns, myself included, and she indicated to us to help Jeanne pick up the rest. But when we started, Jeanne turned on us and very angrily yelled. 'No, stop! It's my fault! I'm the one that hurt Our Lord. It's my responsibility.' We could hardly understand her. As I said, she was crying uncontrollably. The other sisters and I looked at Mother for guidance as to what to do, and Mother, almost inconceivably to us, waved us off and indicated that she wanted us to leave the chapel... leaving Jeanne alone, crying, kissing each host as she put it into the chalice and muttering over and over, 'I'm sorry Lord. Lord... Lord, please forgive Ron and me. Please, Lord we're sorry.'"

At this point I reluctantly interrupted, "I know you said, sister, that the Mother Superior gave Jeanne Trudeau a little leeway, but this seems more than just a little. I know I wasn't there, but Jeanne's conduct in this case sounds more like she had gone berserk than that she was expressing a rational respect for the... 'The Blessed Sacrament,' as you call it."

Sister Mary Agnes affirmed my opinion, "Several of the sisters had the same thought. Later in the day, one of them asked Mother why she didn't take charge in the chapel and make Jeanne let us help her. Mother said calmly, 'Sometimes you follow your head and sometimes you follow your heart, at least when you're sure it's speaking from love and not just sentimentality. But there are times, not often, but sometimes, when you just listen to the essence of all truth.' Then she added, 'Besides, our foundress said that we should respect new postulants because, 'The Lord often reveals to the least that which is best." To this day I'm not certain exactly what she meant, but I think maybe she felt the Holy Spirit was speaking to her and to the rest of us through Jeanne and we just couldn't recognize His voice.

"After a short while I returned to the chapel to see how Jeanne was doing. It was obvious that she had found and picked up all of the hosts that Ron had strewn around, but Jeanne was still on all fours on the floor between the pews looking for any hosts she may have missed. I walked around the chapel looking for any that might have been lying under the pews or kneelers and then observed, 'I think you found them all, Jeanne.'

"But she shot back, 'I have to be certain. I'm going to keep looking until I'm certain.' Her tone was still very sharp and absolutely insistent.

"I knew I could not dissuade her from her search, so I left. There were two other nuns in the chapel for their hours before the Blessed Sacrament and my time was due in a while so I left with the intent of checking again later.

"Ron had arrived at about 11:00 AM and it was mid-afternoon when I arrived back at the chapel. When I walked in, Jeanne was kneeling in one of the pews just staring at the Monstrance and the chalice on the altar where she obviously had placed them. Her facial expression was stern, but she had stopped crying. I approached her and asked how she was feeling, but she just knelt there, frozen, with her eyes glued to the altar. When she failed to respond to my first inquiry, I tried again, but she gave up the same reaction... nothing. I looked over at the other sisters to see if Jeanne had responded to them but they indicated she had failed to react to them also. I asked one of them, as she was leaving, to tell Mother what was going on.

"After I had completed my time in prayer, I tried again to get a response from Jeanne but again I received nothing in return. When Collation passed with Jeanne still in the chapel, I really began to worry. It meant that she had missed two meals. But still, Mother insisted that we leave her alone.

"I was having difficulty getting to sleep that night, and, since we were scheduled for another period of prayer in the chapel at 1:00 AM, I just stayed awake. I was anxious to return to the chapel to see if Jeanne was still there and to check on how she was doing. When I entered the chapel the thing that caught my attention first was that Jeanne did not appear to have moved a bit. She was still kneeling rigidly upright and staring fixedly at the altar.

"When prayer time was over, I was very tired and went back to my room to try to get some sleep. I think I got some, but very little. I woke earlier than I otherwise would have and sneaked down to the chapel, again to check on Jeanne.

"Entering the chapel I felt a strange warmth. The sisters that were there for their scheduled prayer hours seemed unaware of Jeanne, who appeared less rigid than earlier. When I slid my way into the pew in which she was kneeling, she noticed me and turned her head towards me. On her face was the most beautiful and happy smile I have ever seen. Looking directly into my eyes she said simply, 'It's alright, now. Everything is alright. I feel kind of hungry. Is it near mealtime? What time is it?'

"When I told her that it was in the early morning she acknowledged matter-of-factly, 'Oh.' Then she rose, slid into the aisle, genuflected and left.

"Since Mother did not make an issue of the event of Ron's invasion of our cloister, everyone else just acted as though it didn't happen either. Both the incident and the non-acknowledgement of its happening were very strange, to say the least.

"Jeanne and I became very close over the next several months. She was a perfect postulant and a model of Christian charity, except for her private prayer time, of course. I don't think she ever changed concerning that matter. But all of the sisters knew about it and just avoided any contact with her when she was in prayer. Before long it was as if there had never actually been a problem. Even Mother Superior seemed to put in an effort to avoid giving Jeanne chores that might conflict with her scheduled private prayer time. On one occasion I heard a couple of the sisters talking about this minor privilege that Mother was extending to Jeanne and asked them if it bothered them. One of them joked, 'Absolutely not. I just ask her to say a short prayer for me during those prayer periods, and since I started asking her to pray for me, my world somehow just seems happier. I don't know if her prayers have anything to do with it, but I'm not going to complain.'

"I don't know whether it was Jeanne's prayers either but the spirit in the convent seemed to be happier... not that it wasn't happy before. But the happiness seemed to rise to a higher level. It may have been the prayers, but I think it was also Jeanne's personality. Sometimes I would watch when Jeanne approached a sister who appeared a little grumpy that day, and when she started talking to Jeanne, the grumpiness disappeared. Jeanne had a very infectious smile. When someone saw her smile, they automatically smiled too.

"We all have chores that are assigned to us for our work periods. Mother always tried to give sisters work in keeping with the talents God had given them. Jeanne had an artistic bent, especially in poetry and music. She was also a fair, though obviously untrained, artist. So Mother assigned her to create religious greeting cards with original pictures and original poems and sayings that the convent could send to prospective donors. It was one of the ways the convent supported itself. Jeanne took to the chore with delightful enthusiasm and produced some beautiful cards. Rather than a chore, it was as though Mother had given her a precious gift by directing her to create the cards. We had a small printing press and one of the sisters would run off multiple copies of the cards for mailing. There were two things that always stuck in my mind about the cards, however. The first was the artwork. It was very attractive but concerned the same topic on all of the cards. It was like her signature: deep peach colored roses, which Jeanne told me were her attempt at Sonia Roses, and also white camellias. She usually put the roses on various shades of beige backgrounds and the camellias on various shades of green and blue-green backgrounds. The other thing that I remember so vividly is the wording on one of the cards. I liked it so much I subjected it to memory. It was a Mother's Day card. The front flap showed the usual 'Happy Mothers Day,' greeting in fancy lettering, flanked with the rosebuds and camellias, and the first part of the wording, which said, 'Of all the creatures in the universe, God put the most amount of His own goodness and beauty into a mother's love.' And when you opened up the card, the left panel said, 'The proof is in all of the similarities between God and mothers.' Then the right panel read, 'They are both intensely concerned about their children's well-being and they both want their children to learn to say, 'Please,' and 'Thank you.'

"Most of the other cards were in poetic form, sometimes putting to rhyme meaningful well worn pious thoughts. Though I think some were original. However, all bore Jeanne's familiar Sonia Roses and white camellias.

Jeanne was also an accomplished pianist, so Mother assigned her to be the organist for our services and Masses. A couple of the other sisters had taken piano lessons as children but hadn't played an instrument for years and, consequently, struggled. I don't want to say badly... let me just say, they were not very good accompaniment. A few others had played other instruments in their school bands and orchestras, but, all in all, we were very much in need of someone with Jeanne's skills on a keyboard. Before Jeanne came, Mother had suggested that the sister playing the organ just use one finger for the melody. I don't think Jeanne ever played the organ before, but she made the transition from the piano with very little difficulty.

"The sisters enjoyed Jeanne's playing and a few asked Mother if we could sing the Divine Office prayers rather than simply reciting them. I heard Mother explaining to them that singing the Divine Office was against the rule of our order, but I think Mother wanted to sing the prayers too. A few days after the sisters made that request Mother announced that once a week Jeanne had agreed to spend some of her early evening recreation time playing the Gregorian Chant for that afternoon's Vesper prayers, and if any of the sisters wanted to spend some of their own recreation time saying the Divine Office prayers a second time silently to Jeanne's accompaniment, she wouldn't mind. Mother said she was certain God would not have given Jeanne her musical talents only to let them lay unappreciated and not enjoyed by His beloved People of God. She told us she did not want to scandalize us by a direct act of disobedience allowing us to sing the Divine Office, but she felt it was in the spirit of St. Francis who told us to love and enjoy God's natural gifts to us...and a musical talent like Jeanne's was certainly a manifestation of God's generosity.

"I might add here that at no time did Mother Superior ask Jeanne to give up any of her private prayer time. On occasion that issue became a subject of light amusement among the sisters, but never uncharitably. We knew she was praying ardently for the benefit of all of the souls in the world, and, since we were part of that group, we could only benefit from it.

"One morning, during coffee, I overheard Jeanne telling Mother that she wished the convent had a piano because some melodies had been running through her head and she wished she could work them out on a piano. She said she thought she might be able to put some lyrics to them for new hymns. She pointed out the organ was in the chapel and she didn't want to distract the sisters in their periods of prayer and adoration before the Blessed Sacrament. A week later a used upright piano was delivered to the convent. I found out later that Mother had called a frequent benefactor who had donated other items to the convent, and that very day, he saw an advertisement in a newspaper from a local university that was selling old musical instruments from their music department almost for the cost of moving them. Naturally, Jeanne was elated and immediately began putting her new melodies on paper and writing hymn type lyrics for the songs. I know I'm prejudiced, but I think they were beautiful. The sisters immediately started singing them at Masses and other occasions. All of the sisters decided that we would all say a special novena to St. Anthony for the benefactor who found and donated the piano. Probably because of the moving, it was slightly out of tune, but we were so delighted about receiving it and Jeanne's playing on it that the, 'slightly-out-of-tune' sound became an occasional source of good humored fun."

Sr. Mary Agnes then interrupted her tale saying that was as far into the story as Father Steve wanted her to go at that time and that she had to return to her duties in the convent. She did offer a short addendum, however, that I feel she could not allow herself to omit. She elucidated, "About Jeanne's piano playing; I have to add that it wasn't just the songs or the sound that was so enjoyable. I would watch Jeanne playing and it seemed like her fingers hardly touched the keys at all. When she was playing, the piano was definitely not a percussion instrument. Her hands just floated over the keyboard effortlessly; like, as I said, her fingers never made contact. But most importantly, everything she played increased and decreased in volume and speed in a way that made each song sound perfect. When I mentioned that to her, she just smiled humbly and uttered, 'Dynamics. That's what gives music its esthetics and esthetics is what makes music an art form. Dynamics have always been very important to me'"

Sister Mary Agnes concluded the interview by adding, "Jeanne's artistic skills at the piano and the organ are why Mother suggested that, if and when Jeanne took her vows, she should take the name, Sister St. Cecelia, which she eventually did." Then she inquired, "Do you know who Saint Cecelia was, Mr. Becks?"

When I indicated in the negative, Mother Superior explained, "Saint Cecelia is the Patron Saint of music, and probably musicians too, because she, herself, was purported to be a musician and, in religious art and folklore, was said to have played so beautifully that angels left heaven to come down to earth to listen to her music. That's why Mother suggested the religious name for Jeanne, but also why Jeanne, in her humility, resisted the suggestion, at least at first. But, eventually, out of obedience to Mother's wishes she reluctantly agreed. I don't think she was ever comfortable with the idea, but by the time she took the name, it didn't matter to her."

After Sister Mary Agnes had related this last bit of information I began gathering up my tape recorder and pad and, since I had already shut off the recorder, I decided to ignore the last remark. I accompanied the Mother Superior back to the vestibule from where we could see Father Steve sitting alone in the other parlor. The nun who had joined him earlier had obviously returned to the convent proper. Father joined us in the vestibule and after the usual, "Did everything go well?" inquiry and positive response we exchanged salutations and Father Steve and I left.

The first comment in the car on our way back came from Father Steve in the form of a simple, "Well... reaction?"

I was expecting a query of that sort, so I responded without hesitation, "A few reactions, actually. Naturally, I don't think I have to tell you that your sister seems like a very nice person. What probably struck me most was her open, outgoing personality. She was telling me the story of Jeanne Trudeau's early days in the convent as though I was an old friend. She didn't hesitate on anything... you know, weighing words or thoughts, or concerned about impressions the way people usually do when they meet someone for the first time. Her words just flowed from her mouth like she was eager to tell me everything about everything about Jeanne Trudeau. Was she always that openly conversant?" I asked.

"I really can't say," was the priest's response. "When I last knew her at home she was a young teenager busy trying to be a farm mother with all of the chores that job involved. I entered the Jesuit Order when she was only about sixteen. She was always reasonably pleasant, but I don't think she was happy until she entered the convent. My father knew she wanted to become a contemplative nun when she was quite young, but he needed her on the farm after our mother died. My feeling was that, for her sake, he was as anxious for her to enter as she was. She and our father were very close. My father was in the habit of saying a rosary after supper, while our mother did the dishes, and in good weather he would say it sitting on the circular bench that surrounded the trunk of a cherry tree that stood in the center of our yard. I can still see him there with little Agnes... this was when she was as young as three or four... sitting with him holding the part of the rosary that he had finished or hadn't gotten to yet and trying to say the prayers along with him. When he finished, they would often just sit there talking. They were both smiling constantly, so I assumed he was telling her happy things... probably about Mary and Jesus... possibly the Holy Family." Then he added, "I have to admit, the openness you've described surprises me a bit though. She and I haven't had a great deal of contact over the years, but we haven't avoided each other either. Our callings just didn't lean towards a lot of family togetherness. It's possible she wants Ron's story told as much as Ron did... because it's her friend Jeanne's story as well."

"Her living so long in a cloistered convent, I guess I assumed she would be more... I don't quite know how to phrase it... verbally subdued may be it," I conjectured reflectively.

Father Steve laughed, "Nun's behind cloistered walls do laugh, you know. I suspect that a few of them are quite witty and, when appropriate, even tell jokes."

For some reason this comment seemed funny and we both laughed out loud.

After a short pause I inquired, "Well, who's on tap for my next interview?"

"Sister Mary Agnes again," he quipped with a playful smile. I assume Sister only went as far today as I told her. I had two reasons for that. First, being Mother Superior, she has quite a few duties in addition to her normal contemplative activities and prayer life, so I didn't think it would be appropriate to take up too much of her time on any given day. Secondly, I thought it might be beneficial if I gave you a break at this point in the story so that you can ask any questions which you might have concerning the things Sister related thus far."

Actually, I failed to think of any except perhaps a clarification of Sister's last remark concerning Jeanne Trudeau's loss of concern or embarrassment about taking the religious name, Sister Saint Cecelia, to which Father Steve again evaded a direct answer, merely saying that it would become evident shortly in another interview.

When Father was assured that I had no further questions he began his own story telling, relating Ronald VanderLinde's conduct after his outburst at the convent. Again, Father Steve told me that, though his brother had given him permission to tell anyone who might be writing his biography anything he ever told him in the Sacrament of Penance, the priest could not bring himself to reveal such matters. He added, however, that there were things that happened outside of the confessional that he could talk about.

Father Steve started, "Ron came directly to see me from the convent. When I answered the door, he just stood there with his eyes glaring at mine, his face was red as a beet and he had an expression of pure hatred. I was so taken aback that I could neither move, nor speak. I didn't even know he was back from Europe.

"As I think I told you before, Ron was a total person. He loved and hated completely, without limit. He pronounced in the most demonstrative tone that I have ever heard, that he fully intended, not just to do as many evil things that he could, but, more importantly, to destroy goodness wherever he found it. He actually included a statement that was the most egregious remark I have ever witnessed. He declared, 'I understand that nuns consider themselves brides of Christ. Well I'm going to seduce every girl I can that is planning to become a nun, so, if any of them do become nuns, their heavenly bridegroom is going to get very used material.' He blared out all of this with tremendous force, then turned abruptly and left. Most of the evil he did do over the next year or so I cannot relate because I learned about it later, in the confessional. But a lot can be imagined and some of it you will learn in subsequent interviews."

As we approached my apartment I asked, "Where and with whom is my next interview after Sister Mary Agnes?"

Apparently, Father Steve had established a definite order for the interviews because he responded without hesitation, "As I said, the next one is with Sister Mary Agnes and that will be followed by an interview with another sister in the convent. This other sister prefers that you interview her indirectly. She understands the importance of the biography and how necessary what she has to tell you is to it, but she is quite shy and feels very awkward about her part in the story. I think we might be able to have you interview her through a screen similar to the confessional or something like that. Anyway, I'll call Mother Superior tomorrow to set up these two interviews and she and I will try to work out the required logistics."

At this, the car came to a halt in front of my building. Assuming our day's work together was finished, I began exiting the car. Father Steve, however, introduced one last piece of business. Reaching to the backseat of the car he brought forward an attaché case. Laying it on the seat between us, he opened it and took out a manila envelope from which he withdrew a photograph. Handing the photo to me he exclaimed, "I found this among Ron's things. I didn't know if or whether you would be interested in it, but you can use it, if you want... or not. When you're finished with it you can just put it with Jeanne Trudeau's letters for future storage."

I took the picture, which showed a pretty little girl standing in what appeared to be the living room of a modest home wearing a feminine flowered dress, but also wearing well-worn shoes. She was obviously posing for the camera, displaying an intense but entirely delightful smile. "Is this Jeanne Anne Trudeau?" I asked almost rhetorically, since I was pretty certain of the answer.

"Apparently," Father Steve responded, "at least according to the scribbling on the back."

At that remark I turned the photo over, revealing what Father Steve described as scribbling. As best I could comprehend the writing it said, "Jeanne Anne–May 12, 1921."

"I'll see if I want to use it in some way," I acknowledged and with that I hopped out of the car and entered the apartment building. The first thing I did when I reached my suite was to phone Helen at work. It was almost noon so I invited her to lunch and filled her in on the day's happenings.

I invited Helen to come to my place from work for an early supper and then spent the afternoon used-car shopping. Lo-and-behold, I was finally successful. For the first time in weeks, I had my own set of wheels again. And considering what I had been driving around in over the past several years, they seemed reasonably reliable.

Helen was her usual supportive self during this letter reading and interviewing period, and I kept her well abreast of the information I was garnering for the biography. She read all of the letters, listened to the tapes and did a reasonably decent job of translating the notes I had taken. She assured me that she was very interested in the whole thing, and I had no reason to doubt her. She never contributed anything directly to this project, but on occasion she would ask questions concerning things I had not considered. There were occasions when she offered explanatory comments concerning religious matters, which were quite helpful considering my lack of religious upbringing. Our relationship at the time and her positive attitude toward everything added an element of fun to the biography researching, all of which made me feel confident and comfortable during the process, at least at the beginning.

Also, my cousin and her husband were still out of town for which I was very grateful. And, lastly, I never opened a newspaper until I got back to work at the paper a few weeks later.

As Father Steve had planned, the next interview was with Sister Mary Agnes. As I learned, this interview was totally about Jeanne Trudeau and her first year as a contemplative nun. Because of this, I would like to spend a little time discussing the photograph that Father Steve gave me.

After supper that evening, during our conversations, I showed Helen the picture. She picked up on some very interesting details. We both laughed about the incongruity of the very feminine dress with the old shoes and the unbrushed, almost tomboyish hair. Helen mentioned the piano in the background and wondered if that might have been the instrument on which Jeanne began developing her future piano skills. I acknowledged that it very well might have been. But what struck both of us most was the intensity in the expression on her face and in her eyes. I told Helen about Father Steve's comment that both Jeanne Trudeau and Ron Vander-Linde were, what he called, total people, who not only lived life to the full, but lived it passionately and aggressively. I also added Father's comment that Ron loved and hated completely, without reservation. At that, Helen abruptly blurted out, "That's it! That's the expression on Jeanne Trudeau's face and especially in her eyes. She is living with absolute intensity."

When I looked at the photograph with that in mind I nodded my head in agreement, but also uttered a disclaimer, "But, according to the date on the back she was only about four or five years old. Wouldn't 'living with total intensity' require more maturity, or, at least, more experience than a girl of that age would possess?"

Helen agreed, but mused, "Some things just don't make perfect sense... especially when you're dealing with matters of the soul."

Naturally, I ended that conversation quickly. However, my instinctive efforts at skeptical agnosticism went for naught, as I was to find out within a few days. As I mentioned earlier, the next interview was to be with Sister Mary Agnes and concerned Jeanne Trudeau's first year in the convent, but, sadly, it also concerned her last year on this earth.

CHAPTER *Nine*

It was two days before Father Steve got back to me. He apologized for the delay, explaining that a few unexpected things came up at the University which required his attention. He acknowledged that he was finally able to call his sister to set up those next two interviews, which he tentatively scheduled for the following two mornings, pending my approval. He explained that the convent activities only allowed the sisters a little over an hour of uncommitted time starting at nine in the morning. He also offered to drive me over on those two days, but I was delighted to inform him that I was no longer among the carless in our society and also agreed to that schedule. He expressed his happiness for me but added that if anything adverse happened, I should give him a call. Then he requested that I contact him each afternoon following the interviews to see how they went and to answer any question that might come up. With that, the priest offered me God's speed and, though I did not realize it at the time, he sent me blissfully into the lion's den.

I arrived about fifteen minutes early and was greeted by the External nun who informed me that, "Mother will be available at nine, but, if you are interested, you can wait for her in the chapel. We have perpetual adoration." She then directed me verbally around the outside of the building to the side door of the chapel in a manner that expressed her belief that, of course, I would want to spend my waiting time in the chapel praying or something like that.

My reaction was a mental, "When in Rome. . ." so I followed her directions and entered the side door of the chapel. The interior decor was much as would be expected: simple, definitely not ornate with wood sidewall paneling similar to that in the vestibule and parlors. It was not very large. There were the usual wooden church pews that could seat fifty or so worshipers. A few small chandeliers and a lesser number of minimally artistic, mostly clear, stained glass windows provided the little light that there was. Prayer books or hymnals lay in the pews, but I questioned whether they could be read unless the sun was blaring outside.

The altar was extremely plain, apparently constructed of wood that could not take another coat of varnish and was sometime in the past simply painted over with white paint. Above the altar was an opening in which stood a reasonably large golden object with a flat, white, circular article in the center from which a golden, sunburst effect spread outward. Though I had been to Catholic churches, or at least one church, with Helen and had attended services there, I had never seen this object. On reflection, I surmised it was probably the monstrance, or one like it, that Sister Mary Agnes said Ron VanderLinde threw against the wall during his eruption in the chapel. From the Mother Superior's description of that upheaval I assumed that there was a second area similar to the one in which I was standing and that the two were separated by the altar, the other one being for worship by the cloistered nuns.

Though I was certain that the External who directed me to the chapel expected me to spend my waiting time in prayer and meditation, I actually spent it mentally turning the chapel around and, in my imagination, watching young VanderLinde yelling and throwing things against the walls, albeit to the horrified nuns, sacred things.

After a while the External entered my side of the chapel from the cloistered entrance and after genuflecting towards the altar whispered, "If you go back out and over to the front door, Mother will see you there." Then she genuflected again and exited back into the cloistered side of the chapel. On my way out I almost genuflected too, but then caught myself muttering, "That's carrying the 'When in Rome...' thing a little too far."

Sister Mary Agnes met me at the door and after a cordial greeting led me into the same parlor wherein we conducted the first interview. I requested her approval again for my use of the recorder, which she of-course-ishly granted and we were on our way.

Sister Mary Agnes began relating Jeanne Anne Trudeau's life in the cloister in the same manner with which she left it a few days earlier: openly conversant... almost bubbling. "As I ended the other day, Jeanne fit into contemplative life very well. She obviously enjoyed the chores Mother gave her and though some were creative, utilizing Jeanne's artistic talents, Mother saw to it that the new postulant also shared in the more mundane necessities of communal life such as scrubbing floors and washing dishes. And Jeanne took to this too, which was no surprise to anyone." At this,

Sister chuckled, "A lot of people don't realize this, but in a contemplative convent where everyone spends so much time reading spiritual books and quietly praying, physical labor can be very refreshing and almost fun."

I had noticed when we first met that day that Sister Mary Agnes had brought a folder with her to the interview. Though I was curious as to what was in it, I deliberately ignored the folder, assuming that, if what it contained were pertinent, she would mention it at the appropriate time, which, apparently, was now. "But it was her artistic activities that were the most impressive," the nun continued. "I mentioned her greeting cards and holy cards the last time you were here, but there were some much more impressive creations." At this, Sister Mary Agnes opened the folder and handed me several hand written pages explaining, "Mother asked the Sisters to put down on paper some of their personal thoughts and feelings about contemplative life and especially their lives in this community. She explained that the diocesan weekly newspaper was planning to print a 'Vocation' supplement and that the bishop was asking each religious house in the diocese to draw up a page, or at least a half page, explaining the particulars about their order and its activities in a manner that might be appealing to any prospective young candidate to whom God may have blessed with a calling to the priesthood, or brotherhood or sisterhood. She added that she considered it her responsibility to make up the actual advertisement... she thought that Ad was an inappropriate word for an invitation to religious life, but the only one she could think of... however, she felt she could use some help from the rest of us. Then the Holy Spirit must have been talking to Mother because she added, 'On reflection this morning it came to me that most people probably see our solemn vows as negative things... things we don't do. Maybe one of you can describe them in the positive way in which we see them.'

"Over the next week Mother received several papers from the sisters for which she was obviously very grateful. But the day before she was directed to submit the newspaper ad concerning our convent to the diocesan office, she seemed disturbed because Jeanne hadn't turned in anything. When she questioned the postulant why she hadn't contributed her thoughts, Jeanne simply told her that she had been working on her ideas and was almost finished. The next morning Jeanne gave Mother the sheets of paper I just gave you. This happened in the hall outside of the chapel. After handing the papers to Mother Superior, Jeanne simply walked back to her cell. Mother started reading them right there in the hall. Several of us were coming and going to and from the chapel. By the time Mother reached the second or third page, it was obvious that our usually quite stoic Abbess was becoming very disturbed and when she finished, she rushed into the chapel sobbing uncontrollably. Several of us followed her in, naturally concerned. We had never seen our Mother Superior that emotional. She was always under control and to see her so upset frightened us. She fell down onto a kneeler in the pew starring up at the Blessed Sacrament, weeping out loud and murmuring, 'They're so beautiful!" She turned to us and repeated, 'They're so beautiful." Then she turned back to the Blessed Sacrament, 'Oh, Lord, Thank You for sending us Jeanne. Thank You! Thank You!'"

Sister Mary Agnes broke off the narrative at that point to inform me that she could only stay until 10:30 AM and that the amount of the story which Father Steve had instructed her to cover that day was quite lengthy, so she asked if I could wait with reading this material until I returned home. She also added that, in her opinion, the various items were very important. Naturally, I agreed to wait.

Sister Mary Agnes described that final "advertisement" for the "Vocation Supplement," which the then Mother Superior drafted as first stating the name of the religious order and the local address followed by the statement, "'Our cloistered Sisters, unite daily with Our Divine Lord in contemplative prayer and penance and, through our faithful adherence to our four blessed and solemn vows, care for souls everywhere.'" Sister Mary Agnes continued, "Then Mother included this material Jeanne had written followed by the invitation, 'If you feel God may be calling you to join with us to live the joy of these vows now and forever, you are welcome to visit our home or simply contact us for more information.'"

I did wait to read the papers until later but they are appropriate to this section of the narrative and, therefore, they are being inserted here:

The Blessed Paradoxes Of Contemplative Solemn Vows

Each of the solemn Vows of Contemplative Orders involves a Holy Paradox that manifests the creative nature of our omniscient God.

POVERTY: Our most basic instinct of self-preservation instills in each human being a strong intrinsic concern for the necessities of our physical existence and well being. This instinctive need generates in all God acknowledging individuals the virtue of hope that our loving Creator will provide what we need to survive in this life. However, the virtue of faith of the Contemplative, which is the foundation of our Vow of Poverty, supercedes the virtue of hope, which is now no longer necessary for the concerns of our human needs and replaces it with an absolute trust in the caring of our ever-loving God.

CHASTITY: The noblest and most appealing dream of any healthy woman is motherhood...to experience all that is involved in the nurturing and caring for those precious beings issued from her own womb so that they may know and love and be loved. And yet, our Vow of Chastity, which negates this personal dream, rather than eliminating its fulfillment exacerbates it to the extreme. Through our Vow of Chastity we take on the brideship of Our Divine Savior, which then, through our union with his Sacred Heart grants us motherhood of all the human souls in God's creation.

OBEDIENCE: The most difficult of our Solemn Vows is most easily recognized as difficult. The human will, which is necessarily free in order to love...to freely choose to sacrifice one's self for another...is asked through our Vow of Obedience to use the freedom of our wills to choose to surrender that freedom for the blessed harmony and peace of our loving home.

ENCLOSURE: By willing vow we freely choose to stay within the cloistered walls, but not as prisoners...the opposite is true. Through loving prayer and holy penance the Contemplative, restricted within the cloistered walls, so unites personal self, not just with Christ, but also with all of the members of His Mystical Body. Thus, with compassion and empathetic love, her spirit flies out from the cloister, like a beautiful cloud covering the entire world with love.

Love has always been a Blessed Paradox: In loving others, we receive our greatest happiness by doing things that give them happiness.

R. Francis Becks

A Sonnet On The Noble Vow Of Poverty

When those with newly vows of poverty
    Lay full their trust in Providential Grace
They sudden know a mystic liberty
    Made real by faith's secure embrace.

We know through faith all needs our God will fill;
    A banishing of hope as requisite for such;
Thus leaving love alone to prepare the will,
    The heart and mind to feel the Spirit's touch.

Yes, hope, a wholesome virtue, they no more
    Have need: for faith has taken charge
To free the eager soul but to adore
    And give and love and virtues breadths enlarge.

    Sweet Poverty gives lightness to the air:
    A freedom rich, both blissful and most rare.

On The Joys Of Universal Motherhood Within The Contemplatives Vow Of Chastity

The happiness and joy that now o'erflow
    This soul know all the boundless bounds
    That only human hopes can know
And move beyond but shallow sights and sounds.

Such joy, by mystic view, is only born
    Of mother loved and loving, and, relieved
    Of pain is from the womb soft torn
With spirit's bliss, since spir'tually conceived.

And loving such, without condition known,
    Is mothered too by all the good
    That we behold in Christ alone
And beauty formed as only goodness could.

Our motherhood's reflection shows
    A finite image of our God.
    And joys of heaven such love knows,
Will always know, while on this soil we trod.

A Sonnet On The Vow Of Obedience

This willing will, so eager to surrender all
    For love of Christ, by nature, still resists
Surrender of itself. Yet, our communal call
    To harmony obedience insists.

With ease our love can offer life as gift.
    And, yet, how hard accepting this priority
Requiring outward peace with inner rift
    Ev'n to wise and just authority.

Great joy! Our wills, by nature free to choose; to love
    In holy paradox do freely choose
To gift our freedom to our God above.
    Yet giving all, a nothing do we lose.

    Most difficult of gifts begets the greatest joy;
    As loving gift will e'er the heart and soul buoy.

A Short Ode On Our Sweet Vow Of Enclosure

Oh, blessed solitude in our enclosured house
Where silence sings those holy songs
    With beautied words of love sent from the Dove
And melodies that only angels know.
    Removed to live a deeper union with the world;

Drawn inward in our prayer
    The fuller to embrace all other souls without
Through union with the beauty of His Mystic Self.

Sweet silence; blessed solitude; all virtues hope;

A depth of soul made deeper and a universal love
That grows with limitation that is limitless
Through love of Christ...
Through love of Christ!

My loving God!
Through loving Christ....

Sister Mary Agnes obviously enjoyed telling the accomplishments of her fellow nun whom, in my opinion, she was painting as too good to be true. And for quite awhile I simply let that aspect of the chronicle be. But, finally, I politely interrupted to point out her unrealistic description, or perhaps more accurately, caricature of her young nun-to-be friend. To my surprise, Sister Mary Agnes did not disagree with the exception I took to her portrayal of Jeanne Trudeau and in agreeing blurted, "You're absolutely right." However, then she added, "But the non-realism of Jeanne Trudeau was not an attribute of her character, but in her commitment to us and the contemplative life. When she first entered the convent her primary interest was to the contemplative life. But after Ron's outburst, her total concern and dedication were directed to my brother and his eternal salvation, which resulted in Jeanne leaving us far too soon... which brings us to the next major episode.

"Two or three months after Jeanne joined us here at the convent, Mother noticed her wincing a bit from some apparent pain. When Mother questioned her about it, at first, Jeanne passed it off as nothing. However, it soon became too obvious. So, after a day or so, Mother told Jeanne that she was setting up an appointment for her to be examined by a doctor. Jeanne offered no objection and, since Mother had noticed that Jeanne and I had started to develop a friendship, she assigned me to accompany Jeanne to the doctor's office.

"When we arrived for the appointment I asked Jeanne if she wanted me to accompany her for the examination and she shrugged indifferently, 'If you like.' The doctor was quite jovial. When he entered the examination room the first thing he said was, 'Well, why are we here today, ladies?'

"Jeanne responded illusively, 'Mother Superior wanted me to see a doctor.'

"The physician looked at her inquisitively and asked again, 'Why?'

"This query was directed at me as much as Jeanne so I answered, 'She's been having a lot of pain lately.'

"'Ah, now we're getting somewhere,' the physician responded. And where is this pain we've been having lately?'

"Jeanne reached her arm around to her back and pointed to an area on the right side above the hip. At this the doctor instructed Jeanne to get into an examination gown and sit on the table and then stated he would be back shortly.

"When he returned he asked Jeanne how long the pain had been there and if it were constant or if it came and went. Jeanne's answers were, 'For a couple of weeks.' And, 'It was constant.'

"'Have you noticed any other strange things lately?' the doctor inquired.

"Jeanne's response startled me. 'I think the water in the bowl is pink when I finish going to the toilet.'

"The doctor immediately began pressing her abdomen. As he did, he inquired, 'How's your appetite lately?'

"Jeanne shrugged her shoulders and muttered, 'I haven't been very hungry. I figured it was God helping me with my fasting.

"'How about fatigue? Do you feel unusually weak or more tired than usual?'

"Jeanne answered, 'I thought that it was because I was having difficulty adapting to the 12:30 AM Matins prayers.'

"With this the physician completed the physical part of the visit and elucidated, 'There is a lump in your abdomen that could indicate something serious.' The doctor admitted that he could not be absolutely certain what it was, but that the problem was probably in the kidneys. He recommended that Jeanne be checked out by a kidney specialist. Then he lectured, 'You know, if you lose your appetite or feel tired it might not be Divine intervention or a lack of sleep. It might be your body trying to tell you that there's something wrong inside, which needs fixing.' He concluded with, 'While you're getting dressed, I'll have my girl set up an appointment with a good renal doctor.'

"Two days later Jeanne and I were in the examination room of a kidney specialist. After an in-office x-ray, several tests and various examination procedures the doctor told Jeanne to get dressed and that we should meet him in his office. In his office the doctor invited us both to sit and then began by asking Jeanne if anyone in her family had ever been diagnosed with cancer. Jeanne replied, 'Yes, they said my father died of kidney cancer.' The doctor's eyes opened a bit. Then he interjected, 'People your age usually don't succumb to renal cancer. However, there is evidence that there could be an exception to that rule when there is a family tendency such as when a parent or grandparent has acquired the decease. It appears from the x-rays and the tests that you have a malignancy in that right kidney. The only way to know for sure is to perform an exploratory operation, and, if the biopsy proves positive we can remove the diseased kidney and any other tissues that are affected. We can hope that, if the initial diagnosis is correct, the cancer has not spread beyond the lymph nodes, which would mean your prognosis is good. And, of course, with only one kidney you could live to a ripe old age.'

"Up to this point, everything was congenial and the doctor displayed a gentle, professional concern for his patient with the obvious intent of curing her illness and eliminating her pain. And, during all of this, including the kidney specialist's diagnosis and prognosis, Jeanne sat calmly with an expression that I would describe as mild indifference. I, on the other hand, was terrified. But, for Jeanne's sake, I tried to hide my devastating concerns. However, all of our demeanors would soon abruptly change.

"The doctor explained with a sympathetic voice, 'It's best, naturally that we perform the exploratory procedure as soon as possible, so that if it is cancer and if it has not yet spread, we can get rid of it before it does. I'll have my secretary set things up at the hospital and she or the hospital will contact you about the when, where and what you'll need to know to prepare.'

"Then the doctor began flaunting the many medical advances, especially in the field of renal disease, that had been made since the beginning of the century. It became rapidly obvious that he was extremely proud of his profession as well as his personal accomplishments therein. He started telling us of the many patients that he had cured of different kidney ailments and especially those whom he had diagnosed and cured of renal cancer. He even gave us a medical history lesson. He expounded, 'You know, the first x-ray taken for medical purposes was done in 1906, and it was of the kidney. And we've come a long way since then.'

"Jeanne listened quietly to all of this and then interjected, 'your diligence speaks highly of your patient concern and dedication to your healing profession, doctor, and your successes are certainly admirable, but I'm okay. I was just curious to know what was causing the pain. But now that I know, I'm fine.'

"At that the doctor became very stern, 'what do you mean you're fine!

You're not fine! You could have cancer and, if untreated, you could be dead in a year... two at the most. And, let me tell you, young lady, it will be a very, very painful death.'

"Unbelievably, Jeanne smiled and reacted like the doctor had given her some very good news. She said simply, 'Thank you, Doctor,' then turning to me, 'I'd like to go home now.'

"The doctor became furious. 'You can't do this young lady.' He turned to me, 'Isn't it a sin to risk your life like that?' Then he turned back to Jeanne, 'I'm going to contact your Mother Superior and tell her to order you to have the operation.'

"By this time we were at the doorway. Jeanne repeated her, 'Thank you, Doctor,' and we left.

"We had walked to the corner and taken a streetcar to the doctor's office. So when the appointment was finished we returned via the same route. Jeanne apparently underestimated the doctor's tenacity. The doctor must have jumped in his car as soon as we left his office because when we got back to the convent, he was standing in the parlor animatedly attempting to convince Mother Superior of the seriousness of Jeanne's possible condition and the necessity of an exploratory operation. God, forgive me. I may have committed a sin of rash judgment, but the thought ran through my mind that he saw Jeanne's rejection of his proposal to operate on her more as a lost opportunity to show off his medical skills to the world than as a failed chance to cure a patient. With that possibility, the famous phrase of St. John Chrysostom came to mind, 'Vanity of vanities, and all is vanity.'

"The doctor became so vehement and so loud that he frightened the sister who was serving as External that day. When Mother saw her distress she nodded to her to leave, which she did in a hurry.

"The doctor presented argument after argument why Jeanne should undergo his exploratory operation explaining that if he finds cancer he can probably cure her. He admitted to Mother that there would certainly be some follow up radiation treatment but that would be over in a while.

"As I said, he was loud and animated but the three of us sisters just stood there quietly and motionless, which probably made him more frustrated, and in turn made him more loud and animated. Finally, Mother interrupted him, 'I understand, doctor, and I will speak to our postulant, here, about your proposal. I'll get back to you when everything is settled.'

"Mother started walking to the door in an obvious but polite invitation for him to leave, but he refused and continued his tirade. At this,

Mother interrupted again, 'I'm sorry, doctor. I don't want to be rude, but we are due in chapel shortly for Vespers. I must insist that you leave. As I said, I will notify you of the result of our discussion on the matter.'

"At this, the doctor was more than frustrated, but he was helpless to the demands of our prayer schedule, so he finally left but not without a last insistence on the need for the operation as the door closed behind him.

On our way into the chapel to say Vespers, Mother suggested we pray over the situation and then said we would discuss it in her office after Benediction. Through hand gestures, Mother indicated that the invitation to her office included me.

"When we got seated in her office a while later, Mother began speaking to Jeanne in a tone that was not stern, but was definitely serious. 'I wanted Sister Mary Agnes to join us because I don't seem to be receiving complete answers when it comes to your health.'

"'I'm sorry, Mother,' Jeanne began, 'but everything is fine. You needn't concern yourself with my health.'

"Mother appeared frustrated. 'Why did you go to see the doctors if you weren't planning to follow their advice?'

"Jeanne answered in an extremely calm tone, 'I just wanted to know exactly what God had in store for me. Now I know and it's fine.'

"Mother was becoming perturbed. 'Since the doctor told me of your reaction to his advice, I've been trying to figure out what to do with you. I've never had a situation where one of our sisters refused medical treatment, especially when it involved something as serious as possible cancer. As Abbess of this convent, one of my most important duties is to see that the sisters in my charge remain healthy and receive the best medical care when they need it. The question of whether I have the power under our vow of obedience to order a sister to accept the recommendations of her doctor has never come up. The sisters have always been eager to do what their doctors say is necessary for their good health. I don't know if I have the power or the right or the duty to order you. God forgive me...all the way through Vespers and Benediction I wasn't saying the Office or worshiping Christ in the Blessed Sacrament. I was thinking about your reluctance, and my prayers were simply for enlightenment as to whether or not to order you to have the exploratory operation.'

"Mother hesitated there and then added, 'Will you explain to me why you do not want to follow the doctor's orders?'

Jeanne hesitated before answering. Then she looked at me thoughtfully and then back at Mother Superior. 'I can tell you, Mother, but it is very personal.' Turning back to me again she asked softly, 'Sister Mary Agnes, can I speak to Mother alone for a little bit?'

"There was no way I wanted to leave at this point. I wanted to know Jeanne's reasons just as much as Mother did, but I couldn't refuse her request for privacy, so I reluctantly rose and exited the room. I closed the door firmly, making enough noise to make Jeanne and Mother believe the door was closed and then I opened it slightly, in the hope that I could hear Jeanne's explanation, which subterfuge was successful on all counts, at least until later when Jeanne exited Mother's office.

"What Jeanne told Mother takes some degree of faith to believe, but if you knew Jeanne and have faith, it's easy to believe.

"Jeanne started with a directive, which sounded strange coming from a postulant and spoken to her Mother Superior. 'You must never tell anyone what I'm going to tell you, Mother. I told Bishop Simpson in confession and he said that if what I told him was a fact and not an elusion, such things are personal, between God and an individual soul... that they're for that soul's spiritual edification and not for public knowledge... and, consequently, I was never to reveal it to anyone else except for a very important reason. I've been praying to the Holy Spirit to help me know whether this is an important enough reason and I think it is. But you must promise me that you will never tell anyone else.'

"I waited for Mother to scold Jeanne for giving her Mother Superior orders, but, remarkably, there was no rebuff. Mother must have affirmed Jeanne's stipulation with a nod or other gesture because Jeanne went right into her tale. 'Do you remember the day Ron VanderLinde broke into the cloister and the chapel and desecrated the Blessed Sacrament? Well, after I picked up the Hosts and put them on the altar, I stayed in the chapel to pray for Ron... that God would forgive him and that He would give Ron the graces necessary for repentance. Ron was so angry when he left here, and I knew he wouldn't get over my rejection of his proposal of marriage easily. I know Ron. He is a good person but I knew he would hold the bitterness in his heart for a long time... maybe forever. So I spent some time that day asking God to give me penances to earn the graces that Ron would need to be truly sorry for what he did. But then I remembered learning in a course I took that St. Thomas Aquinas said that no one could earn grace... that grace is a free gift from God. However, he also said that if God gives someone grace because of the prayers of someone else, it's not because those prayers earned the grace but, rather, God did what the prayer wanted as sort of a favor to a friend. So I decided that I would spend the rest of my life becoming the closest friend to God that I could be, so that He would grant my prayers for Ron. And what better way to become someone who God the Father would want to befriend than to become as much as possible like God the Son... like the Father's Son, Jesus Christ. And all I could think of was Christ's willingness to accept His horrible suffering and death for all of the souls in the world. I thought, if I would be willing to accept a horrible suffering and death for just one soul... Ron's, God the Father would see me as a miniature reflection of his Son and He would want me to be His friend and, if I was His friend, He would grant my prayers for the grace Ron needs to be sorry for what he did in the chapel. Our Divine Lord suffered and died to redeem all the souls who ever lived. I can't actually redeem any souls. But, if I unite my pain and my death with Christ's, God might let me share in one soul's redemption... in Ron's. So I asked God to let me suffer and die a painful death for the grace of Ron's salvation.'

"There was a short pause. Then I heard Mother's voice, 'That's very deep. And it certainly sounds very generous of you. But I'm not a theologian, so I don't know whether what you're saying and praying for agrees with Church teaching. Have you discussed these thoughts with Bishop Simpson?' Mother questioned.

"'Oh, yes,' Jeanne blurted out in what sounded like enthusiasm. 'And he said what I proposed was probably all right theologically. But that's not all I told him.'

"Mother cut in again, 'And am I going to be as agonized as I am now from what you've told me thus far?' She queried. 'I'll tell you, the prospects of watching you or anyone as young as you suffering and dying a painful death is not at all attractive, especially for those of us who have come to enjoy you and love you and all of your wonderful talents. Consequently, what you've told me so far has not convinced me to let you avoid a cure for your apparent kidney illness and I think I'll have to say no.'

"Standing outside of Mother's office door I almost cheered when I heard Mother's very rational argument for making Jeanne let the doctor operate.

"The thought of watching my newly acquired friend suffer a painful death was agonizing. My eavesdropping took me on an emotional rollercoaster from the depths of imagining Jeanne dying of cancer to her rescue through Mother's conclusion that she should seek the means of a cure.

"But then Jeanne rendered everything thus far, irrelevant. She completed what she had admitted to her confessor. 'What I've told you thus far, Mother, is what was running though my mind and heart during the evening and early morning hours in the chapel after Ron burst into the convent. Then something happened. And, as I told Bishop Simpson, I don't know whether it really happened, or if I simply fell asleep and dreamed it. In either case, it was too real not to be God telling me the things He did. I found myself in a long hall with a door at the end. The door was open and through the doorway I saw a brilliant, beautiful light. It had a slightly golden hue. Though I wasn't able to step through the doorway, I knew if I did, I would be engulfed in the Light, and that it would be everywhere infinitely in all directions. And I knew the Light was the infinite Goodness that is God and the infinite beauty that radiates from Him. As I said, I couldn't step through the doorway, but I heard a beautiful voice say, 'Because of our love for Him, so be it!'

"The voice said, 'Because of our love for him.' If the voice would have said, 'Because of your love,' I might have thought the whole experience was staged by the devil to flatter my ego and seduce me into a sin of pride, thinking that I could save Ron. But the voice said, 'our love'... meaning God's love is doing the redeeming and my love is just attached to it, kind of. At any rate, I believe God was telling me that I could and would suffer and die and would be able to unite my suffering and dying with Christ's for Ron's salvation... and the graces for that salvation would be given by God to Ron because of my prayers as a gift to me, as His friend.'

"I was still standing in the hallway outside of Mother's office, but I now wondered if I wasn't actually asleep and just dreaming... and a dream that was both beautiful and nightmarish. Jeanne's offer to suffer and die for Ron was one of the most beautiful things I had ever heard. And, yet, the thought of her suffering and dying from a painful death like the doctor described was terrible. I waited anxiously for Mother's response, but there wasn't any. Suddenly I realized that Mother probably couldn't respond. She probably didn't think she had a right to say no to Jeanne's intentions, but she couldn't bring herself to actually say, 'Yes,' either because to do so was to condemn Jeanne to the awful suffering. But, of course, by not saying anything, Mother was, in fact, giving Jeanne tacit approval.

"I was standing quite close to the door hoping Mother would say something that might discourage Jeanne's plan when the door swung open and I was confronted face to face by Jeanne, who became obviously aware that the door was not shut all the way and that I had probably heard most, if not everything, of her conversation with Mother Superior. As I stepped back in embarrassment Jeanne simply closed the door behind her and inquired, 'Did you hear much?'

"'Everything,' I admitted sheepishly.

"She just admonished without expression, 'Then, I have to tell you that you can never relate any of the things I told Mother to anyone... ever.'

"I nodded my head in agreement, and that was the last time she and I ever talked about that incident, nor have I told anyone else until today... not even my brother, Steve. When Steve first notified me about Ron's desire that a biography be written and told me that I would be required to relay to someone, such as you, about Jeanne's experiences at our convent, I've been agonizing over the question of whether I should tell you what I had promised Jeanne I would never tell anyone. But I knew that the information was absolutely necessary if Ron and Jeanne's story was to be told, and, since I remember Jeanne telling Mother that Bishop Simpson qualified his instruction to Jeanne about not relating her mystical experiences unless there was an important reason, I thought this might be such an important reason. I've been praying to the Holy Spirit for guidance ever since Steve called. God forgive me if I'm wrong by telling you.

Sister Mary Agnes broke off the narrative for a short while. I was not certain whether she was simply gathering her thoughts before continuing or giving her throat a little rest. During this short break, I deliberated about Jeanne's "mystical experience" for a few seconds. Needless to say, the deliberation made me feel very uncomfortable... so much so that, in an impulse of abject cowardice, I even considered pulling the plug on the interview. It took considerable courage to simply stay in my seat and continue listening. "Mystical experiences," were not part of my reality, nor did I want them to be.

Fortunately, Sister Mary Agnes broke my negative musing with the continuation of Jeanne's narrative. "A year or two later I respectfully confronted Mother about her decision to allow Jeanne her fateful resolve, and Mother said that this was the most difficult decision she faced during her tenure as Abbess of the convent and by far the most painful. Needless to say, it was equally painful for me and most of the other sisters too."

With that, Sister Mary Agnes picked up the saga again. "In the subsequent months, Jeanne tried to hide the pain and we tried to ignore her wincing, since it was obviously instinctive and she wasn't able to hide it. Mother did cut down on her physical chores while still leaving enough to allow our postulant to feel useful. However, Jeanne was able to continue her greeting and holy card creations unabated. And, of course, she continued playing the piano and organ. Which brings us to this." "With this," meant another set of papers, which Sister withdrew from the folder she had brought to our interview... only these sheets were obvious musical compositions. The score showed handwritten notes on the usual staff lines and hand printed lyrics with a title printed at the top, which read, 'DEAR LORD.' Sister Mary Agnes explained, "I also brought a few samples of Jeanne's songs and poems with me. This is an Offertory hymn, which she composed within the first few months she was with us... not too long after we received delivery of the donated piano. The Sisters loved it and we still sing it quite often during Mass. I had one of the Sisters, who took piano lessons for a few years as a child, make a copy, so you can take this one with you. I want to keep the original here."

(Following is the copy of the manuscript "DEAR LORD." Some of the handwritten lyrics are a little difficult to decipher so with Helen's help translating, I typed up what we thought the lyrics should read. That follows the musical score.)

Dear Lord

Dear Lord, here are my labors; they're yours now.
Here are my sorrows; refresh me.
Here is the peace that you promised.
Here is the heart that you won.
Dear Lord, make my eyes mirrors of beauty.
Make my voice sing only love songs.
Make my ears hear all who need me.
Make my heart one with your own.
Dear Lord, you are the way leading.
Dear Lord, you are the light guiding;
Dear Lord, you are the truth that we long for;
All that I am is now you.
All that I am is now you.

Sister Mary Agnes continued thoughtfully, "I don't want to leave anything out, but I don't want to overwhelm you with too much detail, either." As she handed me another paper she explained, "This is another poem I would like to give you. But this one was written about six months later... well after Jeanne's health started fading. She began getting weak and started to require more bedtime. On occasions like this I asked Mother if I could help Jeanne with any of the things she couldn't handle for herself. To my delight, Mother assigned me that duty, which wasn't a duty at all, but a real joy. There was a problem, however. Some of the other sisters were sort of envious. One told me only half joking, 'With what your doing for Jeanne, she'll probably feel more grateful to you than to the rest of us when she gets to heaven and you'll get the benefit of most of her prayers of gratitude.' So, during a recreation period when everyone was present I made a point of asking Jeanne to pray for all of the sisters equally when she sees Our Divine Lord in paradise. It was the first time any of us openly mentioned Jeanne's malady and her prospective near term entry into heaven. Everyone looked at Jeanne to see how she took reference to her impending death and Jeanne responded perfectly and in complete accord with Jeanne as Jeanne. She chuckled and said, I'll make all of you a deal. I'll promise to remember each of you constantly to Our Lord, if you remember me in your prayers occasionally.' We all laughed too. After that we were relaxed about the topic of her illness and prospective death.

"Mother asked Jeanne occasionally whether she wanted her to ask the doctor to prescribe something to relieve the pain, but there wasn't much in the form of pain relief in those days and Jeanne told Mother that she wanted to endure as much pain as she could. She said, 'I'm not brave and I may not be able to take too much pain... certainly not as much as Our Savior did on the cross. But I want to try to endure as much as I can. I'll let you know when I can't take any more. The unseen problem was that on some nights the pain kept Jeanne awake. When this happened for a week or so at a time, Jeanne told me that she would get down in the dumps. She said the worst part of those feelings was that she had a hard time praying and sometimes felt very alone... like even God had forsaken her. But she said what consoled her during those periods was that she thought that was what Christ was probably going through on the cross when he yelled out, 'Father' why hast Thou forsaken Me?' She said she was hoping in those depressed moods that God was giving her an opportunity to share in that part of Christ's suffering. She also added that, even in the worst of those feelings, she somehow was able to feel close to the Blessed Mother and that's why she wrote the poem I just gave you. Again, I had one of the sisters make that copy, so that I can keep the original. Sister added, "That one's short, so you can read it now if you like," which I did. (The poem follows.)

A Sonnet To Mother Mary
(In gratitude for her counsel during those hours of spiritual darkness)

When that veil of gray drops heavily o'er my soul;
   When day is night and night seems without end;
   When distant church bells raise their mournful knoll
   To note another hour I did spend,
Ill-spent, wand'ring through that wretched state
   Unsensing of God's love. When I would grope
   To find a something that would, at least, abate
   The pain, or offer then some light... some hope.
When naught can then that loneliness dispel.
   When I would seek the way I cannot find,
   Or then some chance laid landmark that could tell
   A weary soul where the road would wind.
Tis then you are the sole star of night;
   In my universe of nothingness... a light.

"Bishop Simpson asked Mother verbally if there was some way Jeanne could take her vows. But Mother explained that the six years as a postulant and novice were set by Rome and that she thought probably the Pope, himself, was the only one who could shorten that time. The Bishop thought for a few seconds and then declared quite forcefully, 'I'm going on a pilgrimage to Rome in a couple of weeks with a group of pious souls from our diocese and somehow I'm going to ask the Pope for permission to rescind that wait for our young postulant. After all, the poor woman is dying. She's not going to take her vows and then change her mind in a few days on her deathbed. The God I believe in is much more flexible than that.' Mother told him to go ahead and try but not to give it much hope. Others had tried unsuccessfully before.

Sister Mary Agnes broke off here for an almost humorous interjection, "You know, Mr. Becks, The Church has a long standing reputation for, "moving exceedingly slow." But what a lot of people don't realize is that, when the Holy Spirit wants to, He can see to it that His Church can move exceedingly fast also... and this was one of the latter cases... which I will get to in a moment. But first, there is one last incident that I would like to relay.

"Jeanne really deteriorated over the next few weeks. She could hardly do anything for herself, so I moved my straw mattress into her room and laid it on the floor so I would be there if she needed anything during the night. As I told you earlier, there were periods where she wasn't able to sleep because of the pain and she would become extremely depressed. One morning she asked me to hand her a tablet of blank sheet music and a sheet of paper on which she had scribbled a poem, both of which she had kept in her writing desk drawer. I had never seen blank sheets like that with the musical marks on the side. She must have brought the tablet with her the day she entered the convent. As I handed her the pad and a pencil and the scribbled papers, she said that she remembered hearing somewhere that you can't think of two things at one time so she had been working on a hymn, of all things, to keep her mind off of her pain. I was taken aback. Then she said that she had been experiencing some things and wanted to express them in music. I felt awkward when she admitted to me quite openly that she was feeling very guilty, because a couple of times she prayed to God to let her die in order to get away from the pain. 'Isn't that terrible,' Jeanne exclaimed. 'I'm such a coward. When Bishop Simpson gets back I'll have to go to confession and confess my cowardice. I'm doing this for Ron; you'd think I'd have the courage to bear it a little while longer. Anyway, I'll need you to help me sit up while I put the hymn on paper.'

Jeanne's self-condemnation was ridiculous, of course, to anyone else, but she was actually serious... and coming from her it almost seemed natural.

"For an hour or so I sat next to her on her bed, supporting her so that she could sit upright and put her new hymn on paper. Naturally, I didn't know what the music sounded like, but I was reading the barely readable words on the papers. It was very difficult. I figured she probably wrote the poem a while back when she could still sit at her desk. But her hand must have been shaking from pain and weakness at the time. The lyrics reflected her somewhat depressed mood but, oddly, they didn't really seem sad. They expressed more of a longing to be home with Christ in heaven, which is a longing many of us have though probably not as intensely.

As the time wore on, my back and arms became tired and achy. Reflecting on Jeanne's expression of a need for confession for wanting to rid herself of the pain from her cancerous infliction, I thought to myself that, if she had to go to confession for that, I should probably go too to confess my desire for her to hurry up and finish writing down her hymn so I could let her down onto the bed and relieve myself of my meager aches. When Jeanne finished with the song, she uttered, almost apologetically, 'I only wrote the melody line. I didn't have the strength to try to chord it.' I didn't want her to know how much my back and arms were hurting, so I didn't tell her how happy I was that she didn't feel well enough to write a complete score."

As Sister Mary Agnes concluded this statement, she handed me the final papers from her folder. They were a musical manuscript entitled simply, "Lord." Sister commented that both the music and the words were understandably hard to read, considering Jeanne's condition, but the sister who copied the previous Offertory hymn tried to make a readable copy for me. (That copy of the manuscript follows. But, again, the lyrics on the more readable copy were also difficult to decipher, so, again, Helen and I translated them. Those typed lyrics follow also.)

LORD

1. Lord, forsake me not I'm so a-
3. Lord, my lamp is full; my vig-il

1. lone. Where is the joy You've al-ways
3. true. The dawn has come but where are

1. shone to me, oh, Lord, my Lord,
3. You, oh, Lord, my lov-ing Lord,

Lord

Lord, forsake me not I'm so alone.
Where is the joy You've always shone
To me, oh Lord, my Lord.
Lord, my soul longs for You, oh Lord,
Nor will it rest until it rests
In You, oh, Lord, My Lord.
Lord, my lamp is full, my vigil true.
The dawn has come but where are You
Oh, Lord; My Loving Lord.
Lord, Your bride awaits, please take me home.
Forsake me not; my hour has come.
Oh, Lord, have mercy, Lord.
Oh, Lord, have mercy, Lord.

"As Jeanne slipped more and more into an immobile state, the convent was also declining in spirit. The occasional innocent playfulness that frequently springs up in a cloister and adds so much joy to our lives was waning along with Jeanne's health. Finally, on Palm Sunday morning, when I stood up from my mattress on the floor next to Jeanne's bed I could see that she could hardly move or talk and as the week progressed her condition worsened to the point where she could no longer do either. She could move her eyes slowly and nod her head and move it slightly from side to side to answer, 'Yes,' or, 'No,' but that was all. Mother spent more time with us and the other sisters came frequently to express their concern and I'm certain Jeanne appreciated it because, when they did, I could see her try to smile. However, this all changed on Good Friday. When I looked at Jeanne that morning, I sensed that she probably would not last the day. Then, about 10:00 AM, Bishop Simpson arrived in a big hurry and was extremely excited. When Mother greeted him they both hurried to Jeanne's room. The Bishop was holding a paper with the Papal Seal on it. He told Mother that somehow he, an unimportant, Auxiliary Bishop from the United States, was able to talk to the Pope. 'It must have been a slow day at the Vatican, if they have such days.' He joked. He related briefly how it came about. "Each group was ushered before the Holy Father who was seated with a priest standing in attendance next to him. I watched the groups ahead of us and the attendant would read off the name of the group and the Pontiff would nod and make the sign of the cross over them and then the attendant would indicate that the group should move on. But when we came up in front of the Holy Father I blurted out, 'Your Holiness, there is a young nun in our diocese who is near death from cancer and her wish is to take her final vows even though she is just a postulant.' The attendant immediately stepped forward to silence me, but the Pope waved him off. When the Holy Father asked why Jeanne wanted so much to take her vows before she died, I told him the reason Jeanne gave, 'That when she meets Christ for the first time in heaven, she wants Him to recognize her truly as His bride.' At this, I think I saw the Pope's eyes water and he indicated his approval to his attendant with a nod. The attendant drew me aside as our group was leaving and told me to return in an hour. When I came back later the Pope handed me this document and with a very warm smile he said, 'Tell Our Lord's new bride that I'm granting her request on the condition that when she meets her new bridegroom for the first time, she asks Him to bestow His blessing and guidance on His poor Vicar back here on earth.'

"The Bishop said the pilgrims on the plane were all supposed to meet downtown for a brief discussion and reflections on the trip to Rome, but that he begged off and came directly to the convent from the airport. He wanted to tell Jeanne the good news as quickly as he could. At that point Bishop Simpson looked down at Jeanne and for the first time realized how far gone she was... that she was no longer able to move or talk... and, of course, would not be able to say the words of the vows... and his face dropped. Mother knew what was going through the Bishop's mind so she suggested, 'Jeanne doesn't have to actually say the words. We can say them out loud and she can say them in her heart. That's where they count anyway... can't she Bishop?

"Bishop Simpson smiled and answered, 'Of course.' We all looked at Jeanne for approval and though she could barely move she nodded her head very slightly in approval.

"Mother told me to get the other sisters and the ceremonial book for Final Vows from her office and added, 'One of our own is going to take her solemn vows here today.' I rounded up the sisters in a hurry and retrieved the ceremonial booklet and rushed back to the room. By the time I arrived, Mother had explained the plan to the other sisters, one of whom suggested that we sing the vows to the music Jeanne had composed for them. One of our other novitiates was scheduled to take her final vows in a couple of weeks and several of the sisters had been practicing Jeanne's musical accompaniment for that ceremony. They obviously felt they were ready now to sing them. Mother agreed, and off they went in melodic vows. I was more interested in Jeanne's reaction than to the singing so I watched her eyes. They glossed over, I think with joy, and then a tear slowly rolled down the side of her face.

"I might add that part of the vow taking is the taking of a sister's new name. During and after the ceremony, Jeanne didn't seem at all bothered by our speaking to her and about her as Sister Saint Cecelia. One of the sisters even said, "I wonder if the angels came down from heaven to listen to us singing Sister Saint Cecelia's beautiful music."

"When all was over, Mother said, 'There. That should make Christ stand up and take notice when you meet Him for the first time. But you are probably very tired now, so why don't we all leave and let Sister Saint Cecelia try to get some rest.' Mother looked at her watch and added, 'Besides its almost noon and time for our Good Friday Service.' Then she nodded to me to stay and everyone else left, but not before Bishop Simpson laid the Papal permission paper on the bed next to Jeanne and gave her his blessing.

"I watched Jeanne's eyes close and suddenly became aware that she didn't seem to be suffering the pain that plagued her all this time. I was tired myself and, since Jeanne appeared to have fallen asleep, I decided to try to catch a nap, so I lay down on my mattress but I never went off to sleep... at least, I don't think I was asleep when what happened a few hours later occurred. I just stayed there relaxing, delighted that Jeanne seemed without pain and able to sleep. This went on for, as I said, about three hours when suddenly and unbelievably Jeanne sat up straight in bed and with a very clear, strong voice started reciting what I recognized as a kind of poem. I was thoroughly startled and stood up looking at Jeanne who was wearing that same indescribably beautiful smile that she wore when I visited her in the chapel the morning after Ron's outburst. I didn't recognize the poem and I understand you'll learn more about that when you talk to Father Steve about Ron's death. But I can say that it sounded like a woman's side of a poetic conversation between her in heaven and her beloved on earth. I was trying to remember what she was saying, but I never studied poetry so what she said didn't mean much to me. But I was able to remember the end and I wrote that down shortly after. She said,

'For love that binds is ever true.
No need for foolish tears.'

"I always wished I knew what that meant."

I immediately recalled Jeanne's recitation from Rossetti's poem the *Blessed Damozel* that she quoted in one of her letters to Ron but I hesitated distracting Sister Mary Agnes from her tale of Jeanne Trudeau's apparent passing to engage her in an explanation of the poem.

Sister concluded her story, "As I said, her smile was radiant and when she finished the poem she slowly laid back, closed her eyes and stopped breathing. Immediately thereafter, the chapel bells began their slow peel indicating it was 3:00 PM: the time Christ was purported to have died on the cross. When I heard her stop breathing I simply felt her pulse to be certain she was gone and, not sensing any, I left to tell Mother that our beloved Jeanne had finally passed away. When I entered the chapel all of the nuns were still there from the afternoon service and when they saw me they knew Jeanne was gone. Mother began some of the usual prayers for the dead. But for me, I didn't that day nor have I ever prayed for Jeanne. I pray to her asking her to intercede for me with her beloved bridegroom."

At that, Sister Mary Agnes ended the interview abruptly, informing, "That's all the time I have today. You will probably be back in a day or two to interview one of our other sisters. I may or may not see you then, but I'll make certain everything is ready for you when you do that interview. I don't know if Steve has informed you, but we will have one more session near the end of your research and I'll see you then.

Sister led me to the door and I was on my way home with my head spinning like a top. As I entered the car, I repeated over and over, "I don't need this. I don't need this. How did I ever allow myself to get into something like this?"

CHAPTER Ten

It was a little past noon when I arrived back at the apartment. The drive from the convent allowed me the opportunity to reflect on Sister Mary Agnes' portrayal of the saintly, Jeanne Ann Trudeau during her last year on earth during which she was required to associate with mere mortals. Mother Superior had forced me to enter into her world of mysticism again, which, as I have mentioned, is neither a world in which I believed nor wanted to believe. I had grown to like Sister Mary Agnes just as I liked Father Steve, but their beliefs and experiences were not of the world with which I was comfortable. As a result, I hesitated calling my Jesuit mentor as he had asked until I could fully regain confidence in my skeptical convictions. Consequently, I phoned Helen first, hoping that she would have her lunch break available for some congenial small talk. Unfortunately, she had taken an early lunch to be available to interview a new prospective employee, so I decided to replay some of the tapes and eat some lunch myself.

About 1:30 PM I phoned Father Steve who commented that he was thinking about me all morning wondering how the interview with his sister was going and, perhaps more importantly, how I was receiving the information Sister Mary Agnes was unloading on me. "Not very well," was my admission.

"I thought you would have some problems with that part of the story," he admitted. Then he added, "I hate to tell you this, Fran, but, for you at least, the worst is probably yet to come."

"I suppose that will be tomorrow?" I inquired sardonically.

"Only part of it," the priest replied. "Only part of it."

"I can wait," I groaned. "And, I mean, I can really wait. You know, I almost walked out on your sister this morning when she started talking about Jeanne Trudeau's doorway to infinite goodness and beauty."

"Why didn't you?" the priest inquired.

"Nothing profound," I quipped. "I just didn't want to hurt Sister Mary Agnes' feelings. She seemed so enthused about telling her friend Jeanne's story."

"That was as good a reason as any for listening to the whole thing," Father Steve replied.

"By the way," I continued. "Do you really want me to believe that a young woman in extreme pain, only a couple of months from death and suffering depression from lack of sleep would compose a song. I'd probably be screaming and throwing things at the wall."

In response, Father Steve simply commented, "But you're not Jeanne Anne Trudeau, are you?" Then he reminded me of my interview with a second nun at the convent the following morning, and we ended the discussion.

When I arrived at 9:00 AM, the parlor in which Sister Mary Agnes and I had conducted the first two interviews was set up for this one. I could see a screen with a chair on one side. The External who let me in indicated that the nun whom I was to interview was already in the room on the other side of the screen and that she had asked that I merely take notes rather than use my recorder. The External left the door open, but the screen arrangement was far enough from the doorway to provide privacy from anyone in the vestibule. When I sat down I said simply, "Sister?"

The nun behind the screen responded softly, "Yes, I'm here. Mother asked me to tell you about Ronald VanderLinde and me. I hope you don't mind the screen but I have always been so ashamed of what I did. But Mother and Father Steve said it was very important that I tell you what happened on that Good Friday afternoon. As I said, I'm embarrassed and ashamed. I hope you won't use my name."

I quickly assured her that I did not know her name nor would I use it if I did. She seemed convinced by my assurances.

"Mother told me to be as honest as I can be and to tell as many details as I can remember. She said that's important."

With that she began her tale. "I was a nurse at a hospital in town when I met Ronald. He was a lawyer and was visiting a patient concerning her injuries in an automobile accident. I was attracted to him immediately, but I was confused. I had decided to enter a religious order in the summer. I planned to go into a nursing order so I could continue to use my nurses training and serve both God and sick people at the same time. But then, as I said, I met Ron. I don't know if you've ever fallen in love, but it was overwhelming for me. I had never felt anything like that before. In our first conversation in the hospital he asked if I was going with anyone and I told him right away that I was going to be a nursing nun. His eyes opened wider, I remember that, and he asked me if I were certain that was what I wanted. Then, in a very playful, boyish manner he insisted that I let him take me out just once so that I would know what I was missing. We both laughed and I agreed to go out with him just once. He was so charming that, by the end of that date, I was very infatuated. It's important that I tell you he was a perfect gentleman at first. He told me he really liked music so we went to concerts at the symphony hall. He especially liked piano performances. It was wonderful. As I said, I was very confused. I was caught between my desire to become a nursing nun and my desire to be with Ronald.

For several weeks we went out a couple of times a week, but we were never intimate, which was one of the things I admired so much about him. Then one night, when he was dropping me off, he wrapped his arms around me and kissed me very passionately. That night, while I was falling asleep, I decided I wanted Ronald more than I wanted to be a nun.

Then, one morning, a day when my shift at the hospital finished at 11:00 AM, Ronald asked me to spend the day with him at his place. I knew he had a condominium in the downtown area, but when he picked me up he drove to one of the eastern suburbs. It was a very cold day for that time of year and there was a heavy, early spring snowfall. It was beautiful, but I hadn't dressed for it when I left for work the previous night.

When we got to the house, I mentioned to Ronald that I thought he lived in town. He answered, 'This is my special place. This is where I entertain beautiful girls.' At this he laughed playfully, so naturally I thought he was just kidding.

When we got inside, he had champagne chilling in the refrigerator. He also had an assortment of fancy hors d'oeuvres. He even had caviar. We chatted and drank and joked around. He played some music on his phonograph player and we danced. Then he said, "Why don't you go up to the bedroom. I have a phone call I have to make. I'll join you in a few minutes. I knew what he had in mind and I wanted it as much as he did. When I got upstairs I looked at the alarm clock on the dresser and saw that it was 2:30 PM I suddenly realized that it was Good Friday afternoon. Usually I'm in church on Good Friday at that time. I felt terribly guilty for doing what I was planning to do on Good Friday, but I was so much in love with Ronald that I drove the thought out of my mind. I got undressed and climbed under the covers and waited for him. While I waited, I looked around the room and saw things that seemed strange. A lot of it was normal though: there was wall-to-wall carpeting and beige walls with soft peach colored drapes. So was the contemporary furniture. I don't know what kind of wood it was, but it was brown and quite nice. The bedspread was paisley with a lot of green and orange and brown colors."

I suddenly realized that my interviewee was describing the bedroom Jeanne Trudeau depicted in one of her first letters to Ronald VanderLinde in Paris. I asked her if there were any pictures on the wall.

She said there was one and she thought it might have been a painting of flag lilies.

"Irises?" I inquired.

"It could be," she responded. "I know them as flag lilies. And I was surprised to see a rather large crucifix hanging on the wall above the bed. But what really seemed strange was that in one corner of the room was a baby cradle and a rocking chair."

"Was there a valet and flower stand," I asked.

"Yes, I think there was, now that you mention it. How do you know? Have you been to that house?"

Not exactly I answered indirectly.

She continued, "I think there were some long stemmed roses in a vase on the stand. I remember the roses because they seemed to be the same color as the drapes"

The similarities to the description in the letter were more than coincidental, so I inquired about the outside of the house. "What color was the outside of the house and the trim painted?"

"It was snowing and I was excited when we got there, but I think the siding was sort of tan and the trim was sort of chocolate brown. So was the roof. I remember that because the house was different from the other houses on the street."

The nun hesitated, but then went on, "This is the part that is so hard for me. I hope you won't mind if I stop occasionally. I choke up sometimes when I even think about it. After a short while Ronald came up to the bedroom. As I said, I was under the covers. After he removed his shoes and socks, he took off his shirt and trousers and was standing there in his underwear. I was watching every move he made. Then suddenly, the expression on his face turned to pure agony. He was looking over my head at the crucifix on the wall over the bed. I couldn't imagine what he was so anguished about. Suddenly I was aware of something dripping onto the headboard and splashing down onto the pillow. I wrapped the sheet around me and sat up to look at the crucifix. It was horrible. I know when I entered the room the crucifix had the image of Christ on it. But now there was a young woman in a nun's habit nailed to the cross. And, unbelievably, she was alive. She had a crown of thorns on her head and the blood was pouring from there and from the nail holes in her hands and feet. And I heard her say, 'See how much we love you, Ron.'

"Ron yelled, 'Oh, God!' When he yelled I turned my eyes away from the crucifix and saw Ron grab his trousers and run out of the room. When he disappeared down the stairs, that's the last time I ever saw him. When I looked back at the crucifix the woman was gone and the image of Christ was back on the cross. But the blood was still on the headboard of the bed and on the pillow. I got dressed in a hurry and left the house. But before I left the bedroom I took the pillowcase off the pillow. I've slept on it every night since, to remind me of my sin and I ask God to forgive me every night before I go to sleep. I didn't physically do anything, but I willed it and that's where sin is... in the will."

I broke in at this point and asked how she ended up in this convent when she wanted to be a nursing nun. She continued her story, "When I left the house I was on foot. Ron had taken the car. I was terrified. I thought that, if I died before I went to confession, I would certainly spend eternity in hell. So I asked the first person I saw where a Catholic church was. After she told me, I hurried there and asked for a priest who took me over to the church and heard my confession. I told him what happened and after we were done there I asked him what he thought the image of the woman meant. He said he didn't know. Then he asked what her habit looked like... what order of nuns she belonged to. I couldn't tell, so he took me to the rectory and showed me a book with religious habits in it. When I saw our habit I knew it was the one the nun on the cross was wearing. He said, 'Maybe it was God telling you He wanted you to enter the Order that wears this habit. So I got my things in order that afternoon and evening and came here the next day. And I've been here ever since."

"I hesitate to ask this of you, Sister, but have you ever regretted joining this order and spending your life as a contemplative nun?" I asked.

"Sometimes." She admitted. "I'm usually quite happy. But once in a while I wish I were working as a nurse; helping to make sick people well. But I tell myself 'It's more important to do what God wants than what I want.'"

Naturally I winced at that. I could not help but wonder if this nun really belonged in this convent and how many people she might have helped as a nurse. It always bothered me when I heard someone say that they are acting on some kind of message from God. How can they possibly know what He wants, even if He does exist.

At that point in the narrative, my companion behind the screen declared she did not have anything further to tell me and hoped that what she had said fulfilled what Mother wanted. I assured her it had, but that I had one last question. "How did Father Steve and Sister Mary Agnes know that you were a part of Ronald VanderLinde's life before you entered the convent?"

The nun explained, "I arrived here the day after Sister St. Cecelia died. All of the sister's were talking constantly about her and her final vows and the manner in which she passed into the next world. Sister Mary Agnes frequently referred to the name Ronald. After a while I asked her who he was and sister said he was her brother. I don't know why, but I asked her what her maiden name was and when she said, VanderLinde, I almost fainted. The sisters helped me sit down and got me some water. After I was calmed they asked what the problem was, but I couldn't tell them. You can probably imagine how down on myself I was when I came here. Even though I had gone to confession, I still felt terrible about myself, especially because of what I was planning to do on Good Friday afternoon. But a couple of weeks later, Mother Superior saw that I was depressed so she asked if I wanted to talk about what was bothering me. I thought that if I told her it might relieve my bad feelings about myself and I'm glad I did. She said that though God never causes or condones evil, He sometimes uses it to do a greater good. She quoted St. Thomas Aquinas who she said called Adam's fall a, "blessed fault," because it enabled God to express His infinite mercy and love by sending His Son to suffer and die for the sins of man. She said that God was probably using my sin to do a greater good. When I heard that, those bad feelings just lifted off of me. Since then, every morning I ask God to help me avoid committing sins, but, if I do sin, I ask Him to do some good with it."

The nun seemed very happy about what she was telling me, so I hesitated to interrupt her but I did. "But how did Sister Mary Agnes and Father Steve learn about you and Ronald?"

She responded that the then Mother Superior told her that her story would please Sister Mary Agnes very much. Mother said that I didn't have to tell Sister Mary Agnes, but, if I could bring myself to tell her, she felt it would be a great act of charity and would make another sister very happy.

It was hard. But I prayed for the courage and finally told our current Mother Superior who probably told her brother, Father Steve, since he was the one who convinced me to tell you the story."

That was the end of that interview so I thanked her and with the External as an escort to the door, I exited the convent.

This time I arrived back at the apartment before noon and was able to make a lunch date with Helen. We met at a popular cafeteria a few blocks from the newspaper office and, though it was crowded with the lunchtime crowd, we were able to find a table in a corner with some privacy... at least, enough that we could hear each other without shouting... sort of.

Helen naturally began by asking how that morning's interview went to which I related the details, including the unbelievable and abnormally grotesque bedroom scene between Ronald VanderLinde, his prospective seductee and the illusionary figure on the wall. Helen grimaced a bit at my description of and reasons for the blood dripping onto the bed but, fortunately, she did not completely lose her appetite.

I knew when I returned to my apartment later, I would be required to tell Father Steve that I had definite reservations about the validity of the repulsive tale of which I was the recipient that morning, so I began formulating my words and phrases and practicing my rationale with my lovely luncheon companion. By this time in our relationship Helen had become accustomed to my cynical and sometimes sarcastic skepticism concerning spiritual and mystic matters, so my personal analysis of what had transpired in that bedroom many years ago came as no surprise to her. She commented once that she actually enjoyed my colorfully portrayed disbeliefs. She said it was like watching a one-act stage play in which the main character, actually the only character, was trying to jump through a dozen hoops at once in an effort to stay upright. Fortunately, in this case, she just listened to my horror story and my cynical barbs. But as we were leaving she mused, "But, if everything that nun said is actually true, that's a very beautiful story. Wouldn't you like to be loved like that. Fortunately for we Christians, we believe we are."

I reacted in the manner with which I had a life long history, "I hope you're not trying to encourage me to become a believer."

She cajoled, "I promised you I would not do that, at least not directly. But I do think, if you were a little more open you would be a lot happier." It was then, for the first time that we were together since I returned from the Capital that I remembered the speech by Ronald VanderLinde about love at the girl's college, so I mentioned it to Helen. I told her that the former Justice must have taken his thoughts on the definition of love from Jeanne Trudeau's letter when he was in Paris. Since Helen had recently read the letter she knew exactly to what I was referring and said simply, "That's what I was talking about: 'No greater love...'"

Shortly after I arrived back at the apartment there was a not too surprising phone call from my missing cousin and her wayward husband notifying me that they could no longer cover their half of the rent and, since our lease required a thirty day exit notification, I would have to cover the entire December rent as well as any future rent for time I wanted to stay in the apartment after that. Knowing I was getting married in January, I decided to stay through the wedding, but only that long. Helen and I had planned to get a much more reasonably priced apartment anyway, so my cousin's retreat from our luxury style accommodations was not a serious problem... as a matter of fact, it was a relief not having to endure my cousin's negativism. What was a bit of a problem, however, was my call to Father Steve.

When I told him that I had serious doubts about the sanity of my last interviewee, I think the priest was a little concerned. "I was hoping you would listen to the stories with somewhat of an open mind. I know you're skeptical, but you said you were an agnostic, not an atheist."

I agreed that he had me there. But I told him, even with the open mind of an agnostic, I found the story of blood and such from a live miniature figure on a cross on the wall more than hard to believe.

I really wanted to leave that conversation as quickly as I could, so I asked with whom the next interview was with to which Father replied, "Me. I'd like you to come out to the university this afternoon or tomorrow morning. I'll fill you in on Ron's life from that day in the infamous house until he died. There are some interesting facts that will make good biographical material. Besides, I'd like you to meet Father Castione. You probably know the name from the letters I gave you to read."

I assured him that I was familiar with his colleague of camellia fame and that I could be at the university the following day about 10:30 AM

We had made arrangements to meet outside of the registrar's office in the main building of the university because that was the easiest place to which to direct me. After we met we went to the science, faculty office and after pouring us each a cup of university, faculty office coffee, which I quickly discovered was only one step above the colored, hot water served at football stadiums, Father Steve began his portion of the interview process.

"As I'm certain you know, Ron bolted from the house with hardly any clothes on, even though it was very cold and there was a considerable amount of snow on the ground. He apparently drove straight here to see me. When I greeted him at the door he only had on his underwear and a pair of trousers... no shoes or socks, no coat and not even a regular shirt. I can say that he asked to go to confession, which he did. As I have told you, I will not reveal what he told me in the sacrament. But, after I gave him absolution, we talked for some time about his past life and his plans for the rest of that life. I can say he told me after confession that when Jeanne entered the convent he decided to destroy goodness wherever he found it and that his experience that day at the house, seeing Jeanne nailed to the cross and speaking to him made him take a 180 degree turn around. He now planned to do good wherever he was able. And then the priest added, "As I told you, he was a total person. When he said he wanted to destroy goodness wherever he found it, he really meant that. The same with doing good."

I was inquisitive about the house, since it resembled perfectly the one Jeanne Trudeau described in one of her first letters to Ron in Paris for their future home. Father agreed that Ron built it and decorated it to Jeanne's description. I asked if he had it built that way and furnished the way Jeanne described so that he could use the house as a place to do evil things and destroy goodness. Father Steve was reluctant to admit that but he did not deny it either.

Next, I asked what happened to the house after Ron's conversion. Father Steve said that the future Justice, "Donated it to the county as part of a Social Service Department experiment."

I suddenly remembered the case that catapulted Municipal Judge VanderLinde into the limelight and resulted in his being made State Supreme Court Justice VanderLinde. "Did that experiment involve a blind couple and their child," I inquired.

"Yes," the priest said enthusiastically. "Do you know about that case?"

I admitted that I had read the story as part of my initial research into Ronald's judicial career."

"I read Judge VanderLinde's decision but I never learned how the experiment turned out. Was the blind couple able to care for their daughter with the help of young single mothers," I asked.

"Yes and no," Father admitted disappointedly. The program worked very well for several years before the county became careless and failed to adequately screen the young helpers. Since the couple couldn't see and were extremely dependent on these women, it only took one miscreant to sabotage the program. The couple woke up one morning to find almost all of the furniture, fixtures, clothing and money gone... as was the helper. Even the dishes and tableware were missing. The authorities surmised that the appointed caregiver probably had a boyfriend who helped her clear everything out over night. That killed what could have been a good social program."

"That's a shame, I agreed. I bet the judge was disappointed."

"For the young couple, of course." Father replied. "As I mentioned, he wanted to do whatever good he could. He cared about the people like the blind couple, but what was of the greatest importance to him was that he was constantly trying his best to do everything good that he could. Literally, that was, apparently, all he wanted out of the rest of his life. That's what happened on the battlefield in the South Pacific. It wasn't that he wanted to die or that he didn't care whether he lived or not. He was totally focused on doing whatever good he could do... helping the wounded, friend or foe. I wasn't there, of course. But knowing who Ron was at that time in his life, I don't think he was even aware that he was in danger in the middle of a crossfire. He may not even have been aware that he was wounded. All he cared about was doing good. That's what total people are like. I haven't met or even read about many, but there are a few and Ron was one. And so was Jeanne Trudeau, I might add."

"Maybe your brother... but I'm still having problems with the stories of our saintly nun," I objected.

The priest looked at me sympathetically. "We know for certain what Ron did in the war because there were many witnesses. Why couldn't Jeanne be as heroic as he was... willing to suffer terribly and die for someone else?"

I'll give you that, Father," I acknowledged. But Ronald VanderLinde did not become a few inches tall and hang on a bedroom wall crucifix dripping blood on the bed. There's a huge difference. A difference between believable and unbelievable."

"A difference between belief and disbelief." He responded attempting a correction. "But let's continue with Ron's story."

Father Steve relaxed a bit and commented that he assumed I knew most of what there was to know about Ron over the next decades from the summaries of his legal decisions while on the State Supreme Court that I read at my alma mater's legal library and from the speeches I reviewed while in the hospital. I agreed with his assumption but added that I had not read much of the legal decisions, since I believed that I had learned enough about Ron's mental disposition from my other research.

"Then the only thing left of Ron's life is his death," Father announced with a grin.

"I'm not sure I'm happy about that smirk," I complained with a touch of irritation.

"Very discerning," the priest observed. Then he continued. "I knew Ron was very ill for some time and about a month before he died I asked him if I should come down to the Capital to help in his care giving. He said he had a nurse with him that took care of those things, but that he did want me there at the end, which he guessed would be in a few weeks. As a result, I organized things at the university and planned a trip to the Capital to stay at Ron's house for as much time as he had left with us.

"He was taking some strong painkillers but he still remained fairly lucid. We had some good conversations and he was very grateful for things I had done for him. He wasn't in much pain and seemed quite happy. One of the first things he told me when I first arrived at the Capital was that he wanted me to get someone to write Jeanne's and his story. And that's when he gave me permission to tell anyone anything he told me in confession and when I told him I couldn't bring myself to do that. But I promised him I would do everything I could to get their story told.

Then, one night, he passed into a coma and began what I recognized as a death rattle. I knew the end was only hours or even minutes away, so I sat with him waiting for the end. And it did come but not as I expected. Suddenly, Ron sat straight up in bed and looking straight ahead with a wonderful smile on his face he spoke, and with a strong voice.

"When he asked me to try to find someone to write the biographies he also steered me to all of his personal papers including the letters Jeanne wrote him while he was in Paris and which I gave you to read. During the two weeks I was there, when he was asleep, I read through his papers including Jeanne's letters, one of which quoted lines from Dante Gabriel Rossetti's *The Blessed Damozel*. When Ron spoke there, sitting up in bed, I realized he was quoting poetry, and then suddenly, I recognized those lines. They were from *The Blessed Damozel*. Then, as soon as he finished reciting the lines from the poem he lay back slowly and stopped breathing. I called to the nurse to verify that he was gone and then I rushed to his desk to find the letter with the Rossetti poem to confirm his last words. I'm certain of what he said because the words kept going over and over in my head:

Alas! We two, we two. Thou say'st!
Yea, one wast thou with me
That once of old. But shall God lift
To endless unity
The soul whose likeness to thy soul
Was but its love for thee?"

Then, after a pause he said,

'For love that binds is ever true.
No need for foolish tears.'"

As was and still is my wont in such situations, skepticism immediately came to the fore and I challenged Father's obvious assertion that Ron and Jeanne had each recited their gender respective Rossetti lines on their deathbeds, miles apart from where each had died and decades apart in time as though they were together in their deaths in both time and space. I asked the priest if that was what he was driving at. He confirmed that he was. "Father," I charged, "Your sister... Ron's sister... was present at Jeanne Trudeau's death. She had over twenty years to tell Ron what Jeanne said and did on her deathbed. And, if he knew what she was doing when she died, under the circumstances of the trauma of their relationship, he could have acted through reflex when he died."

"Playing psychiatrist?" Father Steve accused sardonically.

"Your right," I admitted. "But, yes, wild things may or may not have happened. But there are possible explanations other than divine or spiritual interventions. I need more than what you've given me thus far to become, "a believer." I said the last two words with as much sarcasm as I could muster.

Father did not wince. He merely replied, "Maybe your next interview will do just that."

"There's another interview?" I asked.

"One more. With Sister Mary Agnes." He answered. "Tomorrow morning, at 9:00 AM, if you can make it."

"I thought I learned everything there was to know about Jeanne Trudeau. After all, she's dead... even in your sister's story," I asserted with a touch of disappointment.

"Not everything," Father replied as he rose and then added, "I told you I would like you to meet Father Castione. I'm certain you learned from your readings of Jeanne's letters, Father was her spiritual advisor prior to her entering the convent. I don't know how much influence he had on that decision... we spiritual advisors don't talk to each other about our advisees the same way psychologists don't talk to other psychologists about their patients... at least not by name... so you might ask him about Jeanne's vocation decision. I don't know whether he will tell you anything, but it might be pertinent to the story, if he does."

On the way to see Father Castione, Father Steve described his fellow, faculty colleague as... a bit eccentric, but harmless." He joked, "The biology students really liked him because he makes his courses interesting and even entertaining, or at least as entertaining as cell structure can be." He added,

"I asked Father Castione to wait for us in the biology, faculty office. I hope he's still there."

The biology, faculty office was at the extreme opposite end of the main administration building, so Father Steve continued his description of Father Castione as we walked. "He's a very practical man... very down to earth. He's moderator of our house: the priest whose job it is to pass out the toothpaste and toothbrushes and, of course, the car keys."

As Father Steve introduced us, I did some of my patented "mental sizing up' of the biology professor. He was short, but not diminutive, probably about six inches less in height than Father Steve or myself, with a tannish, Mediterranean complexion. He appeared almost wiry, or, at least lively, and exactly the type of professor who could make cell structure entertaining.

It was approaching noon. Since I hadn't bothered to eat breakfast that morning, I was getting quite hungry. After Father Castione acknowledged that he knew that I had been asked to write the story of Jeanne Trudeau and Ron VanderLinde, I went right to the point. "I know that you were an advisor to Jeanne before she entered the convent. Was there anything you may have said that made her so abruptly break off her engagement to Ron and enter a convent?"

"I don't believe so," the priest replied. "As a spiritual advisor, we're always trying to get souls to love God more each day. Whether anything I said had a direct bearing on her decision, I can't say. Steve has informed me about everything that transpired since she entered the convent, and I have to say that I have mixed emotions about it all. A young girl deciding to give herself to a life of prayer is certainly beautiful. But, then there was all of that pain and death. However, if what Steve says happened, there was a happy ending. The whole thing was a dramatic roller coaster ride wasn't it? For myself, I like growing in sanctity to be a slow, gradual, lifetime process. None of those sudden, lightning bolt conversions."

At this, Father Steve chimed in, "That's my preference too. But there has to be room in God's redemptive plan for both processes, doesn't there."

Father Castione nodded his head in agreement.

Father Steve walked with me to the main entrance and again asked me to contact him after my last interview with Sister Mary Agnes.

Again, I was a little early for the interview at the convent, but this time I declined the offer to wait in the chapel, opting instead to wait in the parlor. When Sister Mary Agnes joined me, we sat quietly for a few seconds. I tried to ascertain why the nun was apparently reluctant to continue the story of her friend, Jeanne, or by this time in the story, Sister St. Cecelia. I also noticed that Sister brought a book with her this time. It appeared to be a Bible. Finally Sister Mary Agnes began my last interview. I had no idea of what it was going to be about or what affect it was going to have on me. She began slowly and rather quietly... almost in a whisper. "Shortly after Jeanne, Sister St. Cecelia that is, died, Ron sent me a note explaining the last letter he received from her before she entered our convent and he included the poem she had written about the white camellia."

Then Sister changed the subject on purpose. "Keep what I just said in mind while I describe Jeanne's funeral and burial. You may have noticed our grounds here. Attached to the building is a wall that surrounds our outdoor area where the sisters grow fruits and vegetables and flowers and where they can just sit and meditate and pray and admire the beauty of God's creations. It's the better part of an acre. The entrance is from the convent. But there is a wall in the yard separating the growing and meditation space from another small area that serves as our cemetery for the nuns when they pass away." There is a wall with a door between the two yards.

With that explanation completed she continued her tale. "When Ron sent me the note about the poem he promised to send me a white camellia every year on the anniversary of Sister St. Cecelia's death and asked me to place it on her grave. And he did. Every year, on that anniversary, a white camellia was delivered to our door, first by one of Father Castione's students; but later by a local florist. Needless to say, I faithfully followed Ron's request and placed the flower on Sister's grave."

I acknowledged with a smile that I considered this a nice touch. But then came the blockbuster. Sister Mary Agnes, with a certainty in her voice I had not heard before declared the following: "About 5:30 AM, on the morning of Ron's own death, Father Steve called to let me know that our younger brother had died. He also told me about the strange sitting up in bed and reciting of the lines from the poem. When I heard the lines I wondered about those that Jeanne recited many years before and I told Steve about it. He read me the portion of the letter Jeanne had written that included the poem and, though it was many years earlier, I firmly believe Jeanne said the girl's lines in that poem before she died. And we agreed they both probably said the same, last two lines as their last words here on earth. But I'm getting away from that morning. After I hung up the phone, I put on a wrap and went out to the graveyard to say a prayer at Jeanne's gravesite. A cold rain had been falling over night and there was still a cold, mist." Then Sister stopped. She apologized, "Forgive me. I tremble every time I even think of that morning." After a short hesitation she continued, "When I opened the door from the garden yard to the cemetery area I almost fainted. There, in a cold, late November fog, was Jeanne's grave, completely covered with dozens of beautiful, white camellias in full bloom. As I said, I almost fainted and then I must have screamed very loud because, within seconds, all of the sisters started pouring out of the convent expecting some intruder or something and when they came to the door that separated the two yards and also saw the camellias, they started falling on their knees... praying out loud. Some of them were not properly dressed for the cold, but they all stayed for upwards to an hour. They started by saying the rosary and then continued praying just about every prayer we knew by heart. At one point one of the sisters started singing the Offertory hymn that Jeanne had composed and, naturally, everybody joined in. Since our previous Mother Superior was long deceased, I was the only one that knew the full story of Jeanne's sacrifice and Ron's conversion, but all of the sisters were exploding with joy. I thought to myself, 'This must be God confirming to us that Jeanne joined Our Redeemer in the saving of Ronald's soul.' As I said, the sisters stayed there for some time. And I have always considered one of the miracles of that day, was that not one of the nuns came down with pneumonia."

Sister then opened the bible she had brought and took out a white flower. "This is one of the camellias from the grave." It was crushed and dry, but it still looked attractive.

I know she wanted to believe that the camellias on the grave were a miracle from God and that Sister Mary Agnes wanted me to believe it also. But I just could not bring myself to accept that theory. I thought to myself that anyone could have climbed over the wall during the night without being seen and spread the camellias on the grave. My idea of a miracle, if there were such a thing, would be a happening for which there is absolutely no other possible explanation. And this happening had another possible, albeit, improbable explanation. But, as I said, I knew Sister wanted to believe this to be a miracle and also wanted me to believe that. And I had really grown to like the VanderLinde kids, so I made no effort to explain my misgivings to my interview companion.

After a short while I expressed my gratitude for all of the time she had given me for which she promised to pray for me and my biography-writing project. And with that I left.

This drive home from the convent was the most difficult. In spite of the fact that I had struggled through all of the reading and interviewing and was finally finished, I had this strong desire to chuck the whole project. This was a story full of, not just bigger than life, but bigger than reality, extreme personalities, performing more than generous acts of sacrifice, followed by miraculous, "love is greater than time and space" experiences and ending with a supposed miracle of white camellias. I was again feeling, "I don't believe these things and, above all, I don't want to believe them. I was so exasperated that I almost prayed, "God! Don't You believe me! I don't want to believe in You!"

When I arrived at my apartment, I was still questioning what I was going to tell Father Steve. Was I or was I not going to actually write Ronald VanderLinde's biography. Though I had promised the priest at the beginning of all of this that I would indeed write the story, because of the extremely strange anomalies that I uncovered during the interviews, which departed so dramatically from, not just my beliefs, but also my attitude towards life, the thought of spending weeks or months putting all of it on paper was repulsive. However, the pressure of deciding immediately whether or not to write the biography evaporated within minutes of my arrival home. When the phone rang and I answered it, I heard Father Castione's voice. "Father Steve died of an apparent heart attack during the night. We found him when he failed to show up for Mass this morning."

I was speechless, and in real pain. Finally, I asked if plans had been made for a viewing or funeral. The priest said that they were yet to be scheduled, but that he would let me know personally when they were, because he had some papers Father Steve had given him to give to me if he wasn't able. Father Castione commented that Father Steve might have sensed something was wrong. Otherwise, why wouldn't Steve plan to give me the papers himself at our next meeting? Father Castione said that he would give them to me at the wake, which he did.

The wake was held at the university, naturally, and, after I showed my respects, I looked for Father Castione and found him easily. He was surrounded by a group of admiring students. When he saw me, he excused himself from his fans and we greeted each other warmly. I expressed my condolences, but he said, "Jesuits don't mourn their deceased. They celebrate because one of their own made it home."

I told him it sounded like an Irish wake mentality and he laughed. Then he handed me an envelope. He advised it contained some scientific thoughts and theories of Father Steve's that the physicist just didn't want discarded with the rest of his non-useful belongings. He said, "Steve didn't know what you could do with them but for some reason he felt he should get them to you." With that, Father Castione added, "I have developed some theories of my own during the years and, since Steve felt you would be a good repository for his weird ideas, I put some of mine in the envelope as well." (Even though I read these papers several times over the next several days, I could only grasp the general concepts. I also failed to understand what I could do with them. So, as the reader will see, I added them as a pseudo-appendix to this book. I thought perhaps by publishing them, someone of wisdom could see a purpose for the ideas.)

The next several weeks were hectic with the wedding coming up and, of course, I did return to work at the paper.

The wedding went off well with only a few of those usual unforeseen calamities, but nothing earth shattering. We were married with only a weekend honeymoon, so shortened by my infamous failure to recognize the City Hall, kick back fiasco.

At first, I could use, "I'm too busy," as my excuse for postponing the writing of the biography and, as time passed and the children started coming in rapid succession, that excuse seemed actually valid. With Helen's legitimate request for a little help with the rug rats, I considered and finally adopted the scenario Father and I semi-agreed upon in the drive back from the Capital to wait with the writing until after the children were raised. Of course, my reluctance to face, for me, the torturous considerations of mystical happenings was probably a subconscious rationalization for putting it off as well... and probably the main reason for the procrastination.

Though I remained writing for the paper all of these years, I never moved up the journalistic ladder: partly because, though Blakesley and I learned to tolerate each other, he never offered me any advanced positions.

And, of course, my innate laziness suppressed any desire for further responsibilities. Though hard to believe, Blakesley actually made it to retirement with the help of a lot of antacids and only one stomach operation due to a bleeding ulcer. When Blakesley left, my best friend, Hank Chapman, who was also godfather to one of our boys, was appointed Managing Editor, thus continuing my job security. Holmes, on the other hand, though holding on until after Blakesley's retirement, did succumb to the tensions of his occult interests. Actually, he did die, what would have been for him, a happy death... with his astrological boots on, so to speak. They say his secretary found him slumped over his desk, with his head and arms lying on those precious horoscope materials on his desk, and basking beneath the rays of that garish astrological wheel on the rear wall of his office. They said his demise was due to either a heart attack or a stroke. I could not help but wonder if his horoscope predicted his final departure that day.

As I mentioned much earlier, I had the extreme pleasure of watching Helen's sisters grow to maturity, marry, and start their own families. The three girls were bridesmaids at our wedding and added considerably to the fun of the occasion. Bridget, in spite of her freckles, found a very attractive young man who, apparently, found those "ugly spots" as beautiful as the rest of us did. Colleen was the only one in the family to enter college, having won a scholarship at a teaching school down state. She eventually became a teacher at the parochial school connected to the family church and, I understand, and not unexpectedly, became relished and appreciated by her students and the school administration. And, as predicted, Kathleen, to the happiness of everyone, was spoiled by whomever and wherever she went.

Helen's father, unfortunately, succumbed to emphysema from decades of smoking cigarettes before the dangers of that vice were known, and only a couple of years before his retirement. The matriarch of the family helped all of the girls, including Helen, with baby-sitting, at least until she could no longer chase after the little ones. She is now in a diocesan operated, senior, assisted living facility where, I understand, several retired priests reside. Consequently she is able to attend daily Mass and other religious activities without leaving the building. The girls visit her frequently and she seems very content.

When our children started into their teen years and we were looking forward to college tuition costs, I accepted some freelance writing assignments to supplement my income, which, of course, cut into my time as well, and which gave me another excuse for postponing the biography.

Then, when the last one's college tuition was covered and I had some real time to myself, Helen calmly counseled, "Why don't you take up that book on Justice VanderLinde. It could give you something to challenge your mind." She had been extremely understanding through the years and never brought up the biography even though we both knew it was gnawing at me from within. But finally, when she noticed me expressing a slightly depressed, uneasy demeanor, she mentioned it. And so, ever eager to please, I did. And so, here it is. I am not endorsing the story or even claiming it is true. It is just what I learned and have expressed as best I could. But there is something that has changed in me. Most of my life I did not know whether spiritual things existed and did not want to know. What has changed is that, though I still do not know, I am, for some reason, uneasy about not knowing. Now I want to know, but I do not know how to know. So, as I said in the Prologue, if anyone has successfully exorcised anything like what I am going through or if someone is wise enough to instruct me in the solution to my dilemma, please write my publisher with your thoughts. He has promised to forward them to me.

And one last anomaly...at least for this skeptical agnostic. I think I actually want there to be a human soul now, if for no other reason than somewhere, somehow Father Steve can know that I finally wrote the story of his brother, State Supreme Court Justice Ronald VanderLinde and, of course, of our beloved Jeanne Anne Trudeau, a.k.a. Sister Saint Cecelia, OPC.

EPILOGUE

I mentioned earlier that I had changed over the past thirty years, which, I am certain, comes as no surprise to anyone, since we all change over time. However, a series of recent incidents and reflections have led me to believe that I now know, not only that I have changed and how I have changed but, more importantly, why I have changed.

Since there was a thirty year break between my initial research for this book and its writing, I had to spend considerable time reviewing again the notes and audio tapes and letters and speeches, etc., that I had accumulated during the interviews and other fact gatherings. Two things quickly became evident during this review: first, matters that seemed relatively unimportant decades earlier now appeared considerably more significant. And situations and concerns that created the greatest impact, as Father Steve referred to the incidents, lessened in importance. I was also able to review a considerable amount of material in hours rather than days or weeks as the information was originally acquired, which enabled me to connect several different items of varying themes together to form multi-colored chunks of reality.

One morning, when I was sitting at a table in the family room, which I had set up for the reviewing, my peripheral vision caught Helen carrying a basket of dirty clothes to the laundry room and, when she emerged several minutes later, she said, "I'm going to make a fresh pot of coffee. Would you like another cup?" I nodded my head affirmatively and low and behold she reappeared a little while later with a fresh cup of coffee that she placed on my table.

Naturally I murmured a, "Thank you," and then added "I don't want to frighten you, but, if you keep spoiling me like this, I might ask you to marry me."

To which she replied, "Yes, you are scaring me," and then added in the same breath, "I have to do some grocery shopping this morning. What would you like for supper?"

That type of silly banter was common in our household over the years, but that morning, with my mind still on several items in my review, a bell went off in my head. I saw this, as I said earlier, as a multicolored chunk of reality: Helen caringly bringing her husband a cup of coffee and then asking what I would like for supper, the conversation between Father Steve, Father Castione and myself in which the two priests expressed their view that they preferred the long, slow lifetime growth in holiness to the lightning bolt conversion type, Jeanne Trudeau's supposed remark from the crucifix, "See how much we love you." And Helen's reaction, asking me, "Wouldn't you like to be loved like that? We Christians believe we are." And Jeanne Trudeau's observations that the reasons the women in the Correction Center were living the lives they were was because they had lost their self-esteem and Jeanne's job was to give it back to them by making them feel important to themselves. It all came together.

Suddenly, I saw Helen and her life over the last thirty years as a slow growth in holiness by day-in and day-out giving of herself to make her husband and, especially her children, feel important and special in their own eyes.

I would like to give one obvious example, though I am certain, there are thousands of subtler ones. Like most parents we tried to guide our children to learn to like most foods by insisting they take at least one mouthful of everything offered them. But one year, I believe it was for Thanksgiving dinner, Helen took a detour. One of the few good things that I brought to our marriage was a file card holder full of my mother's old recipes, one of which was her recipe for chicken or turkey stuffing, which, together with the bread crumbs included, chopped parsley, raisins and sautéed chopped onions. As children of pre-school and early school age are prone to do, ours expressed their varied tastes. One just wanted the breadcrumbs, another did not like the raisins, another liked the raisins but did not care for the parsley and onions, etc. As noted, in spite of his or her tastes we insisted that everyone take at least one mouthful.

But, the year in question, instead of buying a large turkey, Helen brought home six little, Rock, Cornish game hens. She then made the stuffing individually for each bird according to each child's tastes and stuck a varied colored hors d'oeuvres pick in each hen to identify what bird belonged to whom. When I discovered the reason for the substitute of the six hens for the traditional one large bird I scolded Helen for spoiling the children, to which she explained, "During the holidays, everyone should be made to feel special. We can make them eat a mouthful of everything on the rest of the days of the year." And, Helen continued this Rock Cornish game hen practice on Thanksgivings and Christmases for years thereafter.

Reflecting on these incidents I had to wonder if those women in the Correction Center and the girls in the Detention Home would have been in those institutions, if their mothers had made them feel special by making them individual meals to their likings on the holidays.

And then my mind shot rapidly over all of those many, many other, as I noted, subtler occasions when Helen put herself out to do things that pleased the other members of her family. One, though very personal, I believe should be told.

Obviously, because of Jeanne Anne Trudeau's admiration of Sonia Roses, Helen requested her florist to include them prominently in her bridal bouquet. Naturally, I considered this a nice touch, especially on reflection of what we both had been immersed in during the previous few months. But seeing my bride at the wedding with her Sonia Rose bouquet in no way prepared me for what she planned for later. That night, when my bride approached our wedding bed, she wore a white camellia in her hair. When I asked her why, she whispered, "It is a perfect symbol of my new husband: with his skeptical agnosticism he...

> Cold appears, and feigns an artificial form.
> Shallow eyes would see him as austere,
> Though he be delicate and sensitive and warm.
> One white camellia now adorns my hair.
> Look upon it love. Behold your soul there.

Needless to say, I did not then, nor have I ever since, considered myself deserving of that night.

However, more importantly, though Helen, by herself, would never have thought of saying such a thing, I have to ask now, "Were not her actions during those past thirty years one big, 'See how much I love you!!' to the members of her family? As the narrative at the beginning of this book displays, I did a lot of dumb things when I first started writing for the newspaper. But I never felt more stupid than I did on this recent morning, when I realized that I had spent thirty years living with and looking at this huge expression of love without recognizing it.

R. Francis Bechs

My final reflection that morning was on the quote from Jeanne Anne Trudeau's summary on the *Blessed Paradox of Contemplative Solemn Vows:*

Love has always been a Blessed Paradox: In loving others, we receive our greatest happiness by doing things that give them happiness.

Appendix A

Speech by Justice Ronald VanderLinde before Labor Union Convention:
I was very pleased to receive your invitation to speak before you today. Now, I know you hear that opening sentence at the beginning of every address given on such occasions, but I actually mean it. And in due time I'll tell you why. But it will take me a few remarks to lead into it.

First of all, for anyone to say anything of any real significance to a labor union body, such as yours, he must include in his remarks at least a fleeting reference to the primary purposes of the labor union movement, which, in turn, requires that you, the audience, understand the initial history or birth of that movement. Many labor union members are not aware why labor unions really exist and how they really came into being. It is important, however, that you do so, so that when you send your leadership out to negotiate a new contract, they do so with the intent of fulfilling the real purposes and goals of the labor movement and do not come back with a contract that may seem good in the short term but is actually self destructive in the long run.

Now, I'm certain that most of you believe, and rightly so, that labor unions exist to assure the working class a living wage and safe working conditions. And that is true. But it's only part of the story. There is much more to the labor movement than that. The dignity of man, for instance, is constantly at stake when you leave your homes to go out into the world to earn the bread for your family's tables. Unions exist because, not just human beings, but also human dignity was being scornfully trampled under foot during the first century or so of the Industrial Revolution. And that is the real reason your unions came into being. And it almost didn't happen. The amassing of obscene wealth by only a few at the expense of and through the brutalization of the masses was so blatantly perverse in the industrialized countries of Europe and here in the United States that many of the rational minds and men of good will, in a passionate search for justice, became irrational. Instead of seeking corrective remedies for the prevailing socio-economic system that we call capitalism, they chose revolutionary change by totally abrogating capitalism and man's right to ownership of property, replacing it with socialistic concepts of society and economics.

Many of you may be aware of the pamphlet entitled *Communist Manifesto* published by Karl Marx and Friedrich Engels in the middle of the nineteenth century. It was an intellectual rebellion against abusive capitalism and became the rationale for the rise of Communism in Europe during the first half of this century and resulted in the Communist Revolution in Russia. Communism and its sister, Socialism, were, of course, such a far left socio-politico-economic reaction to capitalism that one could almost certainly predict a counter reaction to the right that not only did, in fact, come into being, but became an even worse form of totalitarianism. It was called Fascism... a human abomination, which this and other nations recently paid a dreadful price to abolish.

I have often asked myself why the United States, within its boundaries, was spared the conflict between the radical opposites of Socialism and Fascism. After all, this country suffered just as badly from the abuses of the wealthy few that resulted in the poverty and misery of the many. The best answer I have come up with is that our founding fathers were absolute geniuses in drafting a constitution with the checks and balances of our ternary form of governance as a firewall, protecting this nation from the economic and governmental extremism that inflicted Europe during the first half of this century.

However, there was another force playing behind all of this. It was the force that originally gave both moral and intellectual validity to the labor union movement and, though that movement was, earlier in this century, suppressed under Communist and Fascist regimes, and still is, in Russia and Eastern Europe, that force has enabled the labor movement to again flourish in much of the western industrial world. That force flowed from the words of that powerful intellect Pope Leo XIII in his *Encyclical Rerum Novarum* promulgated in May of 1891.

I told you at the offset that I was happy to be invited to address this body. And one of the reasons, though certainly not the only one, was that, in order to research this speech, I knew I would most certainly be required to reread Pope Leo's *Encyclical On The Condition Of Workers*. I have always enjoyed reading the Encyclicals of Pope Leo for several reasons, sometimes only for entertainment. First, he is, in my humble opinion, the most brilliant pontiff in the two thousand year history of the Church. His thinking is not only deep, rational, and insightful but he expresses his ideas with crystal clarity. And in addition to that, even in translation, his words flow like lyric prose.

I am going to draw extensively from pertinent concepts in the Encyclical; some verbatim, and only occasionally will I interject my own thoughts. Yet I believe it will serve you well to listen carefully because the long-term survival of your movement may lie in balance.

The first half of the Encyclical offers a lengthy dissection of the errors of socialism, which was gaining a great deal of intellectual momentum at the time the Encyclical was written. And the document includes in that dissection a profound, logical explanation as to why the right to the ownership of private property is an essential attribute in the nature of man. The second half of the Encyclical, however, is of most importance to you today. Pope Leo presents an irrefutable defense of labor unions as a means of attaining labor justice while avoiding the pitfalls of socialism and other such extremist economic ideologies.

In extolling the benevolence of the labor union, Pope Leo also offered several, practical admonitions, which is why I am here and what I intend to leave with you today.

The first is to counter what Leo calls, "The great mistake... the notion that class is naturally hostile to class, and that the wealthy and the working men are intended by nature to live in mutual conflict." The pontiff argues, "So irrational and so false is this view that the direct contrary is the truth. Just as the symmetry of the human frame is the result of the suitable arrangement of the different parts of the body, so in a State is it ordained by nature that these two classes should dwell in harmony and agreement, so as to maintain the balance of the body politic. Each needs the other: capital cannot do without labor, nor labor without capital. Mutual agreement results in the beauty of good order, while perpetual conflict necessarily produces confusion and savage barbarity."

Leo then directs both the laborers and the owners to their just duties. The workers should, "...fully and faithfully perform the work, which has been freely and equitably agreed upon; never to injure the property, nor to outrage the person of an employer; never to resort to violence in defending their own cause, nor to engage in riot or disorder; and to have nothing to do with men of evil principles, who work upon the people with artful promises of great results, and excite foolish hopes, which usually end in useless regrets and grievous loss." The Encyclical then lays out the duties that bind the wealthy owner and the employer, "...not to look upon their work people as their bondsmen, but to respect in every man his dignity as a person ennobled by Christian character. They are reminded that, according to natural reason and Christian philosophy, working for gain is credible, not shameful, to a man, since it enables him to earn an honorable livelihood; but to misuse men as though they were things in the pursuit of gain, or to value them solely for their physical power - that is shameful and inhuman."

Pope Leo also commented on the duties demanded of those to whom God has given various talents and in doing so, the Pontiff laid low the fundamental argument for Fascism. "Whoever has received from the Divine bounty a large share of temporal blessings, whether they be external or material, or gifts of the mind, has received them for the purpose of using them for the perfecting of his own nature, and, at the same time, that he may employ them, as the steward of God's providence, for the benefit of others. 'He that hath a talent,' said St. Gregory the Great, 'let him see that he hide it not; he that hath abundance, let him quicken himself to mercy and generosity; he that hath art and skill, let him do his best to share the use and utility hereof with his neighbor.'" Leo then spoke to the workers, "As for those who possess not the gifts of fortune,...in God's sight poverty is no disgrace, and that there is nothing to be ashamed of in earning their bread by labor. This we see in Christ, himself, who...did not disdain to spend a great part of His life as a carpenter Himself."

Leo also dealt with what we call, "The government," and its roll in management/labor relations. He asserted, "As regards the State, the interest of all, whether high or low, are equal. The members of the working classes are citizens by nature and by the same right as the rich; they are real parts, living the life, which makes up, through the family, the body of the commonwealth; and it need hardly be said that they are in every city very largely the majority. It would be irrational to neglect one portion of the citizens and favor another, and therefore the public administration must duly and solicitously provide for the welfare and the comfort of the working classes; otherwise, that law of justice will be violated, which ordains that each man shall have his due....Among the many and grave duties of rulers who would do their best for the people, the first and chief is to act with strict justice...towards each and every class alike." Further, in discussing the provision of commodities within a society Leo asserts, "...the labor of the working class—the exercise of their skill, and the employment of their strength, in the cultivation of the land, and in the workshops of trade–is especially responsible and quite indispensable. Indeed, their cooperation is in this respect so important that it may be truly said that it is only by the labor of working men that states grow rich. Justice, therefore, demands that the interests of the working classes should be carefully watched over by the administration, so that they who contribute so largely to the advantage of the community may themselves share in the benefits, which they create—that being housed, clothed and bodily fit, they may find their life less hard and more endurable. It follows that whatever shall appear to prove conducive to the well being of those who work should obtain favorable consideration. There is no fear that solicitude of this kind will be harmful to any interest; on the contrary, it will be to the advantage of all, for it cannot but be good for the commonwealth to shield from misery those on whom it so largely depends for the things that it needs."

Pope Leo had one further instruction to the state; this one concerning taxation. "If working people can look forward to obtaining a share in the land, the consequence will be that the gulf between vast wealth and sheer poverty will be bridged over, and the respective classes will be brought nearer to one another... The right to obtain private property is derived from nature, not from man; and the state has the right to control its use in the interest of the public good alone, but by no means to absorb it altogether. The state would, therefore, be unjust and cruel if under the name of taxation it were to deprive the private owner of more than is fair."

Pope Leo XIII then, after extolling the benevolence of associations and organizations that unite people together to help a wide range of the helpless, states, "The most important of all are workmen's unions, for these virtually include all the rest. History attests what excellent results were brought about by the artificer's guilds of olden times. They were the means of affording not only many advantages to the workmen, but in a small degree, of promoting the advancement of art, as numerous monuments remain to bear witness. Such unions should be suited to the requirements of this our age–an age of wider education, of different habits, and of far more numerous requirements in daily life." Pope Leo then made reference to the fact that labor unions had already begun to spring up even then, in the last century. "It is gratifying to know that there are actually in existence not a few associations of this nature, consisting either of workmen alone, or of workmen and employers together, but it were greatly to be desired that they should become more numerous and more efficient. We have spoken of them more than once, yet it will be well to explain here how notably they are needed, to show that they exist in their own right, and what should be their organization and their mode of action."

The Pontiff then proffers his reason for the need of labor unions. "We read in holy Writ, 'it is better that two should be together than one: for they have the advantage of their society. If one fall he shall be supported by the other. Woe to him that is alone, for when he falleth he hath none to lift him up.' And further, 'A brother who is helped by his brother is like a strong city.' It is this natural impulse, which binds men together in civil society; and it is likewise this, which leads them to join together in associations, which are, it is true, lesser and not independent societies, but, nevertheless, real societies."

It is obvious that Pope Leo foresaw what was to transpire a few years hence when both Communism and Fascism suppressed the labor movement for he added, "Private societies, then, although they exist within the body politic, and are severally part of the commonwealth, cannot nevertheless be absolutely, and as such, prohibited by public authority. For, to enter into a 'society' of this kind is the natural right of man; and the state has for its office to protect natural rights, not to destroy them; and, if it forbids its citizens to form associations, it contradicts the very principle of its own existence, for both they and it exist in virtue of the like principle, namely, the natural tendency of man to dwell in society.

Pope Leo offered a few other important admonitions. First he talked about prudent wage negotiations: "Let the working man and the employer make free agreements, and in particular let them agree freely as to the wages; nevertheless, there underlies a dictate of natural justice more imperious and ancient than any bargaining between man and man, namely, that wages ought not to be insufficient to support a frugal and well-behaved wage-earner. If through necessity or fear of a worse evil the workman accepts harder conditions because an employer or contractor will afford him no better, he is made the victim of force and injustice.

Leo also suggested something that was to become reality many decades in the future, i.e., worker ownership of stock in the companies for which they work. He wrote, "If a workman's wages be sufficient to enable him comfortably to support himself, his wife, and his children, he will find it easy, if he be a sensible man, to practice thrift, and he will not fail, by cutting down expenses, to put by some little savings and thus secure a modest source of income. Nature itself would urge him to this. We have seen that this great labor question cannot be solved save by assuming as a principle that private ownership must be held sacred and inviolable. The law, therefore, should favor ownership, and its policy should be to induce as many as possible of the people to become owners." Isn't it interesting to listen to that and realize that the Pope wrote this in 1891?

Leo elsewhere in the Encyclical inserted another passage relative to this same theme. Though he was speaking about farmers and their working of the soil, his remarks can easily be applied to factory workers and their labors as well. "If working people can be encouraged to look forward to obtaining a share in the land, the consequence will be that the gulf between vast wealth and sheer poverty will be bridged over, and the respective classes will be brought nearer to one another. A further consequence will result in the great abundance of the fruits of the earth. Men always work harder and more readily when they work on that, which belongs to them; nay, they learn to love the very soil that yields in response to the labor of their hands, not only food to eat, but an abundance of good things for themselves and those that are dear to them. That such a spirit of willing labor would add to the produce of the earth and to the wealth of the community is self-evident. And a third advantage would spring from this: men would cling to the country from which they were born, for no one would exchange his country for a foreign land if his own afforded him the means of living a decent and happy life." As I said, it is easy to switch the word 'land' to 'factory' and see how the three benefits Pope Leo envisioned would apply there: the chasm between rich and poor would be bridged or at least abated, factory workers would be inclined to work harder if they themselves owned shares in the company and thus benefited additionally from their labors, and few workers would be prone to leave their own company to work elsewhere.

And lastly, Pope Leo saw the need for what we refer to as reserve funds and pension funds. He concluded, "Among the several purposes of a society, one should be to try to arrange for a continuous supply of work at all times and seasons; as well as to create a fund out of which the members may be effectually helped in their need, not only in the case of accidents, but also in sickness, old age, and distress."

In 1931 Pope Pius XI also wrote an Encyclical entitled *Quadragesimo Anno*, which dealt with the same topic and which I reread in preparation for this address, but for all practical purposes, Pius simply reiterated and reaffirmed the declarations offered by Leo XIII in *Rerum Novarum*, so I had no reason to include anything from that Encyclical here today.

However, in closing, I would like to present some thoughts of my own: First, we are currently in a workers paradise, if you will. Everyone was so deprived of the niceties of life during the recent war and many people were also wanting during the economic depression preceding it. Consequently, they are now catching up. Currently, manufacturers in this country can sell almost anything they can make and are, thus, willing to give into most of the demands of labor unions. And I don't want to rain on your parade, but be careful that you don't demand too much, too quickly. History certainly tells us that there will come a time in the not too distant future when competition either from within our own boarders or from without, or both, will force the companies for which you work to curtail expenses in order to stay profitable. In that case you may be forced to give back some of the benefits you now enjoy lest the company for which you are working be forced out of business and you forced into unemployment.

And one last caution: As I'm sure most of you know, I am a jurist and have been for several decades. I know the jurist mind, having spent most of my time during those years conversing with, eating with and, yes, even playing golf with my fellow jurists. Though we love a good debate and conflicts of all sorts are what we are constantly involved with, there is one thing about which we always turn negative. We strive very hard to be fair to all parties before us, but, if there is physical violence involved anywhere, at anytime, the one exception being obvious self-defense, the perpetrator of that violence, no matter how righteousness his cause, is automatically considered dead wrong. So my admonishment to you today is, negotiate to your hearts content. Argue your heads off. Call your adversary insulting names. Even go out on strike, if that's necessary. But do not, under any circumstance, get violent unless you are attacked first and even then, only react in a defensive manner.

With that I close this address. Thank you for inviting me and I hope that what I have said will be, in some way, beneficial to your organization in particular and the labor movement in general.

Appendix B

On Cosmology... By Steven VanderLinde SJ

1. Man has constantly limited his growth in knowledge because of various applications of personal pride. There has been a jealous pride within each academic discipline that refuses to consider the ideas being developed in the other disciplines as being pertinent to their own. Instead of the practitioners of each discipline, while examining the results of their experiments and discoveries whether material or cerebral taking into account results and discoveries within other disciplines, they put up walls between the various disciplines thus hindering the full advancement within all of the disciplines. Inter-disciplinary cooperation and inter-disciplinary active research should be and should always have been a primary criteria for all fields of knowledge including, not just the sciences, but also such materially evasive disciplines as philosophy and theology and even mystagogy. Of practical import is the constant and flying battles between science and theology that have plagued academic development since the dawn of academia.

2. One of the obvious limitations for both disciplines created by the conflict between Physics and Theology is the apparent non-understanding of timelessness and spacelessness.

When Moses asked the Person in the burning bush who he was, God answered, "Yahweh," which literally means, "I am who am." A free translation is, "I am the eternal present." However, apparently neither theologians nor scientists seem to understand this revelation either in theological considerations or in scientific matters.

Theologians, when speaking of God having no beginning and no end often use phrases such as, "Before all time God knew such and such." But there is no such thing as before time for God. God has no before and no after. He lives in a totally timeless and spaceless environment. He lives in the constant present.

There are two considerations of time and space that appear at first glance to be contradictions of each other, but are not. First, time and space are not distinct entities. They are integral parts of matter and energy. Where there is no matter or energy, there is no time or space and vice versa. Secondly, time and space are not something. They, and we have to add here, matter and energy also, are the absence of something. They are the absence of timelessness and spacelessness, which is a real and absolute and ideal state or condition or environment, if you will. When God created the universe he allowed timelessness and spacelessness to be invaded and corrupted by matter and energy, which brought with them the further corruption of time and space.

3. Cosmologists either do not understand Einstein's two theories of Relativity or they don't believe them. Someday, somebody is going to combine the two theories and there will be an enormous intellectual explosion, at least in the discipline of general physics."

Time and space are not discrete entities. They do not exist apart from matter and energy and, therefore, where there is no matter or energy there is no time or space. It follows from this that the more matter and energy are compressed, the more time and space are compressed. At the center of a black hole, not only matter and energy are being compressed into an infinitesimal point, a singularity, but so are their space and time.

If we could make one of Einstein's wormholes big enough for a person to climb completely through, he would be in another universe altogether and the only place in that new universe where there would be time or space would be where the atoms and molecules of his body were. There would be no time or space other than that in that entire new universe. There would be only timelessness and spacelessness outward infinitely in all directions. And there would be no way he could get back into this universe or any other existing universe, since to do so would require a corruption of a corruption: the invasion of the absence of something, i.e., timelessness and spacelessness, into the absence of another timelessness and spacelessness. Every wormhole is a path to another, as of now, timeless and spaceless universe and every black hole of sufficient mass is another matter and energy filled universe about to be created... a big bang, if you will, as the matter and energy in the black hole implodes out of our universe into or through a worm hole and, thus, creating another universe. And, through the predictions of the Inflationary Theory, the mass of one large star compressed into the core of a black hole would inflate in the new universe to the matter and energy mass of a universe similar in size of the universe from which the black hole originated.

Reasoning: If the mass within a black hole were sufficiently large, the gravitational pull within the black hole would attempt to create a singularity, not just of the matter and energy within the black hole but also of the time and space. When that singularity takes place, the matter, energy, time and space would all be at infinite levels, since no more of these entities could be taken into the infinitesimal singularity. But since space in the singularity was infinite, gravity would also be infinite and would be attempting to pull more mass into the singularity, which, of course, means that gravity was attempting to exceed infinity. This effort would cause the mass within the singularity to try to explode, but again gravity would prohibit an outward explosion. Consequently, the mass within the singularity, including its time and space, would implode and in the process create a wormhole through which to implode... a worm hole path into a new universe with its timeless, spaceless environment, thus creating a new universe similar to ours.

4. I don't know why scientists and theologians insist on limiting a limitless, omnipotent Being.

God could easily have created one universe such that it would, through the process described above, spawn other universes that would spawn others and so on. There could be a near infinite number of universes out there. To understand how man try's to limit God we need only look at man's picture of the universe only a few hundred years ago when our earth was considered the center of it all.

On Biology... By Anthony Castione SJ

One of the most prominent questions in the field of contemporary biology involves the uncertainty of the force or biological law effecting biological evolution. Charles Darwin, while holding firm to the basic principle of biological evolution, himself, questioned whether his theory of selective genetics through random mutation or, the survival of the fittest, was in fact, the cause of evolutionary change.

The obvious first question is whether the multitude of complex biological entities we currently observe around us could have evolved from the first life forms on earth, one cell amebas, through Darwin's theory of selective genetics through random mutations, and have done so in only about three billion years as the span of life on earth is currently estimated to be. Further, the one cell life forms were all that were present for the first two of those three billion years, meaning the vast majority of the evolutionary process must have occurred in only about one billion years. It is apparently mathematically impossible to calculate the number of years required for one-cell amebas to mutate to the current multiplicity of species on earth, but it is probably many times longer than one billion years. Consequently, there must be another force involved in the evolutionary process.

There appear to be some species that mutated almost regularly and others, which hardly mutated at all over hundreds of millions of years. Those that did mutate frequently seem to have done so in a manner producing species more adaptable to the environment, if that environment was threatening but not lethal, whereas the species that did not frequently mutate were already sufficiently adaptable to their environment. In other words, threats within an environment seem to cause the adapting mutations. Another answer could be that something in the many species is capable of sensing a danger and ordering mutations to adaptability in the next generation.

That process of preferential biological mutation to adaptability indicates an innate process within all biological entities that must have begun at the two billion year point in the life cycle of the one-cell ameba forms on the planet. At about the two billion year mark of existence in the depths of the ocean, amebas, through Darwin's theory of selective genetics, or purely random mutations, could have finally created a mutation, which included a "threat of danger" sensing gene with a DNA instructive means of mutating future entities more adaptable to the threatening environment, thus setting in process the evolutionary activity.